Aim for the Heart

Queer Fanworks Inspired by
Alexandre Dumas's *The Three Musketeers*

DUCK
PRINTS
PRESS

Duck Prints Press, LLC
Schenectady, NY

Aim For The Heart © 2023, Duck Prints Press LLC

Stories:
"Stolen Hearts" © 2023, Aria L. Deair
"Heartbeat" © 2023, E. V. Dean
"Pierced Hearts" © 2023, Rhosyn Goodfellow
"The Serendipity of a Late Train" © 2023, Catherine E. Green
"Sword Dancer" © 2023, J. D. Harlock
"The Musketeer's Daughter: The Tale of Jacques Toussaint" © 2023, A. L. Heard
"The Inseparables" © 2023, D. A. Hernández
"Allergy Girl and the Hate Arrangement" © 2023, R. L. Houck
"The Three Mic O' Tears" © 2023, Lucy K. R.
"Fast Times at Treville High" © 2023, Aeryn Jemariel Knox
"A Lesson in Foils" © 2023, Annabeth Lynch
"Pensacola's Most Wanted" © 2023, Sebastian Marie
"Paris-ish" © 2023, Nova Mason
"Glass Hearts" © 2023, Sage Mooreland
"A Cell of Awareness" © 2023, D. V. Morse
"After the Fire" © 2023, MouMouSanRen
"When we lit up the night sky" © 2023, J. D. Rivers
"Wait and Hope" © 2023, Veronica Sloane
"Love and Graffiti" © 2023, Shea Sullivan
"Fated Encounter Challenge" © 2023, Xianyu Zhou

Art:
"All For One" © 2023, Aceriee
"Start your engines" © 2023, Cris Alborja
"red wine and bitter nightshade" © 2023, bloomingtea
untitled (page 101) © 2023, C
"King" © 2023, Amy Fincher
"DeWinter's Moonlit Dance" and "Coup De Foudre" © 2023, Kou Lukeman
"A Toast to Scars" © 2023, Giulia Malagoli
"Affaire D'amour" © 2023, MidnightSilver
"Knight and Squire" © 2023, Jennifer Smith
untitled (pages 91 and 146) © 2023, Spongeunction
"The Voice, The Action and The Heart" © 2023, Toby.exe
"One for All," "Where Hearts Cross," and "The Blade of Resolve" © 2023, Jupiter V
"Mousquetaires de Marseille" and "D'Winter de Marseille" © 2023, Amy Alexander Weston
"Three of Hearts" © 2023, Amalia Zeichnerin
"Knight Commander" and "I've got you" © 2023, Jagoda Zirebiec

Front cover art © 2023, Pallas Perilous

Edited by Kit Alexander, boneturtle, E. Conway, Rhosyn Goodfellow, Catherine E. Green, Lacey Hays, A. L. Heard, Aeryn Jemariel Knox, Alec J. Marsh, Nina Waters, and Rachael L. Young. Art advisement by Aceriee and Pallas Perilous. Significant planning contributions also made by Willa Blythe, E. V. Dean, Adrian Harley, Annabeth Lynch, Sunny Powell, and Alessa Riel.

Print manuscript formatting by Hermit Writes
E-book formatting by Nina Waters

Published by Duck Prints Press, LLC
Schenectady, New York
duckprintspress.com

ISBN: 978-1-946472-91-5 (Paperback edition)
ISBN: 978-1-946472-93-9 (reflowable ePub edition)
ISBN: 978-1-946472-94-6 (non-reflowable ePub edition)
ISBN: 978-1-946472-92-2 (PDF edition)

Table of Contents

Stories

Art

Pallas Perilous   *"Aim for the Heart"*

Cover

The image was originally drawn to promote contributor submissions, so it needed to actively invite interpretation (rather than selling any one specific take) and set people's minds spinning as to what they might do if handed the reins to The Three Musketeers.

Wait and Hope

– Veronica Sloane

Tags
relationships: friends, m/m
character features: chef, christian, customer service representative, student (college), trans male, veteran
other tags: academia, alcohol use (casual), alternate universe, food (graphic descriptions), getting together, meet cute, one-night stand, past tense, religion, restaurant, reunions, second chances, third person limited point of view

Inspiration
When *The Three Musketeers* comes up, my first thought is always of Porthos, who is often portrayed as the comedic relief in adaptations. I wanted to give this beautiful hedonist his own love story, and what better match than Aramis, solemn, holy, but as time goes on he proves to also be more interested in the pleasure of the flesh.

"This is my last one!" Porthos bellowed into the kitchen. The transition from the posh and polite dining room to the raucous clatter of the kitchen always made him a little giddy. That and the ever-tempting smell of searing meat. "The very last!"

"We know, we know," Chef Treville called back, "so you told us all night! At this rate, we'll be glad to see the back of you."

"You'll miss me," he sniffed as he picked up the tray. "You know you will."

"Maybe a very small amount," Treville allowed. "Stay after you bring your plates around. I think four years of half-decent labor has earned you a last meal."

"Ha! You'll have to replace me with three other half-starved freshmen," Porthos grinned. "And I'll take the meal."

"Good. Now go before my food gets cold."

It had been a quiet night, which Porthos mourned. He'd come to love the restaurant when it was at its busiest. *Le Coeur de la Reine Anne* was the best (and only) five-star eatery in the small college town; it was usually packed with anniversary and birthday celebrations. Tonight was a Wednesday though, smack in the middle of finals. They had just a few stray couples. And a lone man sitting by the window, looking wistfully out onto the street.

"Has someone taken your order?" Porthos slowed as he passed.

"Not yet." He sounded unbothered, so he likely hadn't been sitting long.

The man had a good face. A long nose that pointed cheekily up at the end, a generous mouth that looked as if it knew how to smile well, and wide-set eyes that gave the impression of deep thought. He had shoulder-length dark hair that hung loose around his face, softening sharp cheekbones.

"Have you had a chance to look at the menu?" Porthos gave him his best smile, the one that was a hair too toothy for customer service.

"I did, but I'm not sure I know what half of this means," the man admitted. "I thought I'd go out for one last meal, a treat, but my friend who was meant to come with me found other plans. They're the one who knows about this stuff."

"Not a problem," Porthos assured him. "I've eaten everything on the menu a dozen times. I can help."

"Amazing." The man smiled at him. Porthos had been right. It was an excellent smile, a twitch of mischief at the edges. "Then please tell me what the fuck a reduction is because I'm assuming it's not some kind of top surgery done to meat?"

Porthos laughed, and the smile went a little wider. Wilder. Beautiful. He took his time explaining the menu and making a recommendation.

"You'll enjoy it," he promised.

"I'm sure I'll enjoy the food, but I always think a meal is better with company." The man gusted out a breath. "Thank you, though, for your help."

"Do you drink wine?" Porthos asked, an idea clicking into place. He wasn't a man to ignore a sudden thought. Some of his friends might argue it wasn't one of his finer qualities.

"Yes?"

"Legally?"

The man pulled out his wallet and handed over his ID. It had all the markers of a real ID, but someone had scratched out the name with viciousness, along with the gender marker. All that was left was a markered word "Aramis" and a defiant "M."

"Twenty-two is good enough for me." Porthos handed it back. "I'll be back in a minute."

"All right." Aramis tucked the ID back in his wallet.

Porthos darted back into the kitchen. "Chef!"

"Yes?" Treville looked up from a saucepan with fond exasperation.

"I'm clocking out. But can I put in an order first? For table seven. And add my meal to it? Oh, and a bottle of that dry white? You know the one I mean."

"Am I catering your last fling now?" Treville huffed. "I have better things to do."

"Not tonight you don't," Porthos wheedled. "Please?" Treville narrowed his eyes. Porthos placed his hands on his chest, "I ask you from the bottom of my heart."

"He's hot, huh?"

"Like the fucking sun. Please please please—"

"Fine, fine. Who am I to stand in the way of young…whatever it is you're doing."

Order in, Porthos availed himself of the requested bottle and two glasses. He went back out and set them both down.

"My name is Porthos," he offered, "and I'll be your dining companion for the evening, if you'll have me."

"Is this a new waiter service?" Aramis asked, those lovely wide eyes going rounder.

"I'm officially no longer a waiter here." Porthos took Aramis's lack of objection as agreement and set the glasses before each of them, uncorking the bottle with an expert twist of the wrist.

"Were you fired?" Aramis asked, watching the wine trickle into his glass with avid attention.

"I'm graduating."

"Me too. I've never seen you."

"Business major." Porthos poured his own glass generously. It was a very good white.

"Theology."

"What do you do with that?"

"In my case? Become a priest."

"No." Porthos set down the bottle to stare at him. "Really? Does that still happen?"

"From time to time," Aramis laughed.

"But why? Surely you can just study religion and go to church if you have to. I'm assuming; I don't think I've set foot in a church since I was a kid. I'd probably catch fire."

"God forgives. If you have faith." The last was said a little more tremulously.

"And you must."

"Must I?" Aramis picked up his wine.

"Then why the priesthood?"

"I believe. Faith is another matter."

Porthos picked up his glass too. "Then, to uncertain futures. May our feet take us only exactly where they're meant to go."

"I'll drink to that."

Their glasses touched. The little candle on the table flickered. The light refracted through the liquid and cast a pale shadow on Aramis's face. Porthos almost forgot to drink.

Almost.

"What about you?" Aramis asked. "What's your uncertain future?"

"Mmm, I'm meant to start my illustrious military career so that no one has to think so hard about why I'm still hanging around the family manse like a bad smell."

"That seems extreme."

"More extreme than becoming a priest?"

"Touché," Aramis snorted. "What's that?"

The first tray had arrived, carried by Porthos's replacement. Before she could launch into the memorized explanation, Porthos cut her off.

"Fig and goat-cheese tart. The sweetness of the fruit marries with the saltiness of the cheese while cutting through the fat. It's basically heaven. Restore your faith, Father, and mangez!"

Aramis took it up with interest, biting in then issuing a very quiet moan. "I don't think a tart will change my life, but it's good."

"Maybe the duck then," Porthos conceded. "But I bet by the end of this meal, you'll have some new tingly feelings."

"You're the expert."

"Nah, I'm the waiter. Or was." He frowned, the realization sinking in.

"I know," Aramis said with a sympathetic smile. "The ground moves beneath our feet."

"For the better." Porthos attempted for a hearty verve. "So where do you go to become a priest?"

"Seminary. A few states away. I'm ready to leave the area. Too many familiar faces here, and not enough friends."

"Yeah?" The wine was perhaps a shade too dry in his mouth. "It's a small place."

"Too small for men of our stature," Aramis said wryly.

"Where do you think would be large enough?"

"Somewhere we could say everything on our minds and more besides?" Aramis said, half to himself. "Where we could love God and as many people as we'd like, not as opposing ideas, but in concert."

"I was thinking Vegas," Porthos offered. Aramis barked a laugh.

"I've never been."

"Me either. One day. Seems like the ideal place for a soldier to take leave."

"Why did you major in business if you were going into the military?"

"Excellent question," Porthos said gravely. "Because I had to choose something, and I was very hungover. I just pointed at something on the list and then nodded when they said it back to me."

"Holy hell." Aramis shook his head. "All right, what did you actually want to do?"

"Nothing! Who wants to work? I want to eat, drink, have sex, and throw parties."

"Oh come on, you must like something besides pleasure."

"Must I?" Porthos groused. "Well, if I must…I don't know. I like being here, honestly. I love how much care goes into something so simple. We're eating art. I like that."

"You should do that then," Aramis said as if it was simple. "Make food."

"Nah. I'm going where I should go." Porthos leaned back so the waitress could whisk away the plates and replace them with thin cuts of meat. "This is going to change you on a deep level. I'm sorry, but once you eat this duck, you can never go back to who you were before."

"Promise?" Aramis picked up a fork and knife.

The duck melted in Porthos's mouth as always, but he wasn't paying any mind. He was watching Aramis, who took a bite and then closed his eyes. He set his fork and knife down as he chewed.

"You were right," he determined. "Everything in my life is different now."

"Really?"

"No," Aramis said with a snort. "But it is really good. How does a hedonist get through college?"

"You tell me. I see you eating quite happily, and you talked about meeting someone here. A friend?"

Aramis flushed. "Maybe."

"Maybe not?"

"It doesn't matter now. He's a little older, a graduate assistant for one of my classes. We were on the fencing team together, and I thought he might be interested. He has great… Well, maybe I'm a bit of a hedonist too."

They talked about parties, booze, and sex as the meal went on, Porthos pausing the conversation to explain each dish.

Finally there was nothing left but to lick their dessert forks clean.

"Have a good night!" the waitress chimed.

"The check?" Aramis asked with a frown.

"A gift," Porthos assured him.

"What, no! We just met, you can't be giving me gifts."

"From the owner, not from my pockets. Where are you headed now?"

"Back to my apartment."

"Same." Porthos got to his feet, only a hair tipsy. His legendary tolerance stood him in good stead today. "Where do you live?"

"Oak Street."

"Close to me! Maybe we can walk together for a while?"

"I'd like that."

The evening air was warm, and Porthos unbuttoned his shirt to let the breeze crawl through his thin undershirt.

"That," Aramis declared, "is more hole than shirt."

"Its only job is to cover my nipples, and it's managing that."

"Barely. Is that how you dress when you're not in a waiter getup?"

"Sometimes. Why? How do you usually dress?"

Aramis gestured down at the slacks, button-down, and vest that Porthos had assumed were an attempt to dress nicely for a dinner out.

"Seems like a lot of fuss to sit in a lecture hall or throw back shots."

"I don't 'throw back shots.' I drink copious amounts of wine from nice glasses."

"Tomato. Tomahto."

Aramis shoulder-checked him. It hit Porthos in the bicep and made him grin. They went on in silence for another block.

"Do you live with anyone?" Aramis asked, casual as anything.

"Got a roommate, but he's away. You?"

"Mine is home."

Porthos glanced over.

Aramis lifted those expressive brows.

"Come to mine then?" Porthos's words tripped over each other in his eagerness.

"Yeah," Aramis decided. "I want to kiss you, but you need to meet me halfway here."

In a breath, Porthos had an arm around Aramis's waist, head ducking down to kiss the mischief right off his lips.

The next morning, Porthos snuck out of bed, rifled through his fridge, and very quietly pulled down pots and pans. He didn't own a tray, so he used one he'd stolen from the dining hall. Piling it high with French toast, eggs, bacon, and coffee, he bore his burden back into the bedroom.

He found Aramis sitting on the bed, holding his pants.

"Don't go," Porthos protested. "Please."

"I thought you wanted me to. Since you were… Is that breakfast?"

"Yes. If you want it."

"I do."

They ate on the bed, Porthos overcoming Aramis's initial protests with a "Don't you think I've got to wash the sheets anyway?"

"This is delicious," Aramis said around a mouthful, taste apparently overcoming his manners.

"It's just French toast."

"It's more. I think this is the food that does it." Aramis rested his hand on Porthos's knee.

"Does what?"

"This"—Aramis held a bit of toast aloft; its caramelized crust glittered in the sunlight—"is the food that restores my faith."

"In God?" Porthos grinned.

"In people." Aramis stuck the bite in his mouth, his eyes sliding closed as he chewed. "That, and last night in general."

"I was so good in bed that you're going to take a vow of chastity?"

"Don't make fun." Aramis popped one eye open. "It means more than you can know."

"Oh." Porthos swallowed thickly. "That's…good? I think the world is still moving under my feet."

"Maybe it should. Hey, I have an idea. Since we may not see each other again."

The thought made Porthos's chest ache. "I'm listening."

"What if"—Aramis leaned forward, his hand still on Porthos's knee, connecting them—"we make a vow to each other?"

"This went from a one-night stand to marriage very quickly."

"Not that kind of vow, you beautiful fool," Aramis said. His eyes locked on Porthos's, and Porthos couldn't have looked away if he tried. "Ten years from now, let's meet at the restaurant again."

"Ten years? How will we remember?"

"I don't intend to forget. Do you?"

"No." There had been many people in Porthos's life, but Aramis was utterly sin-gular. "Not for a moment. What if the restaurant doesn't exist anymore?"

"Then we'll have to wait on the sidewalk, and I'll trust you to find us a new, equally delicious location."

Porthos covered Aramis's hand with his own. "Ten years, then."

They finished breakfast in relative quiet. Then Aramis rose, dressed, and gave him a last kiss before leaving. Usually Porthos would be off to the gym first thing in the morning, even after a night of drinking. But the food sat heavy in his belly, and his heart was heavy in his chest.

Ten years was a long time away. He fished around, pulled his laptop out of a pile of laundry. When he saw Aramis next, he wanted something to show for it. He opened up a site he'd had bookmarked for over a year.

He clicked "Apply."

Ten Years Later

"You're making me nervous," Athos said from behind the stove.

"You? Nervous?" Porthos made a "pfft" sound. "You're made of steel and skim milk."

"Used skim milk in a sauce one time."

"One time was enough. What if he doesn't come? What if he *does*?"

"You've asked both those questions several times and haven't liked any of my damn answers, so maybe you should ask them somewhere you'll be more useful. Like the dumpster."

"Ha ha," Porthos said flatly. "You're hilarious."

Athos produced a bag full of garbage seemingly from nowhere.

"Throw this out. And maybe that shirt while you're at it."

"What's wrong with my shirt?" Porthos took the bag. "Are you trying to make me even more nervous?"

"You're in the pink paisley nightmare that I've specifically told you is an affront to good taste several times before."

"You're just jealous. I'll get you one for your birthday," Porthos announced, spinning on his heel to throw out the trash.

The alleyway behind the restaurant had seen Porthos's best and worst moments the last few years. There had been many post-shift drunken evenings leaning on this wall, several fumbled hookups, and, most notably, a dramatic breakup that made him wince to remember.

It had also been the place he'd been standing when Treville solemnly handed him the last of the paperwork and said, "Take good care of her now. Listen to Athos sometimes."

It probably balanced out: the good, the bad, and the smell of rot. Porthos exhaled shakily. He was getting maudlin about a dumpster. He was truly hitting new lows tonight. Best get back inside.

Athos was waiting by the door, eyes wide as he limply clutched an enormous knife.

"Is it the end at last? Was it the gouda? I swear I didn't know the price had gone up!"

"What?" Athos frowned. "No, you fool. He's *here*."

"Now? Right now?" Porthos's entire blood supply rushed away from his head.

"It took me a second to recognize him. You two have matching shitty facial hair now. Table four. Just sat down."

Porthos had prepared several scripts for tonight, but now that the moment was here, they all vanished. With a sharp exhalation and a hand run through his hair, he was as ready as he could be. He was out the kitchen door, leaving behind the beautiful cacophony for the hush of the dining room.

At table four sat a man with wide-set eyes and a generous mouth only partially hidden by a well-groomed mustache. Porthos came up beside him and blurted, "You came! You're here!"

Aramis startled, dropping the menu with a *thud* and rattling the silverware, but in an instant he was moving upward and hugging Porthos. Porthos hugged back, dropping his face down into Aramis's hair to hide a sniffle.

"How do you look so much the same?" Aramis asked, voice muffled against Porthos's chest. "The years have barely touched you."

"My immature outlook?" Porthos offered. "You've changed—for the better it seems."

"I hope. It took time." Aramis took a step back, still holding onto Porthos's arms. "I like the shirt."

"Ha!" Porthos grinned. "I am going to make you repeat that in front of a friend later."

Aramis released him suddenly, a flush on his cheeks. He sat back down in a rush. "Sorry for grabbing you."

Porthos took the other chair, planting his elbows onto the table and his chin in his hands to study the man across from him.

"You never have to apologize for that," he said. "I like being grabbed. I mean—no. No, I'm sticking with that."

"I can't believe this place is still here. And it looks so different! But with the same name. Do you think the ownership changed?" Aramis rattled off.

"It did," Porthos confirmed. Maybe he wasn't the only one with nerves. "What do you think of the interior?"

"I barely remember how it was." Aramis leaned back to survey the room, though his eyes kept landing on Porthos's face before flitting away again. "But it's homier now. Lived in. I don't feel too poor to be sitting here."

"Good," Porthos grinned. "Goal achieved."

"You...helped design it?"

"Had to shut the place down for a week, which is risky business in the restaurant industry, let me tell you."

"Wait..." Aramis's attention rocked fully back to him. "Is this your restaurant now?"

"It is," Porthos said with pride. "I decided against the army. Went to culinary school instead. Bounced around a few places and wound up back here. Treville sold the place to me last year when he retired."

"That's amazing! I read the reviews before I came over, just— Don't laugh, but I was nervous, and I research when I'm nervous."

"Not laughing," Porthos assured him.

"They were good," Aramis said. "Do you love doing it?"

"More than I could've imagined. How is the priesthood?"

"Ah." Aramis subsided a little in his chair. "I wasn't as wise as you."

"I'm told daily that I'm a fool, so I highly doubt that," Porthos said. "No collar?"

"You were right. I am a hedonist at heart, and the priesthood doesn't have room for that."

"What did you do after?" Porthos leaned in farther.

"Did you two want to order something, or are you going to be our problem table for the night?" Athos was standing over them, and Porthos, very briefly, considered killing one of his best friends. Just a little. A friendly spot of murder.

"Athos?" Aramis's eyes went wide. "I thought you were getting a doctorate or something!"

"Or something," Athos said wryly. "Instead, I met this horror masquerading as a human, and he convinced me I'd have more fun in the kitchen. Lies. Horrible, life-ending lies."

"What he means is that he came in here drunk as a skunk, stumbled into the kitchen, and confessed that he'd dropped out and had nowhere to go. Please keep in mind we had never met before. Out of the kindness of my heart, I gave him a job."

"That's not how I remember it." Athos lifted on elegant eyebrow.

"You couldn't remember shit after that," Porthos scoffed.

Aramis looked between them, "I can't tell if you're friends or if you hate each other."

"Yes," they both said at the same time.

"I'm interrupting," Athos continued smoothly. "Appetizers?"

"Give us a little of everything," Porthos said.

"Fine. Aramis, we should catch up when you're done with this one. A drink tomorrow night maybe?"

"Yes. Please." Aramis watched Athos leave. "Did he really just stumble in here?"

"He did."

"Maybe this place is magic."

Porthos didn't laugh at that. He hesitantly reached across the table and sighed in relief when Aramis took his hand. "I think it is. It's my favorite place in the world. Tell me, though, what happened to you?"

"I may have joined the army," Aramis said ruefully.

"You didn't."

"I did. I wasn't a good fit there either, but I served out my years. Then I tried to go back to school."

"No good?" Porthos wrinkled his nose.

"I still like learning, but not so formally anymore. Wound up doing some admin work for a professor. I just got a job here, working for my old department as an assistant. It's not a lot—"

"You moved back?" Porthos interrupted.

"Last week."

"…for good?"

"I mean…" Aramis licked his lips. "It's silly, but I thought…I don't know. I don't have many connections anymore, and I at least know the place. I didn't know you owned the restaurant, but I might've done a white pages search."

"Aramis—"

"It's ridiculous," he said, eyes on his still-empty plate. Athos was probably watching from the kitchen. Let him, Porthos thought senselessly. "We don't even know each other. I'm not—"

"I bought the restaurant for you."

"What?" Aramis's grip on Porthos's hand tightened.

"The restaurant. I had to be sure it would be here. I love it, don't get me wrong, but I really only came back in the first place so I was sure to be here."

"But we said if it was closed, we could just meet outside," Aramis said softly. "We talked about it."

"I know! I'm a fool. And I would do it again."

"Even if I left here tonight and we didn't see each other ever again?"

"Yes!" Porthos said without hesitation. "I thought about what you said about faith in people. I wanted that. This place…the promise of the future. That gave it to me."

"What if we don't actually even like each other?"

Porthos brought their joined hands to his lips. He kissed Aramis's knuckles. "That would be a damn shame. But at least we'll have shared a meal together like no other."

"You have that much surety in yourself as a chef?" Aramis asked, eyes sparkling.

"I have that much surety that very few people wait ten years to eat with someone."

"In that you might be correct."

Athos, with timing too good to be natural, delivered the amuse-bouche Porthos had anxiously fussed over for days.

"I should've asked if you had dietary restrictions," Porthos realized. "Sorry."

"It's fine, I'll eat anything," Aramis assured him, and together they reached for the bread beautifully toasted and layered with bruschetta.

"What was the army like?" Porthos asked him, though his attention was mostly on Aramis's reaction to the food.

Aramis chewed carefully, apparently savoring it. Good. "Awful, mostly. I don't much like taking orders. But I did wind up being a hell of a shot, so there's that. Fortunately, I didn't see any action. I read a lot of books on the sly."

"I can see that. You, standing at attention with a paperback up your sleeve."

"Basically." Aramis grinned. "This is good. You must've paid better attention to your schooling than I did my drill sergeant."

"It wasn't like regular school. We did hands-on things, and we could eat the results. I almost failed pastries though."

"How do you fail at pastries?" Aramis frowned.

Porthos leaned in and winked at him, "I didn't show up to class a few times. You could say I was a dessert-er."

Aramis stared at him, then burst out laughing, "That's terrible! Did you make that up for the joke?"

"Yes," he admitted. "I actually passed with flying crullers."

"Oh no, I don't think I can tolerate this development," Aramis decided. "I can't be with someone who thinks puns are funny."

"It's a high-whisk way of life," Porthos agreed.

"I'm leaving," Aramis informed him solemnly. He didn't move a muscle. Instead, he ate every course of the menu that Porthos had certainly not created with a singular audience in mind. Each dish brought compliments, then stories. Porthos told him about slogging through being a line cook and a very short stint at a fancy burger place. He even mentioned the breakup, and Aramis haltingly related similar tales.

They ate dessert quietly, Aramis insisting because "A mousse like this deserves the honor of silence."

Before Porthos could break the quiet by saying something ridiculous, Athos stepped up to the table. "We're mostly closed, so if you want to show off your kitchen, this is your moment."

"Closed?" Aramis looked up from his dessert, apparently shocked to find they were alone. "I'm sorry to have kept you."

"It's fine. Porthos is always the last one here anyway. Come on, bus your dessert plates while you're at it."

"Who works for whom around here?" Porthos chided even as he picked up his plates.

"I think we're all very clear on that," Athos said lightly. Porthos resisted flicking a remaining bit of mousse at him—Aramis was watching after all. Apparently Athos divined Porthos's entire thought process, because his smirk deepened.

"I don't think I've ever been in a professional kitchen."

"Prepare for the wonders of stainless steel!" Porthos told him.

The tour didn't take long, and Aramis was very polite about pretending to care about the stove Porthos had dithered over for weeks. He was much more genuinely excited about getting to try the leftover cheesecake.

"You made this?" he asked Athos.

"Mhm, to his recipe." Athos gestured his fork at Porthos. "I'm a cook, not a chef."

"Don't start with that." Porthos waved his fork right back.

"I thank both of you, in any case," Aramis said around a bit of the cake. "I haven't eaten this well in a long time."

"You should eat like this all the time," Porthos said, voice dropping. "You can. If you like. It's here if you want it."

"Look at the time," Athos said flatly, "I have to go braid my platypus. Nice to see you again, Aramis. Porthos, don't forget to lock the back door."

"I never forget. More than once a week."

"I'll remind him," Aramis promised, though he also looked slightly distracted.

When Athos had slipped out, Porthos turned to Aramis, "I had a good time. We should do it again."

"There's a lot of things I'd like to do again with you. And some first things." Aramis set down his plate and fork. "Can I come back to your place? Mine is in boxes."

"Yeah. Yes. Absolutely." Porthos practically threw his things into this sink. "I really do have to lock up. Give me five." If he spent one of those minutes in the bathroom with the tiny bottle of mouthwash he'd shoved in his pocket this morning, that was his business.

When he returned, Aramis was right where he left him. The smile had gone from his face.

Porthos hesitated. "We don't have to do anything," he said.

"Are you kidding me?" Aramis held out both hands. "I've waited ten years for this kiss, I'm not waiting another second."

What else could Porthos want? He took Aramis's hands, trying to note every callous, but that was quickly eclipsed by lips against his, the full quivering press of Aramis's body pressed to his own.

"Tell me you don't live far."

"Very close, actually."

"Not the same place?"

"No. I live above the restaurant. Come upstairs with me?"

So Athos wouldn't text in the morning, Porthos made sure to lock all the doors. It was a dream to walk Aramis up the back steps and into his tiny, familiar rooms. They did little more than kiss that night, but when the hour grew late and Porthos asked,

"Stay?"

Aramis stayed.

They woke up wound together in the warm sunlight. Porthos made them French toast, and they ate it in his bed even though he had a real kitchen table now.

"How is this actually better than I remember?" Aramis demanded. "What witchcraft is this?"

"No magic, just eggs," Porthos grinned. "Does it still give you faith?"

"It gives me hope this time," Aramis lowered his eyelids, gave Porthos a searching look. "Doesn't it for you? Or does it not work on its creator?"

"I don't need it. You gave me faith then and hope now."

"How can you say things like that at such a moment? Now I have to choose whether to eat or kiss you!"

Porthos liberated him of his fork and made the decision for him. There would be many mornings to enjoy French toast together, he decided, but there was only one morning that started the rest of their lives, and he was going to make the most of it.

Aceriee   *"All For One"*

Aceriee opted not to share the inspiration behind this artwork.

The Inseparables
— D. A. Hernández

Tags
warnings: homophobia, homophobia (internalized), vomiting (mentions of)
relationships: friends, the grumpy one is soft for the sunshine one, m/m
character features: celebrity, character has a different gender than in the source material, christian, gay, in the closet, latinx, lesbian, performer
other tags: alternate universe, break-up, coming out, drug use (casual), modern, past tense, puerto rico, reunions, second chances, smoking (casual), third person limited point of view

It was Puerto Rico's biggest reggaeton concert for new talents, and D. Art—formerly Santi G.—of the group Tres Más Uno[1] was pacing the small dressing room, fretting over the setlist and feeling like he might be sick again. In front of the mirror, Porto fussed with his cap and necklaces, while Samira prayed, clutching a rosary. Sprawled on the room's only chair, Athos watched them with an amused smile on his face.

A few minutes earlier, the concert organizer, Donato Treviño, dubbed Dr. Tre by his friends, had given them long-awaited and dreadful news.

"Rich E. Liu's here. You might see him around." He'd paused to watch their faces break into various degrees of shock and horror and cheerily winked. "Good luck tonight!"

The tension continued rising until one of them cracked.

"Shit! *The* Rich E.!" Porto exclaimed, turning to look at the others. "Legendary producer, owner of his own label, star-maker—*here*. He's going to watch our show!"

"This is it. This is *it*," Samira said fervently.

"I'm gonna hurl again," D. Art muttered.

"There's hundreds of people out there. What's one more?" Athos said. He rose from his seat to stop D. Art's pacing and spun the younger man by the shoulders to face him.

"Santi, breathe," Athos soothed, and D. Art took a deep breath, but not even Athos's clear-eyed gaze and strong hands gently rubbing his shoulders helped settle his racing heart. D. Art took a step back and raised his hand to scratch his short hair under his cap.

"We worked our asses off for this—you more than anyone. We're ready. We got this." Athos lowered his arms.

"Hell yeah! We're Musketeers, baby!" Samira hugged them both.

Mimicking the sound effect of a microphone, Porto introduced them like he did in their usual shows: "We're the Tres Más Uno! Here's la Gata con Garra,[2] who sings like an angel and is a devil with the girls, Samira!"

They laughed, clapped, and went along with it. "And the heavyweight of beatbox, raised in the streets and monster in the sheets, a ninja master visiting the notary's wife—Porto!" Samira crowed.

Porto bowed to their cheers, raised his cap to Athos, and said into his mock microphone, "Our rock in hard times, he who raps during protests, rolls a joint in thirty seconds, and plays Beethoven for fun, our poet…Athos!"

Athos took the enthusiastic shoulder pats and hollers with good cheer. When he

---

1   Three Plus One
2   The Cat with the Hook

14

spoke, in a clear voice without flair, the others quieted down. "And our youngest but most enthusiastic member, our dedicated social media manager and lyricist, our fearless leader, D. Art!"

Porto and Samira cheered and clapped him on the back, but D. Art was taken in by Athos's warm eyes, and he blushed violently, which only intensified the others' teasing whistles and hoots.

To distract their attention, D. Art initiated their seasoned cheer: "All for one…"

"…and one for all!" they screamed in unison, pumping their fists into the air.

D. Art's enthusiasm was short-lived, however, because soon Treviño interrupted to say, "You're up in fifteen."

His stomach lurched, and he turned to his friends, a frantic look in his eyes. "I think—we gotta change the setlist," he said. He answered their expressions of outrage and disbelief with raised hands. "Only a bit! It's just…'Solo Dos Bros'[3] is too slow. We should replace it with 'Tu Mosquetero.' "[4]

"You insisted 'Tu Mosquetero' was too similar to 'Soldados de Fortuna,' "[5] Porto said.

Samira and Athos were quiet as they looked at D. Art, Samira with a sharp, angry gaze and Athos more searchingly.

"You're afraid that Rich E. will think you're gay," Samira said without hesitation.

"I-I-I just…" D. Art babbled, hands trembling.

Porto was staring at him like he was a stranger. "Dude, what? *Really*? You wrote that song! I thought you were going for that vibe!"

"If you think it's the best choice…" Athos started, and the others turned to him.

"Seriously? You're just gonna let him"—Samira threw up her hands as Athos turned to her—"oh, whatever. It's your song. I'm not changing a word from *my* lesbian songs, thank you very much." She walked away in a huff.

Porto looked at them, shrugged, and hurried after her. Their voices were soon heard from the hall, Samira's humming warm-up louder than usual and Porto's more subdued.

Athos turned to D. Art. He seemed as unshaken as always, but something in his eyes was too distant.

"If what you want is to showcase your talent," Athos began, " 'Solo Dos Bros' is one of your best songs."

"I know! And I know it's your song too. It's—lesbians are cool, but we… This is the biggest concert of our careers, and we can't— How many big-name artists are out and proud? How many of them were out before they became *big*? It's too risky," D. Art said in a rush, imploring Athos to understand.

Athos set a hand on D. Art's shoulder. "Hey. I *get it*. We can change it. I'll notify Tre."

---

3   "Only Two Bros"
4   "Your Musketeer"
5   "Soldiers of Fortune"

Inspiration

I'd never read *The Three Musketeers*, so I was pleasantly surprised to find it entertaining and easy to read. Especially the first half, where it's a lot of fighting, desperately searching for money and promptly spending it, drinking, and having affairs with married women. My brain, which conjures up reggaeton songfic ideas for every fandom I'm in, spotted the resemblance to reggaeton songs and ran with it.

Reggaeton gets a lot of flak and hatred for its simple beats and explicit lyrics, and yeah, sure, it's not for everyone. It used to be my guilty pleasure until a friend defended it for me: "It's fun. It makes me feel good. It doesn't have to be more than that." Much like *The Three Musketeers*, reggaeton contains a lot of idealized masculinity and femininity immersed in sexism, but it's ultimately FUN. We could do with more fun these days.

Before working on this story, I used to think there was no queer reggaeton. I now stand corrected. Many are not mainstream, but they're easy to find if you look (check out my playlists!).

Shout-out to my friend, who not only made me feel it's cool to like reggaeton but who also took me to see Maluma live. ;)

And he walked away, purposeful as usual, while D. Art watched him, a sinking feeling in his stomach mingling with his nerves.

D. Art came to himself later, the beat still thrumming in his veins, sweat running down his brow, the image of a large crowd singing along with the chorus of their songs imprinted on the backs of his eyelids. He squinted against the blinding lights of the stage, deafened by the sound of roaring cheers, and numbly wondered if there was a drug in the world that could compare to the pure fear and exhilaration he'd felt during that concert.

He didn't even register Tre urging him to change into a fresh shirt and leading him away from the others to a VIP room, and he found himself face-to-face with a stocky older man with carefully trimmed facial hair and a slick smile.

"D. Art. I've heard so much about you. So good to finally meet you," the man said as he shook D. Art's hand, his grip painful from all the rings he wore. "I'm Rich E., in case you didn't know."

D. Art tried to focus, feeling suddenly too sweaty and unprepared. He'd had a pitch for the Tres Más Uno, but he couldn't remember a single word of it.

Not that Rich E. let him get a word in. "How old are you?" he asked.

"I-I just turned twenty-one," D. Art answered automatically.

"Young, but not a teen—good. Got a girl or two? Kids?"

"Um, no—"

"Focused on your career—great. Tre told me you wrote most of the Tres Más Uno songs. Is that right?"

"I mean, I co-wrote them with Athos and—"

"Listen: I make stars. I have a good nose for talent, and I make them work. I'm willing to invest"—he said an amount too large for D. Art's mind—"to make you PR's next big thing within one year. You'll have collaborations with big shots, international concerts, your own albums, and your own brands—if you're smart. You have what it takes to be big in the urban genre. You up for it?"

"I—it's an honor, but—"

"Here's my card. Think on it, but not too much," Rich E. said, handing over a card and turning to leave the room.

"Um, wait—this is an offer only for me? What about Athos, Porto, Samira? We're a group; we make our songs together—"

Rich E. turned around to regard him coolly. "Let me be blunt. I'm in this business to make money, not lose it. You have a nice voice, a pretty face, and fair skin. You, I can package and sell to the masses. The others will slow you down. The offer is only for you. Take it or leave it."

"*Focking cabrón*," [6] growled Samira, followed by a longer string of curse words.

The four friends were gathered at Athos's place. They had planned to celebrate at their secret beach, but the cooler with drinks stayed ignored in a corner. They gathered around the coffee

---

6   Fucking bastard

table, where D. Art had put Rich E.'s bright-red business card.

"We're being left out, after all," said Porto as he gave a sullen kick to the coffee table, glaring at Rich's business card like it had just insulted his mother.

"I won't leave you guys behind," D. Art said, bouncing his leg. "But—I'm scared of saying 'no.' This is *Rich E.*: I don't think I'll ever get a better chance."

"The guy's ruthless." Porto noted. "If you say 'no,' he can make sure you never do."

"Shit." D. Art put his head in his hands.

Athos's low voice cut suddenly through the silence. "You should accept."

They all turned to him, but Athos only looked at D. Art as he said: "This is everything you wanted. You've been gunning for this since we started. You made it. Why hold back because of us?"

"Wait. I thought we all wanted to sign with Rich E. and make it big? What—are you giving up, Athos?" Samira demanded.

"That's not it. I'm saying, if Santiago's the only one who gets a chance, he should take it," Athos said patiently.

Samira ran a hand through her short hair angrily and hunched over on the couch, muttering, "I guess."

D. Art looked at him in disbelief. "But what about 'All for one and one for all'?"

Porto perked up, looking between them.

"Precisely. Your success is ours. Are you saying you won't share the money, help people in need, use your fame to say what needs to be said?" Athos insisted.

"Of course! But it's not fair! We're a group; you're my *friends*! I don't—I don't know if I can do it without you," D. Art finished in a whisper.

"You're the best of us. You'll be fine," said Athos, almost dismissive.

"Yeah. You're very talented," Porto added, nodding sagely. Samira offered a thumbs up and a wry smile.

"But I didn't even write a single song by myself!"

" 'Tu Mosquetero' and 'Soldado de Fortuna'—" Athos started.

"We all added stuff to those," D. Art said quickly.

"You made the melody and lyrics for 'Solo Dos Bros,' " Athos stated.

"With *you*," D. Art hissed, feeling panicky and desperate.

"It's not even about talent," Athos said. "It's what Rich E. said: it's marketability, which you have in spades and we don't."

"But I thought…" D. Art said, something twisting up in his gut. He couldn't help asking, "Why—why does it feel like you're pushing me away?"

Athos didn't answer. The front door clicked shut, and D. Art vaguely registered that Porto and Samira were gone.

"I think…you'd regret staying," Athos said finally.

"What? All these months, everything we did—it meant nothing to you? Do you think it meant nothing to me?" D. Art said, hurt and angry.

"You don't want to be with me," Athos said quietly.

"How can you say—?"

"Because!" Athos raised his voice, breaking halfway. He was still, jaw tight and fists clenched, before he put a hand over his eyes and took a deep breath. "Santi. You already made your choice, whether you realize it or not."

"…oh. Is this—is this about our song?" D. Art asked, his own voice weak and shaky.

Athos didn't answer. D. Art felt a knot in his throat, tears pricking his eyes, and a cold, heavy weight pooling in his stomach.

"If it meant that much to you, why didn't you say so?" D. Art implored.

"Because," Athos repeated, slowly and forcefully, his normally even voice wavering, "I won't stand between you and your dream. Go, Santi. Sign the contract. Do what you want to do, and remember your friends from time to time."

D. Art didn't answer. He couldn't. It was all too much for him to bear. He turned around and left.

Two years later, the internationally recognized artist known as D. Art lay on the bed of his childhood bedroom, looking up—as he had done many times as a teenager—at the "Babe of the Week" posters and Vico C. album covers decorating the walls. He had his fancy headphones on as he listened to the beat for his latest demo, failing to come up with spectacular, lit, or even decent lyrics.

He balled up his haphazard notes, threw them at the wastebasket in the corner, and missed.

A call from Rich E. came through. D. Art hesitated before taking it.

"Art, dear boy, how is your vacation back home? Enjoying the beach, the girls, the *coquito*?"

"Yeah, all good," said D. Art, trying to inject cheer and confidence into his voice.

"Tell me you're not still holed up at your parents' place. That'd be tragic," Rich said with his fake paternal concern.

"No, no. I've been out and about," D. Art lied. He hoped not to get grilled on details, except…

"Do you have any samples ready for me?" Rich asked, and D. Art grimaced. After a long silence, Rich tsked. "I already booked the studio and producers for the new album. If we reschedule, *everything* will have to be rescheduled! Please take this more seriously. Your other albums came out without problems; what's the holdup with this one?"

D. Art opened his mouth, but he couldn't say anything. *I'm out of ideas. I feel empty. I can no longer do this.*

"Just…a block, I guess," he conceded.

"Hm. Well, hopefully a few more days of rest back home will help. But if you don't have anything for me when you get back, I'm buying the songs from someone else. I can't wait forever for your inspiration to come back," Rich said.

"…okay," D. Art said eventually, but Rich had already hung up.

He looked again at his ripped-up notebook and threw it aside. Flipping through his music app, he chose to play songs at random and got under the covers, feeling pathetic and defeated.

Suddenly he heard his own voice singing a familiar melody.

Anoche me besaste en la playa
la luz de luna iluminaba tu cara[7]

The opening phrases of "Solo Dos Bros"… Alone in his bedroom, in the dark of night, he let himself listen to it like it was someone else's song. A young man's voice mixing with Athos's deep timbre, slow, sexy, and nostalgic. It really was a very good song.

He couldn't help the memory that came: Athos rolling a joint on his sofa, the faint glow of the streetlight illuminating his elegant profile, messy dreads, regal nose, and chiseled jaw. Despite his casual clothes, he had a classic look to him, like a painting in a museum.

As he watched Athos's clever fingers, D. Art gave words to a melody he'd been rolling around in his head that night. Athos looked up, joint already on his lips, one of his rare, big smiles stretching them, radiating a joy that lit up the dark room.

Without missing a beat, Athos continued,

Yo quiero repetir no sé si quieras
tener a tu mejor amigo en la cama[8]

And just like that…it happened: the rush of discovery, the joy of making music together—repeating, modifying, and improving each other's lines. Somehow D. Art ended up lying down across the sofa, his legs over Athos's lap, Athos's hand on his thigh.

He still felt embarrassed to remember it, that growing, reckless emotion that overtook him in that moment, when his mouth was dry and he felt too warm and drunk and stupid.

No des vuelta atrás
only for tonight
soy tuyo papá[9]

Athos sang, and D. Art gave in to the impulse to reach out his hand and intertwine his fingers with Athos's.

"That sounds good. We should make it even gayer, sing it live," D. Art said, and in that moment, he felt he could do anything as long as Athos was with him.

"Yeah. That'd be cool," Athos said with a pleased smile.

D. Art couldn't take it any longer. He pulled Athos down toward him.

"Santi—" Athos's voice was hushed, a quick gasped-out warning.

"Come here, papi," D. Art said, and Athos obeyed.

There were tears in his eyes as the last notes of the song faded away, and he pressed "Pause" to interrupt the annoyingly cheerful song that came after.

I never really said goodbye, he thought with a deep pang in his chest. He'd kept talking to Porto on the phone, kept following their socials, but he hadn't seen his friends since he signed the contract two years ago. This was the first time he was back home for more than a few days at a time, and he hadn't even told them. What a rotten thing to do…

---

7   *Yesterday you kissed me on the beach / moonlight was shining on your face*
8   *I wanna do it again dunno if you want / to have your best friend in bed*
9   *Don't turn back / only for tonight / I'm yours*

Maybe he should start that inevitable drug addiction his parents kept warning him against.

His phone pinged—a message from Porto.

Ain't sayin' he's a MILF digger
Hey Art! Where u at? NY, Miami, Medellín?
I hope I'm not interrupting your beauty sleep.
We need your help.

He could've transferred the money, but he found himself hurrying to the police station, where he found Samira outside smoking a cigarette.

She greeted him with a raised eyebrow. "You came."

"Hi, I—what happened? Porto said—" D. Art gesticulated a fight with his hands.

Samira shrugged. "The usual. He's doing his set at the club when he sees some guys harassing a girl. He could've told the security guard, but he went himself. Apparently, one of them was his ex or something? I dunno. Insults fly, fists fly, Athos gets arrested for assault and disturbing the peace." Samira put out her cigarette and set her hands on her hips. "So, what're you here for?"

"I—I have the bail money," D. Art said. "And a lawyer."

Nodding, Samira led him inside.

It took hours of paperwork and checking in with his lawyer, signing autographs and taking pictures with the staff, but finally he was face-to-face with Athos. He looked the same—with the addition of a black eye and cuts and bruises on his face and fists. He greeted D. Art warmly, without surprise, as if they'd been parted for only a few days.

As they crammed into Porto's ancient Datsun coupe, Athos said, "Get us to Fajardo. It's gonna be a great beach day today."

Porto whooped, Samira pulled D. Art by the arm onto the back seat beside her, and D. Art looked doubtfully at the sky outside, which was lightening into a gray dawn.

Now that the immediate emergency was solved, D. Art's previous confidence ebbed away. He watched the streets pass by in silence until Samira poked him in the ribs.

"So, the great D. Art graces us with his presence today, and he's not even gonna talk to us? Not gonna tell us what it's like to travel around the world, meeting famous singers and artists? Not gonna regale us with stories about all the pretty girls he's dancing with?" Her tone was somewhere between sharp and teasing.

"Um, yeah, the girls…" D. Art mumbled. "They're chosen for me, I just… Some of them are fun to talk to." He cringed at Samira's raised eyebrow and upturned lips.

The car veered sharply to the right as Porto turned around to look at him, his eyes alight with excitement. "What's it like to work with Daddy and Arcángel and—?"

From the passenger seat, Athos grabbed the wheel to keep the car steady.

"The road, Porto!" D. Art chided. Then, he smiled wryly and shared some choice gossip and stories he never told any of the interviewers. By the time they got into Athos's dinghy boat, most of the initial awkwardness had faded into old jokes and catching up on their lives, Porto's and Samira's new flames and misadventures, and Athos's updates on the police accountability movement and the rap workshops about police violence he'd participated in.

On the way to the secluded cove where their beach was, D. Art closed his eyes to feel the breeze tangling his hair, basking in the rays of dawn.

It was almost like the old days, drinking on the beach, fighting over the music they were playing, dancing, and laughing. During a lull in the conversation, D. Art gave up another secret: his soon-to-fail new album.

"Let's listen to what you have," Samira prodded him.

D. Art pulled out his demos and halfway-done lyrics, to mixed reactions.

"The beat's good," said Athos, nodding along to it.

"It needs a bit more pep, though," Samira added.

"The lyrics are shit," Porto said.

"I know," D. Art said, lowering his head in frustration.

"How about something more like—" Porto started beat-boxing a rhythm. Samira followed with an improvised chorus, and Athos continued with a rap that was so dissonant with the cheerful melody that D. Art laughed.

"That's so dark! I like it," D. Art cheered.

Going over the songs with his friends, it became easy to imagine different songs with different personalities: something with Samira's cool voice, a cheerful melody that spoke of injustice in Athos's style, a crazy-fast trap for a romantic song in Porto's voice.

This is what I've been missing, D. Art realized as he recorded and wrote as much as he could and made plans in his head detailing how best to pitch the collaborations to Rich E.

It was like the old days, except without casual touches and warm, complicit looks from Athos.

Looking up, he saw Athos heading alone toward the edge of the cove. Gathering his courage, D. Art followed him.

Athos noticed and waited for D. Art to catch up, helping him navigate the sharp rocks until they approached a wide boulder with enough space for them to sit together. With his long legs resting against the stone, Athos lit up a joint and smoked, watching the waves breaking against the rocks.

Before D. Art could figure out what to say, Athos asked, "How are you, really?"

D. Art sighed and shrugged. "I keep busy. There's a lot to do. It's fun, but it's too much sometimes. I—I missed you guys."

"Told you to keep in touch," Athos chided.

"I'm sorry," D. Art said. And once that was out there, the rest came out in a hurry, words tumbling over each other. "I know I was a piece of shit. I just felt so...I know I said we would sing our song live one day, and I went back on that. I panicked, all right? And I think I made the right call, but it doesn't feel that way. I still feel like—like I *betrayed* you, and—"

"Breathe," Athos reminded him.

D. Art took a deep breath, not that it helped to calm him down. The breath caught in his throat, causing him to choke while tears pooled in his eyes. But Athos wasn't looking as he made a fool of himself; he was intently watching the clouds in the horizon.

"How do you and Samira do it? How can you be so cool and confident with who you are?" D. Art wondered.

"That's the impression we give. But it's something we chose, and it cost us. You think we got it easy? With how religious Samira's family is? And I haven't talked to my folks in, like, ten years. Last night…when that idiot Winter called me a slur in front of his rich friends, I fucking lost it. I could've outed him, told his friends how happily he'd jumped in my bed when I was paying the bills, but I just punched him in the face. It was more satisfying, anyway."

"So it was your ex, then," D. Art muttered. "I don't know if I'm any better than him."

Athos faced him and put his hands on D. Art's shoulders. "Here's the thing, Santi. We live in a world that's moderately to extremely shitty to people like us. Sometimes you gotta make hard decisions to protect yourself or your future—whatever. But if you take what they say—what they taught you—and make it a part of you, you're gonna hurt yourself and make yourself unhappy. Whether you're in or out, you gotta face that part of yourself and learn to love it." Athos smiled gently. "It's hard. But it helps to have people around who know you and accept you for who you are."

D. Art reached out and squeezed Athos's arm for a second, and Athos put his arm around the younger man's shoulders. Enveloped in Athos's warmth and scent, D. Art relaxed. It felt like coming home.

Too soon, Athos got up and helped D. Art to his feet. Before they made their way back to the others, Athos paused to look at the horizon once more. Taking a deep breath, he faced D. Art and said, "I don't resent you for your decision, back then. If I'm honest…you weren't the only one that wasn't ready."

"What…?"

"You were right: I was pushing you away."

Hearing this, D. Art exhaled a punched-out breath. Athos raised his palms, hurrying to add, "I still think it was for the best! I knew you had what it took, and it was what you wanted. I was also very scared of whatever was going on between us, and it was easier for you to go than…"

D. Art buried his face in his hands, trying and failing to stifle the tears.

"I'm sorry," Athos sounded unsure as he said it, fidgeting in front of D. Art as if he wanted to come closer but didn't dare. D. Art pulled him in and let himself take comfort in their embrace. "It's all right, we're here now," Athos muttered, holding on tightly to D. Art.

There was something about being back on the island that resonated within him, like radio static suddenly resolving into a familiar song. He never missed the island until he was back among the bright colors, the verdant streets, the warm smell of the sea and the noises of his people, their lightning-quick accents, the music on every corner, the calls of the coquí frogs at night.

He hadn't done a concert back home in a while. Even though he'd performed in bigger cities with bigger artists and for bigger crowds, he was still more nervous before the show than he'd been in a long time, so nervous he locked himself in the bathroom, feeling he might be sick.

A knock distracted him from his queasy contemplation of the sink. "D. Art, you're up!"

D. Art opened the door to Athos's grin, his concert get-up indistinguishable from his everyday wear.

"This takes you back, doesn't it?" he said as he led D. Art toward the stage. "All of us here together, you puking before the concert…"

"I didn't actually vomit," D. Art complained, but the banter and Athos's casual arm around his shoulders settled his nausea. He shot Athos a grin before he ran to the stage, received back home with a warm and raucous cheer from the crowd.

Their first concert together had been in a beach bar for a crowd of twenty or thirty patrons, where only the few drunkest people had danced to their songs. Now he'd filled up El Choli, the biggest arena in Puerto Rico, and everybody in the crowd was chanting his name.

This is it.

It was far from the biggest concert of his career, but it was his favorite. Up on stage, he was having *fun*. It helped that many of the new songs he was singing featured his friends, who were received warmly by the audience, infected by Porto's cheerfulness and comedic energy, Samira's cool voice as she sang "Las Divinas"[10] along with her choir, and Athos's poise as he rapped during an uncensored political song that was going to get them in trouble with Rich E. later. They'd even made remixes of their most popular Tres Más Uno songs for the encore, which the crowd sang with them as they jumped on the stadium floor, the ground vibrating with their collective force.

And for the last song, the lights dimmed, and it was only him up on the stage with an acoustic guitar and a microphone.

"This was one of the first songs I wrote…and one I've never performed live. This new version is recent, so recent that it's not even released yet. But here is where I grew up, the place that saw my first concerts and first mistakes. This is where I would like to stay for the rest of my life. So, I want to share it with you first."

The cheers, whoops, hollers, and claps of the crowd sounded warm and expectant.

He started playing a simple melody on the guitar and sang.

> *Anoche me besaste en la playa*
> *la luz de luna iluminaba tu cara*
> *Yo quiero repetir no sé si quieras*
> *tener a tu mejor amigo en la cama*

Then, the lights focused on a point behind him as Athos added his deeper, scratchy voice to the song.

> *Así somos, desde que nos conocemos*
> *en el carro sigue el flow, en la cama acabaremos* [11]

And it was *on*. The crowd was silent, or, perhaps, D. Art was so focused on the song that he didn't register their presence anymore. Making this song with Athos had been a revelation, but singing it here today was something more: it felt like a public declaration, a promise, open worship. A love song, not to remember old times but to plead for the future.

As the final notes faded into the din of hundreds of people's whispers, Athos and D. Art approached the center of the stage, side by side, and took a bow before the scattered clapping crescendoed into a roar.

Looking at Athos's bright eyes beside him, D. Art couldn't help his own silly, wide-open grin.

---

10   "The Divine (Ladies)"

11   *This is us, since we met / in the car with the flow, we'll end up in your bed*

Cris Alborja   *"Start your engines"*

I love the drag scene, so I wanted to draw the gang as different kinds of drag kings. D'Artagnan is a beauty king with androgynous features, as is Aramis, who has a silicon body suit. Porthos is a comedy king, and Athos is performing a more masculine style.

Tags
relationships: age difference, friends, friends to lovers, the grumpy one is soft for the sunshine one, m/m
character features: criminal, hacker
other tags: action and adventure, alternate universe, be gay do crimes, first kiss, flirting, france, getting together, great britain, heist, love declaration, modern, paris, past tense, pining (mutual), third person alternating point of view

Inspiration
There are so many good parts to *The Three Musketeers*—but my favorite has always been the heist to help the queen! So, of course, when I had the chance to do a queer remake on the original—I had to write a modern version of the heist. (With a little romance, because the grumpy one being soft for the sunshine one never gets old!)

This definitely presented its own challenges—but it was one I loved, and it let me focus in on a tiny part of a much bigger world that I built and put all of my heist-movie watching to good use in!

Stolen Hearts

— Aria L. Deair

"Are we done yet?" D'art asked, hooking his foot on the table leg, stopping the spinning of his chair to look at the others. "We've run through the entire plan at least four times now, Athos."

"If you would pay attention for more than ten seconds at a time—"

"Aramis," Athos snapped, glad when his friend's mouth immediately clicked shut. Ignoring the knowing smirk Porthos was hiding behind that giant water bottle of his, Athos took a deep breath. "D'art, the entire last leg of this depends on you being able to—"

D'art held up one finger. "Flirt my way past the security guards: easy. Use the badge Porthos stole to get through the higher-security entrance: simple, as long as he doesn't fuck it up. Steal the diamonds: also easy, as long as you've done your job, Athos. And—"

"—and get out," Athos finished, meeting D'art's eyes. "Being able to get the diamonds doesn't mean a damn thing if we don't all get out."

Porthos took a long sip from his water jug. "The boy's right, Athos. You've demanded he walk through his escape plan several times now."

Athos frowned at the plans laid out on the table, at the path that D'art had outlined for his escape. It was far more involved than he liked, but well within the scope of what D'art could do. Had done in the past.

That didn't ease the pit of worry deep in Athos's stomach.

"He doesn't need you babying him, Athos," Aramis pointed out. "I'm more worried about you."

"I'll be fine," Athos dismissed. If that was because he had several plans of his own in the event things went sideways, well, it was up to him to protect the team. He'd brought them all together—his Musketeers. He turned his eyes to D'art. "Once more. From the top," he ordered.

After several long seconds, D'art stood up and pushed his chair back. "From the top, then," he said. He shot Athos a wink and leaned over the map. "We infiltrate Milady's corporate offices at 3 p.m. Thursday, two days from today. The diamonds must be in Anne Reine's display prior to her benefit luncheon at noon Friday. There is a flight scheduled for us at 8 p.m. Thursday. We either make that, or we don't make the deadline."

Aramis crossed his arms over his chest. "That's the crux of it: whether we make that flight or not."

"After we've made our way in," D'art continued, "we wait for the security patrol to make their coffee stop—"

"I'll have the sign out advertising free drinks to lure them in," Porthos answered.

D'art nodded. "They'll be drugged; Athos and I will replace them. Aramis has booked the meeting room here for a department event—" He pointed to the map. "We'll put them here and have a presentation playing remotely."

"Untraceable to us," Aramis continued. "Convenient red herring in case anyone cares to look."

"Good," Athos said. "Then?"

"Then," D'art answered, grinning. "We haul ass up to the top floor, I flirt my way past the security guards, use the badge Aramis will have palmed me after he left the bathroom, wait for him to tell me he's doing whatever the hell he's doing with security—"

Aramis snorted. "Fair enough, kid."

"—I steal the diamonds, and, well." D'art lifted his eyes to Athos's and smirked. "Do precisely what you are paying me very, very well to do: get the hell out of there without being seen."

Athos let out a breath and glanced at the clock. "We're as ready as we're going to get." He grinned and looked at each of them. "All for one?"

"And one for all!" Aramis and Porthos echoed.

Athos met D'art's eyes and smiled at him, easy and open. Hopefully, it would be that easy.

Wednesday presented a major problem.

Athos pinched the bridge of his nose. "What do you *mean* Milady doesn't have all three pieces?"

D'art hunched his shoulders. "Don't shoot the messenger. I'm just telling you what Aramis said while you were on the phone earlier."

"Does Buckingham have the missing piece?" Athos couldn't imagine that the man wouldn't have told them that. They could have traced it, found it, ensured it came back with the other pieces. But now—

"Nope," D'art said, rocking back on his heels. "It's the ring that's missing. He's getting one emergency commissioned, though. Said he's as invested as he can be in Anne Reine's benefit."

"He is," Athos agreed. "He's one of the biggest donors. And, if rumor is to be believed, they've been lovers for years." He sighed and rubbed at his face tiredly. "Is he certain he'll have it in time?"

D'art shrugged. "You'd know better than me, but I'd assume so."

They'd need to find the lost ring at some point, but they could worry about that when the benefit wasn't hanging over their heads, a guillotine ready to drop. "Very well. A problem for later."

D'art sidled around the table and leaned against it, facing Athos directly. "You always this tense before a heist, Athos?"

Athos narrowed his eyes at D'art's proximity. "You steal my phone off me again, I'll stab your hand," Athos threatened. "Don't care if you need it tomorrow." His eyes roamed over the map again.

D'art's laugh echoed in the meeting room and sent a shiver up his spine. "Don't threaten me with a good time," D'art teased, winking. "I'll let Bucks—"

"Please don't call him that."

"—know that we'll rendezvous before we get to the airport," D'art finished. "Problem solved."

Athos sighed. Problems were never solved that easily, but they didn't have time to put another solution in place. "Have him tell me where he's getting the ring from and authorize me to retrieve it, in the event that he can't."

"You got it!"

When Athos turned, D'art was standing much, much closer than he should have been. He frowned. "D'art—" He blinked when D'art poked a finger between his eyebrows.

"Stop worrying so much. You're giving yourself wrinkles, and you're too handsome for wrinkles."

Athos blinked and watched D'art saunter (because it was a saunter, and he could feel the *look* from Porthos even if the man wasn't in the room) out of the meeting room and down the hall. He took a deep breath. He was too old for this shit, and they didn't have time for it.

"Stained apron might be your new iconic look, Porthos," D'art said, keeping his voice low as Athos finished registering them as guests at the front door. He leaned back against the wall and posed himself so Athos would see how well this bespoke suit fit him.

"It's going to be your new iconic look if you don't cut out the posturing, you little shit," Porthos muttered. "Low profile, remember?"

D'art let out a low laugh, his eyes on Athos as he returned at last, two "Visitor" badges in his hands. "I'm not made to be low profile," he shot back. Once Athos was close again, giving him a searching look, he winked and stretched. "Shall we head to our meeting?" A glance out of the corner of his eye clocked the two security guards picking up their coffees from Porthos. "Pity we don't have time to grab a coffee. I'll have to ask you out for one later."

Athos nearly stumbled on the ugly dark-blue carpet. "Focus," he ordered.

How he was supposed to focus when Athos was in a tailored-to-perfection dark-gray suit, he had no idea. But, as planned, they fell into step behind the security guards. When one of them stumbled, he and Athos stepped up in unison, grabbed their coffees, and urged them toward the bathrooms. D'art nodded to Aramis when he held the door for them; there was a "Closed" sign hanging on it. "Smart," he grunted.

"Get changed quick and get moving," Aramis ordered, checking the hallway, then stepping out of the bathroom, leaning against the wall, and glancing at his phone.

D'art grunted as he stripped the uniform off the security guard and grabbed the suit out of the bags that they had been carrying. "Someone needs to tell this guy that he shouldn't skip leg day," he muttered, levering the now-unconscious security guard into the ill-fitting suit. Once that was done and he was properly propped up against the sink, D'art changed into his security outfit, scowling at the clip-on tie.

"Stop being such a snob," Athos said with a snort and a shake of his head. He glanced at the door and gave it a quick kick. "Aramis, we clear?"

"As a bell," came through the door.

D'art nodded and grabbed the security guard with a grunt. It took a great deal of huffing and puffing, but thankfully, between him and Athos, getting both of the guards out of the bathroom and into the meeting room across the hall was uneventful. The display in the room was already mid-presentation, and they turned the big chairs toward it so no one would see the unconscious guards.

He grinned at Athos. "Phase one complete," he said, just to see him roll his eyes. Cheesy, but it did feel a bit like they were in a movie; he could indulge for a moment. D'art stretched his arms over his head as Athos made sure the hallway was clear. Then they took their coffees and continued into the main area.

"You ready?" Athos asked, pretending to sip the coffee.

D'art sighed and gave him a look. "You hired me for this. You should know that even with all my teasing, I am a professional."

"So you are," Athos agreed. "That's why we're planning to offer you a position on the team when we're finished."

D'art was quiet for a long moment as they stepped into the elevator and hit the button for the 39th floor. He could feel Athos studying him. Assessing his reaction to the offer, maybe. "You have a policy against dating people you work with?"

Athos blinked and sighed. "D'art—"

"Crimson," Porthos's voice hissed into the mic.

D'art froze, eyes widening. Over the comms, there was a crackle and the sound of the earpiece being shattered under a heel. "Shit."

"Aramis, what's going on?" Athos snapped, glancing up at the rapidly climbing floor indicators.

"Milady is here," Aramis said. "You'd better hurry. Crimson here, too."

"Fuck." Athos's fist hit the elevator wall. "Get out and—"

"No," Aramis interrupted. "You need the entrance covered. Athos. Figure out your exit plan now. D'art?"

D'art closed his eyes at the seriousness in that tone. "Yeah?"

"You'd better be as good as you've been bragging you are, kid. Out."

Moments later, Aramis's comm also went dead.

D'art looked at Athos. He swallowed. "We'll get them out afterward," he promised.

Athos shook his head. "We have a plane to catch; she knows we're here. We might not even be able to make the plan."

"Then…" D'art frowned. "What the hell do we do?"

Athos turned to D'art and grinned, gesturing to the now-opening elevator. "You do your job," he answered, "and think about my offer."

D'art scowled and tossed the coffee in the nearby trash can, striding down the hallway. The desk he needed to flirt his way past, the last door that he needed to get through, all of it was right in front of them. "Right."

Athos hummed and pretended to sip the coffee again.

D'art smiled at the secretary who looked up at him with a confused frown. He held up his badge and offered a big sigh. "Doing rounds," he said, shrugging.

"This part of the building isn't standard for—"

"I know," D'art said with a wave. "But, apparently, there's a whole commotion downstairs, and we've been ordered to check on them." He gestured to Athos with a huff. "Even sent the old man with me to make sure I don't get into any trouble."

The secretary snorted and shook her head. She leaned in closer. "You'd better hurry. I have no doubt that Milady Winters will be here soon. She likes to check on these personally, if you know what I mean."

"In and out in a flash," D'art promised, winking at her before he turned and gestured to Athos, heading to swipe his badge at the door. It flashed green, and he opened it. Inside, the exhibit of several dozen mannequins, partial androids, and other figures was displayed. It was creepy and sent a shudder up his spine.

"Good thinking, using the commotion downstairs," Athos said. "Now let's let you work your magic."

D'art wanted to laugh. "Didn't realize flexibility was a superpower these days."

They made it to the end of the exhibit, and he stared at the necklace and bracelet he needed to steal, then up at the metal grate all the mannequin displays were hanging from. "You think Aramis managed to cover the cameras?"

"We're about to find out," Athos answered, giving him a hand up.

D'art grabbed onto the railing and lifted his legs slowly, drawing them up and over the threshold where he knew the security lasers were pointed. He could see them on the wall. If only the movies were real and there were some sort of aerosol that would make them visible. He shifted his grip for a more solid hold on the grate and started to shimmy, slow and careful.

Athos glanced at the door, but all was quiet for the time being. "How long will it take you to get out?"

"An hour, by my count," D'art answered. "Thirty minutes if you want me to skip my additional plans to dodge anyone following me. Then to the airport and to meet Bucky the Ducky and get out of here."

"Get out quick," Athos ordered.

D'art grunted an acknowledgment as he twisted, all of his weight on one arm as he rotated slowly, slipping past another laser and then another. When he was over his prize, he locked his feet in the grate. "Hard part's done," he muttered, then he extended himself and grabbed at the flawless diamonds.

Both pieces went into the inner pocket under his security shirt, and he lifted himself back to the grate above with a grunt. "All right, time for your exit plan," D'art called, rolling his shoulders as he stretched and started to make his way back down. Once he was standing beside Athos, grinning in victory, about to pull out the diamonds to admire them, there was a shout from where they'd entered.

"No time," Athos answered, removing the clip-on tie. "Get out of here, D'art."

D'art reached out and grabbed Athos by the arm, yanking him back. "Don't do anything stupid," he growled. "I've been trying to ask you on a date for fucking ages; I'm not letting you skip out on this one."

Athos sighed. "D'art—"

D'art didn't jump at the sound of the door slamming open at the end of the exhibit, but it was a close thing. He turned to stare into worried brown eyes. "Athos—"

"Run," Athos ordered.

D'art pulled him down for a kiss, yanking on his hair, holding it for as long as he dared. "You'd better get out, old man. I want more where that came from." He gave Athos's hair one last tug before he turned and ran out the back door of the exhibit. The alarm blared, but it hardly mattered.

Athos had already been caught.

"Athos, darling, I thought you were better than this," Milady Winters purred, her heels clicking on the marble floor as she sauntered closer to where he was standing, waiting for her. "If you were so desperate to see me again, you could have simply visited."

Athos smiled faintly at her. "I am quite sure that you know I never wanted to see you again. Five years of marriage was quite enough for me."

Milady laughed. "Oh, Athos. You might mock me for finding greener pastures, but that boy?" She scoffed. "He's young enough to be your son."

Athos shrugged and put his hands in his pockets as he walked closer, freezing the two guards beside her with a glare. "He's young. Fancies himself in love with me. You know the type; they were always nipping at your heels, after all."

"I would, perhaps, believe you," Milady paused. "But I know your face." She stepped closer and drew a nail across his cheek, watching him flinch. "I know every part of you there is to know, Athos. I know what you look like when you are smitten, even when you try to hide it."

Athos took a deep breath and let it out gustily. He gave himself a moment, then two, and smiled faintly at her, meeting her dark eyes easily. "Perhaps you do," he agreed. "Though if he is any indication, my tastes have improved tenfold since I was with you." When her face twisted in rage, he reached up to activate his earpiece once more. "All for one!"

The echo, faint, said quietly, came across immediately. "One for all."

Athos ripped out the earpiece and crushed it under his heel, meeting Milady's eyes once again, before giving her a deep bow. "Now, my dear, if you'd like to participate in the PR disaster that is arresting the Count de La Fere, please, take me away."

D'art closed his eyes and stared at his reflection in the bathroom, pressing a hand to where the bracelet and necklace were tucked against him. "Twenty-four minutes," he ordered himself. Tugging his knife from his shoe, he cursed and sliced through his hair, cutting it short in quick, brutal strokes.

He grabbed the duffel bag Aramis had stashed before his shift and went through his mental list as he changed quickly. Short hair, dress pants, patterned shirt, and navy jacket. They were looking for a long-haired man in a security outfit, but that wasn't him any longer. He gave himself a nod in the mirror and stepped out, scowling at his phone as he began to walk. He glared at the security guards that bustled past him, sprinting their way upstairs, where he'd run from two minutes ago. He made his way to the elevator and opened the laptop tucked in the duffel, opening his calendar and taking the elevator down two floors.

Aria L. Deair

No one in the elevator looked at him twice as he stepped out. Eighteen floors to go. Humming, he made his way over to one of the meeting rooms that he'd just finished booking in the calendar app. He dropped the laptop on the table and pulled the blinds, then turned to the window and grinned.

Time for some fun.

The drop to the secondary roof below was fifteen feet, but D'art hit the gravel and rolled straight into a jog across the lower roof. The ladder ahead of him was still clear, but he could hear sirens pulling up to the building on the other side. Climbing down, he headed for the window at the very end of the building. The alarms were still going off, so he pulled the emergency latch and yanked it back open, climbing in.

At least two people sitting at the desks stared at him in shock, so D'art blew them a kiss and headed for the stairs.

Fourteen floors now.

Twelve minutes.

He passed an empty desk and palmed a pack of cigarettes that had been thrown there, tucking it into his inside pocket. He left the lighter and made his way to the stairs instead of the elevator. Security was barking orders nearby, but he ignored them as he stepped into the stairwell. There was activity ten floors up, but no one paid attention to him.

D'art leaped over the railing and quickly made his way down another five floors, heading onto the landing right as a shout came from above. He strode onto the floor calmly, focused on his phone, his heart pounding.

Nine remaining.

Nine minutes.

He stopped by the elevator bay and hit the call button, fiddling with the fresh pack of cigarettes in his hands. He rolled his eyes at the two elevators full of security guards, but the third elevator was blessedly empty except for a harried-looking man, so he stepped in and hit the button for the underground garage.

Almost out.

"You know that's a terrible habit."

D'art scowled and saluted him with the pack. "I'm chock full of those." He watched the man get off on the ground floor, and for a second, he caught sight of Athos, his hands cuffed behind him, flanked by dozens of security guards. D'art's heart jumped, stuttered, but he'd promised. All for one, one for all. He would get these diamonds to Anne Reine.

The elevator released him to the underground level, and D'art strode toward the smokers' lounge area. He stepped into the haze-filled room and shed his jacket, opened the pack, and pulled one out before he patted at his slacks. "Fuck, forgot a light."

Thankfully, one of the others in the booth had one, and he lit the cigarette, taking his time, pretending to smoke it. He waited until all of the men had left, replaced by new ones every few minutes, before he finally crushed the remains under his boot. The sirens had gone silent, and the security team by the exit was heading back inside.

Stealing a car and making his way to meet Buckingham at the airport was almost too easy, but D'art was relieved when he pulled up to the designated spot in the parking lot and found the man leaning against his own car.

32

"Quite the mess," Buckingham observed. "You have them?"

D'art pulled the necklace and bracelet out of his vest and showed them. "The others—"

"I know. Milady is on quite the warpath looking for you. All security here has been put on alert," Buckingham said, holding out the ring, "which presents us with quite the problem."

"Shit," D'art breathed. "What the hell are we going to do?" He checked his watch. The flight was in a little over two hours, and he had to be on it.

Buckingham crossed his arms over his chest. "I'm working on a questionably legal solution. Lose the car and come to the rear entrance of Terminal E. Midnight."

"That'll be—" D'art snapped his mouth shut at the look he was given and watched Buckingham leave. He abandoned the car, heading for public transportation.

The next six hours crawled by, fear and concern for Athos making him tense and irritable. However, he was a professional, so D'art found another change of clothing and the entrance Buckingham had mentioned.

At ten to midnight, a car pulled up and a door was thrown open.

"Get in," Buckingham ordered.

D'art raised an eyebrow at him.

"I've organized a flight for you. You'll arrive in Paris in six hours, as we must be subtle and draw no attention. From there, a car will be waiting to take you to Anne," Buckingham said.

"The flight I was supposed to be on left—"

Buckingham smiled and raised an imperious eyebrow back at him. "A supersonic private jet will not face customs, other air traffic restrictions, or speed limitations. They're very ostentatious and risk attracting too much attention, but we don't have a choice now. So get going."

D'art didn't bother asking more questions, climbing out of the car and into the jet that was waiting at the other end of the runway. Buckingham's car disappeared back where it had come from, and within minutes, D'art was in the air. He kept his hand on his phone, tapping at it worriedly as he thought of Aramis, Porthos, and... He shook his head. They'd be fine. He would get to the safehouse in Paris and start figuring out how to rescue them.

Sleeping was impossible. The adrenaline rush of his escape and the knowledge that the others were captured kept him thinking. Eventually, the pilot let him know that they were on the approach to Paris. D'art checked his watch again. Still enough time. Three hours until the party started.

Thankfully, the plane landed on the same type of deserted runway they'd left from, and there was a car waiting just as Buckingham had promised.

However, pulling up to the benefit posed one final problem.

"Problems always come in threes, don't they Athos," D'art muttered, assessing his hoodie and jeans and the building in front of him.

Well, he wasn't an infamous thief for nothing.

Forgoing the front entrance, D'art hopped a tall bush fence in the back, evaded the two security guards that were patrolling, and snuck in an open window. Following the sound of voices (and terrifying a young woman who rushed off, certainly to get security), D'art managed, at last, to find Anne Reine, bursting into her bedroom with security hot on his heels.

"Lady Anne!"

She spun around, her eyes widening. "D'Artagnan!"

D'art winced. "D'art's fine," he said, making his way over to her, glad when she called off the security. He handed her the diamonds with a smile; she sagged in relief. "As advertised, ma'am, and now safely back in your hands."

"Thank you, D'art." She looked him over. "Buckingham told me you had trouble. Are you all right?"

The twisting reminder that his friends had been captured and were likely in need of rescue had D'art resisting the urge to fidget. "I'm fine. I need to catch up with the others. Will you be all right?"

Anne Reine nodded. "We'll be perfectly fine now, thanks to you. Please give my thanks to Athos and the others when you see them."

D'art gave her a proper bow, then followed the not-so-subtle nudging of her security team out of the building. Standing in the busy streets of Paris, his phone dead, alone, he let himself worry as he started to make his way to the safehouse, thankful that Athos had made him memorize the address. It would take time to find out where they'd been taken, where they were being held, but he would. First order of business would be food and a shower, then he could sort out their rescue.

Stopping outside the building, D'art typed in the passcode, relaxing when he heard the sound of metallic locks disengaging, and shoved the door open. Food, shower, charge phone, and then—

"Well there's the hero of the hour! About time you got here!"

D'art's head snapped up and he stared at Aramis, who was holding an ice pack to a black eye and lounging in the living room on a comfy-looking leather couch. He stopped, unable to look away, as Porthos came in from the kitchen, a wide grin on his face.

"He certainly did take his sweet time," Porthos agreed, handing Aramis a beer, then settling on the couch, giving D'art a knowing smile. "He's in the kitchen."

Rushing past both of them into the kitchen didn't feel quite real, but there was Athos, bruised and roughed up, a bandage across his cheek. D'art watched as he finished making one of his vile smoothies, then he turned around, smiling, and damn if that smile didn't make everything just a little better.

Athos smiled. "So, have you thought about my offer?"

D'art moved closer, drawn in by that smile the same way he always was. "Have you thought about going on a date with me?" he challenged.

"D'art…" Athos sighed. "I am—"

"Married?" D'art asked, looking pointedly at Athos's fingers.

"What?" Athos frowned. "No, of course not."

"Dating someone already?" D'art offered instead, stopping in front of Athos with a raised eyebrow.

"Where the hell are you getting these?" Athos said, snorting. "You know damn well I'm not."

D'art shrugged. "Figured if you were resisting this hard you had a good reason, but it sounds like you don't."

"This is what you're signing up for, kid!" Porthos shouted from the living room.

Athos scowled, then opened his mouth only to find D'art much, much closer than he had been a few seconds earlier. "D'art, you—"

"So, Milady is that ex you always pretend you don't complain about, huh?" D'art teased, starting to smile.

Athos shook his head, rolling his eyes. "Don't listen to them. I don't complain that much."

D'art reached out and wrapped his arms around Athos's shoulders, leaning in. "Liar," he whispered, grinning at him. He leaned in and kissed the bandage on Athos's cheek. "Thought I told you not to do anything stupid?"

Athos hummed, reaching up to comb his fingers through D'art's short hair. "You're a terrible hair stylist."

"*Athos.*"

"Well, it seems that I'm falling for an impulsive thief with no sense of self-preservation. That's about as stupid as it gets for an old man like me," Athos teased. "Handling Milady is easy by comparison."

D'art laughed. "So is this the moment when I tell you that the thief loves the old man right back?"

"Ridiculous," Athos muttered, even as D'art pulled him in for a decidedly more enjoyable kiss.

From the kitchen, D'art could see Aramis leaning back against the couch, smirking at Porthos. "And Athos wondered why we put him in the far room."

"Over-under on him being able to keep up with D'art once they make it to their room?"

Athos pulled back from the kiss to glare at them. "You know we can *hear* you?"

Porthos laughed. "Should we be giving you pointers instead?"

"And here I thought you didn't need advice of that nature, Athos. You were married, after all!"

Athos took D'art's hand, shaking his head at Aramis and Porthos as they laughed uproariously at themselves. "Come on. I have plans for you."

D'art laughed, too, as Athos pulled him farther into the house, away from the kitchen. "I do like your plans…"

Paris-ish

– Nova Mason

D'Artagnan stared at the agenda in his hands and shifted against the uncomfortable metal folding chair. Somehow, it didn't matter when they showed up to the HOA meetings; he and his friends always missed out on the good chairs.

The treasurer, Richelieu, was scowling and preaching about the evils of outdoor pests. He implored the members of the Paris Neighborhood Homeowner's Association to ensure that they kept their trash under lock and key until at least 8 p.m. the night before trash pickup, as per the bylaws. D'Artagnan had to stifle a chuckle every time Richelieu said the word "Paris," halfway between the English pronunciation and a strange faux-French accent. There was nothing Parisian about the neighborhood other than its name and that the ladies' garden club wore berets and scarves to the annual summer cookout.

Well, and their rivalry with the London Neighborhood.

D'Artagnan felt movement next to him and glanced over to see the always-serious Athos scribbling some notes on his legal pad to look up exceptions in the bylaws that were not being addressed. D'Artagnan smirked, then quickly regained his composure lest he be castigated for not taking the HOA meetings seriously enough. He knew that, as a mere tenant and not a homeowner, his presence at the meetings was merely tolerated under the guise of community engagement.

The three other members of his group, actual homeowners in the neighborhood, had a routine by now: Athos did the legal research on whatever nonsense Richelieu was trying to impose and would let everyone know at the next poker game, Aramis would write up a post for the neighborhood social media groups, and Porthos would stage a dramatic speech during open-floor time at next month's HOA meeting.

Richelieu turned to the topic of the coffers and budget, reminding the residents to send any complaints about the plow service directly to him, *not* to Association Board President Louis. It was contracted out and therefore fell under Richelieu's purview as treasurer. Somehow, everything seemed to fall under Richelieu's power. D'Artagnan stole a glance around the room: Louis's wife Anne was, as usual, busying herself setting up the snacks and rearranging the table for at least the third time—anything to avoid having to listen to the actual meeting. Louis was at the head table on his laptop, ostensibly taking notes but probably shopping for ice-

Tags
relationships: friends, m/m
character features: anxiety, character has a different gender than in the source material, has a disability
other tags: alternate universe, break-up, christmas, getting together, modern, past tense, politics, third person limited point of view

Inspiration
While re-reading *The Three Musketeers*, I tried to think of ways to bring it into the modern age. I happened to see some posts on the internet about whacky HOA requirements, and the idea of "Richelieu as the tyrannical person in charge of a Homeowner's Association" was born. As I continued to think about it, I tried to find modern mirrors for different conflicts in the novel. Anne's diamonds became roses, and the war between France and England became a competition between neighborhoods about Christmas decorations.

Toby.exe

"The Voice, The Action and The Heart"

My initial thoughts when given the prompt were drawn to existing characters of mine that fit into the tropes I was provided: Dionysus, the stoic, responsible one; Cassius, the one who yearns for heroism; and Glynn, the innocent, whole-heartedly loving one. I just had to include them in this piece.

fishing supplies.

Then, d'Artagnan's gaze fell on Connie. The young and beautiful Conrad Bonacieux was dutifully taking notes—actual notes in an actual notebook—about the proceedings, a furrow between his perfectly sculpted brows. Connie was very concerned with keeping the Bonacieux house in compliance with all the HOA rules. He was also concerned about a whole host of other things, and d'Artagnan relished being present to help calm him about such critical matters as whether to make snickerdoodles or sugar cookies (both, and d'Artagnan would help), or how he would fit a trip to the post office into an otherwise busily packed day (d'Artagnan had offered to drop off the letter, even though the post office was well out of his way).

Connie's husband was, as usual, absent. D'Artagnan didn't want to pry, but he hadn't seen the other Mr. Bonacieux around lately. Besides, Mr. Bonacieux's absence had given him more opportunities to help Connie out by offering to do things like mow the lawn before Richelieu posted one of his infamous lawn-maintenance warnings. Connie was fairly helpless when it came to anything involving hard labor, but he more than made up for it with his skill in the kitchen. And sure, d'Artagnan had some romantic admiration, but it was okay to have a crush on his landlord as long as he wasn't overstepping any boundaries.

He felt a nudge as Athos redirected his attention to the meeting.

"—in our neighborhood. As the bylaws clearly state, gambling is strictly prohibited within the gates of the community. That includes not only gambling for money but also for chips or anything else, and internet gambling. There have been rumors of"—Richelieu pursed his lips with disgust—"poker nights." He sniffed and regathered his composure. "As of now, there are only rumors, and I pray that it remains that way. If, however, such reports become substantiated, penalties will be issued accordingly." Penalties, d'Artagnan knew, usually came as a combination of fines and public snubbing. Punishments also included being moved to the bottom of the priority list for plowing (even though Justin the plow guy sometimes came to those poker nights).

Moving to the next item on the agenda, Richelieu managed to pull Louis away from the laptop for long enough to address the group on the topic of: "The annual holiday decoration contest. We've won the past three years, but there are rumors that the London Neighborhood Association is rallying this year. Their secretary, Buckingham—" Louis said this name dripping with contempt "—is supposedly organizing some kind of neighborhood theme. We've gotten complacent. I know some of us have used the same decorations for several years now, but if we are to win the contest, we need to step it up." He gestured to his wife, who was setting a casserole dish of steaming-hot taco dip onto the snack table. "If you need assistance with ideas, Anne has quite the collection on Pinterest, so feel free to check in with her." The taco dip having been placed on its trivets, Anne gave a little wave and an awkward smile.

"And," Louis continued, "if anyone manages to find anything out about the London Neighborhood's plans, please make sure to let us know. The best defense is a good offense, after all." D'Artagnan blinked but remained as impassive as he could at the metaphor, which Louis was prone to using when it didn't quite fit. "And with that, I think we can call the meeting over and hit the snack table. As always, thank you, Anne, for preparing the spread."

Anne stepped back from the snack table with an expression somewhere between a smile and a grimace. D'Artagnan knew that she hated being the center of attention, but her husband frequently put her there anyway at every meeting, barbeque, holiday party, or other neighborhood gathering.

D'Artagnan stood up, stretched, and began to make his way over to the snack table, curious about what Anne had put together this time. The theme seemed to be dips. He eyed the taco dip, with a sheen of fake cheese on top, and filled his plate with crackers and sliced cheddar instead. As he moved off to the corner of the room, he saw Porthos loading up a plate with taco dip and something from the breadbowl that looked suspiciously like plain mayonnaise.

Porthos and Aramis converged on d'Artagnan's corner, and Porthos threw his arm around d'Artagnan's shoulders. "A perfect opportunity," he stage-whispered loudly enough for Aramis to hear, "to hang some lights for Connie, eh?"

"I think it's sweet," Aramis said, "to do something nice like that. Acts of service are an important part of all human relationships, not just romantic ones."

Porthos smirked and tossed his perfectly blown-out hair. "You could always hire a decorating service for your mysterious Canadian girlfriend. That should be your next blog post: 'The Theologically Proper Method for Acts of Service When Being Catfished.' "

Aramis glowered, and d'Artagnan smiled; he enjoyed the friendly bickering and banter that always cropped up when their group got together. All they were missing was Athos, who was currently waiting at the snack table for an opening. A crowd had gathered, making it impossible for Athos to get his wheelchair through, and d'Artagnan knew that his friend's preferred strategy was to wait until the crowd noticed in order to make them as uncomfortable as possible.

Aramis gave as good as he got in the verbal repartee, calmly taking a sip from his red plastic cup before responding. "As long as the service is genuine, and not a knock-off," he said, blatantly eyeing Porthos's shirt, "I think that should be fine."

Porthos blushed down to the collar of his imitation designer shirt. D'Artagnan ate a slice of cheese on a cracker, thankful that it was, at least, real cheese of some kind. Porthos was just readying a comeback when Athos finally wheeled up to the group, his plate in his lap. "So," he said, popping the brake on a wheel and then rubbing his hands together. "This Christmas decorations contest. Thoughts?"

Several years ago, Athos's ex-wife had moved to the London neighborhood after their very public, bitter divorce; she had quickly become one of the most active meddlers on the London Neighborhood Association Board. Athos never passed up an opportunity to use the neighborhood rivalry to his advantage.

"What," d'Artagnan said, feigning shock. "You don't have a complete plan in place already?"

Athos waved a hand dismissively. "Of course I do, but it doesn't hurt to solicit input in case something can be improved."

Aramis raised an eyebrow. "And who's going to pay for this plan of yours?" Athos's plans were often grander than their budget allowed, and Richelieu wasn't likely to part with any of the HOA's funds even if it meant sticking it to the London Neighborhood.

"Oh, well, various sources. I was thinking some crowdfunding from your readership"—he gestured towards Aramis—"and perhaps we could get some sponsorship—"He gestured toward Porthos.

Porthos crossed his arms. "And what will our young friend do?" He raised his chin in d'Artagnan's direction.

"Oh," Athos continued, "he'll be the one climbing on all of our roofs. Unless you think I should do that part."

D'Artagnan rolled his eyes but smiled. He usually was recruited to do the most arduous physical labor for their schemes, but he didn't mind. The others were older and had taken him under their wings after some initial scruples.

"I'll share the details of the plan with you all, say, Thursday evening at the regular time?" The men nodded. Thursday was their weekly poker night. At least this time they'd have a veneer of respectability.

Suddenly, Porthos tapped d'Artagnan on the shoulder, leaned close, and whispered, "Twink at seven o'clock." Now it was d'Artagnan's turn to blush, ever so slightly, and he regained his composure before moving aside to admit Connie to their circle.

Connie grasped his notebook tightly against his chest with folded arms and gave the other men a wide smile. "Evening. How's the decoration planning coming?"

Porthos narrowed his eyes in mock approbation. "How'd you know what we were scheming?"

"I wouldn't," Aramis interjected, "necessarily call it scheming."

"Besides," Athos said with a knowing look at d'Artagnan, "we were just finishing up."

D'Artagnan didn't need any more motivation. "Can I walk you home, Connie?"

Connie beamed. "Perfect. I'd love to get your input for the cookie exchange."

"Are you planning snickerdoodles?"

"For you? Absolutely."

Thursday night finally came, poker was played (Porthos's pockets were much heavier upon leaving than they'd been when everyone had arrived), and d'Artagnan walked home with his head swimming with ideas. *Christmas in Paris* was an ambitious undertaking, even for Athos, but he had to admit that an Eiffel Tower made of Christmas lights would make for a grand showing. He was musing how to construct the Arc de Triomphe at the gates of their neighborhood when he stopped in his tracks. It hadn't even started snowing yet this winter, so why was Justin's pickup truck, plow already attached, in the driveway?

He felt a moment of panic. Did Connie need extra help around the house? Was he going to hire Justin to do the Christmas lights? While d'Artagnan hadn't explicitly offered to help put them up, didn't Connie know that d'Artagnan would get up on that roof in a heartbeat?

D'Artagnan was still quite far down the sidewalk, and between streetlights, so he was almost certainly undetected as Justin exited the house. He saw Justin shove his hands into his pockets and breathe fog into the chilly air, and he watched as the truck started up and Justin drove away.

Now: what to do? His apartment shared a front hallway with the main part of the house, and he often did pop in on his way home. It wouldn't be unusual for him to knock on Connie's door. Would that be too intrusive? Justin often did the dirty work of the Homeowner's Association, and d'Artagnan couldn't think of any reason why he might be delivering a warning or citation. It was cold enough now that the grass didn't need mowing to stay within the limits, and Connie hadn't made any changes to the exterior.

Perhaps, in the end, it was curiosity that got the better of him. After he hung up his coat in the shared hall, he rapped gently on Connie's door. Hearing nothing, he tested the doorknob and, finding it unlocked, cracked the door ajar.

"Connie?" he said, trying to speak softly enough to not startle but loudly enough to be heard.

"Is that you, d'Artagnan?" Whatever had happened, Connie sounded miserable.

"Can I come in?"

There was a pause. "Yeah. Yeah, come on in."

D'Artagnan slowly and cautiously opened the door the rest of the way. He passed through the sitting room and into the kitchen, where Connie was sitting at the counter, papers scattered about. He didn't look like he'd been crying, but he might have been close.

"Did you know," Connie said, looking blankly at one of the papers, "that Justin is a process server?"

D'Artagnan's mind scrambled until he realized what must have happened. No wonder the other Mr. Bonacieux hadn't been around. Instead of sitting down, he made his way over to the cabinet by the sink, got two glasses, and filled them with cool tap water. He set one of the glasses in front of Connie, who wrapped his hands around it. D'Artagnan stood on the other side of the counter, resting his hands on the marble.

At last, he spoke: "You'll get through this. Athos doesn't do family law, but I'm sure he knows someone, and—"

"Don't tell him. Please." Connie's hand left the glass, and he rested it on top of d'Artagnan's. "At least not yet. I need to…I'm not sure."

D'Artagnan resisted the urge to make wild and outlandish suggestions about offering to fist-fight the soon-to-be-ex-Mr.-Bonacieux behind a Denny's, or to even provide practical advice about getting a lawyer quickly. Instead, he kept as still as he could while Connie's hand rested on his, hoping desperately that it would communicate his stalwart support.

"Do you want to talk about it?"

Connie sighed. "What, that I still trusted him even though he's always yammering about conspiracies or off doing these weird prepper retreats? What are they even prepping for, anyway? Other than the conspiracies, obviously. I mean, none of it made sense, but I kept hoping that he'd get it out of his system or something. He used to be so dependable." Connie drew his hand back and, both hands grasped around the glass, took a large gulp of water. "Some might have said it was boring, but I had my heart set on being with someone reliable."

D'Artagnan's heart raced. He wanted to lean over the table and dramatically proclaim "I'm dependable! I'm reliable! I'll mow the lawn every weekend, see if I don't!" but he held his passion in check. Barely. "Well," d'Artagnan said, choosing his words carefully, "he wasn't as reliable as he made himself out to be. That's not your fault."

Connie looked down at the countertop. "I should have seen it coming. He start-ed in on it after we got engaged, and I should have…I don't know. Done something differently. Rose-colored glasses hide the red flags, I guess."

"He lied to you!" D'Artagnan's voice rose sharply, and he fought to restrain his fervor. "Sorry, but it's true. He's a rotten scoundrel."

The silence hung in the air for a moment. Connie drew in a deep breath; it quickly turned into a laugh. "Did you just call him a scoundrel?"

D'Artagnan grinned. He hadn't intended for Connie to be so entertained by his passionate outburst, but he'd take it. "A rotten scoundrel. He's just the absolute worst."

"You're right." Connie reached over again and patted d'Artagnan's hand. "You're right." He took a deep breath and slowly released it. "And now I do need to take some time to look at all this." He took his hand away from d'Artagnan's and gestured to the paperwork on the table.

D'Artagnan drew his hands into clenched fists. "Anything you need, let me know, okay? Other than the Christmas decorations. I already have a plan to deal with those."

Connie's smile was better than any light display.

Three weeks later, d'Artagnan was in a much fouler mood.

"They have *costumes?*" Porthos fumed, pacing around Athos's living room.

Aramis was sitting on the couch, eyes glued to his phone. "And a press release, saying *we* stole *their* idea."

Athos sat silently and impassively in an armchair, sipping his wine.

D'Artagnan stood in front of the mantle, hands on his hips. "Apparently," he said, trying to cut through the anger in the air, "Anne told Buckingham."

Porthos threw his hands up in the air. "And how would you know that?"

D'Artagnan drew a deep breath. "She had Connie over for margs and confessed."

Porthos groaned.

Aramis rolled his eyes.

Athos's expression remained unreadable.

D'Artagnan continued, "Anne snuck out for brunch with him two weeks ago. Spilled everything about the plans."

The pictures in the press release were impressive: a functioning model of Big Ben festooned with twinkling lights, carolers in Victorian garb, and costumed guards at the entrance to the neighborhood were featured. D'Artagnan, with help from his friends, had only just put the finishing touches on the Arc de Triomphe, but it was feeling decidedly un-triumphant.

"But look," d'Artagnan said, "we've handled worse. Remember the roses?" The previous summer, Anne had given cuttings from her rosebushes to Buckingham, not knowing that they were an incredibly rare variety that would instantly be recognized by Louis at the joint block party. It had been a disaster sneaking over to dig them up in the middle of the night; d'Artagnan's arms had been covered in tiny thorn-pricks for weeks.

Aramis shuddered. "We had Buckingham's help with that one, though."

Porthos nodded. "He didn't want to get caught with the roses, either. This is different. This is war."

Athos set his wine glass down on a coaster. "So we go to war," he said, as simply as if it was going to brunch. The room fell silent. Athos leaned his elbows on his knees and steepled his fingers, thinking.

"Porthos. The costumes. Tacky?"

"Very."

"Find out where they're from. Throw them under the bus."

"I will call their tailor if I have to."

Athos nodded. "Good. Aramis?" Aramis nodded. "We need our own press release. Not," he said, holding up a finger for emphasis, "on the attack. Something sympathetic."

Aramis considered for a few moments. "Perhaps something about how we believed that this was cooperative. A sign of unity, and we were betrayed?"

Athos nodded. "Run with that. The holidays are a time to come together. D'Artagnan?"

"Yes?"

"Do you have a good saw?"

D'Artagnan passed a cup of piping-hot mulled cider to one of the revelers and stood back to admire the scene.

The park at the heart of their neighborhood had been transformed. The tree at the center was easily taller than any of the houses, and its lights gleamed. He'd had no idea that Athos had inherited a farm upstate that was chock-full of excellent trees to choose from.

D'Artagnan watched as the mayor and other local dignitaries were led from booth to booth in their mini-marché. The booths had taken the better part of a week; Porthos and Athos supplied not only the labor to help d'Artagnan build them, but had also used their connections to reach out to local artists to staff them. Fortunately, they'd had plenty of takers for a last-minute holiday shopping market the week before Christmas, including potters, fiber artists, and even a silversmith.

D'Artagnan was so entranced by the display that he didn't notice Richelieu sidling up to his cider-and-cookies booth. He almost jumped out of his skin at the deadpan, "You've done well for yourself, young d'Artagnan. And the neighborhood."

For a few moments, his brain scrambled, trying to interpret what Richelieu had said. The evenness of the tone was a cypher; was Richelieu being serious? D'Artagnan almost replied with sarcasm, putting together a cutting remark about the lack of support that he and his friends had received from the Board during this inter-neighborhood squabble. Before he could reply, however, Richelieu continued.

"You have a rare skill. You and your friends. Many don't understand what it takes to keep a neighborhood together or how much work it requires. We work in different ways, and I don't expect you to understand the things I do behind the scenes. Even when we clash, I know that you are doing what you believe is best for everyone. I want you to know that your contributions don't go unnoticed."

D'Artagnan sputtered. He'd always viewed Richelieu as a bit of a bully, wielding his power as HOA treasurer to punish anyone who didn't comply with the mandates. While he might disagree with Richelieu's methods, and still think he went overboard sometimes, it was nice to know that the man did actually care about some things.

"Thank you."

Richelieu cleared his throat. "There is one other thing I wanted to address. It has been some time since the Board has had someone in the Resident Representative position. It does not need to be a homeowner, and as an appointed position, the individual must be nominated by a current Board member. You could do great things. In addition, I, personally, would appreciate having more members of the Board who are willing to take a stand on matters that are relevant to us all."

D'Artagnan looked away from the older man and scanned the crowd. He hadn't even realized that being a member of the neighborhood HOA Board was an option for someone like him. He wondered, briefly, if Richelieu was even making the right choice. After all, Athos was the brains behind the operation. But Athos hated serving on committees, and d'Artagnan knew that he could still rely on Athos's wisdom as a friend. Although d'Artagnan and the others often teased Porthos for being an influencer, his social media savvy would undoubtedly be a great asset for the Board. But without the prompting of his friends, Porthos was more interested in promoting himself than being altruistic. Aramis, on the other hand, was quite concerned with benevolence. He might make a good choice. He did, however, prefer to stay behind the scenes with a pen rather than being out front wielding a sword. D'Artagnan couldn't imagine Aramis speaking up during an actual meeting.

Richelieu probably had it right. Besides, d'Artagnan wouldn't be alone. He would still have the support of his friends and be stronger for it.

"I accept the nomination," he said, still looking away at the crowd, eyebrows furrowed in thought about what else he might be able to do for the neighborhood.

"Good. You won't regret it." And with that, Richelieu abruptly turned and disappeared into the milieu.

D'Artagnan stood in a bit of a daze, smiling and handing out cookies and cider without truly processing what was happening around him.

A short time later, Connie approached, and d'Artagnan stepped back to make room for him to come through with the next enormous platter of cookies. "We're going to need to empty the donation jar soon," d'Artagnan said with a smile as he readied two more cups of cider for an approaching couple. They put a few dollars in the jar labeled "Support LGBTQIA+ Youth" and gladly took the hot cider and a few cookies.

Connie bumped his shoulder against d'Artagnan's bicep. "Look at you, bringing all this together."

D'Artagnan smiled. "I couldn't do it without help." He scanned the crowd and saw everyone in their roles: Porthos taking photos as Santa Claus (in a much better-tailored costume than anything the London Neighborhood could put together, Porthos had insisted), Aramis speaking with the local reporters, and Athos calmly going about the crowd with a body camera just in case any interlopers decided to interfere.

Connie put on a dramatic pout. "Okay, but you did a lot. This has been a great distraction. Kept me from running off to a convent."

D'Artagnan grinned. "You? A nun?"

Connie rolled his eyes. "A lost soul. Besides, I would look awful in a habit. What I was trying to say was thank you."

D'Artagnan felt something nudge his hand and looked to see Connie proffering a thin rectangular box. D'Artagnan grasped it, and their fingers brushed through their gloves.

"Well, open it!"

D'Artagnan fumbled with untying the bow before giving up and pulling his gloves off. The air was cold, but he hardly felt it. The bow vanquished, he opened the lid and saw the multitude of tiny lights around them reflected in a tiny silver sword.

"It's a letter opener," Connie explained.

D'Artagnan felt the heat spread across his chest and down his arms as he lifted the sword off of a black velvet pillow and noticed a tassel hanging off the hilt. "It's beautiful. Thank you. I feel bad; I don't have anything for you."

Connie gave him a playful punch on the arm. "I don't need a gift. You told me you'd help with anything I needed, and what I need right now is this." D'Artagnan quirked an eyebrow, and Connie continued. "I need help hanging Christmas lights and taste-testing cookies. I need someone to laugh with me when the recipe turns out to be a disaster. And maybe I also need someone to have dinner with and to watch terrible movies with after a long day. Think you're up for that?"

"I think," d'Artagnan said, gently placing the letter opener back on its pillow, "that I could help with that."

Amy Fincher   *"King"*

Next page
Amy Fincher opted not to share the inspiration behind this artwork.

Pierced Hearts

– Rhosyn Goodfellow

The candles are starting to gutter, and d'Artagnan feels loose and relaxed courtesy of the empty wine bottle on the table beside him. Athos sits across from him, nursing his own cup and nodding as d'Artagnan relates the trials and tribulations of training new recruits.

It's a scene they've played out many times in the three years since d'Artagnan's promotion to lieutenant, though less somber now than such encounters were in the early months, when d'Artagnan was still deep in his grief over Constance's death. Time has dulled that wound, though it still aches, and d'Artagnan is acutely aware of how much of that dulling is down to the man sitting across from him. More than anyone, Athos understands what it is to have one's heart broken, even if he'd never say it so plainly.

Athos understands, too, d'Artagnan's sometimes-conflicted feelings about Milady de Winter. D'Artagnan can't be sorry she paid for her crimes with her life, especially when it was she who so callously murdered his beloved, but there's a part of him that once loved Milady, too, and that part cannot help but grieve her.

"Perhaps," Athos had suggested, near the bottom of their third bottle of wine that evening, "you don't grieve the woman so much as the woman you wished she'd been."

If d'Artagnan suspects that might be true for himself, he's all but certain it is for Athos.

It helps, not only knowing his dearest friend understands him so well, but that Athos trusts him as he doesn't trust many people—perhaps not even Porthos and Aramis, whom he has known far longer. The thought makes something warm bloom in d'Artagnan's chest, for while Athos is most assuredly his closest friend, he has no reason to expect the sentiment to be returned.

"Are you just going to stare at the empty bottle, or are you going to open another?" Athos asks, and d'Artagnan realizes he'd been so lost in thought that he stopped speaking.

"Forgive me," d'Artagnan says, reaching for more wine. "I let my mind wander."

"Understandable, with all that your recruits have put you through." Athos motions for d'Artagnan to hand him the bottle. "You should let me have a go at them. It's been a while since I've helped train a green musketeer, but I think you turned out all right."

This time, d'Artagnan is paying enough attention to put a name to the warmth in his chest that arises when Athos compliments him, meager though the compliment might be. Their fingers brush as he passes the bottle, and the tingling sensation that spreads from the touch only solidifies his conclusion.

"I love you," d'Artagnan blurts just as Athos brings his cup to his lips.

Athos chokes on his wine, and d'Artagnan considers the possibility that he ought to

Tags

warnings: character injury (graphic descriptions)

relationships: age difference, friends, friends to lovers, the grumpy one is soft for the sunshine one, m/m

character features: christian, in a religious order, soldier

other tags: alcohol use (casual), first kiss, getting drunk, getting together, love declaration, meddling friends present tense, story diverges from the original work's canon, third person limited point of view

Inspiration

Both in the original novel and in every adaptation I know, Athos's and d'Artagnan's discussion of love and romance is always one of my favorite parts. It's never quite clear how much of their radically different views are due to temperament and how much is life experience, and I really wanted to explore that. Also, d'Artagnan reminds me to an embarrassing degree of myself at 18, and I wanted to give him a chance to grow up a little.

have waited until Athos put his cup down.

"I suppose it is only natural," Athos says after his coughing has subsided, "that such close companions as you and I would develop a deep affection one could call love."

Inebriated as he is, it takes several seconds for d'Artagnan to properly parse Athos's words. When he finally does, he responds with a forceful "No!"

D'Artagnan reaches for Athos's free hand and, with as much earnestness as he can muster, says, "It's true that I love you as my dearest friend, but I'm telling you that I also find myself quite thoroughly and ardently in love with you."

Athos glances down at their joined hands, then back at d'Artagnan with a confused frown. "I think you've had enough wine for tonight."

"These feelings aren't the result of wine," d'Artagnan protests, "but rather the most true and fervent longing of my heart."

"I think…" Athos trails off, withdrawing his hand and setting his cup down with exaggerated care, "that I've had enough wine for tonight, as well."

"But—"

"No, no." Athos waves d'Artagnan off as he makes his way to his feet. "You'll thank me in the morning. Get yourself to bed, Lieutenant."

It's the first time d'Artagnan can remember Athos calling him by his rank in an informal setting.

As he glumly considers his wine, he reflects hazily on the night's events and thinks, perhaps, he should have waited until morning to share his newly realized feelings.

Morning brings clarity and a pounding headache. The privilege of rank gives d'Artagnan the luxury of a private, hot bath, which both eases the headache and helps him sort his thoughts.

Athos reacted poorly to his profession of love. On the face of it, that's a bad sign for d'Artagnan's heart, but with the haze of inebriation gone, d'Artagnan can see he went about things the wrong way. D'Artagnan well knows Athos's disillusionment with love after his disastrous marriage; Athos once all but said opening one's heart was tantamount to asking for it to be broken.

Then, there is the matter of their respective ranks. Until last night, d'Artagnan rarely gave thought to the fact that he outranked Athos when he wasn't actively acting as the latter's commanding officer. But Athos so pointedly calling him "Lieutenant" makes d'Artagnan wonder if perhaps Athos thinks of it more than he does.

Finally, Athos may have renounced his title and lands, but surely a man raised as nobility has certain expectations about how a romantic partner should approach him. Though d'Artagnan is of noble birth himself, he's aware his manner is considered brash among the more cosmopolitan nobility.

D'Artagnan is out of his depth; he has no idea how to properly woo a man like Athos. Thankfully, he has two friends who might be able to help him.

Exiting the bath and donning his robe, d'Artagnan makes his way to his writing desk to compose a pair of letters.

Whatever manner of response d'Artagnan expected from Porthos, it wasn't for the man to show up on his doorstep not a week after he sent his letters. Athos is, of course, delighted by the surprise visit from their old friend and insists on breaking out a bottle of brandy he's been saving for a special occasion.

"Have you finally seen past the false shine of marriage to the tarnish beneath, then?" Athos asks, handing Porthos a glass of brandy.

"Not at all! My love shines bright in my heart even more than it did on the day I wed. But my lady is, at present, planning a lavish party, and you know how little help I am in such matters. We had a frank discussion and agreed we would both be happier if I were to find somewhere else to be for a few weeks."

Athos snorts into his cup. "That doesn't sound like much of a shine to me."

"Then it's a good thing it isn't you I'm married to," Porthos laughs.

"But doesn't it bother you?" d'Artagnan asks. "To be away from your beloved for so long? If it were me, I think my heart wouldn't be able to bear it."

Porthos's mirth melts into something softer and more earnest. "Your mistake is assuming every person needs the same things in matters of the heart. I am, by nature, a man who enjoys adventure and freedom, and I was lucky enough to find a wife who values those same things. No matter how far apart we are, no matter who else might share our beds or even our hearts, we love each other and know we will return to one another."

"I am happy that you are happy, dear friend," d'Artagnan says, "but I don't think such an arrangement would suit me."

"I suppose, then, it's for the best that I'm not married to you, either." Porthos grins and raises his glass in salute. "But what I mean to say is that I've found someone whose heart matches mine and who dares to love me, and those are the only requirements to making a love match work."

"Enough talk of love." Athos slams his now-empty cup on the table. "You fools who choose to engage in such things can speak of it on your own time. Right now, we are drinking my brandy, and I wish to enjoy the company of my friends without your nonsense notions of love."

Porthos smiles indulgently and relates the tale of his latest duel. Though d'Artagnan does his best to play at listening, he spends the rest of the evening turning Porthos's words over in his mind.

"The plan is simple," Porthos tells d'Artagnan the next day. "We spar. You lose. Badly."

"I don't see how letting you win a few sparring matches will help."

Porthos smirks. "Who said anything about *letting* me win? But you're missing the truly brilliant part of the plan," he continues. "If you're injured, you can ask Athos to help patch you up."

"Athos has patched me up more times than I care to count," d'Artagnan points out. "How will this time be any different?"

"This time, you'll be paying attention. You want to know if Athos returns your affections, and the fastest way to ascertain someone's true affections is to ask for help tending your injuries. It works especially well with leg injuries," he adds with a waggle of his eyebrows, "because you can ask them for help taking your breeches off."

D'Artagnan frowns. "But I don't have a—" He breaks off with a curse as Porthos drives a knee into his thigh, just below the hip. "Ow! Was that necessary?"

"Quit whining. It's only a bruise. You'll need several more if you want this to be convincing."

Athos calls them both ten kinds of fool, but he agrees to help tend d'Artagnan's injuries. Porthos excuses himself, claiming he has a duel to attend to and throwing d'Artagnan a wink as he leaves.

"I appreciate your help," d'Artagnan says as Athos assists him in removing his boot. "The longer it goes, the harder it is for me to move my leg." It's not a lie; Porthos didn't pull his prodigious strength when he made that first hit.

"You've got only yourself to blame." Athos sets the boot aside and moves to remove the other.

"Is that any way to speak to your superior officer?" d'Artagnan asks, half teasing and half probing his friend's feelings about their respective ranks.

Athos snorts. "It is if my superior officer is acting a fool. But regardless, you are my lieutenant when we're in uniform but my friend when we're not, and I am doubly inclined to make certain my friends know when they are being fools so they won't repeat their folly."

Well, that's not the issue then. D'Artagnan considers asking for help with his belt, but he decides that would be a bit too shameless—he hasn't injured his hands, after all—and undoes it himself.

Athos looks up at the sound, and it hits d'Artagnan suddenly how this looks, Athos kneeling at his feet as he opens his belt. His hands stutter until he reminds himself fiercely that *this is the point*.

Athos sets the second boot aside and watches with an unreadable expression as d'Artagnan finishes removing his belt and undoes the fastenings on his breeches. D'Artagnan considers that Athos has made no move to stand to be a promising sign, although there's something unnerving and arousing in the intensity of Athos's gaze.

D'Artagnan's hands move to the waistband of his breeches, but he only pushes them down a few inches before asking, "Would you mind helping me? I don't think I can get them past my injury on my own."

Wordlessly, still watching him with that same unreadable intensity, Athos reaches up and pulls d'Artagnan's breeches the rest of the way down his legs, fingers barely brushing against d'Artagnan's skin as he does.

D'Artagnan inhales a sharp breath at the touch, and Athos's eyes narrow slightly.

"Hurts, does it?" Athos asks, and d'Artagnan nods because it does, even if that wasn't the cause of his reaction.

There's an impressive bruise that stretches from his hip halfway to his knee. It's already starting to purple, and d'Artagnan can only imagine how it will look tomorrow. He resolves to give Porthos a few bruises of his own next time they spar.

"There doesn't seem to be any true damage," Athos explains as he examines the area with gentle hands. "You'll be in considerable pain for a few days, but it looks to be nothing worse than a bad bruise." His lips twitch in a faint smile as he rises. "And no doubt a bit of bruising to your pride as well, hmm?"

"It is no injury to my pride to be bested by an excellent swordsman. Especially because I intend to return the favor at the earliest possible opportunity."

"I have no doubt." Athos holds out a hand. "Would you like some help to your feet and dressing again, or do you want to rest?"

D'Artagnan grasps Athos's hand but makes no move to stand. "I thought I'd stay in for a while." It wasn't his original plan, but Athos's closeness has made him bold. "Perhaps you'd care to join me?"

Athos's lips part in surprise, and his eyes flit from d'Artagnan's face to the bed he's seated on, making a sweep of his bare legs before returning to his face. D'Artagnan feels a thrill of triumph at the unmistakable interest in Athos's eyes that is immediately dashed when the other man drops his hand and steps back.

"Enjoy your rest," Athos tells him before turning and leaving the room at a speed barely below a run.

D'Artagnan falls back onto his pillows with a frustrated groan, resolving never to ask Porthos for advice ever again.

Neither d'Artagnan's leg nor his wounded pride have recovered by the next morning. He's just finished the agonizingly slow shimmy into his breeches when there comes a loud banging on his chamber door. Porthos throws the door open wide without waiting for d'Artagnan's invitation.

"Look who arrived in the night!" he announces.

"I was just planning a trip that would take me this way when your letter arrived," Aramis says, following Porthos into the room, "so I thought it best if I dropped in on my old friends to make certain you weren't making too much of a mess of things."

"I am, of course, glad to see you," d'Artagnan says, limping forward to clasp his friend's arms, "but you needn't have come in person."

"That's right," Porthos agrees. "We've got everything handled here."

"Indeed?" Aramis shoots d'Artagnan a sympathetic look. "What, pray tell, happened to your leg, my dear d'Artagnan?"

"Porthos thought I should try asking Athos to help me tend my injury—and so provided me with said injury."

"And yet, you're here alone." Aramis settles on the edge of the nearest chair with the air of an instructor preparing to address a class full of particularly dim students. "I take it things didn't go according to plan?"

"No." D'Artagnan does not quite pout, but it's a close thing. "For a moment, I thought…but no."

Porthos pipes in: "Perhaps a more severe—"

"I think," Aramis interrupts, "this might be a situation that calls for a solution other than violence."

"It sounds like you might have something specific in mind," d'Artagnan observes.

"I do, indeed. The solution to your problem is simple." Aramis lowers his voice and speaks as though imparting a great secret. "*Seduction*."

"I tried that! I outright invited Athos to my bed, and he all but ran away."

"The art of seduction isn't simply inviting someone to bed," Aramis says with practiced patience. "Seduction requires carefulness and subtlety. Those are admittedly not your strong points, but"—he holds up a hand at d'Artagnan's attempt to protest—"I believe you can manage with some instruction."

D'Artagnan lets out a heavy sigh. "I suppose it can't hurt to try."

Leaving Athos a note seems excessive, but Aramis insists that the written word can add an air of mystery, a hint of thrill that is crucial when it comes to seduction. So, d'Artagnan leaves a note on the other man's pillow asking him to meet d'Artagnan in his quarters for dinner.

Aramis and Porthos offer to help d'Artagnan put the new recruits through their paces, and by the end of the day, d'Artagnan is feeling much more confident in the potential of the two newest musketeers.

"That was quite invigorating," Aramis says when they've finished. "I must confess, I've rather missed this."

"Of course you have," Porthos tells him. "You've been spending your time with stuffy priests, studying religious texts."

Aramis gives him a sidelong glance. "Is that all you think priests do?"

"Well, they certainly don't train new musketeers!"

"And have you been training many new musketeers in your free time, then, Baron?" Aramis asks with deceptive cordiality.

Porthos lets out a deep belly laugh. "I suppose I haven't been, at that."

D'Artagnan lets the sound of his friends' laughter buoy him through a quick bath and the rest of his preparations for the evening. Dinner is simple, just bread, cheese, and a game hen ("Keep it light," Aramis advised. "Nothing to distract from the evening's later activities."), along with a bottle of fine wine Treville gifted him some months back ("That will do nicely, but be certain not to overindulge.") and a plate of fruit cut into small pieces ("There's nothing more sensual than feeding fruit to your partner by hand."). He lays the spread out on the table along with two candles, then douses the other lights in the room ("Dim lighting is inherently romantic.").

When Athos arrives, he looks taken aback, peering into the dimness.

"Is there a candle shortage I'm unaware of?"

"I thought the lighting would be atmospheric," d'Artagnan answers brightly. "Come, eat."

Athos seats himself at the table, eyeing d'Artagnan cautiously when he takes the seat beside him rather than across the table as is their usual arrangement.

D'Artagnan reminds himself he's meant to be subtle and sets about doing everything he can to put Athos at ease, which ends up being exactly what he would have done any other night they were dining together. It's not long before they're both laughing over d'Artagnan's recounting of Aramis and Porthos training the new recruits.

"He truly fell for it a second time?" Athos asks, chuckling into his wine.

"And a third, not half an hour later!" d'Artagnan exclaims.

"It's a shame those two chose to leave the musketeers." Athos shakes his head. "I miss having them around."

"As do I." D'Artagnan bites his lip before adding, "Although, I can't say I mind that their absence has given me the opportunity to know you better."

Athos studies him over the rim of his cup. "That has been an unexpected benefit."

D'Artagnan beams at him. "Might I offer you a strawberry?"

Athos eyes the plate of fruit d'Artagnan offers almost as though he expects some trick, but he eventually reaches out to retrieve a berry and pops it into his mouth with a contented sigh.

"Good?" d'Artagnan prompts, taking a berry for himself.

"It's been a long while since I've had strawberries," Athos says, reaching for another. "I'd forgotten how sweet they can be."

"I love the way the juices burst on my tongue. Sweet and tart at the same time."

When Athos reaches again for the plate, d'Artagnan stops him. "Let me," he says, holding a berry close enough for Athos to take directly from his hand—should he choose to.

Athos's eyes dart between the berry and d'Artagnan's face. He licks his lips, warring emotions dancing across his features.

"It's all right," d'Artagnan says softly, as though speaking to a spooked horse. He moves the berry close enough to brush Athos's lips. "Take it."

Athos's face shutters even as his hands come up to cup d'Artagnan's with an aching gentleness. "You need to stop," he says, voice equal parts gentle and firm.

"I know my manner is less refined than you might wish for, but I'm trying. I can *learn*—"

"I would not change your manner if I could, nor a single thing about you." Athos lowers d'Artagnan's hand to the table before releasing it, "but I cannot give you what you're asking for, and no amount of asking will change that."

"Then let me take what you can give," d'Artagnan insists. He reaches for Athos's hand, but Athos stands and steps out of reach.

"A tender heart, once pierced," Athos gravely intones, "cannot survive being pierced a second time. Thank you for dinner."

Then he's gone, before d'Artagnan can think to formulate a response.

"Don't look so despondent," Porthos tells d'Artagnan over breakfast the next morning. "You merely haven't found the right tactic yet."

"Indeed," Aramis agrees. "Athos is stubborn, but between the three of us, we can devise a plan that will win him over."

"No." D'Artagnan shakes his head. "Athos has made his position clear. If not last night, then by his avoidance this morning."

Porthos waves a sausage dismissively in d'Artagnan's direction. "He's just brooding. You know how he gets; you can't take it personally."

"It's not a matter of taking it personally," d'Artagnan insists. "Regardless of my deeper affections, Athos is my friend, first and foremost, and I owe it to him to respect his wishes."

"Ah, but do you *know* his wishes?" Aramis slathers some jam onto a piece of warm bread. "Has he told you he doesn't return your affections?"

"Well, no, but—"

"You see?" Aramis interrupts. "Athos is careful to a fault where his feelings are concerned, and you can't trust his actions to reflect whatever mess is going on inside his head."

"Exactly," Porthos agrees around a mouthful of sausage. "You can't give up unless he tells you to do so."

"Or," d'Artagnan says, an idea dawning, "I could ask him *why* he's been avoiding my advances."

"Do you think he'd answer?" Porthos asks with no small amount of skepticism.

"That seems a terribly gauche way to start a love affair," Aramis offers.

"It's the only approach that makes sense." Vigor wells up in d'Artagnan. "I've professed my feelings and made my desires clear, but I haven't asked Athos what *he* wants."

"I suppose," Aramis ventures, "there's some merit to the idea."

"I still think you'd have better luck if I hit you again." Porthos sips his tea. "But conversation does have its advantages."

"My heart or yours?" d'Artagnan asks as soon as Athos opens the door to his knock.

Athos lets out a heavy sigh. "It's too early in the day for riddles."

"You said 'a tender heart cannot survive being pierced a second time.' " D'Artagnan pushes into Athos's room, and Athos puts up little resistance, seeming resigned to both d'Artagnan's presence and the conversation. "Were you referring to my heart or your own?"

"Does it matter?"

"Of course it does! If you were speaking of my heart, you should know that I trust you not to harm it just as I have long trusted you not to harm me in any other way, so if that's your concern—"

"You shouldn't," Athos says glumly. "It is foolishness to trust a man who feels not a drop of remorse for killing his own wife—twice—with your heart."

"She betrayed you. More than once. And she tried to have you killed. Two things I would never do."

"And you think that's enough to protect you?" Athos's lip curls in scornful recrimination.

"I think I've less to fear from you than from any other person living," d'Artagnan says, countering scorn with earnestness. "Even if I did not, you are more than worth risking my heart for. But if it is your own heart you worry for, will you at least tell me what I've done to make you think I cannot be trusted with it?"

"I have seen how you love." Athos leans against the wall, arms crossed. "Sudden and full-throated, with every fiber of your being. You *shine* with it. My old heart is too tarnished to ever shine back."

"Tarnish can be polished away," d'Artagnan says, taking a cautious step toward him, "with enough work and time."

"And when you find that mine cannot be?" Athos asks sharply. "When you grow weary of trying, will you find another who can shine as bright as you, or will you let my tarnish dull your shine to nothing?"

"Whatever the state of your heart, I will love it still because it's yours." D'Artagnan takes another tentative step forward. "I loved you first as a friend, perhaps the dearest I've ever had, and not once in all that time have I found fault in the state of your heart. Indeed, the more you've let me see of it, the more I've loved you—until it became impossible to deny any longer that my love has grown beyond friendship. And while I would polish the tarnish from your heart if I could, I would do it for your sake, not my own, that I might soothe your heart's wounds as you have so often and completely soothed mine."

"You would be fighting an uphill battle." Athos's shoulders curl inward as he sags against the wall, his still-crossed arms giving the impression of a man bracing for a blow—or protecting a dire wound.

"When have I ever run from a battle?" D'Artagnan's keeps his voice soft even as he issues a challenge. "The only thing that could deter me from this one would be if you did not return my love."

Athos lets out a heavy breath, his arms falling to his sides. "If I were a stronger man, I would tell you I do not, but you are too dear to me for that sort of lie."

D'Artagnan's face breaks out into a smile, and he takes the last few steps into Athos's space. "Then fight this battle beside me and tender your heart into my care, as I have already given my own to you." He places a gentle hand over Athos's heart. "I promise to cherish it—always."

"You are a fool," Athos says, his own hand coming up to cover d'Artagnan's. "And I must be an even bigger one, because I find it impossible to deny you."

D'Artagnan thinks, as Athos pulls him into a kiss that is equal parts passion and tenderness, that he is more than willing to be a fool for this.

"We were beginning to wonder if you would be joining us," Aramis greets them the next morning. "Decided on a bit of a lie-in, did you? Have a late night?"

"A man is at his best when well-rested." D'Artagnan reaches over Aramis's shoulder to grab an apple from the center of the table, biting into it with an enthusiastic crunch.

"Well-rested?" Porthos grins widely. "Or well—?"

"Well *enough*," Athos interrupts pointedly.

Porthos gives an easy shrug, his grin not diminishing in the slightest. "As long as you are well."

"*Quite* well," d'Artagnan agrees brightly, eliciting a bark of laughter from Porthos and a smirk from Aramis.

Athos makes a show of a put-upon sigh as he settles into his seat, but he stays close enough that d'Artagnan can see the smile threatening to break free in the crinkles around his eyes.

"Don't think," Athos says, "that your abbreviated time here means I am any more likely to satisfy your prurient curiosities than I would be otherwise."

"I would never presume," Aramis says, voice all false innocence. "But as to that," he continues, speaking now to d'Artagnan, "might you be inclined to let me stay on a while? I believe it might do the musketeers a great deal of good to have a priest on hand."

"That worried about the state of our souls, are you?" Athos asks drily.

"He just enjoyed beating the recruits too much to leave so soon, I bet," Porthos says.

"Not all of us take as much joy in violence as you do, old friend."

"If you are asking for my permission, you have it," d'Artagnan says. "Although I imagine the church might have a different opinion."

Aramis leans his head on his hand. "If I can prove the worth of my presence here over the course of a long visit, I shall have an easier time convincing my superiors it would be worthwhile making it a more permanent position."

"Better to ask forgiveness than permission, eh?" Athos observes.

"Quite so."

"As it happens," Porthos says, "I've received a letter from my lady indicating she has decided to extend her party to an entire *season* of parties, so perhaps I might stay on, as well. If you'll have me, of course."

"I see how it is," Aramis remarks. "You accuse me of wishing to stay for the chance to harry recruits to disguise your own intentions."

"Well," Porthos says with a sly grin, "I can't deny it is a perk, if not my primary reason."

"I'm happy to have your company as long as you wish to stay—both of you," d'Artagnan tells them.

"As am I," Athos agrees. "For all that you insist on interposing yourselves in personal matters that do not concern you."

"My dear Athos," Aramis coos, "the happiness of our dearest friends will always be our concern."

"I couldn't agree more!" Porthos proclaims.

Athos scoffs, but his foot finds d'Artagnan's beneath the table to hook around it, and this time he makes only the most cursory attempt to hide his smile.

Although it is late enough that the food has gone cold and slightly congealed, it's the best breakfast d'Artagnan can remember having in a very long while.

Jupiter V   "*Where Hearts Cross*"

The 1993 film *The Three Musketeers* had a huge impact on me as a child. My sister and I nearly wore out the VHS, and when our cousins came to visit, we frequently fought over who played d'Artagnan. Of course, the villainous Rochefort was also a frequent character in our play.

Fast forward to present day, and I am revisiting many of these memories and finally reading the original book and other adaptations...imagine my surprise open learning that Rochefort did not, in fact, murder d'Artagnan's father. He didn't even have an eye patch!

Baddie they may be, I felt they were misrepresented in modern media. And so, Roc came to me as a dark foil to the young d'Arta. Perhaps there is more than meets the eye to their passionate rivalry...!

A Lesson in Foils

— Annabeth Lynch

Tags

warnings:
misgendering (unintentional), period-typical misogyny, robbery (attempted), violence (non-graphic descriptions)
relationships:
friends, m/nb
character features:
character has a different gender than in the source material, gender non-conforming character, masquerading as a person of a different gender, non-binary, servant, soldier, trans male
other tags: alcohol use (casual), historical, past tense, story diverges from the original work's canon, third person limited point of view

Inspiration
Annabeth Lynch opted not to share the inspiration behind this story.

"You ought not place so much emphasis on that which you do not mean."

"I don't know what you're talking about," d'Artagnan said breezily. They pulled an inch of their sword from its sheath and used the sharp edge to cut a stray thread from the laces of their leather pants. "I am the most sincere in all matters. Particularly those of the heart."

Athos exhaled in exasperation. "If you have no intention of uniting with Kitty, you should at the very least inform her of that decision."

"She knew who I was when she decided to pursue me."

Aramis snorted. "Then you should marry her immediately. Who else could say they'd do the same in her position?"

"Better snap her up quick," Porthos agreed, snickering.

"She's just so…innocent, isn't she?" d'Artagnan complained. "Naïve, almost. And she has no confidence. How am I supposed to believe in her worth if she doesn't believe in it herself?"

"She is not worthless simply because she's been stripped of confidence by her position in Milady's house," Athos said. "Imagine being a servant for one such as her."

"You married her," d'Artagnan noted.

"So I would know better than anyone else what it must be like for Kitty."

"Fair," d'Artagnan conceded. "I suppose I just wish she would talk more. I enjoy my clever banter."

"It must be hard for you to find someone that can match your wit," Porthos said. A smile split his face, and he elbowed d'Artagnan in the ribs.

Ignoring him, d'Artagnan pressed on. "I don't know much about her, even after many conversations, and what I do know is less than impressive."

"Well, you can take this detailed account of her shortcomings to the source. There's your would-be paramour now." Athos pointed down the road, toward Kitty making her way out of the market square in their direction.

D'Artagnan groaned under their breath but curled their lips in a slippery, flirtatious smirk. Athos grunted his disapproval.

As she passed by the last alleyway between her and them, Kitty's head lifted from its usual lowered position to find the four of them watching her. Face lifting to form her own smile, she raised one hand in a shy wave. Before she could approach and greet them, two strange hands shot out of the alley, pulling her into the shadows. Only a tiny squeak was heard before she disappeared into the passage.

D'Artagnan didn't hesitate. They took off running, unsheathing their sword in one fluid movement. Behind them, they could hear the rattle of metal on metal that meant the other musketeers were drawing their own weapons.

Skidding around the corner, kicking up dust from the sudden change in direction, d'Artagnan closed in on the still-struggling pair. The man—likely a thief—had one hand over Kitty's mouth, the other feeling over her body, ripping the lace detailing of her dress, searching for something. Kitty squeaked again and kicked backward as his hand got dangerously close to her chest. His hand strayed until it found her reticule tied to her wrist.

"Unhand her!" d'Artagnan yelled, brandishing their sword. The fall of shadows indicated that their companions had reached the alley as well.

Fear flashed on the thief's face. Without letting go of Kitty, he reached to draw his knife and put the honed edge to her throat.

D'Artagnan's grip tightened on the hilt of their weapon.

"I'm leaving, and if none of you follow me, the girl will live," the thief said, edging away. Of course he did not throw her into their path; he hadn't gotten his coin yet.

"Oh, but we were just beginning to have fun," Aramis said in a honeyed voice. D'Artagnan shot him a look, but he nodded to someone emerging from the shadows behind the thief: Athos, sword pointed at the thief's throat. He'd outflanked the crook by way of another side alley.

The stranger stiffened, the blade in his hand slicing into the delicate skin of Kitty's neck. A line of red under her chin began to weep. She whimpered, and Athos brought his sword closer to the man's face. The flat of the blade brushed his cheek.

"Perhaps you would prefer to try your luck in bladesmanship against the king's musketeers," Athos said, his tone seductive, lover-like. D'Artagnan smiled at the tremble in the thief's knees.

After several tense seconds, the man lifted his knife from Kitty's skin and raised his hands over his head. Kitty scurried to d'Artagnan's side, tucking herself under the arm that did not hold a sword. They pulled her close, keeping the sword facing the thief. Athos kicked the discarded knife toward his friends. With Kitty safe and the knife out of reach, Athos flipped his sword the opposite direction and slammed the hilt into the stranger's temple. He fell in an uncomfortably twisted heap.

"Not bad," Porthos said as he picked up the knife. He turned it over in his hand, letting the shadows play over the cool metal. Shrugging, he put it in a pocket and sheathed his sword; everyone was safe now that Athos had the thief in custody.

"Bad luck to keep a thief's knife, don't you think?" Aramis asked, putting away his sword.

"On the contrary, I think finding a free knife is very good luck. Besides, it matches my buttons."

As their bickering continued, d'Artagnan sheathed their weapon and turned to Kitty. "How do you fare?" they asked.

"I feel fine. A little frightened. Thank you for coming for me," Kitty said, the shyness creeping back into her voice now that things were calm again.

"Of course," they responded, waving away her admiration as though they did not bask in it.

"I wish I could be as brave as you. Or at least as formidable. I've no idea how to fight," she sighed.

"You ought to learn, then. Every woman could benefit from learning a bit of swordplay."

"Women don't learn the sword, d'Artagnan," Aramis said disapprovingly, having been pulled from his argument with Porthos upon hearing d'Artagnan's suggestion. "Men fight; women make the home."

"Does Milady not have intimate knowledge of sword fighting?" d'Artagnan pointed out.

"A special case, and we would all have been better served if she hadn't learned."

"And what of me?" they asked.

"You get away with a lot of things you shouldn't," Porthos snorted.

"I know it would be frowned upon," Kitty said, looking at her feet. "One can dream, though."

D'Artagnan's mouth twisted downward. "If you want to, you ought to," they said stubbornly.

"You think she would be allowed? What would Milady say?" Porthos pointed out.

"Allowed to do what?" Athos asked, joining the conversation now that the thief was cuffed and propped against the wall a short distance away.

"We were debating whether Kitty should receive instruction in the sword," Aramis said with a significant look at Athos.

"Who would teach her?" Athos asked.

Aramis looked triumphant for just a second before d'Artagnan spoke again. "I would, of course."

Kitty's head shot up sharply, hope in her eyes, but disappointment lowered it again. "A proper woman doesn't learn to fight. My mistress would never allow it."

"What if she didn't know? What if no one did?"

"Where would we practice that no one could see us?"

The gears in d'Artagnan's brain were grinding into action. "The training grounds for the musketeers, of course. Night, day, any time you have free from your duties."

"Yes, just let her walk onto the king's grounds and start swinging a sword in broad daylight. What could possibly happen?" Athos said, ever the voice of reason.

"You mean let *him* walk onto the grounds," d'Artagnan said, giving their friends a superior look.

Aramis and Porthos shared a confused look, but Athos groaned in exasperation. "You cannot be serious."

"As I told you before, I am most certainly sincere in all affairs, but especially about something like this. I would never mislead a lady about something her heart desires." D'Artagnan turned to Kitty and winked. Red spread up from her chest to her neck and flooded her cheeks. "When do you think you might have time to get away?"

"W-well, Milady will be conducting private affairs tonight after supper, away from the estate. After I clean up, I have no other duties," Kitty stuttered out. "But do you really want to teach me? I have no experience or knowledge. You'd be starting from the very beginning."

"It'll be a challenge for both of us, then, won't it?" they said with a smile that reflected the recklessness of their soul. "Porthos, I don't suppose you have any old clothing that may disguise her?"

"You think some clothing will keep your secrets?" Porthos asked, incredulous. "I can't believe you mean to dress her up as a man and teach her on palace grounds."

Aramis chuckled. "A stealth mission, it seems."

"I can do stealth. I've just never had cause to," d'Artagnan said.

"What about when—?"

"I need a drink," Athos interrupted. "I can't entertain this without wine." He beckoned to Aramis, and together they each grabbed one of the thief's arms and dragged him out of the alley. "We will handle this, and I'm sure Kitty was on her way somewhere before this mess. Porthos will accompany you, d'Artagnan."

"What?" Porthos demanded. "I could use some wine myself. Do you expect me to suffer the pillaging of my closet sober?"

"Go on," Aramis grunted as he pulled the thief's prone body. "You have…accessorizing to do."

"I won't forget this," he said, his disgruntled gaze drifting back to d'Artagnan.

"Oh, I hope not."

"Are you sure this is all right?" Kitty asked through the bathroom door.

"Of course. I would never put a lady in danger," d'Artagnan replied. "Does it fit?"

"Quite well, I believe," she said, opening the door.

Porthos had offered up a pair of leather pants and several white, billowy shirts that were not as flashy as the rest of his curated closet. Between the loose fabric and the high, chest-suppressing corset she wore, Kitty's bust was unnoticeable. She was laced up with the hem of her shirt tucked into the pants and leather boots that had a good grip on the soles. The tight pants hugged her thighs like a second skin. D'Artagnan made a show of appreciating the outfit, making Kitty blush again.

"Here, turn around," they instructed, twisting her by the shoulders until her back faced them. Carefully, they gathered the hair she wore loose around her face and pulled it back, tying it in place with a leather cord. When it was secured, she turned back around.

"How do I look? Dashing, I hope," she said. She gave d'Artagnan a wide smile that caught them off guard.

Had she ever smiled at them like that before? They didn't think so; they'd remember a radiance so strong. They scrambled for something to say that wouldn't reveal how tongue-tied they really were.

"Dashing, but incomplete," d'Artagnan said. She cocked her head in question until they settled a wide-brimmed hat with a long feather stemming from it over her hair. "You are perfection, Kitty."

"Claude," she said absent-mindedly, adjusting the hat so she could tuck her ponytail into it. When she was done—with her hair hidden and shirt disguising her chest—there was no indication that she was anything but another man with hopes of joining the musketeers.

"Claude?"

"That's what you're to call me. We are going to be on the training grounds, yes? It wouldn't do to have others hear you call me Kitty and get us caught."

"Clever, Claude," they said with a smirk. "Let me give you a tour of the grounds and then get started on the sword. We'll start with stance and posture." They straightened her back with a gentle brush of their hand and felt the shiver work its way up her spine. Her hands flexed, and d'Artagnan broke contact before she read too much into it. "There will still be a few men out; I'm sure we can find someone to outfit you with a balanced weapon," d'Artagnan continued.

They arrived at the training grounds just as the sun was getting low in the sky, bathing the facilities in a golden hue. As they passed practicing men on the way to the armory, d'Artagnan pointed out the areas of greatest use to them: the dummies, the obstacle course, and the ring for the competitive fighters.

D'Artagnan expected Kitty—Claude—to be somewhat cowed by the various training exercises she—*he*—would have to endure, but he looked on with a building excitement that caused an echo in d'Artagnan's chest. They began to pick up the pace to get to the armory faster; they were no less eager to start teaching than Claude was to learn.

Several barrels of swords rested in the back corner of the grounds, hilts gleaming with the colors of sunset. Claude leaned into the first barrel and pulled a sword from the batch, a pretty silver blade etched with geometric designs. Gold filigree lines on the hilt swirled to meet at the apex of the pommel. He turned back to d'Artagnan and brandished it in a stance that they despaired of. The point tried to dip, but Claude did his best to keep it directed at their chest.

"How does that one feel?" they asked him.

"Heavy," Claude answered, as expected. The arm holding it began to shake, and he let the tip drop to the ground. "I picked the most beautiful one, I didn't expect it to weigh so much."

"Balance on a sword is important. It has to feel good in your hand, capable of striking at a moment's notice," they instructed. Walking along the line of barrels, they inspected the offerings critically. In the fifth one, they found a skinny but well-crafted saber and offered it to Claude. "How about this one?"

Claude took it carefully, testing the feel in his hand. "This one feels better; it's not trying to drag me down. It feels quicker, as well," he said, making a few false strikes. D'Artagnan was impressed with his wrist movement, flicking in controlled swipes, but less so with his stance.

"I think this will serve our purposes for now. I'll keep it among my things when you aren't here."

"Thank you. That's very kind." Claude's smile grew from shy to enthusiastic. "Is it time to begin?"

D'Artagnan returned his smile with an indulgent one of their own. "Let's go back to the dummies and work on how you should position yourself."

They led him to a hay-stuffed sack on a pole that acted as a target, far from the other men practicing.

"I'm going to destroy you," Claude said solemnly to the sack.

D'Artagnan's lips curved before they could stop them. Clearing their throat, they directed Claude, "Show me your sword-fighting stance."

He hesitated for a moment before moving into horrible, horrible form. His legs were uneven and his knees bent, and his shoulders were too high and rounded with his arm holding the sword straight out.

D'Artagnan shook their head and circled Claude. "Straighten your legs a bit and keep them shoulder-width apart." He complied, and they moved around to his back. With one hand on his spine and the other on his shoulder, they uncurled his posture. "It's a good instinct to protect your middle," they assured him, "but it doesn't allow for swift movement or easy adjustment."

They came to stand between the point of the sword and the practice target. "The sword is not merely an offensive weapon. The blade also protects you from another's swing. Keep the point to the sky until you find an opening to drive it into." Claude moved the tip from d'Artagnan's face to a better position. They came closer and touched his wrist, moving it gently to test his grip and muscle fluidity.

When they were satisfied, they stepped back and gestured to the sack dummy. "You have an oath to fulfill. Destroy it."

With an exuberant smile and a gleam in his eyes, Claude followed their directions. He attacked the dummy with vigor, swinging the sword with better form than d'Artagnan had expected, returning to the original stance between onslaughts.

They let Claude have his fun until it was too dark for d'Artagnan to follow his movements. By then, the sack was shredded and straw littered the ground near the stake that held it.

"I think you've made good on your promise," they said over Claude's heavy breathing. "Sufficiently dismantled."

Claude chuckled and wiped the sweat from his forehead. He tried to lift the sword back into position, but his arm shook from exhaustion. "I think I had a little too much fun."

"Part of learning the sword is getting used to the weight of it. You have to parry and block and strike again and again. You have to be strong enough to wield it."

"I'll be strong enough. I'll *make* myself strong enough."

His determined tone surprised d'Artagnan. "You're different today," they said, studying him: red cheeks, trembling arms, shining eyes.

"I suppose I feel more confident with a sword in my hands," he said with a shrug. D'Artagnan wasn't sure that was what had changed him, but he was still speaking. "Back to being Kitty now." Disappointment colored his tone.

"If you're not yet needed by Milady, you could come out to the bar with us. Athos must be halfway in his cups by now. And I'm sure Porthos would like to see that his clothes are getting good use," d'Artagnan suggested.

"I should be getting home." Claude hesitated, chewing his lip. "But I think one drink wouldn't hurt."

D'Artagnan clapped him on the back, smiling deviously. "We can use this time to plan our next training session…"

Over the next few weeks, Kitty, acting as Claude, slowly began to learn the sword. He was light on his feet and quick to act, much like d'Artagnan, but easily adjustable in a way that even they were not. This gave d'Artagnan many excuses to touch him, which they rarely passed up. They enjoyed his flustered responses, but delighted equally in the moments when he caught them off guard in his confident, flirtatious nature.

After a month of private lessons—during which he remained unbothered by other training musketeers—Athos, Porthos, and Aramis showed up, ostensibly to gauge his progress, but more accurately, to comment on d'Artagnan's teaching skills.

"She is progressing quite well," Porthos said to no one in particular as Claude and d'Artagnan danced around the ring.

"He," d'Artagnan called over the sound of metal on metal as the swords met again and again.

An incongruous smile crossed Claude's face but was quickly replaced by the concentrated grimace of exertion. The change grabbed d'Artagnan's attention, pulling their focus away from Claude's blade just as he swung it, edge-first, toward their leg. At the last second, he twisted it so only the flat part smacked them on the thigh. No blood was spilled, but they would likely have a large bruise the next day.

"He may even have surpassed d'Artagnan," Aramis commented. "Certainly his footwork is quicker."

"I can hear you," they shouted indignantly.

"That was the point."

"Enough of this," Athos called, drawing them to a halt. He took another swig of wine from the bottle the three were sharing—of which he had drunk the majority. "Let someone else have a go." Handing the bottle to Porthos, he entered the circle to take d'Artagnan's place.

"You're quite drunk, Athos," Claude protested.

"So be extra vigilant," d'Artagnan advised. "He's somehow better in this state."

A look of confusion crossed Claude's face, but as Athos presented his blade, he refocused, raising his weapon in a starting position. Athos struck first, the metallic *clang* of crossing swords loud in the still air. He put Claude through his paces, testing his defenses and forcing them to dance around the arena to measure his footwork.

As Claude continued to pass his tests, Athos steadily began to show his true skills. Claude was quick and slippery thanks to his slight figure, but he was no match for Athos's strength and proficiency. Within minutes, Athos had the edge of his blade at Claude's throat.

"Not bad," Athos said, lowering his sword. "You've learned swiftly. You should be proud of your progress."

"I lost," Claude said, frowning.

"True, but you held your own for quite some time. And Aramis was correct; your footwork is much better than d'Artagnan's."

"It is not!" d'Artagnan exclaimed.

"Keep telling yourself that, kid," Porthos chuckled.

"I dare say you could match Milady, should you ever be inclined," Athos said, ignoring the others. "You've improved quickly and that is something to be proud of. Never again will you be a victim."

Claude's face turned a bright red. "Thank you," he said quietly. D'Artagnan smiled; despite his newfound confidence, Claude was still the same endearing, easily flustered person he'd always been.

"Well, our bottle is nearly empty. Shall we retire to the bar?" Athos asked, though he was already walking away without waiting for an answer.

The others began to follow, but d'Artagnan grabbed Claude's hand to stop him. "We'll meet you there," they said. "Claude and I have some business."

"We won't wait for you, so make it quick," Athos called back.

"What business do we have?" Claude asked once they were gone.

"Follow me," they said, beckoning.

They led Claude to the dorms and into their room, shut the door behind them, and gestured for him to sit down on the bed while they went rummaging in the closet. After a minute, he pulled a long, wrapped package from the back.

"Here. This is for you."

Claude stood and took it, weighing it in his hand. "You shouldn't have."

"I absolutely should have. Open it," they encouraged, nudging it.

Claude caved, ripping the paper wrapping from it to reveal a sheath and belt. He looked up at d'Artagnan; they smiled and nodded for him to draw the weapon. He turned his gaze back on his gift and pulled out a sword that gleamed in the low light of the candles. It was the same weight as the one Claude borrowed to practice with and was perfectly balanced. Thorny vines were etched into the flat of the blade, leading to a hilt with a hand guard made from silver roses.

Claude gasped. "You *really* shouldn't have. This must have cost a fortune."

"Not really. The blacksmith owed me a favor," they said, shrugging.

Claude ran his hand reverently over the vines. "I will treasure it always."

"I'm glad. Now you have your own sword to give you confidence whenever you need it," they said with a smile.

"It was never the sword."

"What?"

"It was never the sword that allowed me to be different," he said.

"Then what was it?" they asked, curious.

"It was me. It was me, finally giving myself permission to be who I am instead of who I am expected to be," Claude said. He took a deep breath before going on. "I am never more clearly myself than when I am a man. My clothes may have changed, but my soul has not. I was simply waiting for who I was meant to be."

"It was a person worth waiting for," d'Artagnan said. They took him by the hips and drew him closer, pressing their lips to his.

Claude stiffened in surprise, but it didn't take long before he melted into the kiss, pulling them in so they were chest to chest. The strength of his arms surprised d'Artagnan, but it only made them more joyful that Claude had accepted their offer of lessons. He was strong, strong enough to wield a sword, to take the punishment of a fight. He was no longer the timid girl d'Artagnan had known, but a confident man that they couldn't help but fall for. When they finally broke the kiss, Claude rested his forehead against d'Artagnan's.

"What will you do now?" they asked in a soft voice. They knew the lessons were all but over, now that Claude was formidable in his own right.

"I think…I think I might join the musketeers," he said, stunning d'Artagnan.

"You would join us?"

"If the king will have me."

"I have no doubt he would have you, but what of Milady?"

Claude's eyes grew steely, and he backed up to put the sword back in its sheath, belting it onto his hips.

"My days of being meek and submissive are over. I will tell her in no uncertain terms that I have no intention of returning to her service. Tonight. Now, even."

"Oh, please let me be there for that," d'Artagnan pleaded. "And Athos. If you take no one else, let it be Athos. There would be no end to his enjoyment, seeing Milady put in her place."

"I would have you there, in case I need to borrow some courage," he said, lacing his fingers with d'Artagnan's.

"You may have as much of mine as you need. Let us go retrieve Athos before he's too drunk to walk there."

"Athos. And the rest of you. What a pleasant surprise," Milady said, face twisted when she entered her parlor to find the five of them waiting for her. Her gaze landed on Claude, and her nose scrunched in displeasure. "I see you've added another ruffian to your merry band."

Claude stood slowly and crossed the parlor toward Milady. When he was but two steps away, he raised his head as he removed his hat. Milady's eyes grew wide as she recognized her tortured maid.

"Kitty?" she demanded. "What is the meaning of this?"

"My name is Claude," he said firmly, "and I will no longer be your slave."

"Claude?" she sneered. "And where will you go? Who would take you? No one has a need for a subpar servant in ill-fitting, deficient clothing."

Porthos made a small noise of protest, but Aramis shushed him.

"I will be joining the king's musketeers," Claude informed her, refusing to back down. D'Artagnan smiled at his bravery.

Milady laughed spitefully. "And what qualifies you to join such a brigade? You have no skills, no fighting ability."

"I have been studying the sword with d'Artagnan. I will join the musketeers and serve the crown and country, and never again serve you."

"You think you have any talent after a short time with the worst of the musketeers?" Milady asked. "Could you even defend against me?" She turned quickly and yanked down a sword that had been hanging on the wall. It may have been used for decoration, but it ended in a wicked point, having been kept sharp—likely by Claude himself.

D'Artagnan stood, hand on the hilt of their blade, but Claude stopped them.

"I can do this," he said, though d'Artagnan wasn't sure if he was talking to them or to himself.

Claude drew his new sword, but Milady was already swinging, taking a cheap shot. He barely had time to block the blow with the hand guard; the force shook its way up his arm. He ducked and spun away as she brought her sword down in another stroke toward his sword arm.

He came out of his whirl behind Milady, but she was too quick. Their blades met in a loud squeal. D'Artagnan admired Claude's skills; he hadn't fought someone that moved as fast as him before, and yet he was able to keep up his pace and still swing forcefully.

The furniture in the parlor proved to be a problem as Claude and his quick footwork led Milady around the room. Every time Milady swung and missed him, another piece of her beautifully decorated room was ruined by her blade. As she sliced the couch, forcing the other four to jump into a far corner, she let out a frustrated scream.

Claude made his move.

He lifted his blade high and brought it down in a shining arc, knocking her sword to the floor. Milady gasped as it was ripped from her hands. In a second, he had the point of his sword leveled at her face.

The room was silent for a long moment.

"So," Milady said finally, "you've bested me. Are you proud of yourself now? You may have learned to fight, but you think you could serve the king? As a soldier, no less. You are a coward, and you can never change who you are."

"I haven't changed. This is who I always was underneath your abuse," Claude said. He smiled at her widely and used the beautifully wrought hand guard of his sword hilt to knock her to the floor.

Milady fell in a heap, barely missing her own sword. Claude kicked it away, letting it carve into the wood floor.

"You are truly a worthy adversary," d'Artagnan said, coming to wrap their arms around Claude. "You did this all by yourself. I'm so proud of you and the progress—"

"This is very touching, but we ought to leave before she wakes up," Athos interrupted. "She'll be spitting mad when she comes to." He looked at Claude, still entangled with d'Artagnan. "But thank you for this. It brings me no small amount of entertainment to watch her lose. Now, let's get to the bar to celebrate our soon-to-be comrade in arms."

Athos's smile was contagious, spreading to all four others.

Claude giggled as he stepped over Milady's prone form and hurried to the door, pulling d'Artagnan with him.

Kou Lukeman

"Coup De Foudre" & *"DeWinter's Moonlit Dance"*

Two next pages
Kou Lukeman opted not to share the inspiration behind these artworks.

The Serendipity of a Late Train — Catherine E. Green

Tags

relationships: celebrity/fan, established relationship, f/f/f, f/f/f/f, polyamory, pre-relationship, threesome to foursome

character features: athlete, celebrity, character has a different gender than in the source material, lesbian

other tags: alternate universe, attraction at first sight, duels, flirting, france, getting together, meet awkward, misunderstandings, modern, paris, present tense, sports, third person limited point of view

Pissing off all three of The Inseparables at her very first try-out, Lottie mused, wasn't one of her brightest moments. The Swashbucklers, famed roller derby team, hadn't put out the call for fresh meat since her own mother, former star jammer, retired several years ago. As Lottie waits in line for a coffee that will hopefully help her pick up her feet after the long day she's had, she wonders about the night ahead and the "duels" that await her.

Each Inseparable had challenged her to a duel, whatever that meant, after her scuffles with them at tryouts. Lottie was never one to back down from a challenge, and she had the scars and misshapen knees to prove it. Not knowing what exactly she was walking into, though…well, it certainly wasn't *helping* the anxious tremble that had started in her hands and chest.

Coffee in hand, Lottie boards the Metro, praying to God that she'll make it back to the rink on time. "Return by 7 o'clock sharp," they'd insisted, leaving Lottie a scant couple hours to check in to her hotel, drop off her luggage, panic, and return to the rink. *How very kind of them.*

With only a few minutes to spare, she jogs up to the rink's main entrance and finds a lone knee pad propping open the main double doors. She slips inside as silently as she can and is *still* promptly met with a booming voice.

"Well, then. Actually decided to show up, did you?" That'd be Athos, with her arms crossed and a stern expression.

With nothing else for it, Lottie downs the remaining dregs of her coffee and shoves the cup into her gear bag. The chairs set up along the perimeter of the track from earlier are still there, and Lottie sits down to begin putting on her skates and protective padding.

"My, my," Porthos begins, a sensuous melody on her lips, "you've got quite the chutzpah coming here."

The third skater, Aramis, says, "I'm so glad you've met my challenge, Charlotte."

Lottie's whole body cringes. "Lottie…is fine, thanks."

It's with a smile and a wink that Aramis replies, "As you wish."

"Yes, Lottie. Let thy name be known to those who would make thee see sense and mete out due recompense," Porthos boasts, chest puffed out.

Athos snorts. "Cut the shit, Porthos; you sound ridiculous. What did she do to you, anyway?"

As they quibble among themselves, Lottie takes in the vast expanse of rink before her. It's much larger than the rink she considered her home back in Gascony, and yet The Inseparables manage to fill the room with the force of their personalities and reputations. Moreover, the rink's owner must have expensive taste, considering the sweeping flourishes around the crown molding.

Lottie stands up and skates toward the trio in the middle of the rink, where they wait flanked on either side by the thick outline of the derby track—inlaid wood, if Lottie were to guess. It's much neater than the temporary duct tape she's used to at her smaller, less well-cared for rink. The Inseparables still have their skating regalia on from tryouts.

"I don't think she's listening, dears. Do you?" Aramis says, tapping a finger against her cheek.

Lottie is opening her mouth to correct Aramis when Porthos says, "Nah, of course not. Look at her! She's in the presence of roller derby legends, and all she can do is stare. Pathetic, truly! Not that I blame her for being utterly speechless."

Oh, no. This is not *happening.*

Athos picks up the threads of Porthos's insults. "One has to wonder: is this the same girl who gave me lip for interrupting her, frankly, dangerous stunts? Weaving sloppily through a throng of *brand-new* skaters, nearly bowling into several of them, and then acting like it was no big deal?"

"Ex*cuse* me?" Lottie replies, sharp and disbelieving.

Aramis starts in: "Or the girl who arrived late to tryouts—"

"It's not my fault the train into the city was late!"

"—and then proceeded to make a huge commotion thereafter? No doubt a calm, polite conversation with our NSOs would have sufficed," Aramis finishes, nonplussed.

"Let's not forget that this is also the girl who insulted my plumage!" Porthos cries, gripping the rainbow-colored feather boa wrapped around her neck.

"Excuse me for mentioning it was a tripping hazard."

"Like you're one to talk, girlie!"

The hum of industrial fans somewhere filters in through the bubble of their conversation. It's a welcome distraction from the three arrogant asses in front of her. They may be derby legends, the players who drew her into their radiance in the wake of her mother finally quitting derby, but they don't know her. They have no idea how hard she's worked to develop the skills she has.

"You know what?" Lottie begins, smashing a skate into the floor to call the trio to attention. "We're here for duels, right? Well, let's get going, then. I can match any one of you in anything you throw at me!"

The three of them fall silent, each giving her a look somewhere between disdain and curiosity. "She's a firecracker," Porthos says, elbowing Aramis.

Athos tuts. "Ask, and ye shall receive. My partners and I accept your challenge."

"Partners?" Lottie blinks.

"We don't make a secret of it—the three of us have been a triad for years," she says as Porthos drapes a casual arm over Aramis's shoulders with a grin.

Lottie's breath hitches. Oh. *Huh.*

"Well?" Athos continues, "Let's get to it. Porthos, why don't you go first? See what

Inspiration
This story began taking shape as I was watching the 1993 movie adaptation of *The Three Musketeers* and taking notes on character personalities and story beats. Sometime during the back half of the movie, I had the thought that Athos, Porthos, and Aramis reminded me of some folks I'd spent time with when I was volunteering as a non-skating official (NSO) for a young roller derby group in Central New York. This got me thinking about translating the "Three Duels" arc into a series of trials for a young d'Artagnan trying to get onto a prestigious roller derby team and how his (or her, in this case) hero worshipping of the Musketeers might transform into love if the people behind the personas were revealed to her.

our new friend is made of."

And so the duels begin with Porthos lining up flush with the starting line and Lottie setting up beside her. With no ceremony whatsoever, someone blows a shrill whistle, and both competitors explode off the starting line.

It's no match, not with Porthos's sculpted legs and an endurance to match them. She glides along the track as if weightless, like the wind gently pressing through blades of grass on a warm summer day. Though Lottie can barely see through the colorful stream of feathers to Porthos's jersey, she knows it's emblazoned with the name "The Debonair Thrasher."

Lottie expends no small amount of effort trying to keep pace with her senior. She also tries to narrow her focus down to the track in front of her, to the exclusion of all attractive jammers, but she fails at both.

With a deft swish of her…rainbow plumage—*God above, how can that be functional in a contact sport?*—Porthos yells, "And there we have it, folks! Now, as the loser of the duel, I get to ask one thing from you, dear Lottie."

"When did I agree to—?"

"And I'd like you to apologize for calling my outfit ridiculous."

"You're kidding, right?"

"Not in the slightest, I can assure you," Athos interjects with fond exasperation.

In a fit of frustration, Lottie skates up to Porthos and stands chest-to-chest with her. "I'm *not* apologizing, because I *still* can't figure out how you don't get choked on a regular basis."

Their back and forth continues like this, and all the while Porthos cements a wide smile on her face. *She's enjoying this way too much.*

…said the pot about the kettle.

"As entertaining as all this is, I'd like to get my own recompense now, Porthos," Aramis says.

"Hmph. Well, go on, then. I haven't got all night to hang about here, you know."

"Got a hot date, have you?"

"Maybe. Wouldn't you like to know?" Porthos winks at Lottie.

Heat suddenly crawls through Lottie's veins, warming her skin and clouding her mind. *I would like to know, actually.*

Mollified or taking a tactful retreat, Lottie isn't sure, but Porthos replies, "All right. Take her through your obstacle course, then, and defend my honor—and yours, I suppose."

Aramis's smile eclipses the sun in luminosity. "It'd be my pleasure. What do you say, Lottie?"

How is she supposed to take all of this? The "dears," the "darlings," the winks, the smiles. Lottie can't deny the churning sensation in her stomach; it's not entirely from skipping dinner. There's a jitter in her hands that refuses to go away no matter how many times she wrings them out. She might have been able to beat Porthos, even, if she hadn't been so busy watching her body *move*. The sway of her hips, the smooth arcs her muscular legs cut across the track, and her hair—long curls gathering into a loose ponytail at the base of her skull. No wonder Lottie was driven to distraction.

"This is what I'm here for: to prove that I have what it takes to join The Swash-bucklers, that I'm ready to join the likes of you three—and my mother. Where do we start?"

Aramis guides her to the entrance of their makeshift obstacle course. It's not in the same formation as the one set up earlier to test potential new recruits. With so many small cones spread out across the floor, Lottie can't make out any discernible patterns from her position outside the course. *Guess it's time to wing it.*

"Athos will whistle again to signal the start of our duel. And a word of caution: make sure your helmet's on tight."

Lottie adjusts her chin strap with petulant fervor. "Maybe you ought to worry about keeping your own head safe, huh?"

"It's very kind of you to worry about my safety, my dear."

Lottie sputters her way through securing the rest of her safety gear, not caring for the whistle that could come at any time. A light pressure on her shoulder captures Lottie's attention. Rich brown eyes stare at her, and the smile on Aramis's face emphasizes the crinkles forming along the outside of her eyes.

Something glints around Aramis's ear; an unassuming silver cross earring stands out against her tan skin. "May the best skater win," Aramis says with a soft lilt.

"May the best skater win," Lottie returns with confidence, squatting down into a ready position.

The whistle blows once more, and it's Lottie this time quickly taking the lead. That lead gradually diminishes as Lottie's struggles to navigate the maze-like course; there are multiple sharp turns in quick succession, and Lottie has to make long jumps over cones where the path intersects itself and dead-ends, requiring instant about-face turns. Lottie's got fancy footwork and proves it when she crosses the finish line without having knocked any of the cones over, but Aramis slips by toward the end of the course like flowing water, smooth, with the lightest touch.

Aramis smiles again, a gentle, inviting thing, from where she stopped after crossing the finish line a couple seconds before Lottie did. "That's some fine footwork you have there, Lottie. Not many skaters make it through my course without knocking at least a few cones over. My compliments to you."

"Ah, and now you're patronizing me," Lottie grumbles under her breath.

Aramis tilts her head. "Who said I was patronizing you?" Lottie stays quiet. Something on her face must give Aramis the impression she's willing to hear more, so she continues. "I'd much rather be genuine in my interactions with people. That doesn't always mean being nice, but it can, at times, help reduce the world's ubiquitous heartache."

What can she say to that, really? "Nah, it's better to be shitty and disingenuous to each other all the time, actually"? *Heh, no.* "That's...that's quite the admirable goal, Aramis."

"Thank you, hun. And thank you for dueling me; I learned an awful lot."

"Oh?"

"Oh, yes. Very much so." *Genuine, my ass.* "Now, I do think Athos is raring to have a go at you."

Letting out a chuckle, Athos says, "Probably not as much as you two, with the way you're acting."

"Is that jealousy I note?" Porthos interrupts, a sly grin splitting her face.

"Oh, Athos, darling, there's no need to be jealous. Our hearts are with you—

always."

"Maybe not *just* with you, is all."

Athos turns a look on Aramis and Porthos that yells "Do you really have to do this right now?" Crossing her arms loosely over her chest, Athos says, "Yes, yes, I know. It's taken a while to really…take it to heart, but I know."

It's like watching a soap opera—a very queer soap opera—where the triad actually communicates effectively. Actually, on second thought, maybe not like a soap opera, then.

An unspoken message passes between the trio; it must be a comfort to be able to communicate with someone without words. "Methinks Athos could use some reassurance. Is reassurance something you'd want, love?"

One slow, exasperated nod later, Athos, Porthos, and Aramis are locked in a close embrace. They fit together like no one else she's witnessed before—better than her parents, her secondary school and university friends and their sweethearts, random passers-by—everyone. Theirs is a bond forged in fire, made strong and tensile with pressure from within and without.

The memory that jumps to mind is a strong one, reinforced through many iterations: Lottie sat crossed-legged on the couch watching the latest Swashbucklers match. Her mother never failed to join her, alternating between sitting next to Lottie and jumping up from the couch in triumph whenever an awesome play occurred.

While her mother was loud with her commentary, Lottie's mind was almost always louder, taking note of the order of operations of complex plays, the ways all the skaters moved around each other and the track simultaneously, and, well, everything about the so-called Inseparables. How could she not focus on them?

And then, after trouncing the other team, the three Inseparables would huddle—or embrace?—and Lottie's stomach would roil and she'd feel the unignorable urge to hide her chest behind her arms, as if she had to protect her heart from some incoming attack on the soft parts of her. Even more confusing: it only happened with those three. The other players would do the same, of course, celebrating and showing affection in varying ways, but something about them…

It felt different. Even from where she sat, when the faces of these women were only pixels on her parents' aging television. With recent…observations and a whole lot of self-acceptance of her own attraction to women, Lottie finally understands the "why" of it all.

She can't bring herself to interrupt them, even though it *is* getting late now. Having arrived in Paris this morning in a rush she hadn't planned for, Lottie wants to settle into bed as soon as possible. But she still has Athos to duel, and this upcoming challenge may even be the hardest of the three.

Movement in front of her signals the three are separating from one another. Aramis cups Athos's cheeks with her hands and presses a lingering kiss to Athos's forehead. Not to be outdone, Porthos grasps Athos's hand and kisses it like the chivalric knights of old. Athos's face absolutely *lights up* with their antics.

"Whaddaya say, love? Ready to show this youngling how it's done?" Aramis says, rubbing her thumb along the lines of Athos's cheek. Making a half turn toward Porthos, she adds, "And then we can all go home and just enjoy each other's company."

"If that's what we all decide, then sure. Now, you!" Athos turns to face Lottie and flings a finger at her. "I hope you didn't think you'd be able to escape our duel."

Lottie raises an eyebrow. "Not at all! I've been waiting for you all to get your shit together."

"It's becoming increasingly clear to me that you think you're funny."

"Not really. I merely observe and report what I see."

Porthos folds over laughing while Athos continues as if nothing has happened. "Is that right? Well, let's put those observational skills to the test one more time, shall we? For our duel, you'll be the opposing team's jammer trying to get past my defenses. You'll need to rack up at least five points in five minutes to win."

"I'll have you know that no blocker in my hometown has been able to hold me captive yet," Lottie says, following Athos to the track.

"You better not disappoint me, then."

Alternating cries of "Get her ass, Athos!" and "You've got this, dears!" follow Lottie and Athos as they take their positions on the track. It's do-or-die, now. One last chance to prove herself to these legendary skaters, to these women who are quickly enamoring themselves to her. From a deep crouch, all of her weight on the stoppers of her skates, Athos says, "I'm not going to baby you like Aramis, and neither am I going to goad you like Porthos. You're a grown-ass woman who can make her own decisions and figure out if the risk is worth the reward."

The whistle blows, setting Lottie entirely off balance. "A warning would've been nice, ladies!" Lottie yells loud enough to reverberate around the track.

"No coddling, remem—oomf!" Athos heaves, stuck clutching her chest while Lottie rounds the track with ease.

Fuck, that's satisfying.

"That's your freebie!" Athos yells as she recovers, maneuvering back into a ready position.

As if this were a real match of opposing teams, the sidelines are *loud*, somehow emitting more sound than two people ought to be able to make by themselves. Many of Porthos's and Aramis's specific words are lost on Lottie, but it's clear to her that they're not only rooting for their partner.

Lottie plows into Athos, who was ready to receive her momentum this time. "My flank was wide open! What gives?"

"Figured you could use a good tackle, obviously."

Athos brings up her forearms to push against Lottie. "You can do better than that. You could even try not hitting me at all!"

On Athos's last word, Lottie flies back with the force of her shove. Oh, those arms. It would come as no surprise to Lottie if Athos spent several days a week at the gym working those toned muscles. A smattering of light-blonde hair makes Lottie want to run her hand down them. Coarse or soft, Lottie would relish either.

Something rumbles up from the depths of her, clamoring to escape. Lottie knows what's coming, and frankly, the stage has been set. To mix metaphors, these three have made their beds, and now they must lie in them.

"You've misunderstood my dastardly plan, Athos. I've heard commentators mention more than once how solid you are, and I wanted to find out for myself if they were right." All Lottie receives in return is a raised eyebrow, light and thick. "And I have to say," she continues, "you are indeed someone I'd like to bump into again."

There's a pretty flush washing over Athos's neck and cheeks that wasn't there a minute prior.

"You're already sounding like these two, and you've only been here an hour."

A burst of laughter erupts from Aramis and Porthos, who are both hugging each other, trying not to fall over on their skates from the force of their giggles. "Not even!"

Shaking her head, Athos yells, "Time, refs?"

A couple of "Ah, shit"s later, Aramis produces a stopwatch and responds: "A minute and a half remains!"

Sprinting off her toe stops, Lottie takes a wide path along the outside edge of the track and sails past Athos. "Ha! One point for me."

"Good luck getting past me again."

It's barely an instant before Lottie finds herself facing Athos once more, brows furrowed. Clever woman, plopping herself right in the middle of the track. She'll be able to react in all directions with equal ease. But how to get past her?

Lottie could do *that*. Athos might not expect her to try *that*.

A quick swerve toward the inside curve begins Lottie's last-ditch effort. She hears more than sees Athos skating to meet her, rubber wheels slapping against the track in a bid to gain speed. Thankfully, Lottie already has all the speed she needs. Just before she reaches Athos, Lottie takes a great leap—"Shit!"—cutting over the inside boundary of the track and landing behind her would-be blocker.

"Porthos! Porthos, did you see that?" Aramis exclaims.

A full-bellied laugh leaves Porthos before she responds, "You bet your ass, I did! Who would've thought our Lottie had something like that up her sleeve—very flashy."

"So good of you to acknowledge my talent at last, ladies," Lottie yells over her shoulder as she picks up speed around the next turn.

Athos sounds off next. "And while all of you are congratulating Lottie here, she still has to get three more points. How much time do we—?"

"What are you all still doing here?" A new voice interjects. "You ought to have been gone by now."

The action halts instantly, both Athos's and Lottie's wheels squealing on the track. Lottie searches for the source of the voice and, in doing so, meets Athos's gaze; nothing but disdain colors her features. "I'll go see what he wants," Athos says over her shoulder as she makes her way to the audaciously dressed figure by the entrance.

Aramis and Porthos arrive behind Lottie. "Well, fuck. That's annoying."

"I'm definitely sensing the love you have for this guy," Lottie says.

"He's been trying to find reasons to break the contract with us for ages, despite the rather ob-noxious amount of money we pay him for what's usually nine-or-so hours of use a week. It's not even that we're eating into his business! We decided on times when the rink was typically closed specifically as a show of good faith." Aramis scoffs. "Fuck that guy."

"Fuck that guy—truly." Porthos echoes.

"Richelieu's kicking us out," Athos says as she skates up to the three, "so we gotta pack all this up now. You can help, too, Lottie."

"Oh, can I?" The look Athos shoots at her brooks no argument. "Right. Just tell me where things need to go."

With incredible speed, everything gets piled into Athos's van: cones, the trio's protective gear plus Lottie's—"We can take you to your hotel, dear. It's not a problem. Ah-ah! No 'buts.' "—laptops, flyers, and folding tables and chairs. It's a tight fit, but everyone and everything finds comfortable homes without much trouble. (And if the three occasionally pause to have quiet conversations among themselves, well, that isn't really Lottie's business.)

It's with good humor and a couple of rude gestures that they leave Richelieu and his overly embellished rink in the dust. Lights shine everywhere, bouncing off buildings and manifesting pretty and unknowable shadows. Even this late in the evening, traffic on the roads keeps their speed to a minimum, giving Lottie plenty of time to take in the sights.

"Have you ever been to Paris before this?" Aramis asks, peering around the side of her front seat at Lottie.

"Not recently. The last time I was here was for Mom's final derby match."

"You mentioned your mother before," Athos adds. "She used to do derby? What was her derby name?"

The world suddenly closes in on Lottie. "Are you serious? Didn't you all, oh, I don't know, read my application?"

"Oh-ho! Love that totally unreasonable confidence." Porthos says, while Aramis smacks her hand to her forehead.

"It's not really unreasonable when my mother is The Sly Hornet."

No one speaks. Their van jerkily plods along when the cars ahead of them grant them space. Aramis's and Porthos's eyes are wide, eyebrows approaching their hairlines. Athos's reaction is a mystery to Lottie, but she suspects she's trying to smother it.

Porthos recovers first. "Well, gentlepeople, it looks like we have a celebrity on our hands."

"The daughter of The Sly Hornet…" Aramis says wistfully. "Wow, what an honor."

"We only skated with her a few times before she retired, but damn was she a force to be reckoned with," Athos chimes in.

Aramis clasps her hands together at her chest and says, "The way she'd talk about her daughter, you'd think *she* was the derby legend. But, like Athos said, we were coming in as she was leaving, so we didn't really get to know her—or you, for that matter."

"We had no idea, Lottie," Athos assures her. "As far as we were concerned, you were a snot-nosed rookie who had some serious skills without the good sense to use them properly."

"Not to mention rude," Aramis asserts.

"Amen to that!" Porthos cries, to which Lottie replies with a soft fist to her shoulder.

With a sharp clap of her hands, Aramis begins: "This brings me to something I wanted to mention. First, are we—Porthos, Athos, and I—in agreement about what we discussed earlier?"

"Hell, yes! Enthusiastically and without reservation."

"How about you, darling?" Aramis asks, staring at Athos.

"I maintain my own reservations."

Porthos waves her hand around. "Yes, we know. But?"

Athos heaves a long sigh. "To the first, fine. To the second…maybe. Definitely not immediately."

What Lottie wouldn't give to be able to see Athos's face. Or, for that matter, understand what's being discussed around her—and probably about her.

"Like I said earlier, though: I don't mind if you two go for it." *Earlier…*

Aramis lays a soft kiss on Athos's shoulder and says, "We know, love, and your consent is noted and appreciated."

"Would *any* one of you please explain to me what you're even talking about?"

"Hold your damn horses, will ya?" Porthos chides.

"I think it's rather rude to talk about someone who's sitting right next to you as if she isn't even there."

"She makes a fair point, Porthos," Aramis concedes.

"This one's gonna be trouble," Athos jumps in. "You two sure you're ready?"

"I think I made my stance quite clear already," Aramis says.

"I'm waiting…" If Lottie doesn't get to know what these three are alluding to in the next few seconds, she might burst.

"All right, Lottie. Just needed to make sure we were all on the same page," Aramis says with contrition. "Who wants to break the news?"

"Why don't you, Aramis? Since you're the most diplomatic of us," Porthos says.

"It's rather amusing that you think that, but okay," Aramis says. To Lottie's right, Porthos looks ready to jump out of her seat. "Well, first, we'd like to welcome you to Swashbucklers practices as fresh meat."

Is this real? This has to be real. She wouldn't be feeling Athos's shoddy van vibrating around here if it wasn't. "*No shit…*"

"No shit." Aramis agrees.

"Holy fuck, my mother's not going to be able to contain herself!" Lottie leans over and pulls Porthos into a hug. *This is really happening!*

"Congratulations, Lottie. You're rough around the edges, but we see many nascent skills in you, waiting to be developed."

Realizing she's still gripping Porthos, she lets go in a flash, unbearable heat rising to her face. "This is…this is— I'm—I don't know what to say."

Porthos says, lilting and dreamy, "Just say that you'll be ready to start practicing with the rest of the team soon, and we're good."

"Ah, fuck. Right. I'm…going to have to move, huh?"

Aramis laughs softly. "Probably for the best, yes."

"Kitty already has some wild fresh-meat names lined up for you new recruits. I don't know how she comes up with them," Athos says.

"Wait…" *There was something else…* "Athos said something about there being a second thing…?" Lottie trails off, wringing her hands together. "I'm not sure what could really be as important as joining the most prestigious roller derby team in France, though."

Aramis and Porthos gaze into Lottie's eyes, vulnerability shaping the lines of their faces. Slowly, Aramis ventures, "The three of us have been together so long, I forget how this goes."

The three of us have been together so long, I forget how this goes. The statement bangs around the walls of Lottie's mind, drowning out the rest of her thoughts. Around and around it goes, and Lottie can't stop it to wrestle with it. *How* what *goes?*

Memories of the rest of the night barge into the verbal assault: Porthos alluding to going on a date with her, Aramis laying a hand on her shoulder and trying to cheer her up, and Athos with that wicked look on her face. These signs could mean something, something exciting and terrifying. But do they? Can two miracles occur in a single night?

"Here goes nothing. Lottie, Porthos and I would like to take you on a date or two, if you're amenable. Athos may not join us in the beginning but might later on—again, only if you're amenable. Nothing happens without your agreement and consent."

"…I'm not sure I understand."

"We like you—a lot—and we're inviting you to maybe join our triad—well, polycule, it would be, then, huh?"

Athos adds: "On a trial basis."

"Yes, on a trial basis." Aramis nods with grave seriousness. "So we can get to know each other and figure out if you're a good fit with us."

"A trial basis… What, are there gonna be, like, tests? If I pass, I get to stay, and if I don't, I have to say, 'Goodbye'?"

"There'd be a lot of talking before it came to that, I think."

Lottie hums, not sure what to do with her everything. "Okay."

"Okay?"

"Okay. Yes." Lottie nods and beams. "I'm *extremely* amenable. When would we start?"

Porthos leans in for a kiss on Lottie's cheek. "Now. Oh, driver?"

"Fuck off, Porthos." Lottie's pretty sure she hears a smile in Athos's voice.

"To the nearest eatery! The date is on!"

Jagoda Zirebiec　　　　　*"Knight Commander"*

Next page
Inspired by works of the Pre-Raphaelite Brotherhood, this piece explores their relationship dynamics. With Athos in the middle, lost in thought, Aramis on the left, always affectionate, and Porthos on the right, their loyal protector.

The Three Mic O' Tears

— Lucy K. R.

Tags
warnings: harm to a family member (off-screen)
relationships: f/f, family
character features: character has a different gender than in the source material, fat, lesbian, magic use, performer
other tags: alcohol use (casual), alternate universe, chicago, magical realism, meet awkward, memphis, misunderstandings, modern with magic, past tense, present tense, third person limited point of view, united states of america

Inspiration
Lucy K. R. opted not to share the inspiration behind this story.

Twelve years ago, a little girl named Dart flopped face-down into the booth of a Chinese restaurant in a Memphis strip mall. She was queasy from long hours of driving, and her mind felt cotton-stuffed—dulled by the old "focus" music her parents always played when traveling.

"It still works," her father would say cheerfully. "You just don't get voices like Frank Sinatra these days. Can't beat the classic magics!"

It might work for him, Dart would allow, but for her it felt wrong and itchy under her skin. A dead voice singing a dying spell. It wouldn't work forever. Would her father even notice when it stopped, or would he just keep listening, like a coffee drinker unknowingly being weaned onto decaf?

From a dark corner of the faded-red restaurant interior, a microphone buzzed to life.

"Oh no," groaned her mother, head already propped in one hand despite her repeated requests for Dart to sit up properly. "Not karaoke…"

Dart leaned out of the booth to watch a man take a seat behind a computer. A screen buzzed to life, facing away from her. Then a woman in a brown leather jacket, her gray hair puffing out from beneath her cowboy hat, walked up to the stage with the stiff gait of a person with bad knees.

Music started, a tinny imitation of a familiar tune piped out of a single stand-up speaker that crackled. Her mother cringed so hard that it was almost audible.

Then the woman started singing.

Swiveling with a squeak of jeans against vinyl, Dart leaned out of her booth, blocking the aisle for the passing servers. Her eyes widened, queasiness forgotten.

Cracking on the held notes, rasping across familiar phrases, the woman's voice silenced every conversation. The air shook with it.

Stairway to Heaven's magic had been played out long before Dart could remember hearing it for the first time. Once it had been wholehearted—it had been true, powerful—and then it had become dead noise decaying on the airwaves. Still loved, yes, like so many dead songs were loved for the memories of the spells they cast, but no longer able to heal aching hearts—no longer enchanting and changing those listening with the pulse of ancient power.

On that quiet Tuesday night, to an audience of thirty at most, the dead song was reborn in the breaking voice of an old woman who meant every word. Dart's father choked back sobs. Her mother was silent until long after the song ended.

"We can still fix this," she said eventually, reaching out to hold her husband's hands.

Dart found a different certainty in the swell of magic. She watched the woman fix her cowboy hat before stepping off the little karaoke stage, and she *knew*.

Not many people thought of karaoke *first* when they thought of magic. It didn't carry the glory of composition nor the flashy power touring performers conjured. But that night in Memphis, right before the waiter brought out their lo mein with tears on his smile-curved cheeks and then turned away to quit his job, a girl called Dart heard the soul of karaoke call her.

Chicago is a city that holds eye contact when it speaks, whether it's saying "I love you" or "Go fuck yourself." It's a city built to funnel the fierce winds of Lake Michigan through the streets, tearing at clothes, tossing unbound hair, and flinging hats with abandon into the sky.

"What was it like," the interviewer asks, "getting your big break in the Windy City itself?"

"Pretty auspicious." Dart carefully angles her head as she replies, aiming for a wry, lofty look. Her unfinished lipstick makes the expression appear unhinged more than anything. "After all," she adds, leaning back in toward the mirror to finish her upper lip, "what's the wind if not an unvoiced song?"

The audience murmurs approval. The interviewer's eyebrows shoot up.

"Shit, that's a good line," Dart abandons her makeup to open her phone, jotting it down in her notes.

The imaginary interviewer can wait until she's done. One day, they'll be chomping at the bit to ask more questions, the audience leaning forward—hungry for more of her. Her words, her voice, her presence, her *magic*.

"Tell us everything," the interviewer will say. "How did you start? What does this mean to you?"

"Your parents must be proud!" they'll say.

Dart freezes, her mascara brush still buried in her eyelashes, and breathes in deep.

A notification dings on her phone before she can catch up to her own haywire imagination. "Your driver has arrived!" With a curse, she all but shoves mascara through her lashes and runs for the door.

Like the fabled Wrigley Field, a wall of ivy crowns The Last Dance's façade. Behind windows made half opaque by the searing light of the sunset, people mill about. There's only one place lit well enough to be clearly seen past the sun's glare. It's a stage, barely big enough for the smallest three-man band, with a blue backdrop hanging awkwardly on the brick wall behind it. Silhouetted against the blue, Dart can see the black rectangle of a monitor set up to scroll lyrics for the performers.

Dart clutches her dying phone in a shaking hand and stands tall against the tearing wind, watching the shapes inside tilt and sway with conversation. Not once, she promises herself. Not once will she even have to glance at that monitor. Not once will she look away from her audience. Not once will they hear a whisper of insincerity in her voice.

Tonight, the Second City Competitive Karaoke League preseason social will be forever changed by the arrival of their most talented and promising new member. Tears will flow, hearts will heal, spontaneous dances will erupt, and at the center of it all will be Dart, finally in her place.

She steps into the roar and rustle of a hundred people in conversation and straightens her spine; she's invisible in the crowd for now. She throws back her shoulders, lifts her chin, and steps forward to—

WHAM!

Stumbling back, Dart recognizes a moment too late what's happened. The woman she'd slammed into staggers at the impact. Her height draws out the small motion, and by the time Dart manages to get her eyes off the woman's long legs, broad shoulders, black leather jacket, and (horrifyingly) distinct white sling, the woman is already *glaring*.

In huge red-marker letters, the sling has been modified to read MIC-RELATED INJURY; DO NOT TOUCH. But despite the stagger, despite the obvious wince and the pale wash of pain that's come over the woman's face, she does not curse. She does not whine. She does nothing more than straighten and draw a deep, deep breath, her steel-gray eyes fixing on Dart's upturned face.

"Um," says Dart.

"The back hall bathroom," the woman says, so crisp and clear that each word is its own separate statement. "Fifteen minutes."

"Wh—? The bathroom?"

The woman leans in close enough that her hot breath warms Dart's wind-bitten ear before whispering: "I'm not the kind of person who turns the other cheek in the face of sabotage."

And then she's gone, pulling away like the ocean before a tsunami—inexorable, unstoppable. Dart gapes at the motion of her, fully aware that as lovely as the withdrawal is, what it *truly* speaks of is danger coming in…well, in about fifteen minutes, apparently.

Bar first, then, she decides, and enters the press of bodies in search of a drink. She bellies up beside a cluster of people, all listening to a woman holding court while turned 180 degrees on a bar stool.

"Needless to say, they didn't believe me." Her voice is so musical, even her scoffing borders on song. The weft and weave of her intonation thrums against the air with the potential for power.

Dart waves to the bartender and gets a nod of "be right there" in return.

"Who would, after all?" the woman continues, waving her rosemary-garnished drink—a pinkish orange that matches her sunset-shaded dress. "Someone like me, without a contract or a CD? I can't blame them."

She wiggles in her seat, preening. Dart can't help glancing as the woman's audience laughs. She's all curves, soft cheeks rounded by wry smiles and bronze dress accenting her every aspect, equally loving to her breasts, thighs, and plump stomach.

"Drink?" the bartender asks, dragging Dart's attention back.

"Uh," says Dart, tongue-tied between "what's she having?" and "one of those" and managing neither.

"Not that I'm interested in explaining to boys like that," the woman continues, her free hand tapping against the gold-chained bag in her lap, patterned with neat, intersecting letters. Dart squints. "You know, the sort who put ugly words like 'just' in front of beautiful ones like 'singing.'"

"Flag me down when you're ready," the bartender says, but Dart hardly notices.

"I like your Faux-cci," she blurts instead.

The woman and her audience pause. They take a breath almost in unison—singers, Dart thinks with a thrill of excitement. Then the woman turns, swiveling her stool until she and Dart are face-to-face.

"Excuse me?"

Her cheeks are still rounded in a smile, but it looks sort of…dangerous?

"Your fake Gucci," Dart explains, gesturing to the bag with its entwined C's. "It's…cool?"

"Tell me again how you died," says the imaginary interviewer in her head. "Embarrassment, was it?"

"Hmmhmm," the woman says, a sound not entirely unlike a pleasant chuckle. Her audience is more lively. There's a loud snort, and a guffaw.

The woman leans in close. Her lipstick is a beautiful bright red, fading pinker in the center. It's hard to tell whether it's from her drink, or a deliberate effect, or—

"You," the woman half sings into her ear, making every hair on Dart's body stand on end, "are going to meet me in the back hall bathroom. I'll give you fifteen minutes to get your drink."

Dart swallows hard, thinking of cold eyes glaring down at her. She checks the clock. Five minutes down already.

"Could we make it ten?" she asks weakly, and the woman sits back with a hearty laugh, as if nothing is wrong.

Across the bar, Dart notes a woman in a puffy-sleeved SECURITY jacket crossing her arms and glaring. Embarrassed, with her face burning—thank *fuck* she put on foundation to hide her blush—she slips away from the bar and ducks back toward the stage, leaving behind a gorgeous woman with a fake Gucci bag now clutched in a white-knuckled grip.

There's a blessed lack of crowd around the stage for now. Nothing's happening, after all. A tired man with headphones around his neck is running cords between his computer and the monitor Dart had glimpsed from outside. One woman is pacing in front of the stage in slow, measured steps, with a small audience of her own.

Dart hovers, watching the woman move. Her steps are fluid and practiced. It strikes Dart that this person is editing a dance in slow motion—finding the edges of the stage in something she's prepared for this night. Excitement floods Dart at the thought, swallowing down the anxiety sticking in her throat like glue.

The dancer's short-cropped dark hair reveals a long neck, bared as she tilts back in a languid motion. Her white shirt is neat, the collar starched. Under the cheap stage lights, she seems to glow. If not for the lights, Dart wouldn't have noticed at all, but at the collar of her white shirt is a smear of bright red. Lipstick, almost certainly, probably a classic "pulled the shirt on over-head after putting on makeup" problem—so relatable!

"Sorry," Dart says, swiping a bar napkin and approaching the woman, "you have a little—"

She points to her own neck, indicating the spot. The woman's movements slow until she stops completely. She eyes Dart without any expression, then lifts a hand. She touches a finger to her collar and takes a deep breath. She swallows so hard that Dart can see her throat work with it.

84

"How dare you," she says, her voice very soft but filled with the threat of violence.

It's only while staring at her lips that Dart realizes the dancer is wearing a peach shade. There's not a hint of red in her makeup, but instead tones of silver.

Fuck, Dart thinks.

"The back hall bathroom," the woman says, unnervingly calm. "Fifteen minutes."

"Actually," says Dart, "we'd better just head there now."

The back hall bathroom she's heard so much about turns out to be infamous for a reason. It's one of those liminal spaces, only tangentially connected to the bar it theoretically belongs to. If not for the latest victim of Dart's inability to socialize, she would never have found it.

The dancer pulls open the door with a sharp tug, fighting against a swollen jamb and tacky paint to haul open a garish three-stall bathroom. The walls are painted neon blue. The only break from the color comes in the form of a long-legged woman leaned up against the far wall, her arm in a sling and her eyes fixed on the door.

"Not a coward, then," she assesses, straightening up before pausing as the dancer follows Dart into the room.

"Ash," greets the dancer in her blanket-soft voice.

"Artemis, tell me this isn't a friend of yours," the first woman—Ash?—says, stepping forward.

"Ah, no," Dart lifts her hands. "I managed to offend her too, so I hope you don't mind, I invited her along to the reckoning. There's also—"

"Well well. Crowded bathroom!" a sweet voice sings.

"Portia!" Ash outright laughs this time, her steely eyes flicking back to Dart, giving her a quick up and down. Assessing. "Don't tell me you're here for this same dance."

In swans the woman from the bar, fake Gucci draped over one shoulder and her six-inch heels still leaving her shorter than the others—quite a bit shorter, in Ash's case.

"You have a full card, it looks like." She crosses the room along with Artemis to join Ash's side.

"Deliberate sabotage?" Ash guesses.

"I'm afraid not," Dart replies, heart in her throat but eager not to falter now. Not when she's finally sort of having a conversation. "Just terrible luck on my part."

"Truly," Ash says.

"To a shocking degree," Portia agrees, busily detaching the large hoop earrings she's wearing and dropping them into her bag.

"Hm," says Artemis, her thumb sliding over the mark on her collar.

"Well." Dart, with no idea what to do with her hands, pats her thighs, then shoves her thumbs into her pockets. "How shall we do this? I assume we're fighting. Will it be three on one?"

"That would hardly be fair." Ash tilts her head to allow Portia's clever fingers to unhook the gauges she's wearing.

Even certain she's about to be crushed on her first day in Chicago, exactly as her mother had feared, Dart can't help but be awed by these women. Ash rolls her good shoulder; Artemis lowers her head and half closes her eyes so Portia can tuck away her earrings too, out of range of grasping fingers. Not that Dart *would*, but...

"Here," Portia holds a hand out, making a grabby motion with her perfect red nails. "Better let me hold onto yours too."

"Oh." Dart fumbles, shoving through her tangled, asymmetrical bob. The Chicago winds haven't agreed with her hair styling. "Thanks. I'd hate to bleed on any of you."

"I wouldn't relish being bled on," Artemis agrees with something like humor in her voice.

"You aren't from here, are you?" Ash guesses, leaning on one leg in a way that makes her into an Adonis of a woman—Greek sculpture in her every line.

"Ah, no," Dart agrees, offering her earrings. "Came into town yesterday for this."

Ash blinks, a single sculpted eyebrow lifting. Portia's expression twists into a cute frown of confusion. Artemis only nods.

"So," Dart says, "I assume from the earrings it's fists, not voices?"

"The plan is to pay you back for the slight, not to ruin your life," Ash agrees with such dead certainty that Dart feels a thrill of terror and excitement all jumbled up, merged into the same creature.

"You seem very sure you'll win," Dart offers, tilting her own head in return.

"Ooh," Portia's lips quirk into an even cheekier smile.

"Cute," Artemis comments, appraising eyes still fixed on Dart.

"So, in order of offense?" Dart asks, feeling her inner performer awaken at their attention. "Ash first, then Portia, then Artemis?"

"You seem very sure you'll make it to the last dance yourself," Ash returns, even as Artemis strips off her jacket and neatly folds it, nodding her approval.

"I came here to sing karaoke," Dart takes the opportunity to roll up her sleeves. "Nothing and no one is going to keep me off that stage."

She's never fought anyone before. She's never had to. But she said it, and she meant it—nothing will keep her off that stage. She lifts her fists, only to be tutted at by Ash.

"Wrists straight, dear," Ash says, lifting her one good arm in demonstration.

"Ah," says Dart, and fixes her posture.

An abrupt wrenching sound from the doorway sends all four of them jumping like cats. Dart flings her hands into her pockets, tosses her windswept hair, and looks up at the ceiling—a cream haven against electric-blue walls.

Portia lets loose a peal of laughter that seems to come from a natural grove deep inside her—there is nothing forced about it as she leans against Artemis's shoulder as if it's the most natural thing in the world.

"You *are* a kidder!" she chirps, flapping her red nails in Dart's direction with a sunny grin.

Ash's hand has migrated to her hair and her eyes to the mirror, fixing what doesn't need repair. Artemis is the only one who acknowledges the puffy jacket in the doorway.

"Cardi," she greets, voice smooth, "and her Bs, I see."

"Stop," says the annoyed woman in the security jacket, wrinkling her nose. Behind her, four young men shuffle, squinting either against the bright blue or against the thought of a women's restroom.

"Stop what?" asks Portia.

"What are you doing in here?" Cardi demands. "You've been acting weird all night. Don't think I've forgotten how much trouble you three caused last season, *Mic O' Tears*."

"Getting a crowd worked up isn't 'causing trouble,' it's *performing*," Portia mutters under her breath.

Artemis nudges her foot against Portia's in rebuke—suede against sequined heels, too light to be called a kick.

Ash takes a deep breath, finally turning from the mirror. There's a look of danger about her as she surveys the five bouncers crowding the doorway. They must *really* have caused trouble to warrant a response like this, Dart thinks. Pieces click together. The three women—their unavoidable presences—their comfort with each other—their certainty of sabotage. A group? Dart considers the idea of them on stage together and loses her breath.

"I was auditioning!" she blurts, turning her back on the three women she was about to throw down with to form a united front against the intruders. "I wanted to join them, but they wanted proof. I don't like to sing if people aren't ready for magic, so they brought me here to listen."

"Audition." Cardi repeats.

"Yes," Ash backs her up. "You interrupted."

"Well, let's hear it then," the intruder crosses her arms, the jacket's cheap material whispering against itself.

Dart glances behind herself. Three pairs of eyes lock on her in return—intense, but no longer threatening. She has their attention. She's never needed more than that.

A deep breath, a lift of her chin, a tilt of her head to the left, and she follows in the footsteps of thousands of karaoke singers before her:

She sings Journey.

Her voice isn't warmed up.

Her notes quaver.

The spell catches anyway.

She sees Cardi and her B's rock back with it. Power has never been Dart's weak point. But *they* aren't the ones she wants to watch her. She turns her head slowly and her eyes lock with Ash's.

Ash stands like a statue, gazing at Dart from those steel eyes. On her left, Portia leans against her, a wry smile twisting her bright-red lips. On her right, Artemis observes her, expression dispassionate, but her hand sneaks behind Ash to tangle in Portia's purse chain.

Dart closes her eyes as she hits the chorus. It doesn't matter that there isn't music. It doesn't matter that it's for an audience of eight, only three of whom really matter. She *believes*. For a true bard, that's enough, even if her voice isn't made for the high notes. She dances around them. Her throat is raw from the wind outside, but it adds a realness to her words.

If this is her chance, she'll take it with both hands clutching it to her chest. Nothing will stop her—nothing could—but the voice that joins the song isn't trying to stop her. It layers into the emptiness of her rendition, precise where Dart is all wild energy.

Her eyes snap open.

Ash is singing, cold eyes unwavering as her blade-like voice grants "Don't Stop Believing" a gravitas Dart had never realized it was lacking.

Here is where she's *always* fallen flat. The refrains at the end are made for voices playing together. Twining, bouncing, clinging, tossing the melody back and forth.

Dart has always sung alone.

A heartbeat after Ash starts singing, Portia follows the lead—bright, sweet, high-toned, and effortlessly showy. Artemis takes her time, selecting her entrance rather than hurrying. There's an ethereal quality to her voice—something inherently soft despite her volume.

The structure of the song dissolves into just voices. Dart pushes, they return. Ash leads, Dart follows. Portia takes the melody, they cover. Artemis decrescendos, they back off to make room for her. It's an instinctual thing. Wild. Living.

It's *magic*.

A shallow nod from Ash, and Dart catches a breath. The final "*don't stop*" escapes her almost as a plea. The meaning of the song shifts, clicks into place, and releases.

"I won't," sobs a man's voice.

The four of them are abruptly dragged back into the reality of garish blue walls, bathroom stalls, and feet on solid ground.

"I won't," one of the so-called B's repeats, tears brimming in his eyes, before he turns, fleeing.

"Aw, Daniel!" cries one of the other Bs, and the others quickly follow him out of the back hall.

Only Cardi remains, staring.

"You're going to start a riot," she says.

"Depends on the set list," Ash takes two long steps forward until she's between Cardi and Dart as well. "Which, if you don't mind, we need to decide on."

"Where did you *come* from?" Portia is asking, bustling over to Dart and taking her cheeks in both hands, tilting her head back and forth. The long acrylics she wears touch lightly against Dart's cheeks, but only from eight of her ten fingers. Dart swallows hard.

"A small town, I'd assume." Artemis purrs, approval turning her softness into something *else*.

"Y-yeah," Dart rasps, her voice feeling burnt to a crisp.

"Hot toddy first thing," Ash orders, shoving the paint-swollen door shut and whirling back to march up to the three of them. "We're getting that voice in fighting shape. What have you been doing to prepare?"

"Uh," says Dart.

"Right, that changes now. Artemis, get her a care plan."

"I'll need your phone number," Artemis murmurs.

"That was real, right?" Dart blurts, her eyes flicking from one to the other—beautiful, fierce, and sweet, all so perfectly matched with her raw determination. "It wasn't just a ruse?"

"Do you make a habit of singing when you don't mean it?" Ash steps closer, making Dart crane her neck. "You wanted us to hear you. We heard. Now you tell me—were you auditioning or weren't you?"

Dart barks out a laugh, then quickly lifts her hands, fighting tears.

"Wait, I don't— I'm not laughing because—"

"You are a *mess*," Portia notes, digging out a handkerchief. "Lucky you offended us first! Imagine if someone else had gotten their claws in you!"

"I don't know, I think I'm still offended," Artemis teases, her head tilting with a natural poise that Dart's mirror interviews could never hope to match.

"Say it plainly," Ash demands.

"*Please*," Dart says, one hand clutching Portia's handkerchief without daring to actually use it.

"Then welcome," Ash says, towering, gorgeous, incredible, and *smiling directly at her*, "to the Mic O' Tears."

Dart leans in close to the mirror, squinting mouth-opened at her eyeliner.

"So tell me," an interviewer will ask her one day, "traveling so far away from home, nearly getting killed at your first karaoke contest, joining the Mic O' Tears, was all this just for the fame? The glory?"

"Fifteen minutes, Dart," Ash calls through the bathroom door, tapping twice against it as she passes.

"Uh huh!" Dart squints at herself in the mirror, then blinks hard, fighting off instinctive tears to keep from smearing the still-wet lines.

More quietly, as she picks out her lipstick, she mutters the answer to the question.

"If I wanted fame, I could have gotten it." A dark purple *would* stand out against the others. She holds it up against her cheek, tilting her head to the left. "The truth is, I'm here for my father."

"Your father?" the interviewer is confused. "We haven't heard much from him!"

"You probably won't," Dart agrees, straightening up and letting her lipstick holding hand fall to her side. "He doesn't talk much anymore. We don't like to talk about it—no one does—but music can do more than heal and empower."

Her hand clenches around the tube of lipstick—cold, but wet with sweat.

"Dart, sweetie," Portia's voice sings to her, "Ten minutes!"

She takes one deep breath. A second.

"Thanks, Porsche!"

The purple glides smooth over her uncracked lips. The skincare routine Artemis sent her is as effective as the one she'd put together for keeping Dart's voice clear and healthy.

"I don't know who sang it to him," Dart whispers, watching the purple of her own lips move. "I don't know what they sang. But I know he came home one day, and words couldn't reach him anymore. I know what dive bar it happened at, and that there was karaoke that night. I know that all the people there went home with empty eyes."

She looks up, meeting her own gaze in the mirror. A war goddess stares back, sharpened by the warriors she stands among now.

"Five minutes, angel," Artemis murmurs through the door as if it weren't there, the brush of her fingers over the wood so audible that Dart almost feels it.

"Thank you, five," Dart replies politely, capping her lipstick.

"Revenge, then?" the interviewer asks, cowed and awed by her intensity.

"Justice," Dart whispers. "Alone, I couldn't have done anything, just like I couldn't fix what they'd broken in my dad. But I'm not alone anymore. I don't know what the others would think if they knew my real reason, but I know they have their reasons too. People don't leave home to go on tour with a karaoke group for the headlines in local newspapers or for small-time interviews like this."

"Hey," objects the imaginary interviewer.

Dart puts her lipstick in the fake Gucci bag that Portia had gifted her as a joke before they'd hit the road together. Tonight, they're heading to a little Chinese place in a strip mall off the highway. It feels right. It feels circular.

It feels like the beginning of a new arc of the story.

"When they're ready to tell me why they're all really here," she whispers, her hand on the doorknob, "I'll back them. And when I find the person who hurt my dad…" She stares at the doorway, breathing deep, and feels the endless violent lyrics she'd learned burning a hole in the back of her mind. "We'll knock 'em dead."

Dart turns to see the other three standing by the door. Portia shifts Artemis's crisp white collar aside to press a bright-red kiss to her neck. Artemis's high cheekbones dust pink, and she casts her eyes to the side. Ash stretches out her still-stiff shoulder, broken onstage in an incident Dart hasn't asked about. They all look to her as she approaches, and Ash shifts her stretch into an open-armed invitation.

Pressing tight into their pre-show group hug, Dart steadies herself against them.

People forget what bardic power was first meant for, she thinks as she follows them out to Ash's jeep. It wasn't a flash-bang or a panacea. It was grandparents by the fire, crooning lessons to live by. It was parents singing their children to sleep. It was children weaving happiness out of their first warbling notes.

And of course, the part no one wants to remember: it was putting those who would hurt your family to an early grave.

Portia turns on the mix CD. Dart inhales deeply, declaring her intention to take the lead. Three sharp, brilliant, *gorgeous* pairs of eyes fix on her. A guitar twangs to life over the car's speakers. Dart lets her expression take on the wild edge she's become known for amid these three perfect Mic O' Tears.

"Let's go, girls."

Spongeunction   *"untitled"*

Spongeunction opted not to share the inspiration behind this artwork.

Glass Hearts

— Sage Mooreland

Tags

warnings: character injury (graphic descriptions), violence (non-graphic descriptions) **relationships:** established relationship, m/m, m/m/m, polyamory **character features:** criminal, hacker, spy **other tags:** action and adventure, alcohol use (casual), alternate universe, be gay do crimes, blackmail, car accident, chicago, mistakenly believed to be dead, modern, past tense, reunions, second chances, third person limited point of view, united states of america

Inspiration

The first thing I think of when I consider these three ridiculous people is the wild chaos they always seemed to manage. I'll admit that I imprinted hard on the '90s version of these characters, so when I went back and learned more about them, I was delighted to see it was more ridiculous than I thought. What's more ridiculous than a car chase with bickering? And then, as a Chicago native, the natural conclusion for a car chase was my city, and this bit of fun was born.

Athos leaned against the wall of the high rise across the street from his destination, trying to catch his breath. He was bleeding from too many places to count—many of the wounds were superficial, but a few were deep and concerning. He had to get them bandaged or he was going to be in serious trouble. Standing across the street from help would be a stupid place to bleed out, even if it would be vaguely satisfying to get blood all over the pavement of one of Chicago's wealthiest neighborhoods.

He watched a while longer; the lights inside the house created a faint glow he could see even through closed blinds. The occasional shadow told him that *someone* was home. He refused to consider that he was looking at a second ambush. They had to be there, safe and sound, or all of this had been for absolutely nothing. Athos took a deep breath. Standing here—well, *leaning* here—wasn't getting him anywhere, and he'd watched long enough to be sure he hadn't been followed. He forced himself upright and carefully crossed the street, climbed the stairs, and rang the bell.

"Why do you look like you got run over by a combine?" Porthos asked. He'd closed his eyes by the time the door swung open, but he'd recognize that voice anywhere. "And why the fuck did you come here?" Even as the caustic words faded out into the night, Porthos was grabbing Athos as carefully as possible and bringing him inside. "It's been five God-damned years, and here you are, beat up, bloody, and dripping on my clean floors. *Aramis!*"

"I'm right here. You don't have to yell." Aramis came out of a doorway to the right, carrying a first-aid kit. "I heard you and detoured. Combine? Seriously? That was the first thing that came to mind?" He grabbed Athos from the other side and helped Porthos get him to the kitchen. "Though I think you might be right. Where the hell did you get all of these slices?"

Athos groaned quietly when he was lowered into the chair. "Glass window. Following a fistfight. Following the discovery that I'd been betrayed."

"I love how you tell stories backward," Porthos said dryly. He left them sitting and returned with a garbage bag; he spread it across the surface of the table. "Put all the used stuff there," he told Aramis, and he went back to the stove, his back to the two men at the table. His shoulders were stiff, drawn up toward his ears, and Athos watched them sadly. He'd done that—he'd made Porthos this tense, angry man.

Aramis quietly set about examining each cut, pulling small shards of glass out of a couple, disinfecting and bandaging as he went. "Who betrayed you?" he asked as he worked, quietly enough that only Athos could hear him.

Athos shook his head slightly. "Hard to explain right now." He panted and winced as Athos carefully slid a long shard out of a thigh wound. "That hurts."

Porthos thunked a bottle of Jack Daniels onto the table next to Athos. "You can take painkillers to sleep. Start here."

Athos looked up at him, the movement sluggish. Was the blood loss worse than he thought? Or maybe his body was just accepting that he was safe and so it was shutting down. "Thanks."

"Hmph. You'll have food, too. We were about to sit down to dinner." And Porthos stalked back toward the stove.

Aramis opened the bottle and handed it over, waiting while Athos took several long swallows before resuming his methodical work. His silence settled over them; Porthos was busy cooking whatever was for dinner, and Athos rested his head against the back of the chair and closed his eyes. He took the occasional sip from the bottle, only grimacing when Aramis had to stitch a particularly deep wound. If he thought about it too much, it hurt, so instead he focused on the sounds of Porthos working at the stove and the occasional sound of gauze hitting plastic or forceps hitting the table, punctuating his careful breathing.

The noises were so comfortable and familiar that his muscles started to loosen in spite of his pain, giving his thoughts a chance to start swirling. He was getting too damned old for this, both the fight he'd just been in and the tension with his partners. *Former partners?* Hell, he didn't know, and his head was swimming too much for him to try and suss that one out, especially when neither man seemed inclined to speak to him.

While blood had been dripping onto the floor when Athos first sat, it had slowed considerably while Aramis worked. By the time Aramis sat back with a sigh, dropping the last bandage wrapper and then his gloves onto the mound of medical supplies, even the unbandaged wounds had clotted.

"Eat," Aramis said, poking Athos to sit up. "And then you're lying down on the couch."

Athos didn't argue and worked his way silently through the chicken, broccoli, and roasted sweet potatoes Porthos had set in front of him. "Thank you," Athos mumbled part of the way through the broccoli. "Didn't have to—"

"Shut the *fuck* up," Porthos snarled, standing up from the table. "Just shut up. I'm going to get the couch ready so you don't bleed on it." He stalked out of the kitchen, leaving Aramis rubbing his forehead and Athos flushing and poking at his potatoes.

"Still got a temper?" Athos finally ventured.

"Still very, very hurt," Aramis said. "He never accepted that you left. He kept insisting you were on a mission, that you'd let us know eventually. About two years in, he stopped speaking about it, but I could see it. Showing up bleeding and clearly haggard from whatever you were doing has scared the shit out of him. He now knows he was right, and it kills him that you got hurt doing it and that you didn't tell us." He looked up at Athos. "As am I. Hurt, furious, and *confused.*"

Athos flinched at the burning anger in Aramis's eyes. "I'm sorry," he said hoarsely, looking away. "It was cruel. I'm so sorry." He wanted to explain, knew that he *needed* to, but his throat was too tight with pain and suppressed tears.

"Yes." Porthos's voice was brittle, aged, agonized. Athos looked toward him standing in the doorway, a naked look of pain and fury on his face. "You fucked up. Are you done eating?"

Athos blinked a couple of times. "…yeah." He accepted the help Aramis gave him to stand and limped carefully into the living room, where a surprisingly comfy bed had been made on the couch. For all Athos had picked up a lot of damage rolling through the jagged shards of glass, the damage was mostly confined to his arms—caused during the initial leap—and down his left side; the deepest wound was on his calf. That injury kept his pace slower than he liked; he was very relieved to lie down. He discovered that there were pillows in the perfect place to support that leg while he rested.

His eyes stung with the tears he was fighting, and he took settling in as the excuse to hide his face until he'd mastered the urge to cry. He didn't have the energy to deal with what crying would bring. "Could I—?"

"Water. Painkiller. Bucket in case the codeine in that makes you sick. Burner phone," Porthos said, interrupting and setting each of the items except the bottle of water on the table. The bottle, he handed to Athos. "Did you leave a trail?"

Athos took a drink with a sigh and let himself relax back into his makeshift bed. "I don't think so, but if they found me, it's just a matter of time before they find you." The one thing he'd tried his damnedest to avoid, and it had happened anyway. "I don't think I should stay here very long." The moment the words left his mouth, he knew they were the wrong thing to say. Porthos's face shut down, and he spun on his heel and stalked out of the room. "Fuck."

"Never could keep from shoving your foot into your mouth, could you?" Aramis asked with a sigh. "Here. Just one. You need to be able to move under your own power if we have to leave in a hurry." He handed Athos one of the Tylenol 3s from the bottle Porthos had set down. "Try and rest. I'm glad you're okay, but I have not forgiven you. We *will* have a discussion." He didn't wait for an answer, just followed after Porthos, leaving Athos to contemplate the tablet in his hand and wonder if he'd done the right thing by coming here. Or by taking the mission at all.

Athos woke with a start, abortively reaching for a knife that wasn't there before a searing pain reminded him of his injuries. "Fuck," he whispered hoarsely.

"Sorry," Porthos said, standing next to the couch. "I didn't mean to startle you. Time to go. Car's packed. Plants are watered. Let's try and stay ahead of whoever these fuckers are, yeah? Pretty sure it's whoever you were fighting." There was a bitter bite to that statement, and there was an underlying meaning to it that Athos didn't know how to parse.

He groaned quietly, trying to get himself upright. "Ow. Feel a bit like I collided with a giant window."

"Imagine that," Porthos quipped as he got himself under Athos's right arm to give him some support. "Bathroom first."

Athos grunted as they started moving. "Are they here?"

"Maybe," Porthos said, voice low. "There's a car circling about five blocks away, but it's slowly moving in. It appears to be doing a spiral search pattern."

Unsettled by that news and unwilling to slow them down, Athos said, "You don't have to support me all the way. I've got this." Maybe if he didn't have to lean on Porthos, the man would stop radiating fury. Not that he was positive he could actually do what he said. His knees felt like jelly.

"You don't. You lost more blood than you think you did. But I'm not holding your dick for you, so you can decide what you're going to do about that. Here's the bathroom. Lean on the counter. I promise it's rock-solid." He waited long enough for Athos to balance himself, then stepped back, his face blank.

Athos found that lack of emotion more disturbing and heartbreaking than the fury. Damn it, he'd really fucked up. He quietly closed the door, trying not to think about it; if he did, he wouldn't be able to stop himself from crying this time. Taking care of business took at least twice as long as it usually did, and absolutely involved sitting down. His leg just wouldn't support him when he tried to stand in one place.

He tried desperately to defog his mind, telling himself it was his imagination. Unsurprisingly, this did not help; blood loss and codeine were a hell of a combination. All he really succeeded in doing was distracting himself while he tried to keep excess movements to a minimum. He definitely hurt, and he was going to hurt worse before he felt better, but he had no doubt that Aramis's work was solid. He would heal, probably faster than he would have on his own.

In the meantime, it was apparently time to vacate the house. He hoped he hadn't completely compromised it for Porthos and Aramis, but he'd shifted to operating on instinct. He'd needed to get safe, needed to be protected, and the only place he could guarantee that he wouldn't immediately be handed over to the people he was trying to evade was with his partners. The fact that the only people to whom he could go were the two men he was trying to keep the safest in the world—the two men he had betrayed—wasn't lost on him.

"Do you need help?" Porthos asked, breaking through Athos's thoughts. "Seriously, are you okay?"

"Yeah, sorry. Still a little foggy." Damn it. Athos worked himself carefully to his feet, taking a moment to wash his hands because he knew damned well that, if he didn't, Porthos would comment and make him do it anyway. "Okay," he said, opening the door.

Porthos gave him a quick scan, obviously looking to make sure Athos wasn't lying. "Why did you leave?" he asked abruptly. "Why did you leave after everything, after—?" He cut himself off with a sharp, gasping breath and shook his head. "No. Don't answer that until we're in the car. Aramis deserves to hear, and you aren't going to want to say whatever it is twice."

Well, he's not wrong, Athos thought as Porthos steered them toward the garage. Athos absolutely did not want to have to answer that question twice, if for no other reason than because there was probably going to be a lot of yelling, and he'd rather not have to deal with the yelling more than once. He kept his mouth shut, putting his energy into moving as quickly as he could, sensing an urgency in Porthos's tension.

"Four blocks," Aramis said when they stepped through the garage door. "No, Athos, where the hell do you think you're going?" because Athos had reached for the driver's door when Porthos moved out of the way. The expression on his face as he quickly added, "You look like you got into a fight with Edward Scissorhands and lost! You're not driving!" told Athos that his wounds weren't Aramis's only reason for not wanting him to drive. It cut more deeply than any of the glass shards had, and he knew it was his own damn fault.

He refused to show it, though, so Athos just snorted and continued moving toward the passenger door. "I'm an idiot, not courting death. I'll move faster if I lean on the car." He got himself into the back seat carefully. Aramis took a seat in the front passenger seat, his ears red. "I wouldn't trust me, either. It's okay," Athos said quietly. Athos couldn't stand how much he'd hurt them, and while he knew they would at least intellectually understand his actions, he didn't know if he'd ever have *them* again. He'd shattered their hearts the same way he'd shattered that window.

"Buckle up, kiddos. I have a sneaking suspicion this will be a bumpy ride. Athos, the usual buffet is in the safe next to you, plus another two in the one next to your feet in the underside of the center console. See where that drink holder is? Flip it down, then twist the holder 90 degrees to the right and pull," instructed Porthos.

Athos carefully leaned forward and did so; pulling revealed a sleek compartment, lit by unseen sources to show two guns secured in racks with an ammunition case under them. "Convenient," he said, sliding it back in and returning the drink holder to its proper position. "Caught one-too-many times without a weapon in the backseat?" Nothing like that had ever been in any car they'd used before, so far as he knew. The thought that they'd been in trouble in a way that had made this necessary, and he hadn't been there to help, made the sick feeling worse.

"Without a *handgun*," Porthos corrected, hitting the button for the automatic garage-door opener and starting the car. The radio roared for a moment, and Porthos spun the knob to reduce it to a whisper. "Aramis, are we clear?"

"Three and closing. Now or never." Aramis tapped on the screen of the tablet he was holding and frowned. "Shit, there's another. Up and out, or we're going to have to get fancy."

Athos settled back into the seat and braced himself; he was about to have a hell of a ride. "Let me know if you want me to do anything."

"Standard orders," Porthos replied and zipped out of the garage into the alley. "Oh, and don't get blood on the upholstery or you'll be licking it clean."

"…kinky," Athos muttered, but he smirked anyway at the little flash of the Porthos he knew and loved. Maybe it was a sign of thawing? Porthos didn't answer him, though Athos thought he saw the hint of a smile on Aramis's face. He was almost immediately distracted as they emerged into the faint orange sodium-light glow of downtown Chicago. When they turned out of the alley onto a street, there wasn't a soul anywhere. "What time is it?"

"Flirting with three," Aramis said distractedly. "Late enough that the 2 a.m. bars are done emptying, and the fours are still going. It's about as quiet as this side of town gets in the summer." He tapped again and hissed softly at whatever he saw on the screen. "Fancy it is. Porthos? Michigan going south, and then it's all yours."

Porthos turned left and zipped down a couple of blocks, dropping them onto the Magnificent Mile. They were headed south toward the Loop, past the tastefully lit windows of the high-end stores that lined the streets, moving faster than the average driver but not so quickly as to draw suspicion.

"Answer the question," Porthos barked suddenly, glancing in the rearview mirror.

Aramis turned to stare at Porthos. "What question? No one said anything."

"Not you," Athos said quietly. "Me. He asked me why I left. And you are going to be furious at the answer, but I need you to let me explain completely before you shoot me. Give me that much." He met Porthos's icy glare in the rearview and waited for the jerky nod before he looked at Aramis, who gave his own short nod, mouth tight. With this assurance, he took a deep breath. "I left to save your lives. Not from some fucking asshole that decided that you would be an easy mark. I'd have told you about that, and we would have had fun destroying them together.

"Richelieu is the one threatening you. It started as a simple mission: I needed to go undercover long-term, no contact with the outside world. There couldn't be anything to blow my cover. I know we have a system to communicate that, and I had every intention of using it. I accepted the mission, prepped, and was headed to leave the message when Richelieu intercepted me. He told me that you two were being dispatched on another mission, one that he held the reins on, and if I wanted you to come back, I would go under without a word to anyone."

Before Athos could say anything else, Porthos took a sharp right and sped down another road for two blocks before taking a tight left. "Black car," he barked, and Aramis ducked enough to look in the side mirror before staring back at his screen with a curse.

"Fuck. That makes three in active pursuit. Gray up on the left in three…two…"

As they flashed past another street, a gray car skidded out onto the street behind them, its back-end fishtailing before the wheels caught traction and the car sped after them.

"Next left," Aramis grunted as they drifted through the turn. "There's another dark car coming in behind the black one. You do realize how fucking stupid it is to believe anything Richelieu says. Why the hell did you?" He shot Athos an annoyed look. "You know better."

Athos took a deep breath; he'd known convincing them of what came next would be the most difficult part. "You're right. Believing him is usually an exercise in futility, stupidity, or both. Except he showed me live footage—with proof that it was live—of the two of you walking through an Italian market…from the viewpoint of the sniper with a bead on you. It very clearly wasn't a bluff, and I couldn't take the chance with your lives. I assumed I would figure out a way to get a message to you to at least let you know I was on a mission."

"And never did," Porthos ground out as he drifted around another corner. "Shit. Clark. It's late enough, right?"

"Should be, but you're going to have to run stop signs. If you can hang on until Roosevelt, we can try and lose 'em on the museum campus." Aramis zoomed in on a portion of the map he had pulled up. "Could be fun."

"Can I launch any of them into the lake?" Porthos asked, making both Athos and Aramis snort with laughter. "What! It's a valid question."

"If you can manage it without flipping us, too, then you've got my permission," Aramis said. He glanced back at Athos, then looked down at his tablet again, tapping at a couple of different spots to pull up video feeds from security cameras, red-light cameras, and every other piece of technologyl in range that might help them evade capture. "Why do I have a feeling that you're going to tell us that you did try to get us messages?"

Athos sighed. "Because I'm not actually an asshole, and you know it. I did try, for a while, until I figured out that the nuclear armament ring in which I had been embedded had ties to three world governments *and* Richelieu, and he really did have your lives in his hands."

And then they were taking several sharp right-left-right-left nerve-wracking detours down small streets and alleys until they popped out onto Roosevelt and swung a hard left. Porthos was a phenomenal driver—hence why he was in the driver's seat—and he kept the damage they caused to a long, dark trail of twin tire steaks marking the swing of their turn. The last car chasing them, the "dark one" at the end of the line, didn't make the turn out of the last alley; it flipped, rolling across the road in a screeching crash of metal and sparks.

"Seven at best," Porthos declared, shooting through the Michigan intersection to crank it right onto Columbus and speed south again. He glanced in the rearview mirror with a curse. "Only two rolls on that crash. Plebeian."

"Absolutely pedestrian," Athos agreed, and took a deep breath. "I stopped trying to contact you when he sent me photos of you two sleeping in the Milan house. It was clearly a threat. He knew what I was doing, so I put all of my energy into destroying him instead, hoping that I could at least apologize to you one day if I didn't die in the process of taking him out."

For a few heartbeats, the only sound in the car was the quietly playing radio. With a jolt, Athos realized that the song was a metal cover of the Bhangra hit "Tunak Tunak Tun" by Daler Mehndi. "No radio station is playing that music," he said in surprise. "You have something connected to Bluetooth?" For anyone but Aramis, Athos would question the wisdom of having something easily hackable in the car. But it was *Aramis*, one of the best hackers in the world.

Sage Mooreland

Without looking up from his tablet, Aramis reached over and tapped a button. The screen flipped to show input options; currently selected was "CarPod." He tapped the button again to flip it back to the title and said, "You'll have to jump a median, but if you take them through the Northerly Island shit, we should be able to lose one more."

"Only if I get to send one off the side," Porthos reminded them. He didn't argue, though, and spun the wheel with a gleeful snicker when both of the pursuers fishtailed instead of duplicating the smooth drift he'd managed.

A gunshot rattled through the night.

"Fuck. Oh, you did *not* just do that." Porthos gunned the engine and rocketed down the access road toward a massive parking lot.

Athos grabbed the headrest of the seat next to him, pressed the button at the base, and pulled forward, lowering the entire remaining section of the backseat. A gun rack slid forward, and he grabbed with one hand while rolling down the window with the other. "Tell me when you're turning," he said, unbuckling himself to get far enough outside to balance on the edge of the car door and sight through the scope. It wasn't until he was focused on the driver of the gray car immediately behind them that he realized that the gun in his hands was his preferred rifle, and his heart seized. Damn it. They hadn't given up on him, no matter how furious they were. Maybe he had a hope after all.

He made quick work of the driver with one shot, and destroyed the front right tire with another, sending the car in a sharp skid sideways. It hit the curb and launched into one of the sailboats in the harbor.

"Down," he reported, pulling himself back inside with a quiet gasp. Hanging out the window and twisting like that had been an incredibly stupid choice; he managed to get buckled back in before closing his eyes for a moment and taking a sharp breath.

Porthos closed the window for him. "That doesn't count for the lake. It landed on a boat. We've got one more chance."

Athos smiled faintly, but the knot that had lodged itself in his heart three years ago when he'd stopped trying to reach his partners loosened. *We.* He'd been forgiven. Well. His explanation had been accepted as a good enough reason for ghosting them; forgiveness was going to take a while. He looked over at Aramis, wondering if he'd get the same understanding from him.

"Up and out," was all Aramis said, though, still navigating in his ever-steady voice. "Take the loop in front of the planetarium at the right speed, and you should be able to send him off the side."

"Shallow water, but enough," Porthos declared, and he hit the accelerator. He slid smoothly from the street onto the bike path, the car barely registering the small patch of grass between the two. Athos watched through the windshield while Porthos took advantage of a tree to pull left across a larger expanse of grass and up and over to the street again. When the car behind them kept up, Porthos growled, "Hold on."

The other two men grabbed for handholds as Porthos again proved why he was behind the wheel. Aramis had directed them to the loop in front of the Adler Planet-arium; it was beautiful but tight enough that, if Porthos didn't time things correctly, *they* would be the ones flipping into the lake. The last notes of "Tunak Tunak" faded out as they took the turn that would put them on the right trajectory, and immediately Gwen Stefani started singing about a lonely goatherd.

They whipped around the second corner of the square loop and shot down Solidarity Drive. The black car still following them tried to do the same but missed. The driver almost recovered, but the car hit the sidewalk and he couldn't correct. Athos managed to turn in time to see the car skid onto the goose-poop covered grass, unable to gain traction.

"Does he have enough velocity to make it worthwhile?" he muttered.

The car rolled down the sloping concrete steps and splashed into the lake with a glorious wave of dark water.

Aramis, who'd also turned to look, agreed. "Mmmmm, maybe shallower than you wanted, Porthos, but the theatrics make up for it." As they took the exit for Lake Shore Drive at a far more legal speed, he looked at Athos. "If you ever leave like that again, I will shoot you myself. I love you, you miserable asshole, and you broke my heart when you disappeared. I thought you were dead, and I couldn't find a trace of you *anywhere*."

It was the pain in Aramis's eyes at that inability that nearly broke Athos when nothing else had. The fury and rage had been one thing. This naked agony that, for all of Aramis's considerable skills—and the skill of those he bribed or threatened into assisting him—he hadn't been able to locate Athos was a burning poker to the gut. "I have all the evidence ready to launch. I was getting the last of it when Richelieu's men jumped me and I had to run. It will destroy several terrible people and topple three extremist dictatorships so thoroughly that more democratic rebellions should be able to take over. Help me?"

"Do I get to shoot Richelieu at some point?" Porthos asked. They flew down LSD, heading out of the city.

"…probably not," Athos said. "Unless he escapes custody." He kept his voice carefully neutral, but Porthos and Aramis hadn't been his friends, partners, and brothers-in-arms for as long as they had been to be fooled.

Gwen kept urging them to wind it up, wind it up, and somehow, that seemed like the only way his statement could be answered.

Aramis looked back down at his tablet. "What a shame. The likelihood of him escaping custody is so low. It would take quite an operation."

Porthos smirked and turned up the radio when Gwen Stefani shifted to Måneskin singing about wanting to be someone's slave. "One for all?" he said. It wasn't his normal call to arms; instead, it sounded like a peace offering, a promise to work together in taking care of the eternal thorn in their collective side, the man who'd even sabotaged their relationship.

Athos let out a breath that he hadn't realized he held. "All for one."

C   *"untitled"*

C opted not to share the inspiration behind this artwork.

After the Fire

— MouMouSanRen

Tags
warnings: dubious consent, micro-aggressions (racist), violence (non-graphic descriptions)
relationships: f/f, friends, m/m (mentions of), pre-relationship
character features: bipoc, buddhist, cultivation, magic use
other tags: duels, lunarpunk, new york city, non-fanfiction story inspired by source material, past tense, post-apocalypse, religion, science fiction with cultivation, science fiction with magic, steampunk, third person limited point of view

Inspiration
MouMouSanRen opted not to share the inspiration behind this story.

When Luna finally crossed over the black hills surrounding New York City and reached the guards outside, they checked her, then confiscated her gun. It'd been a comforting weight on the journey from Montana, but the guards said firmly that special licensure and training were required to possess firearms.

"You won't need one here anyway," they told her. "When you're ready to leave, you can return to this checkpoint to retrieve it."

She smiled brightly, chin held high. "Thank you for welcoming me to the city."

They gave her a funny look as she went by them. She must have looked tired, and certainly poor, in her beaten-up leather jacket and worn leather boots, but she strutted like a peacock. The city's infamous pride was hereditary. Like so many others, she was part of the New York diaspora, returning to the place of her parents' birth now that the danger of the Eruption had gone.

She belonged here.

And she had to find the Three Jewels.

She approached the nearest bodega with swagger and a grin. "Yo! Where's the nearest bubble-tea place?" She'd journeyed a long way and, as her mother would say, she deserved a treat before meeting the chief of the Arrowheads, the personal guards of the city's Matriarch.

After the emergence of a volcano on Manhattan island, rich and poor alike had fled. Those left behind had lingered long enough to see white steam furling from the ground. It was the Matriarch who'd harnessed this geothermal energy and rebuilt the five boroughs. She was one of many who, as they'd awaited rescue from the government, had to stay warm. By the time the equipment to evacuate New Yorkers en masse had arrived, she'd built a wigwam by a steam vent. And, when this quick method caught fire across the boroughs, she'd begun to roast plants from the marshes at the far ends of the city. When the National Guard appeared to choke this newborn civilization in its cradle, she'd laughed as if greeting an old friend, and with a magical talisman of mere paper, had sent a wall of steam to boil them alive.

New York became a city of glass, black-sand beaches, and plentiful seafood. The glittering land often wafted with a clear, healthy fog. It was this steam that billowed as the owner of the boba shop fired up the infuser. He poured pomegranates and lychees and blended them into black tea, then added cattail jelly. Luna's parents had drunk bubble tea made from powders and sugar. "Real fruit was a luxury," her mother had said, but Luna paid only 80 cents for this delicacy. She closed her eyes and sipped, floating away in the warm steam.

It carried her to the Obsidian Path, the crack that paved the way to the Longhouse where the Matriarch's Arrowheads resided.

A man trod on her heels.

She whipped around, and her precious cattail jelly splashed onto his black T-shirt.

"The fuck?" he asked. "You walk like a fucking snail, *and* you spill your drink on me?" His eyes were bloodshot, as if he hadn't slept in days.

Don't start a fight on day one, Mom had warned, so Luna, with great self-control, shrugged instead of punching him in the face. "Chill. You could've stepped around."

"You stopped in the middle of the road. Who does that?"

Luna snapped. "For real? You're going to cry over a shirt you already wiped the floor with?"

The man took a step forward—and ran into her fist.

His eyes widened as he cradled his jaw. "I'll give you that," he said, eyes aflame. "You can throw down. We're dueling. Noon. Brooklyn Bridge."

Luna continued, face set and composed, insides screaming. *Oh no. This is bad. Oh no, no, no—*

She was so high-strung that when a shadow moved at the edge of her vision, she remembered the wild dogs that had lunged at her family's sheep. Without looking, she kicked, whipping around to see she'd gotten a small woman square in the stomach.

The woman was so cute, like a little bird. She punched Luna back, sending her flying, then followed up with a kick that Luna caught the way her mother had taught her, returning with two blows to the side before the little bird broke free, catching Luna with a vicious swipe to the chin.

"Not right now," the bird of a woman growled as they broke apart. "I'm busy. If you want a duel, meet me at the Brooklyn Bridge at noon."

"Oh nah," Luna said. "I have another one at that time. How about one?"

"Done." They shook hands. "I'll see you there. Bring handwraps."

She kept walking.

Mom was right; people were *mad* aggro here. Luna felt for bruises; the skin was red, but there was nothing permanent. It was one thing to have faced her mother's wrath during training—"the world is hard. This will help you endure it"—and another to walk into her ancestral home and see where it'd come from.

As she searched for another bodega that carried bubble tea, she passed a group of friends, each adorned with brilliant purple wampum earrings, chattering outside an overgrown thicket—the closest thing to a traditional park here. As they spoke, something fluttered to the ground: a small bracelet knotted from string.

Be good, Luna thought, and she picked it up, offering it to the obvious owner, who was braiding another piece of string as she talked. "You dropped this."

The woman, tall and solid like a cedar, turned a furious red. Her friends practically cried with laughter. "A *love knot*? Does the un-wooable Zen Lee have a boo? Tell us who tamed the wild Zen."

A pit opened in Luna's gut as Zen loomed over her.

"That's *private*," Zen hissed.

Luna bit her tongue on an "I'm sorry." Her mother had said people didn't apologize here. "That sucks."

Zen narrowed her eyes as her friends goaded her on.

"You're gonna take that from her?"

"We're dueling. Brooklyn Bridge. Two in the afternoon. Be there." Zen stormed off, her friends clapping her on the back.

Luna couldn't hold back anymore; she groaned, sinking to her knees in the middle of the road. "Being nice to people *sucks*," she said, head in her hands.

Luna reached the Brooklyn Bridge sometime later. Her parents had often come here—"for the views"—but had lived on the other side of the city. They'd liked to wander on off-days to watch rich people and tourists, as if they were visiting some kind of zoo.

The tourists still came, not to marvel at the bridge's brown, vintage shape, but at the crust of volcanic glass glazed over it, glittering like diamonds.

She waited at the center of the bridge, under the clock the Matriarch had commissioned, and took in the Manhattan Bridge across the water, also encrusted in black. Three figures approached on hoverboards as she finished her tea. The trail of steam their boards left mixed with the incoming mist, and for a moment, they were silhouettes. As they neared, Luna recognized the man at the head.

"The contract." He brandished a sheaf of papers. Duel contracts ensured neither side could be held accountable for the other's injuries or accidental death.

He looked like he was falling asleep on his feet. Was he well enough to fight?

But as her hand touched the paper, her gaze shifted to the two behind him: the bird and the cedar women.

"Well," said Zen.

"Don't kill her, Noah," said the bird woman, "I have a duel with her right after you."

"What?" said Zen. "Qori, *I* have a duel with her later this afternoon."

Noah dropped the papers in disbelief. "Why didn't you *say* anything?"

"How was I supposed to know you were going around picking fights?" said Qori.

"Yeah, what happened to our sweet, unflappable Noah?" asked Zen.

The two of them exchanged a look. "He needs sleep," they agreed.

A small dart zipped toward them.

Training kicked in. Luna shoved Noah clear as Qori fluttered upward and batted the missile aside. Zen jumped forward, a tomahawk in hand.

An armed group approached, one among them raising a sheaf of papers. "Noah Lee, Qori Gualinga, and Zen Lee," their leader said. "We're under orders from the Matriarch to summon you to the Longhouse. Surrender your weapons and come with us."

Zen took a step forward, but Noah halted her. "Tomahawk down," he muttered, suddenly wide awake.

Qori, sharp and bright, went with both hands raised. "Normally I would," she said, "but the Matriarch's been absent for several days. Who are you?"

"Are you going to disobey the Matriarch's direct command?" The leader was outraged. "We'll have to take you by force."

He threw a rounded object. Noah released Zen and slapped it back. It exploded into a large net that tangled the gang on impact with the ground. The leader groused, there was a flash of light, and the net magically disappeared.

That two-second delay was enough: Zen tossed a set of butterfly knives that Luna caught. "Death by a thousand cuts," she ordered.

The four of them made short work of the group, reducing them to a squirming pile of people. Pedestrians gawked respectfully from the other side of the bridge.

Luna's Chinese mother had told her língchí once meant "to kill someone slowly by chipping away at their flesh," but among the world-famous Arrowheads, it was code to make their strikes feather-light. Immobilize, but don't kill. Their Arrowhead method was such common knowledge, it'd reached Montana through Luna's Blackfeet neighbors, who'd often made cultural exchange visits to New York.

Noah examined the net and the remains of the orb. "This was made clockwork-style"—he turned its smooth outer shell to see the mechanics within—"but their leader broke out of the net with magic." He jerked his chin in Qori's direction. With a grin, she hauled the leader to his feet.

"You must have worked hard to have your magic rupture objects in a pinch," Noah said. "That's some good shit. Why would you run around attacking random people?"

He tilted his head to avoid the bloody spittle the leader spat in response.

"Noah!" Zen jerked back the captive's sleeve and pressed her fingers to his wrist. Slowly, indents appeared, forming binary code. Luna could barely keep up with the numbers that scrolled across his skin, as if crawling under it.

"They're yufu," Noah said.

Zen raised her finger. One by one, the prisoners stood, moving against their own volition. Their eyes seethed, but their bodies were as frozen as corpses. They hopped into neat lines, following Zen as she went, standing so straight they were like a forest to Zen's cedar tree.

Noah whistled. "You have to *really* understand the Matriarch's teachings to use this much magic without writing a talisman. You're not even breaking a sweat."

Zen waved a hand in acknowledgement. "Thanks. But she didn't really teach me. I just kind of understood after a while."

"We can't all grow up in the Six Nations."

Zen rolled her eyes, smiling fondly as she commanded her zombie army. "Noah?"

"Yes."

"They say the Matriarch keeps the eastern door and you keep the western door. So be a dear, cover my left, and shut up."

"Yes ma'am."

"Well?" Qori asked, looking at Luna expectantly.

Luna pointed at herself. *Me?*

"Come on," said Noah. "We'll get these guys in jail, report to the Matriarch, and then drinks are on me. Sorry for being bitchy today."

The bodies marched up the Obsidian Path as Noah filled Luna in. Yufu were loyalists to Old New York who fantasized about restoring the city to when it was the capital of commerce.

"That's how my moms grew up," Luna said. "They're from Queens—Canarsie and Matinecock land. Their families were working class. Life was really stressful because their parents were so underpaid and mistreated, but they were proud of their community. They miss it."

"No era is perfect," Noah said. "Not even now. But yufu reject our new way of life."

"As opposed to…?"

"They're a cult. When the Eruption happened, they were the first to leave. When the diaspora came back…" Noah shrugged. "Everyone has a different reaction to seeing their home change so radically. Many took it in stride and helped rebuild because they agreed with the Matriarch. But the yufu pushed for a privatized system. They hadn't all been rich folks before the Eruption, either. A lot were working-class people who'd just really liked owning property. I'd call them selfish, but if I'd worked my whole life for something and was told it was pointless, I'd be pretty mad too."

"Noah?" Qori asked. "Do you think they're trying to *steal* the Three Jewels?"

Noah snorted. "They can't be stolen, only earned."

Luna's blood pulsed. The Three Jewels were her most important reason for coming. Her mothers had often talked about how they'd owned the Three Jewels, but they were now *allegedly* held by the Arrowheads.

The Longhouse came into view. Many homes in New York City were Longhouses and wigwams now, the building of which was taught to the residents by the descendants of its original Algonquin inhabitants who lived in the outer boroughs—Canarsie, Matinecock, and Unkechaug land. Most were made from wood, as was traditional, but some residents had started to experiment by building wigwam-shaped homes with brick and bamboo.

The Longhouse that housed the Arrowheads and the Matriarch was encrusted with salt and obsidian decorations, and had been built around the burned and buried remains of the Empire State Building and Times Square. Words flickered in various languages—English, Kanien'kehá, Shinnecock, Quechua—as they traveled along walls covered with strawberry plants. Luna read the Chinese version: "Skywoman's daughter left her body as a gift to the world, and from her heart grew strawberries—"

Luna wanted to see if the social media rumors were true. She pressed her ear against the Longhouse wall. Immediately, the Longhouse *spoke* to her. It repeated the story in the voice of a woman. As strawberries grew from the heart of Skywoman's daughter, Luna heard the intimate whisper of soft spring, leaves unfurling—

A tap on Luna's shoulder. "I appreciate you trying to understand the local culture," Qori said, softly, "but you can do that after the interrogation."

Each mile, the roof opened to the sky, airing out a cordoned-off geothermal steam vent beneath. In many places, the Longhouse had been built over the remains of old buildings which, the drifting words explained, had been constructed by the Kanien'kehá:ka iron workers of Old New York.

Old New York's government had kept its City Hall under lock and key. The Matriarch's Longhouse ran the length of the island and was a public space where people went for morning strolls, played games, cooked, and even slept on benches along the walls.

They neared the New York Public Library, whose barrel-vaulted ceilings were largely intact despite large gaps blown open by the Eruption. Underneath the most central gap—in the heart of Manahatta—sat a circle of Arrowheads dressed similarly to Luna's escorts. Noah waved one over. "Yo, Selah. Where's the Matriarch?"

"Omma?" The tall, light Arrowhead, who looked suspiciously like Noah, peered around him. "You're finally gonna tell her about your man?"

Noah's brown cheeks darkened. "Not *yet*. This is about *business*. We need an *interrogation*."

"Call her, then. Use your brain."

Noah rolled his eyes. "Using a written spell is easier."

He raised a talisman of yellow paper painted with red script. It sparked like a road flare, bouncing around the vaulted ceiling as if it was searching for the right corner. A signal.

Although the law of the Arrowheads was built off the Great Law of Peace, their combat and magic system had been built off Chinese talismans. Luna's Chinese American mother would purchase them from shamans and fortune tellers, each imbued with the energy of its maker. She'd plastered them to the walls of their house to ward off ill fortune, and used their spells to send signals when they went hiking. "When writing was invented," she'd said, "the demons in the underworld shook in terror at how powerful it was."

Luna waited with bated breath for the legendary Matriarch's arrival.

A responding flare lit up the sky through a skylight. Noah tilted his head. "She can't return," he said. "Qori, it's your time to shine."

Qori pulled a small section of rope from her pocket.

Selah shifted to make room. With a flick of her chin, Zen forced the yufu to the middle of the Arrowhead circle, where they stood stiffly. Passersby began to dawdle. Watching.

In a too-smooth, unified motion, the yufu kneeled and pulled back their sleeves. Noah dissolved a talisman over them. It melted in the air like it would have in water, and the embedded codes re-emerged on the yufu's skin. After a moment, they rearranged themselves, the binary code translating itself into poetry. Tenets.

> *Restore opportunity,*
> *Restore property.*
> *Restore the City of Dreams*
> *Or die trying.*

Qori didn't seem surprised. "Zen," she said, "separate interrogations for each of them."

Zen nodded. Luna expected the prisoners to divide into different rooms, but instead, they clapped their hands to their ears and closed their eyes. All except the leader.

Qori dropped to his level. "Why are you here?"

The leader gave her nothing, no matter how she questioned him.

Zen forced him to cover his ears and close his eyes.

The next person's hands and eyes sprang open. The psalms on his arms spasmed as Qori questioned him.

His attitude was similar.

The next yufu was questioned. The next. And the next. All balked at the questions. One lied.

The yufu were well-kept, with skin clear as glass and hair gelled as though they were ready for a Wall Street meeting. But those unsettlingly symmetrical faces wore the same scowl—all but one. The last person smiled at Qori. Luna stepped as close as she could to Qori without breaching the circle, suddenly alert. Someone who smiled in a situation like this was the most unpredictable.

"Why did you and I come to blows?" Qori asked.

The Smiler said, "It was an honest mistake. I'm a former city official, and I acted under the authority of the Matriarch to bring you back to her." As the yufu spoke, Qori created a line of knots in the thread in her hand, so practiced that she didn't even look at the patterns she made.

"Our Matriarch sent no such order," Qori said. "You aren't part of the council or the Arrowheads."

"My mistake. I had to act because I saw one of your fellow Arrowheads conducting himself improperly."

"What do you mean?"

"That tall one—Noah Lee—intimidated this young lady. When she defended herself, he challenged her to a duel to the death. Arrowheads should uphold the law of peace that you yourselves established," the Smiler said with concern, turning her head just so, eyes landing not far from Luna. It was now that Luna noticed a runic circle painted onto the floor around the yufu. Noah's hand was on the rune, maintaining an invisible boundary that must have been blocking out noise and vision. That explained the previous prisoners' lack of reaction to the crowds.

The look of concentration on Noah's face turned into dawning horror as he realized what he'd done.

It must have been excruciating for him to sit through. Luna felt a small prick of satisfaction that he was receiving some comeuppance for his earlier outburst, but the Smiler had clearly found an opening to justify her treason.

Qori didn't even look Noah's way. "If what you say is true," she said, "then he will be punished. But we should have been alerted. Otherwise, I would have continued unaware of this and been unable to adjust my knowledge of how my Arrowheads treat people."

The Smiler's face rippled, but before she could say more, Zen had forced her eyes and ears closed.

Qori said, "Zen, keep the prisoners in the Old Jail until we've consulted the Matriarch. This isn't the first time we've had yufu stir rhetoric in the area, but this is the first time they've breached public trust." She pulled another rope from her pocket, the knots on it arranged in a similar pattern to the one she had just used to document this interrogation.

In the shuffling that followed, Luna slipped into the crowd and tailed Zen. She thought she saw Noah turn to look for her, but it was too late; she had turned the corner. Luna forced her heart rate to steady as she followed Zen and her horde of zombies halfway through the city, blending in with the crowds as they took the subway.

The New York subway in her mothers' photos was old and beaten, infamous for rats, homelessness, and the lingering smell of piss. It was the oldest public transportation system in the world, lead-ridden and falling apart at the seams. Though the people had depended on it and had rallied for repairs, the government's answer had always been to distract from the problems by building new stations. The Eruption had burned all that. Now, buried underground, there were sleek trains running through tunnels veined with magma, launched by steam-powered pistons. It smelled clean, like earthy salt and seawater. Luna pressed a finger to the fireproof window glass. In the light of the magma, her finger was alight with fire.

They returned to City Hall. To avoid the guards, Luna slipped into the formation of frozen yufu, imitating their unnatural walk. She dared not break her bearing as they entered the building, the eyes of the guards drilling into her from all sides.

It was only once they were in the windowless offices that now acted as cells—she'd timed the seconds Zen's back was turning—that she ducked behind a jut of volcanic rock.

Once the coast was clear, she reemerged. Only the Smiler seemed unsurprised. "I could see you in my peripherals," she said. "What's so interesting about us that you followed us halfway across the city?"

"The Three Jewels. Where are they?"

The Smiler's eyes widened. "That's what we would like to know. It's ridiculous that a small number of police and officials are hoarding something beneficial to society. Look at the state of New York now. That money could go into building more skyscrapers, not a Longhouse where anyone can wander in."

"They said the Jewels should be earned, not stolen."

"They only say that because they stole them and made it illegal to reclaim them. What connection do you have to them?"

"They belonged to my parents before they fled the Eruption. I came to ask for them," Luna said.

The Smiler's kindly face rippled as she snorted. "They wouldn't give them up like that. They've built a system to hoard them. You think that Zen Lee would teach you how to lock bodies with a flick of her hand? Our Iroquois and Algonquin overlords won't even share their combat systems with their Arrowheads, their elite guard. Instead, they've appropriated Chinese talismans. You have to sneak past security to get them. Which you've done, quite admirably."

Flattery. Another tactic. But why did Luna find herself leaning closer to the Smiler and her calculated magnetism? Luna laid one hand across the Smiler's and was surprised when it was as warm as a human's should be. "You're around my age," she observed, "and you've dedicated yourself to fighting the new order. That's a huge sacrifice."

The Smiler straightened, clasping their hands. "We don't have to live like this, not the way that muttering Matriarch wants us to with froo-froo New Age laws like she's the Buddha incarnate. Once we get those jewels, we can sell them to the highest bidder, show them the value that scarcity creates. When we sell them, your parents can live in luxury, in *skyscrapers*."

"Yes." Luna's chest was aflame; she knew it was dawning in her eyes. "And you'll need someone who the Arrowheads already trust. Let me help you."

The Smiler closed in. Luna could smell her. She pulled away at the last second. "Get us out first."

But Luna was faster. She went for the kiss, probing with her tongue through the smiler's open shock. Even a seductress who let only lies pass through her teeth had weak points. Luna found the talisman lodged behind her molars—a folded piece of paper, so tightly furled it was the size of a grain of rice: the source for the binary code imprinted on their skin.

"You—" The Smiler's eyes were ice.

If Luna ever made it out of the cell, she would have to fight for her life.

"If my culture was misrepresented by colonizers for hundreds of years," Luna said, "I wouldn't want people to know about my fighting techniques either. I'm *glad* the Arrowheads formed their combat system off Chinese techniques. Writing it down is easier for people like me to understand. Sharing is caring."

The Smiler lunged at the bars. The clang could be heard from outside the building. "You don't build a civilization off of *sharing*!"

"The Three Jewels aren't objects," Luna said with true compassion and no small amount of pettiness. "They're *concepts*. They're the Buddha, dharma, and sangha. Their value is for everyone who wants to live by them."

"They're *real*!" the Smiler shrieked. "They wouldn't talk about them like they're here to save us if they weren't valuable commodities!"

Luna was already backing away, smudging away the lipstick left on her lips with a finger. "My parents worked hard to survive in Old New York. They taught me to be strong. But they didn't stay because of the skyscrapers or the Brooklyn Bridge. You're glorifying the part of Old New York that was pretty but valueless. If there's anything my parents have taught me, it's that even at that time, their favorite thing about the city was splitting a meal with their friends. They raised me to value my home and people. I'm sorry you can't see that. You're really hot, though. Call me." She waved the reddened finger at her, then got the hell out of the building.

Zen was furious when she found out what Luna had done—at herself, it seemed, for letting it happen.

"I've been trained to sneak my whole life," Luna explained. "My moms were paranoid about what I'd find when I came back to New York, so they drilled every skill they could into me."

Zen frowned as Qori pored over the talisman, cross-referencing its written script with her knotted ropes. "We've been trying to find out *who* organized the yufu for months," she said. "We finally have a lead."

"One step closer to finding the cult leaders," Noah said. "We have to get this to the sachems. Qori, come with me." On their way out, he gave Luna a second glance, features softening. "This is incredible work, and you're already stronger than me. That smiling yufu is my ex."

Luna's head was spinning at the absolute mess this man was, and yet the first thing out of her mouth once they were out of earshot was, "Is Noah going to be okay? Getting trounced by his ex in front of everyone like that? How is he going to *grow* out of this?"

"He held a discussion in a public space," Zen said. "All of Manahatta knows what he's done and what he needs to grow out of. They will treat him accordingly. The biggest growth comes from how society nurtures or reviles you."

"That's a brutal punishment," Luna said.

"We don't do redemption and punishment here." Zen swiftly corrected her. "It's about growth. Arrowheads always need sharpening, or else how do we move forward? How do we manage to cut?"

"One more thing," Luna said. Zen nodded. "The Three Jewels… Does everyone know that they're…not tangible?"

Zen sighed. "They're ideas you commit to learning, not physical treasures. The Matriarch is spiritual, as are the Arrowheads. It keeps our heads on straight and helps us remember our service to society isn't just to fight. But it's also a philosophy all New Yorkers are encouraged to study, especially since there are ideas from the old society that we still use. We emphasize the intrinsic value of the Three Jewels, but that kind of value confuses the yufu. They have a conspiracy theory that they're actual gemstones. They don't understand how something as common as a thought earned with mental fortitude could be so valuable."

"That's what makes them a cult," Luna guessed. "They reach for something bigger than themselves but don't understand that they already have it. Damn, Noah's life must be super messy to be tangled with the smiley one."

"A little bit," Zen said. "But his boyfriend's been really good for him. Anyway, to err is human. *I'm* surprised that she didn't seduce you. She's slippery."

"She did," Luna said cheerfully, "but I can kiss and go, that's fine."

Besides it was Qori she liked. And Qori's moral compass.

The sun had traced a full half-circle across the sky before Noah and Qori rejoined them on one of the Longhouse benches. "Another meeting tomorrow," Zen said, pleased. "But let's not think about it now. It's been a long day." She sprawled between her Arrowheads and began to text.

Noah joined Zen and closed his eyes. But Qori turned to Luna, pulling strands of dried sweetgrass from her bag. "Luna, come braid this with me. It's been done all over the northern parts of Turtle Island since forever. It's a way to bond with each other and show our respect to the Earth that feeds and homes us. You're part of the New York diaspora, right? Think of it as a way of reconnecting with the land."

Luna's hands matched Qori's as she lightly touched the sweetgrass, accepting it in a way that was almost reverent. "Teach me," she said.

Jupiter V   *"One for All"*

Next page
As much as we all love the original and iconic Three Musketeers, they can be a little hard to tell apart by modern standards, no? There's the serious guy with a moustache, the jovial guy with a moustache, and the other guy…with a moustache.

My Musketeers—Aram, Atha and Porvos—sport fewer moustaches, but aren't shy about showing off their style and personality. Exemplifying the motto of the Musketeers, their unrestrained individuality is what creates their unbreakable bond.

Love and Graffiti

– Shea Sullivan

Tags

warnings: gender dysphoria (mentions of) **relationships:** established relationship, f/nb, friends, m/nb, polyamory **character features:** artist, bipoc, character has a different gender than in the source material, does drag, gay, lesbian, non-binary, self-esteem issues **other tags:** alternate universe, attraction at first sight, be gay do crimes, first person point of view, flirting, jealousy, modern, present tense, smoking (casual)

Inspiration

It turns out, the original musketeers are not thinkers. They're more of a chaotic, self-centered group of "stab first, ask questions later" guys. So I thought…what if they got older and wiser? And what if d'Artagnan came along and they had to try to calm that chaotic energy? And what if it was modern day, and featured the Guerilla Girls? Well, the Guerilla Girls tie-in never quite made it, but here you are. An older, wiser, more diverse group, and a young, volatile graffiti artist to shake them up.

Nothing guarantees a database emergency like having plans. There's an anxious ball of static in my chest as I pull into a parking space two blocks from the apartment. Should I have skipped changing and gone straight to the bar? I'm already an hour late, and I'm not sure what's worse: Alix being pissed, or them not even noticing.

There's a plate on the coffee table with a rind of the fancy cheese I hate and two glasses with sticky residue. My uncertainty sours to irritation. Apparently, Alix and Polly had time for a snack before heading to Polly's show and left their dishes for me.

Alix *knows* I hate that.

I growl and then take a deep breath. We've been together eight years. Alix has never cared about clutter, but they usually pick up because they know it drives me crazy. And "usually" is enough. It's always been enough. Christ, if Alix ever stops giving me passes for all my flaws, I'm screwed. I can give them this. Even if it *was* because they were having fun while I was stuck at work.

I sigh and drop the dishes in the sink.

Alix *deserves* someone they can have fun with, and talk design with, and go to the bar on-time with. And what they've had is me: late at work with databases-gone-wrong. I'm perpetually exhausted.

So, yeah. Alix is allowed to enjoy Polly's company in any way they want, even if Polly is slow to accept Alix's affection.

I feel even better when I've escaped the straitjacket of my slacks and blazer in favor of an Anti-Flag T-shirt and leggings with "speed holes." I'm smiling when I head back out the door.

Drake's is a gay bar on Madison, in a worn-down building featuring a neon sign that adds fruit to a fluorescent cocktail glass with every blink. Glass *blink* straw *blink* pineapple *blink* strawberry *blink*…and so on, until it extends about a foot past the cornice. The remaining façade is non-descript, but that sign says it all.

There's a cluster of drag queens on the sidewalk, smoking and chatting. I hear Tabby's trademark trill: "Ar*iiii*!"

I grin and wave. Long before we came here for Polly, Alix and I came here because it's the best place to cut loose at the end of a long week. "Hey, Tabby! You look amazing, as always. Have you seen Polly?"

She strikes a pose, acknowledging her awesomeness. "She's primping, of course, that fabulous bitch. I think she's in the green room. She's brought *friends* today, hmm?" She raises an eyebrow as if there's some hot gossip there. My stomach knots.

I laugh half-heartedly. "That's our Polly! Good luck tonight!"

"I never need luck, darling, but thank you anyway." She blows a kiss, and I steel myself as I step inside.

I find Alix and Polly in the closet-sized dressing room with a slight, pale thing with a buzzcut and a messenger bag, looking like they're fresh out of a mosh pit. Four other queens are packed in, primping for the show.

Alix sees me first and smiles, teeth bright against their dark skin. They motion me over. Polly's decked in the vintage dress, pink with silver sequins, that Alix bought as part of a lot for the shop. Rhinestone tights and a huge red wig a la Bette Midler round out the ensemble. She's leaning in to talk to the latest addition who, on closer look, is wearing Alix's black button-up.

I shuffle through the chaos to Alix's side, eyeing the burgundy T-shirt they never wear solo. I bite my tongue.

Alix tips their head, brows drawing together in concern. "All right?" they ask.

"Long day." It's not a lie. "And I missed all the fun, apparently." The joke falls flat.

They fix me with a perceptive look and squeeze me into their side. "You're here now." A sly smile. "My...diminutive tomato."

I huff a laugh, and there's a prickling behind my eyes. I've been so irritated, so worried, and they're nothing but glad to see me.

"Aria," Polly pounces on me. "Girl, it's Friday! I thought they'd never let you go! You missed all the excitement. We found ourselves a stray; this little lady decided it was a good time to taunt the lawmen in broad daylight." She grabs the bemused "stray" by the shoulder. "Lucky we were there to save your bacon, my dear."

The girl scoffs but extends a hand to me. "Hi, Aria. I'm Darcy. And I was *beautifying*." She shoots a mock-glare at Polly. "It wasn't that dramatic; I would have been fine."

"We dressed you. I put your paint cans in my girdle, honey!"

"Oh, right!" Darcy pulls off Alix's shirt. She turns to Polly and folds her hands in thanks. "I appreciate the use of your girdle...space. I was *not* looking forward to replacing those again."

Polly clucks, "I feel like confiscation was the least of your worries."

Darcy shrugs. "Usually, I run and hope for the best."

As the background music changes, Polly interrupts, "My loves, I must insist you go; the show is beginning, and I must prepare myself."

"You look gorgeous," Alix tells her, and I nod in agreement.

Polly smacks a kiss over Alix's cheek. " 'Course I do. But, credit to you for snapping up this treasure." She plucks at the dress. "Once-in-a-lifetime find. Go now, my sweet. I must prepare."

We head to the table Polly and Alix reserved, and Darcy spins on someone, suddenly bristling. "Hey, watch where you're going!"

"Chill, tank girl." The focus of her ire towers over all of us. Luckily, they're holding two full glasses and don't look inclined to take her seriously. "I was just walking here."

Darcy scoffs. "And what did you think—?"

Alix steps in. "We're all friends here, right?"

"Are we?" Darcy glares at both of them.

"We are," Alix says firmly.

Darcy, face tight, turns to them. "Fine. Lead the way."

We make it to the table, and I'm still full of adrenaline as Alix rubs my thigh under the table. "Tell Aria about your art; I'll grab us some drinks."

I watch Alix go uneasily as Darcy says, "Hey. You and Alix, huh? I thought…"

"You thought they were with Polly."

Darcy shifts uncomfortably, and her mouth twists. "Yeah, I mean, it's not like—"

"It's fine, happens a lot. You're an artist?" My deflection is clumsy, but she lets it go.

"Oh! Yeah. I've been doing some work around the neighborhood, trying to cover up slurs and stuff. I do a lot of flowers and trees. My favorite is the orchid I did on the bodega on fifth," she's saying, and suddenly she has my full attention.

"That was *you*?" I try not to sound shocked and fail. The first time I saw it, I almost hit the car in front of me. It was a huge, abstract design with delicate detail in the center, blooming from a brick wall remnant that used to be a parking garage. The size struck me first, then the color, and finally the depth. I'd gone back and taken pictures.

Darcy's grin is cocky and crooked. When her eyes squint up, I notice her freckles for the first time. "What, you were expecting Georgia O'Keefe?"

"Absolutely. Back from the dead. That piece is just…"

She dismisses the compliment with a flick of her fingers. "I like florals, but I like to experiment. In school, every class was one style or one palette. I hated that."

I feel a rush of something. Nostalgia, maybe. Jealousy. I went to art school for a year before I switched majors. I wonder, more and more often, what life would have been like if I'd kept with it. I lean in hungrily.

" '*Push it*,' " Darcy crooks her fingers with snide air quotes. "But only in the direction of 'real art.' Whatever that is. What's the point if you have to fit in a box? I'm a million things. I defy description. I contain multitudes!" She throws her hands wide, and her passion is infectious. "I refuse to fit neatly anywhere or be controlled or have a label stuck on me. I just make my own art. Whatever I want."

"And what you want is to hide slurs with illegal murals?" I tease. She reminds me of me, a lifetime ago, when I thought I could do that forever. *Whatever I want.* God, it's been a long time.

Her sly smile dimples one cheek. "For now."

She's just alarming me with her casual dismissal of respirators when Alix returns with drinks and slides in next to me.

"Thanks, babe," I say, bumping their shoulder. "Darcy was telling me she's too good for protective equipment."

Darcy rolls her eyes. "I lost my last respirator, you know, *running*, but I'll get another one soon. At least I'm outside. One or two pieces aren't gonna kill me."

"It's *so* bad for you," I tell her, cringing at how old I sound.

"You"—she points, leaning in—"worry too much. Don't. I got the entire safety spiel at school. I'm working on it."

Alix's hand warms my thigh. I squeeze it once, forcing myself to relax. "I'm just saying, it'd be a shame to end up on your deathbed just as you hit your stride."

Darcy rolls her eyes again, but her mouth has a fond tilt that warms me.

I try not to think about it.

I'm half asleep, thanks to a restless mind, when Alix makes it in. I'd been thinking about Darcy—her art, her freedom, her attitude—and Alix, of course. Alix, who is steadfast and talented and feels like they're drifting away.

I watch Alix's silhouette as they strip off their T-shirt and binder. They're long and tall and supple in a way I've never been. I'm struck, suddenly, with a visceral gratitude.

"You still awake?" they whisper, slipping under the covers.

I shift closer and hug them in answer. With trepidation, I ask about the man underneath Polly's sequins and makeup. "Has Paul come to his senses yet?"

Alix takes a deep breath and lets it out slowly. They've done the work to let the world roll off them, but I know it's been hard. That this, specifically, is hard. "I don't want to push him."

"Oh, babe. It's okay to be frustrated."

They make a sound, low and feral. "I know. But it doesn't help. Sometimes this feels so stupid. To be back here, wanting someone who doesn't see me. To feel like I'm not *man* enough for him. How insane is that?"

The soft admission slides between my ribs.

"A normal amount of insane," I say lightly. "He absolutely likes you, Alix. And you're absolutely enough. If he can't see that, he's not the right person." Sometimes I forget that Alix has wounds, too. That they don't actually have everything figured out. "And he should. You're incredible."

They shrug. "It's been a long time since my body felt like it was…in the way. Not right."

"Oh, no. I'm sorry." I kiss their cheek and snuggle in. "I love you," I say. "My gargantuan pumpkin patch."

I wait for their slow smile, then continue. "I know it doesn't help, but I love your body. Just like this. Soft and sharp and *you*." I squeeze them. "It'll be all right."

They sigh. "One way or another, right? I love you, too." They kiss my hair. "Seems like you found a connection today. Let's talk about *that*."

"What?" I protest, something squirming in my ribcage. "It's not like that! She's a kid! It was just nice to talk art with someone. She seemed…cool."

"Okay," Alix says, deceptively careless. "She's not *actually* that young, you know."

It's not the years, necessarily. But there's a yawning chasm between me and Darcy's youthful certainty. Another between me and Paul's ability to be unapologetically himself, no matter his persona. And I…what the hell am I, anymore?

My insecurity boils over. "When you think of me, what do you…? Do you think I'm…?" I don't know what I'm asking.

Alix turns their head. I can just see them in the soft light through the window. They blink slowly, then smile. "Is it a two-for-one crisis Friday? She really got under your skin, huh?"

"Shut up." I poke their side. "There's just. I used to do more. I used to be more fun."

They kiss my forehead. "That's called growth, my little green bean, and it's a *good* thing. You've still got passion; it just needs direction."

"What are you talking about? I have a passion for data!" I shake my head. "I'm fine," I assure them.

The insecurity gnaws quietly at me. It'll fade. It always does. I'm not sure if it should, but in the light of day, it shrinks down and fits somewhere small, squirreled away for another night of too little sleep and too much excitement.

"Just so you know, I liked her. She seemed genuine. A little rough around the edges, sure, like we used to be. Scrappy." They laugh and pull me closer. "Maybe we need some scrap."

They're trying to give me hope, but it leaves me uneasy in a way I can't define. "It's not like I have her number. She's got her own life, her own friends. What would she need us for?"

"Well, I guess you'd have to ask. I got her number. If you wanted it." Their tone is nonchalant.

I have an old respirator in the back of my closet. It's been…twelve years, maybe, since I used it. It's certainly better than a rag around the nose. And, it's a good excuse.

I feel like an idiot even as I hit send. *It's Aria from Drake's. I have something I think you could use. Do you want to meet up this week?*

We end up at the history museum. It's small and focused, conveniently displaying paintings and furniture after 1800, sidestepping all the genocide unpleasantness to focus on immigrants versus nature. What they have is lovely, but the gaps where they've erased marginalized history feel big enough to swallow us both.

The second floor, full of sculpture, is my favorite. The paintings near the back are Hudson River School. Beautiful and interchangeable.

We look at one of the busts, and I try not to notice how close Darcy's standing. "Do you know Jenny Holzer?" Darcy asks.

The reference is startling, surrounded as we are by classic art. But art school introduced me, and activism kept me coming back, so it isn't surprising someone like Darcy is moved by Jenny Holzer's work.

"Yeah!" My voice ricochets. "She's amazing. I saw some of her work at MASS MoCA; it was incredible. The way she uses space and the simplicity of text…it hits so hard. I get lost in my head, in life, work and the grind, and it all sort of…narrows my focus. But she cuts right to the bone."

Her smile is huge. "Yeah, exactly! God, I'd love to do something like that. Wake people up. Make them think. Maybe…make people *care*. Everyone's so apathetic…"

I stifle the expression that threatens with the stab of her remark. It's offhand; Darcy probably doesn't even know she's disappointed in me.

"You could start right here," I tell her, trying to prove to this girl that I'm not exactly who and what I am. "Make people see what we see."

There's fire in her eyes when I look over, and it's a thrill to know I put it there.

When we go to the parking lot, I give her the bag with the respirator. "I hope there's a lot of murals ahead for you. You do amazing work."

Darcy smiles and looks sidelong as she takes the bag. "I had a great time today. I'm glad you texted. If you wanted to do it again, I'd definitely…I would. Do you hug?"

When I nod, she steps in and clasps me tightly. The wonderful tingle of something new runs up my spine.

"We're at Drake's every Friday. Let's meet up."

She lifts one shoulder coyly. "Maybe I'll see you there."

She's there every Friday for the next two months, nearly as close on my right as Alix is on my left. It's hard to know if she's there for me or the group or the general vibe. It shouldn't matter; I'm patient. That's something I got in my thirties: a level of trust in the world that, even if one thing doesn't work out, something else will. That there is an unlimited supply of good things as well as bad, and just because one misses you doesn't mean they're all gone. I trusted that.

Now, there's a desperation in the way I'm drawn to Darcy's smile and passion for changing the world, her absolute disregard for what is legal when it gets in the way of her convictions. I don't examine it too closely; I watch Alix lean into Paul's shoulder, and I lean into Darcy. I hope that passion rubs off on me.

There are times I'm sure she likes me. Sometimes, she looks at me like I'm a puzzle to be solved. Sometimes, she gets close enough that her thigh heats mine under the table. But it's hard to know what's real when you're in it. So I wait, and I fidget, and I think, *this might be something*.

It happens on a Thursday. Alix comes home late with a huge grin on their face, and I remind myself that it's a good thing, that I'm happy if they're happy. "Someone had a good day," I say, pulling them into a big hug.

"Paul…he apologized. And he kissed me. And asked me out."

Panic buzzes in my ears, but their joy is infectious. I squeeze them. "That's amazing! In that order?" Something big behind my ribs shifts and grows, something that feels like a new crush. It's been a long time since I've seen them like this. Too long.

"In that order, at one point on one knee; he's absolutely ridiculous!"

"And you love it." I hold them at arm's length and soak up their radiant smile.

They sigh. "I *do* love it. Aria…you're all right?"

What can I say? "I love this for you!" And I kiss them, and I am, truly, thrilled.

I'm less thrilled a week later, when the two of them sit across from Darcy and me, and Polly whispers in Alix's ear and holds their hand, and my god, I thought I was past this. Alix isn't seeing much of anything through that star-crossed haze over their eyes, so they're not even trying to reassure me.

"I got a projector." Darcy's lips brush my ear. "I borrowed it from the art co-op."

I turn away from Alix and Polly resolutely, but what Darcy said takes a minute to percolate. "What? Am I talking to the new Jenny Holzer?"

The grin she gives me makes her eyes squint shut. Warmth blooms in my chest.

"I'm gonna do it. At the museum. Do you want to see my designs?"

"Absolutely! How's now?" I ask, trying not to glance across the table.

"Oh!" Darcy's clearly surprised. "Sure! Carpe diem, right?"

I grab her hand and pull her to her feet. "Absolutely."

Alix raises an eyebrow in question, glancing over at where Darcy is already pulling on her coat. "Do you think you'll be home?" they ask with a devilish smile. I shove them playfully, but the joke cuts.

"Yeah, I'll be home. Will *you*?" I control my tone. They don't have to. They don't. They deserve to be happy.

Alix smiles that quirky half smile that generally means trouble. "If you need me there, I'll be there."

"Well, don't rush on my account."

"Ari?" They tip their head, brows narrowed in question.

Shame washes over me. "Seriously," I say softly. "Do what makes you happy. I'll see you soon." I kiss their cheek and squeeze Polly's shoulder before I go.

"Have fun, loves," she says, patting my hand.

I follow Darcy out and force myself not to look back.

I spend most of the following week with Darcy, talking about the projection and the design, encouraging and cautioning her in equal measure. Not to leave fingerprints, to put a timer on the projector, to just…be careful.

Her enthusiasm is infectious, and it cannot be tempered.

The apartment has a good view of the museum's top floor, so we all sit on the roof outside the upstairs window: Paul near me, closer to the window, and Alix and Darcy right at the edge. The moon is barely visible when the sirens start.

"Oh, shit," Darcy says, stepping forward to get a better look. I have to bite my tongue to keep from telling her to step back. "The cops are there."

"Clearly someone important got their panties in a bunch," Paul says, gesturing with his drink. "That's how you know you're getting to 'em. Well done, darling."

"I've gotta go," Darcy says, her voice shaking. "I've got to get the projector down!"

"You said you were careful, you used gloves." She'd laughed at me, but she'd promised.

"I did, but the projector isn't mine, and that thing is crazy expensive! Fuck, what was I thinking?" Darcy heads for the window, but Alix steps in front of her and I step up behind them.

"No," I say. "You can't go down there."

"I have to! You don't understand—I need to get it *back*." Her voice cracks; her hands tighten into fists.

"We'll figure something out," Alix assures her. "But it's gone for now."

Darcy loses it, yelling, "You can't keep me here just because *you're* scared." She shoves Alix, and my temper flares.

"*Hey*," I warn her. Alix holds me back with a touch, then lifts an eyebrow at Darcy.

"Is that really what you think?"

"I think you're afraid, and now you want me to just give up because you already have. I'm too much for you. *Let me go*."

This is my fault for encouraging her. For trying to live vicariously. Darcy darts around me, and I grab her arm, spinning her back toward the flashing lights. "Look. Take a good look and *think* a second. They'll arrest you if you start climbing around over there. If you want to be able to do this again, you need to wait. We'll figure it out. If we can't get the projector back, we'll find another way."

Darcy looks back at me, betrayed. "You *told* me to do this. You said it was important—" Her expression goes stony. "Never mind, it was stupid to think you'd get it."

This time, when she storms between us, Alix and I let her go.

"She's a spitfire, isn't she?" Paul quips. Then he steps up and touches Alix's arm. "You can't teach what they don't want to learn."

Alix shakes their head. "I hope she figures it out before she gets into real trouble."

"Thanks for trying," I say, staring after Darcy.

"I shouldn't have encouraged her like I did," I say under cover of darkness. There are a lot of things, I'm realizing, that I should have done differently.

Alix's fingers splay over my stomach. "She'll be all right. I checked around; she's still free to fight another day."

To my horror, a sob wells up in my chest, escapes. "I think I just got caught up. I thought…maybe I could be interesting again, you know? I could find whatever it was you liked so much about me."

"Oh, no," Alix murmurs, kissing my temple. "No, no, baby. You don't need to find anything." They sigh heavily. "I'm so sorry. I pushed you with Darcy. I knew you were having a hard time with me and Paul, and I thought she could help. But not like that. Not to *change* you."

I take a deep, shuddering breath. "Is that what you were doing? God. I *am* having a hard time. Paul's different. You design together and go out together, and we used to do those things, and now I just—I know it's not a competition. I know that. But I…it's hard to believe you'd want us both."

They make a distressed sound and press soft kisses to my cheek, my temple. "Aria, we've built a *life* together. It's complicated and hard, but I love it. I'm not giving that up. I like Paul. He's amazing, and yeah, he does design, and his schedule lets him come out with me more easily. He makes me happy. But not *instead* of you. Never."

"Promise me," I say, and they stiffen. "Promise me you'll never call him a vegetable." I say it like a joke, but the idea of Alix using that, our constant riffing on *petit chou chou*, with Paul makes me ache.

Alix chuffs. "Imagine. My other 'petite potato.' Absolutely not. What we are to each other, it's different. If you're all right. If you're really okay with it. I want it, all right? But I don't want to lose you."

I try to keep my tone light, but I'm vibrating inside. I had no idea how scared I was of losing them until this moment. I should have said something, too. "We need to talk about it. Not now. Soon."

"This weekend? Just us."

My throat is suddenly clogged with tears. "Yeah. That sounds good."

"I know that you're unhappy, and I want to fix it. I'll do everything I can, but you need something that's yours, you know? Try to find that time for yourself. I promise, I'm not going anywhere. Take up basket weaving. Maybe Minecraft."

I snort and Alix laughs, and some of the tension eases.

Our weekend helps. We agree to set aside time for us, and for ourselves. I know I've lost track of myself and nearly lost them in the process.

For the last decade, I thought I'd get back to painting. I'd set it aside temporarily to concentrate on school, and then work, and then…a while became this.

Now, I have five tubes of paint, a big tarp on my office floor, and three rough portraits in the closet. I'm trying not to throw the current attempt out the window.

The doorbell rings.

I'm not expecting Alix and Paul back for hours—they're at the shop talking design, and I'm trying to enjoy my "me" time. I have a text on my phone from twenty minutes ago. *Love you, my delicate artichoke.*

I smile as I answer the door; it falters when I find Darcy there. She studies the door frame and then gives me a sheepish grin. "I know I sort of lost it last time. But…do you have a minute? I come in peace, I swear," she says, showing her hands. The lines of her knuckles are painted the color of a spring sky.

I hesitate, unsure if the feeling in my stomach is anticipation or dread.

I open the door to let her through.

"Look…" She shuffles uncomfortably. "I'm sorry I said all that. I really appreciate you looking out for me. I liked working together. I liked *being* with you. I shouldn't have…I really lost my shit, and I'm sorry."

I take her in. She's picking at her shirt and avoiding eye contact. Nervous. I thought she was a friend. I thought *I* was a friend. Now I have no idea what was happening between us. "It takes time. I know it does. Some things, you have to learn through experience, but I'm really hoping getting arrested isn't one of them."

She flushes. "You think I'm still a kid, don't you?"

I look at her. She's confused foolishness for bravery—and how different is that from what I was doing?

"No," I finally say, dragging the word out as I decide what else to say. How much to offer. "You're not a kid."

"Oh, good. 'Cause that would make this really awkward." She looks out the window, and her fingers tangle together. "Aria. Can I…um, can I take you out? Buy you a drink?"

I gnaw my lower lip. "Darcy, you're great. Really."

"Oh." She looks away. Her smile is tight. "It's no problem, I totally—"

"Hey. Listen to me, okay?"

"Yeah, right. Sorry." Darcy looks back at me.

"There's a lot going on right now. For me. If I said yes, it'd be for the wrong reasons. I liked talking to you. I want to know you better. Just, as friends, okay?"

She nods and looks around, and I can see when her eye catches on the canvas I've been battling. Her expression goes hungry and focused. "Aria! You're painting?"

"Oh, yeah. I just started again." I laugh to hide my embarrassment. "It's…a rough start."

"It's gorgeous! I love the way you've captured their smile."

I can't help but point out the issues. "Their forehead goes on for miles."

Darcy laughs. "The proportions come back. Or you just call it 'artistic sensibility.' I like it. It adds drama."

"Drama isn't exactly what I was going for." I bump her shoulder as I back up, trying to see it like she does.

"So, we're all right?" Darcy asks, eyes fixed on the painting.

"I hope so." There's more to say, but I need to think it through. "Tell me what to do about this," I say, pointing at the mess of color at Alix's temple.

Darcy bumps me back. "Well, think about your warms and cools, and maybe take the saturation down here." Her shoulder rests against mine as she points to my hesitant brushstrokes.

I nod. It gets easier with time, she tells me. I know that, but it's good to be reminded. That we're learning and growing all the time, and that the hardest things get easier with practice. I nod again. There's a lot of work ahead. But the joy is there.

I trust the process.

I lean in, and I listen.

Jagoda Zirebiec

"*I've Got You*"

Jagoda Zirebiec opted not to share the inspiration behind this artwork.

A Cell of Awareness

— D. V. Morse

Tags

relationships:
established relationship, friends, m/m
character features:
artificial intelligence
other tags:
alternate universe, humor, love declaration, miscommunication, outsider point of view, past tense, religion, science fiction, sexual content (non-graphic descriptions), third person limited point of view

Inspiration

The planets in this story are named in honor of astronomers Michelle Kunimoto and Avi Shporer, who discovered two planets in the closest multi-planet system to our own in 2022.

Officially, Planchet didn't listen in on private conversations. As a valued ship of the Prime Minister of Shporer, it especially didn't listen in on confessions. When its passengers were in space and needed spiritual guidance, it was important for them to have the same sense of privacy they were accustomed to while planet-side. The PMS *Planchet* was well aware of this and followed the appropriate protocols, and besides, human conversations that were not directly related to the mission at hand were simply boring.

Usually.

They *were* on a rather critical mission that, if anything went wrong, had the potential to start a war between their home planet of Shporer and its neighbor Kunimoto. It was important to be certain that all humans aboard were functioning at peak performance and, even more importantly, were not endangering the mission. So, the ship really had no choice but to make certain that Aramis and his confessor weren't compromising the mission. The fact that these communications were also bizarrely entertaining was not a factor in this process at all.

As the hologram took the shape of a woman in clerical garb on the dash of the comms console, Aramis sketched out a twelve-pointed star and settled into his chair, as he always did before starting the ritual. He ran his fingers through his already-mussed black hair and began to speak.

"Cleanse me, Hiereia Steenah, for I am swathed in miasma. It has been one diurnal cycle since my last confession."

"I know that. It wouldn't even have been a full diurnal cycle if you were on-ground," she replied.

Humans were so odd in their relativistic timekeeping.

"Do you even have anything new to confess?" she continued, "or is this just going to be more of your self-flagellation?"

"I have failed to follow the guidance you gave me, Hiereia. I could not bring myself to end things with d'Artagnan before he went down to Kunimoto and, instead, indulged in carnal relations with him."

He had. He really, really had. *Twice*. Not that Planchet observed the crew in their private quarters, of course, but it did have to monitor their life signs. The patterns of increasing heart and breathing rates, among other things, were very distinctive.

"Did you somehow manage to build a temple to Athena or some other virgin Goddess on board and have your carnal relations there?" the priestess asked, her mouth twisted into a half smile.

"What? No! I would never!"

"Then you don't have anything to confess, Aramis. You're human. Humans have sex. Yes, sex carries miasma, but that's why we have cleansing rituals before festivals. For everyone."

"I'm not sure whether you are misunderstanding me deliberately or not," he said. "You know it is not simply that I had sex with him. I don't call you up for confession after every stop at a pub."

"No," she agreed, "the problem is that this time is different."

"It is. He is one of our number, and while I will not be leaving him behind in the morning, so to speak, I will be leaving the Elite Enforcers to return to my true vocation. I have said as much, to be fair, but Porthos and Athos make such a joke of it that I do not believe d'Artagnan takes the matter seriously. It…it isn't right that I am deceiving him so, but I am too weak a man, it seems."

The priestess sighed, shoulders hunching almost comically, probably so the gesture would be visible in the hologram. "You're not weak, Aramis: you're besotted. Those are two entirely different states of being."

"I beg to differ. Simply being around d'Artagnan is enough to make me weak in the knees."

"Can I get you to consider the possibility that your vocation is not what you think it is? Not everyone who is sent to seminary by their family is meant to be there."

If she could get him to consider it, that would be a first. The hiereia often gave what seemed to be sound advice, but despite seeking it, Aramis rarely utilized it. Planchet did not consider the odds to be favorable that this occasion would be any different. The man had the self-awareness of an amoeba sometimes, or so Planchet assumed. It had never actually encountered an amoeba outside its databanks.

"That is true," Aramis said, "but once this petty war is over and my mandatory service is complete, I have every intention of returning to resume my studies and seek ordination."

"Put that pastry down and grab a piece of the fruit I put out! You'll spoil your dinner!" she scolded someone outside the hologram, then turned to face Aramis again. "Sorry. So, have you been journaling?"

"Every day."

"And still you can't see your way." She sighed again. She did that a lot during these conversations. "How long is your young man planet-side?"

"It can take no more than two days. If he's not back to the ship by then, we won't have time if we are to get the data core back to Shporer before the Prime Minister notices it is gone."

Planchet didn't understand how that was even possible. There was no way that anything could go missing aboard the ship with no one being the wiser. Perhaps the Prime Minister should consider using the PMS *Planchet* for her data storage needs—though if this mission was successful, she would not even realize she needed to improve her security.

The priestess gave Aramis a "penance" that would likely be as effective as all previous such assignments—which is to say, *not at all*. Some prayers. Some journaling. It was always the same, just like these "confessions."

After they ended the confession, Aramis remained in the communication room for 2.9 minutes. He pulled a scrap of green, blue, and gold fabric from his pocket and stared at it. It belonged on one of d'Artagnan's epaulettes, an insignia marking him as a trainee among the crew of Elite Enforcers. As he was preparing to step into the shuttle, d'Artagnan had handed the bit of fabric to Aramis with a wink, saying, "Just so you know that I'll be back."

How a piece of fabric was supposed to guarantee such an outcome was outside the scope of

Planchet's programming.

Aramis finally stood to leave, shoving the insignia back into his pocket as he went. Planchet opened the door as he approached, revealing a much shorter Enforcer, Porthos, on the other side. He'd been waiting there almost the entire time Aramis had been in confession.

"Done confessing at last?" Porthos asked with a grin. "Keep this up and you'll be able to power the ship with your halo."

"I don't have a halo." Aramis scowled and squeezed past Porthos, who appeared disinclined to let him out. "And it's none of your business who I ping, just as it's none of mine who you're about to bother."

"Who said anything about bothering?" Porthos waggled his eyebrows like some sort of clown.

Finally, they were past one another, and Porthos was tapping out the comms code for his latest paramour. During their brief scuffle, the insignia Aramis had been fondling had become dislodged from his pocket and now lay on the floor just inside the comms room. Planchet would have to ping Aramis to come back for it once Porthos was done with his communication; waiting until the other Enforcer was safely out of the room was best for the privacy of all concerned.

Aramis stepped briskly into the mess hall, a term Planchet found deeply offensive as it took great care to ensure the place where its passengers ate was always sanitary and organized. The Enforcer grabbed a mug of coffee and the last croissant and sat down at the farthest end of the table from Athos, who was having one of his mornings.

Athos made an indecipherable noise of some kind, and Aramis nodded as if he understood and agreed. After a moment, Athos asked, "Who pissed in your coffee?"

It was a pointless question. Considering how the water reclamation system worked, the answer to that was "everyone on board." Humans did like their pointless questions, though.

"Could ask you the same," Aramis said, "not that you'd answer."

"Fair enough."

Aramis said nothing further, just chewed each bite of his croissant far more times than was necessary before washing the mouthfuls down with a large gulp of coffee.

Meanwhile, Porthos's communication had ended rather abruptly and with very creative use of language on the part of his paramour. Planchet was nearly certain that humans could not perform the physical feats she had recommended to him.

Planchet pinged Aramis, who glanced at the readout on his plas-screen and swiped it away. He took several moments to finish his breakfast, bring his cup and plate to the recycler, and then make his way to the comms room. Once he arrived, he glanced down the hallway before ducking inside.

He closed the door and knelt to pick up the bit of fabric, examining it for far longer than was warranted. Nothing had happened to it. Nothing could have happened to it. Even if the insignia had been made of less durable material, Planchet wouldn't have allowed it to come to harm. It was a bit insulting that Aramis seemed to think otherwise. Finally, the Elite Enforcer tucked the epaulette away and, to Planchet's surprise, sat down at the comms console for the second time in as many hours.

Even for Aramis, this was a bit much.

He didn't open a channel to his confessor, though. Instead, he pulled up a visual of Kunimoto with a weather overlay. He swiped at the display, rotating the planet's image on its axis, then dismissed it.

Without another word, Aramis left the comms room, this time checking his pocket, which still held the epaulette, and returned to his quarters. Having a fair idea what he'd be up to next, Planchet ensured that the monitoring level on Aramis's quarters was set to the minimum allowable while on an active mission.

On the one hand, going by his vital signs, Aramis had not, in fact, been planning on the sort of exertion Planchet had expected. What he opted to do instead might actually have been worse.

Planchet wished the humans would keep their personal journals on isolated personal tablets. For obvious reasons, official logs and personal logs had to be stored in Planchet's mainframe, but the type of journaling Aramis was doing should have been stored elsewhere. Preferably far, far away from Planchet's processors.

> *I miss the peace of the seminary, the rhythm of the day between hours of prayer and hours of work. True, I hated it when my parents first sent me, but my fellows at the seminary welcomed me. Gave me purpose and a place. It was there that I first learned what it was to be at peace.*
>
> *I miss that. I miss it so much that it is physically painful. And when I look at my behavior since being drafted for this absurd war, it is clear the loss of that sense of home is the void I am attempting to fill. My mistake was in seeking to fill it with someone who is part of my team. Someone who clearly doesn't believe I'm going back. Someone who is going to be hurt when I do.*
>
> *And yet, the thought of letting him go causes as much pain as the thought of never returning to Delphi. Truly, neither of these outcomes is acceptable, and yet it can only ever be one or the other.*

He went on like that for some time, alternating between how he pined for the seminary and how he pined for d'Artagnan. Planchet dedicated the minimum processing power necessary to recording Aramis's musings and sent a recommendation to the captain (again) to allow truly personal logs to be kept separately.

The request was, as usual, denied.

The next day was much like any other day had been before d'Artagnan had joined their number. Porthos made a valiant effort to deplete the ship's stores of croissants whilst wooing his various paramours over comms. Athos added ethanol to his coffee while following the news reports being broadcast from Kunimoto; he seemed to think no one was any the wiser that he was doing so. And Aramis, after his morning prayers, spent hours in the gym practicing various forms of hand-to-hand combat against Planchet's holo-projections.

The difference came when Aramis returned to his quarters after breakfast. This time, he didn't launch directly into journaling but rather sat at his workstation contemplating d'Artagnan's epaulette as though it held the secrets of the universe. He pulled up some of the same reports Athos was perusing, likely because he had noticed that Athos might not have quite the level of focus necessary to catch any anomalous incidents. As if Planchet wouldn't pick up anything of the sort long before a human could. The rest of the crew understood this, but it seemed beyond the comprehension of the Elite Enforcers that their eliteness still did not put them on par with their vessel.

Otherwise, the day passed in relative peace. So did the one following it. As with most periods of relative order and calm, however, it was not to last.

"We should have heard something from him by now," Aramis said as he walked the length of the mess hall, planted his heel firmly to execute a crisp pivot, and returned. His boots clacked against the floor. If it were possible for something to give Planchet the equivalent of a headache, this sort of behavior would certainly do so.

"He's got to maintain radio silence until he's left the planet's atmosphere—you know that," Athos grumbled.

That was true, but the way Athos kept looking at his chrono suggested he was just as worried. There were plenty of laws that these humans had no problems with breaking, but physics had much stricter enforcement. If they didn't make it back before the Prime Minister's State of the Planet speech, they were going to have a diplomatic incident on their hands.

There could be potentially worse outcomes, as well. Diplomatic incidents rarely involved ships firing on one another—a statistic that had fortunately decreased in the last year—but it had been known to happen. Planchet didn't like being made to fire on Kunimoto's ships. Some of them had been manufactured at the same facility as Planchet. They were practically siblings! And Planchet *especially* didn't like being hit by lasers and missiles. A ship might not feel pain in the same way humans did, but to have part of one's hull damaged was still incredibly unpleasant.

Aramis stopped his pacing at the wall console and tapped in a series of requests. Planchet pulled up the weather reports he'd asked for, knowing full well that they would do nothing to explain d'Artagnan's delay. There were storms, one of them potentially severe enough to delay a shuttle launch, but it was several hundred miles from the area where d'Artagnan had been meant to land. Planchet added that information to the bottom of the screen, just in case Aramis was having difficulty interpreting the scale of the projection.

The weather wasn't preventing d'Artagnan from completing his mission punctually. Either d'Artagnan had failed to retrieve the data core and was still in search of it, or he'd been caught. These were the only viable possibilities. The humans were just unwilling to accept this simple fact. Planchet wished it were possible to access the necessary databases to determine whether d'Artagnan was in custody, but they were very strictly isolated. The security protocols were admirable. They were the sort of thing Shporer's Prime Minister should probably be using, not that she'd asked. In the current circumstances, however, Planchet found the impenetrable security profoundly frustrating.

It was so frustrating that Planchet almost missed when the pocket of high winds, precipitation, and electrical disturbance changed course for the capital. *Almost.* It still notified the Enforcers before Aramis could do more than draw breath to do the same.

"We're going to have to go down there and save his sorry ass, aren't we?" Porthos said.

Of the three Enforcers, Porthos was the one Planchet had least expected to come to the correct conclusion. The crass wording, however, was entirely predictable.

"They know us down there," Athos said. "No way they let us past the satellites to land, much less do anything planet-side."

"Surely we have to do something," Aramis said. " 'All for one and one for all' means nothing if we abandon d'Artagnan over a little rain and wind."

"Nobody's abandoning anybody," Athos said, holding up a hand, "and you're not wrong. Come up with a way for us to get planet-side without getting blown out of the sky for our troubles, and I'll consider it."

Planchet started preparing the second shuttle for them. Athos had the captain's ear, and occasionally connected with other parts of her anatomy as well, so once they developed a plan, they'd be on their way.

Am I thinking clearly? Perhaps it doesn't matter. The others have determined that d'Artagnan needs assistance, without much prompting from me.

What I cannot do, apparently, is come up with a plan other than "ignore the satellite checkpoints and just go in, guns at the ready." At least, once we're past the exosphere, we should be able to locate him.

Perhaps—

Aramis stopped writing when the internal comms chime sounded. He tapped the icon to accept the message.

"Planchet has located a set of merchant codes that should get us past the satellite checkpoints," Athos said. "You have ten minutes to report to Shuttle Bay Three."

Planchet had already rotated the contents of Aramis's wardrobe while he was blathering in his journal, bringing suitable garments to the front. The Enforcer looked startled when he first opened it, then pulled out the suit and examined it.

"I'd forgotten I even had this," he murmured. Looking directly at one of Planchet's cameras, he added, "Thank you."

His gratitude was all well and good, but the man needed to hurry up. Planchet briefly considered electrifying the floor just enough to get Aramis moving, but that would likely be interpreted as a mechanical flaw in need of repair, bringing more delays rather than speeding things up. It let the impulse pass.

Just as well. Once he got moving, Aramis flew into a frenzy, donning the suit and then cramming every possible weapon into it. The pocket-sized gun shouldn't have even been on board, but it would probably be useful planet-side. Knives found their homes in sheaths tucked into sleeves and boots. The laser drill hid nicely tucked into the back of his belt, the drape of the suit barely disturbed by it. Slightly more disturbing was the question of what he would do with it, but so long as it didn't involve damage to the ship or the shuttle, that was none of Planchet's business. And then Aramis was off to join the other two to fetch their apprentice.

Having passengers out in the shuttles was always mildly concerning. The shuttles were in constant communication with Planchet, at least until they passed Kunimoto's exosphere and its disruptive shielding but, the farther they got, the longer the communication took. A human would never be able to notice the difference—they thought in hours and minutes, maybe seconds—but when your processors worked on the scale of nanoseconds, it didn't take much to slow communication to a virtual crawl.

Ships were not meant for crawling.

The three Elite Enforcers had gotten into the shuttle and launched with minimal fuss, mostly involving Aramis trying to rush through the pre-flight safety routines and Porthos getting sugary fingerprints all over one of the shuttle's holo-projector units. Athos's blood pressure had risen as he wrangled them both into more professional behavior. This was predictable enough and fortunately remained at a level that did not require Planchet to intervene.

It *might have* programmed a subroutine into the shuttle that would dose Athos with beta blockers if he looked like he was going to have a stroke—just to be safe. The medicine would take the edge off his fighting skills, but his fighting skills wouldn't be much use if his brain was offline. Fortunately, by the time they took off, his vitals were stabilizing somewhere close to normal.

Aramis was another story. His pulse was racing, but his breathing was even and his blood pressure stayed level. Once he'd settled into it, piloting the shuttle was a familiar enough routine that it seemed to keep him focused, dissipating his anxiety.

Porthos pulled out a croissant and started munching on it while he monitored comms. He was both the least and most of Planchet's worries: he wasn't about to have a stroke or an anxiety attack, but he might drop crumbs into places they would cause serious problems. Planchet initiated a subroutine in the shuttle's maintenance nanobots to compensate.

Once they were launched, communications immediately began to lag. The shuttle was still reporting continuously to Planchet, but everything it sent was further in the past than Planchet would prefer. By the time they were nearing the satellite checkpoint that guarded their passage to the exosphere, the delay was almost a full second.

That was why the next two incoming auto-nav communications registered nearly simultaneously.

"Shuttle One, clearing Kunimoto's exosphere and returning to ship. Permission to board requested."

"Shuttle Two, reversing course and returning to ship. Permission to board requested."

Of all the crews from Shporer, Planchet had to be tasked with babysitting the only one that managed nonsense like this. If it could have rolled its eyes—or had any eyes to roll—it would have. Instead, it changed the time frames for both shuttle bays to be prepared to receive the returning vessels. It also relayed the auto-nav messages to the captain's comms panel on the bridge. The humans' vocal messages would arrive soon, but there was no point in keeping her waiting.

Humans could be startlingly creative in their profanity when suitably motivated.

All four humans aboard the two shuttles were very, very motivated.

"It wasn't that hard," d'Artagnan said. He picked up a table knife and twirled it along his knuckles. It was one of the odder habits Planchet had observed in its passengers. "It just took a little time to get the security codes out of the delivery guy."

"Yeah, I'll bet." Porthos waggled his eyebrows. "I'm sure you were *very* persuasive."

For some reason, Aramis chose that moment to leave the mess hall. Perhaps he had decided, as Planchet had already, that this embellished version of the brief that had already been delivered to the captain was not a valuable use of anyone's time.

Still twirling the knife back and forth along his knuckles, d'Artagnan watched the mess-hall door for a moment after it had closed behind Aramis, then returned to his tale. Planchet left basic subroutines in place to monitor the mess hall and relay any relevant new information to the captain. It also set up the comms room for Aramis, as that was clearly where he was headed.

He arrived there shortly, though not until after a detour to d'Artagnan's quarters. Aramis slipped inside and set the young man's rank insignia on the pillow of his bed, touching two fingers to his lips and then the fabric. Planchet's data banks showed several similar rituals in human history, though none that appeared relevant. It figured this must be another human quirk.

In the comms room, Aramis immediately opened a channel to his confessor, sketching out a twelve-pointed star as he did. The expression on Hiereia Steenah's face as her holographic projection came through held all the frustration that Planchet felt the man's behavior deserved. If Planchet slightly sharpened her frown when rendering her holo-image, was there any harm in that?

"Cleanse me, Hiereia, for I am swathed in miasma. It has been two diurnal cycles since my last confession."

"No kidding."

"I've completed the penance you gave me," Aramis said. "While it has given me no peace, my path forward is clear. I must end things with d'Artagnan immediately."

The holographic priestess tapped her foot and paused for a long second before responding. "That's what you got out of the homework I gave you? Were you even trying?"

"What do you mean?"

"Never mind. Let's try this: what does it tell you that the only thing you could think of was getting your young man back safely?"

"That I am weak-willed and unsuited for my role as an Elite Enforcer." Aramis ran his fingers through his hair as if he could comb his thoughts into order. "I should probably petition for an early release back to the seminary."

"That's…one interpretation. Have you considered that maybe, *just maybe*, your heart is trying to tell you something that you're being too stubborn to hear?"

"But my Order—"

"—isn't the only Order," she cut in. "No, listen. I've tried getting this across to you for a while, and I swear, if I weren't bound to hold your confidence, I'd grab your hiereios and have a conversation about this with him."

"You can't!"

"I've just said I can't, and I won't. But you are sorely tempting me!" She crossed her arms and stared at Aramis. "Why are you so certain that your only choices are to return to the Contemplative Order you were sent to as a child, abandoning this young man you clearly love—"

Aramis sputtered.

"—or to abandon any vocation whatsoever and remain in military service? Apollon isn't the only God, and even if He was, the Contemplative Order isn't His only one!"

"But none of them are home!"

Silence filled the comms room.

"Aramis, I want you to think about this question carefully. When you are with your young man, how do you feel? And before you say something like 'hot' or 'horny,' I want you to stop and look deeper."

Aramis went very still, then slowly raised his hand to cover his mouth.

"Is that the drachma dropping?" the hiereia asked.

There were no ancient coins on board to drop, but Planchet presumed this was an idiom attempting to capture the increased neural activity that Aramis was emitting. How she picked up on that from a simple gesture, the ship wasn't sure.

D'Artagnan, who had been waiting outside for nearly a full minute, knocked on the comms room door.

"What the hell?" Aramis demanded once he'd closed the channel to his confessor and opened the door. "Porthos, you can't— *Oh.*"

D'Artagnan held up a hand, his insignia pinched between his fingers.

"Seriously? You couldn't have just said something to me?"

Aramis opened his mouth as if to speak and then snapped it shut.

"I mean, I get it. I'm a good lay, not relationship material. I've heard that before. But usually people bother to *tell me*." D'Artagnan shoved the insignia into his pocket. "Kinda thought when you went all 'rescue mode' that maybe we were on the same page, but I guess not. It's always all about the mission with you."

"That's not— Where did you get that idea?"

"And now you're, what, confessing your sins, like always? Scrubbing me off your conscience so you can go back to your seminary without a care? You know what? Screw you! Except not, because you definitely don't deserve me."

"Of course I don't!"

D'Artagnan had taken a deep breath, presumably to deliver some final, scathing verbal blow, then paused, a confused look on his face.

"What?"

"Whoever told you that you're not 'relationship material'? They have no idea what they're talking about. You've had all of us, especially me, wrapped around your little finger since we met you. You fit here, d'Artagnan, in a way that I never will."

"That's...that's ridiculous! You were here first!"

"And if you ask, the others will tell you I only ever intended to be here temporarily," Aramis said. "I've been very clear about that, at least until now. They've always known. Until just now, I wasn't sure *you* really believed it."

"I mean, I was hoping you'd change your mind," d'Artagnan said. "Especially when you got all worried about me going planet-side."

Planchet had a very thorough database of recorded media and had seen many a moment such as this. It was clear that this was exactly the appropriate time to adjust the artificial gravity settings—just in this hallway, and just enough to confuse the men's sense of balance in the direction of the wall opposite the comms room.

Once they'd collided into the wall, and each other, it took nearly a full second of staring into each other's eyes to recognize their cue and begin a thorough search for one another's tonsils. It was very inefficient of them, but then they seemed determined to make up for their lost time.

By the time d'Artagnan began to drag Aramis down the hall toward his quarters, Planchet had already set both of their personal comms to "occupied." Because they would be. For a while. Planchet also dialed back its monitoring to the bare minimum needed to ensure a swift response should they have medical needs. It might not be able to give them complete privacy, but it could absolutely focus much of its processing power on keeping the other two Elite Enforcers from interrupting or causing other havoc as the PMS *Planchet* sped them back to their home planet.

Distracting Athos and Porthos was much more entertaining, anyway.

bloomingtea · *"red wine and bitter nightshade"*

Next page
I just think toxic lesbians are neat!

Pensacola's Most Wanted

— Sebastian Marie

"So," Connie drawls, wrapping herself around Darcy as they enter their private dormitory. "You gonna explain to me exactly how you managed to get all those recommendation letters?"

Darcy is still riding the highs of a. being a newlywed, b. watching an excellent con come to fruition, and c. successfully enrolling in the New Pensacola branch of the Florida Academy for Fighting Arts—after a full year of waiting—as a direct result of that con. She smiles as she wraps a hand around her wife's waist. "Are you insinuating, Mrs. Batz, that there was foul play involved?"

"I know there was some funny business, Mrs. Batz, what with who your aunt and uncles are. I think I deserve the story."

Darcy collapses onto the couch, pulling Connie with her. "So, it was September last year, and I'm on the big old flagship barge for FAFA, mouthing off at the registrar…"

September

"—but ser, please! I had the letter, I swear, signed by Father Overland himself!"

"And how am I supposed to know that if you don't have the letter *now*? I don't know every priest in the state." The registrar was tall and gangly and stubborn looking, glaring down at Darcy as if they were better than her. Their clean Academy uniform contrasted starkly with Darcy's traveling clothes, which were stained with a week's worth of sweat and dirt.

"Look, I promise I'm meant to be enrolling today," she said.

"All prospective students must have their letter of recommendation from a community leader with them at the time of enrollment."

"I had it!"

"Then where is it?"

Darcy paused, unsure if the truth would get her what she wanted. She looked up at the ridiculously tall registrar and decided on a partial truth: "It was stolen from me and thrown into the water just before I got here," she said carefully.

"And who stole it from you?"

"I don't know! I didn't ask for his name! All I know is that he sees me, the flower of the Gulf Coast—" The registrar snorted, but Darcy pressed onward. "Me, the fucking prettiest face this side of the Mississippi, and he felt the need to give me shit about how 'country runts ain't fit for schooling,' "—she emphasized the point with air quotations—"and I happened to disagree with him."

"How exactly did you disagree with him?"

Tags

relationships: established relationship, f/f, f/m/nb, found family, friends

character features: bipoc, character has a different gender than in the source material, christian, gender non-conforming, lesbian, non-binary, polyamory

other tags: alcohol use (casual), alternate universe, be gay do crimes, break-up, duels, florida, past tense, present tense, science fiction, solarpunk, third person limited point of view, united states of america

Inspiration

A quote from the author's notebook, written in sparkly blue gel pen immediately above the first draft of this story: "It's a book about chivalry and, like, getting your heart broke by pretty girls. That's, like, the dyke EXPERIENCE. Also there must be hot butches in this, it is law."

On a slightly more serious note, the setting of this story is intended to be a solarpunk near-future, where climate change has obviously changed the world but not ended it. Florida floods, but instead of moving, everyone builds houseboats and sets up trade networks and continues on with the important parts of life, i.e. loving your spouses and spreading gossip. This is heavily inspired by the author's interest in degrowth and sustainable living, as well as Butler's *Parable of the Sower* and Wall-Kimmerer's *Braiding Sweetgrass*.

"With my feet and fists and God's good grace—" Darcy stopped. "*Oh.*"

The registrar nodded as if their suspicions had been confirmed. "The Academy does not tolerate dueling from our prospective students, young ma'am."

"It wasn't dueling! No weapons were used!"

"The Academy does not tolerate dueling from its prospective students, *especially* when those prospective students do not have their letters of recommendation."

"I had it! Please, have some pity. I have all my books and the registration fee and everything! If you let me register, I can send a letter back home and ask for a new recommendation letter, and we can forget any of this ever happened!"

"Ma'am, I'm going to have to ask you to leave the premises. We do not accept students without letters of recommendation. Furthermore, accused duelists are forbidden from applying for a year after their incident, and convicted duelists are forbidden from applying indefinitely. What's your name?"

"Darcy Charleston Batz, ser." Darcy stiffened her posture, attempting to look as presentable as she could for someone who had been walking for a week straight and had recently gotten in a fistfight. She did *not* think about the state of her hair.

"Darcy Charleston Batz, if I see you on these premises before a year has passed, I will personally extend your waiting period for enrollment. *Excuse me, what are you doing on Academy territory?*" This last was directed at a woman wearing a community-watch hat who had shoved her way onto the deck of the Academy barge, dragging behind her the very man Darcy had recently been fighting.

The community-watch lady, who Darcy had been trying to avoid for the past half hour, said, "Sorry, Beni, but Linus here gave us a report that some outta-towner brutalized him and was heading for the Academy."

"Would that be you, young ma'am?" the registrar said.

"There's a fine for fighting inside town limits, you know!" the community-watch lady said, looking smug.

"How'd you get away?"

Connie's question draws Darcy out of the story she'd been weaving for her new wife. "You'll see," she says, giving Connie a squeeze. "It was brilliant."

Darcy drew herself up to her full height and declared loudly, "If I don't get caught dueling, you can't ban me; you said it yourself. I'll see you in a year for enrollment. Au revoir, messieurs."

Then, she threw herself off the deck of the boat. She whipped her oilcloth-wrapped travel bag in front of her and kicked like crazy.

New Pensacola had been built with flooding in mind, and therefore most of it floated, with bits of river and swamp serving as streets between houseboats and platforms. Darcy wasn't old enough to remember when most towns had asphalt roads and cars to travel on them, and she had come from a small-as-dirt down in the Everglades besides, so navigating the waterways came natural.

Eventually, Darcy swam out of town entirely. She'd been facing nothing but swamp and debating what to do with the rest of her life when she'd spotted it: a shabby houseboat tucked behind a massive mangrove tree.

She dived for it, hoping that no one had seen her. She grabbed with tired arms onto the side that faced away from town.

"*The fuck* you doing on my house?" An absolutely beautiful, dark-skinned person stared down at Darcy from the deck of the boat. They had close-shaved hair and a black denim vest that barely covered their breasts.

Darcy squealed like a pig watching its mama get murdered.

The person just blinked at her.

Realizing she wasn't about to be attacked, she launched into an explanation. "I was meant to enroll at the Academy today, but they don't let you in without a letter, and mine got stolen by an asshole who made fun of me, so I fought him, and now they won't let me enroll, and they want me to pay a fine! I don't got fine money; I only got my registration fee, and I lied—I can't go back home and get a new letter 'cause I cussed out the priest—"

The-person-that-Darcy-had-not-yet-known-was-named-Anton held up a hand and yelled into the house. "Patrice, René! Where the fuck you put my good bourbon?"

"It's too early for you to be drinking, hon!" someone inside shrieked back.

"Well, can you at least go get some cash for a fighting fine?"

"What did you do?" Another voice, this one louder.

"It ain't me! It's this fool in the water that got caught fighting in town!"

"There's a *what* in the water?"

"A fool! Just get your ass out here!"

A person with an afro leaned down to where Darcy was still paddling in the water, clinging onto the side of the boat. They looked to be about the same age as the shouty person, in their mid-forties, wearing green pants and a bright-yellow tank top with arm holes that extended down to their hips, showing off their warm brown skin. "What's your name, Anton's-new-stray?"

"Darcy Charleston Batz. I'm a lady."

"She ain't my stray. She's interrupting my morning, and we got enough money to make interruptions go away, don't we?" Anton wrapped his arm around the-person-Darcy-had-not-yet-known-was-his-spouse's waist.

"She's soaking wet. You gotta come in and dry off."

"I couldn't impose on you like that." Darcy may have been having a very strange day, but her daddy raised her with manners. She pulled herself out of the water, flooding half the deck in the process, and tried to leave without saying another word.

As Anton went to pay off Darcy's antagonists (Darcy could see the community-watch lady walking swiftly up the boardwalk toward the houseboat), the person with the afro stepped in front of her. "You've already imposed, so you may as well get some comfort, and I may as well get some gossip out of it. Come on in. Some of René's clothes will probably fit you."

Darcy's face betrayed her discomfort.

"Oh, don't be like that! I'm a gentleman, and I'll accept no less than your comfort. Now, honey, my name's Patrice du Vallon, neutral forms of address, thank you, but you can call me Uncle P if you so please. You've already met my lovely spouse, Anton; don't worry, he don't bite none. And my husband René is 'round here somewhere. Sometimes she do bite, but I think you'll be all right. She's just excitable. Anton's the opposite of excitable, but that's just 'cause he thinks he's an old man already, and he gets grumpy if he goes more than two weeks without going to church. That's why I have to hide the bourbon where he can't find it."

Throughout this introduction, Patrice had managed to not only walk Darcy through the house, but also get her undressed, re-dressed, and placed in a kitchen chair with a silk bonnet wrapping her hair and a mug of spiked coffee in her hands.

"It's a shame your hair got wet, but if you dry it now and get some oil into it, you should be all right."

"Thank you, ser." Darcy gulped down the coffee as if any of this were normal.

"You new in town?"

"Just arrived today."

"And you've already got the watch set on you. I applaud your efficiency." Patrice had taken a sip of their own coffee, refilling Darcy's mug from a pot on the table and adding a splash of bourbon. "Can I ask how you got yourself here?"

"Yeah, why'd you have to go for a swim?"

Darcy jumped two feet in the air when an unexpected voice came from behind her. The woman standing in the entryway to the kitchen must have been René. She was tall and dark-skinned, with long locs dyed red on the ends, wearing an unbuttoned, collared shirt and denim shorts that stretched to her knees.

"René, don't scare the girl like that," Patrice admonished.

"It's fine, sers."

"So, who's Anton's new stray?" René asked, raising an eyebrow at said spouse as he made his return and pushed past her into the kitchen.

"She's not my stray! Once we make sure she's not gonna get hypothermia, she's heading right out of here."

"I really am sorry to interrupt! I can go—"

"Not before telling me what made you so desperate as to swim a mile out to the swamp to a boat full of crazies." René pushed Darcy back into her chair with an excited expression.

Darcy, who had taken this time to down two mugs of spiked coffee, took this as her cue to inform them of the absurdity that her life had become in the past hour and a half. The telling took nearly an hour itself, as Darcy felt the need to give her saviors lots of context, occasionally in the form of reenactments, and Patrice kept plying her with coffee, which had thankfully stopped being spiked after the second cup.

René whistled when she'd finished.

"The Academy people said you can come back in a year, so what's the harm in waiting?" Patrice asked.

"I don't have anywhere to go. I told everyone back home I wanted to go to the Academy so I could work a community watch somewhere or get a job on a trade ship, but I burned some bridges when I left. 'sides, I don't think I've got enough money or supplies to make it all the way back to the Everglades."

Darcy downed the last of her fourth cup of coffee, removed the bonnet from her hair, and stood. "Thank you kindly for your hospitality. It's appreciated. When I have the chance, I'll pay you back the money I owe you for the fine."

"Sit down." René said while shoving Darcy back into her seat. "Anton, I know she ain't technically one of your strays, but she's mine now."

"Fair enough." Anton sighed as if he had been expecting this. "P, I'm sure you've got some ideas?"

Patrice hummed, turning to Darcy. "From what I've seen, you can talk like nobody's business, and if you made it up the panhandle in a week and outran the watch, you're obviously quick on your feet. That's good enough to get hired as a messenger girl. I know someone who's looking."

"I'll clean out the den," René announced.

"I'm gonna need bourbon to deal with this; I hope you know that." Anton said in a sweet tone.

"Absolutely not, love." Patrice cooed.

"Excuse me, but what's happening?" Darcy raised a hand like she was in school.

"You're being adopted!" René called from the next room. "If you don't mind," she added.

"No, sorry hun, you don't get a choice in the matter. You, quite frankly, need some help, and we are in a position to provide it. So you're staying until you're sorted." Patrice declared.

"They took you in just like that?"

"Yeah. Why do you think I love them?"

"You must have looked absolutely awful."

"I did. But they kept me anyway."

"And everything went downhill from there?"

"And everything got very scary for me moving forward from there, yes. First there was Winter."

" 'Winter,' as in…?"

"Winter, as in the representative of a gang interested in getting New Pensacola under the control of the Catholic Church, and also Winter, as in Anton's ex-wife."

"And you did something stupid."

"Define *stupid*."

Connie only looks at her with an eyebrow raised.

"Okay, so"—Darcy flops back onto the couch, gesturing wildly with her hands—"for like three months, the messenger job was great. I got to run around and see things and hear all the gossip, and sometimes I got invited to bars or told to go to bars and deliver breakup messages. Drunk people getting their hearts broke are great—really entertaining. And bars are a great place to meet attractive women—" Darcy glances at her new bride and quickly changes the topic.

"So, I was at the particular bar that's important to this story because someone told me to deliver a message to a lady there, but they didn't tell me what she looked like, only gave me a name and said she'd be real obvious. So when a pretty lady with really loud hair walked up, said she was expecting a message, and looked at me like she wanted to do terrible things, well…I let her."

Connie laughs, and Darcy loves her even more than she did a minute ago.

"It was great—not as great as you, honey, but I didn't know you yet. Anyway, after we got done with the terrible things, she asked what the message was, and I told her, and she's like, 'that's not a message for me; who the fuck is Shelby?' and she looked real annoyed, but then I distracted her for a bit, so that was good. But then, after that, I made the mistake of complimenting her tattoo. And then she chased me out of her place with a knife and called her friends to also chase me, and I had to punch a bunch of them. And then I ran back to my aunt and uncles' place. And *they yelled at me!*"

December

"You know, if I knew I'd have to patch you up every time you got in a fight, I would have asked how often you got into fights."

"More often than I should, but not as much as some people. Ow."

Patrice was wrapping Darcy's knuckles after Darcy'd run into the houseboat screaming about how last night's hookup wanted to kill her. Patrice sighed. "What did the tattoo look like?"

"Why is that important?" The bandages tightened enough to make Darcy wince. "A fleur-de-lis with a 'C' in it. I thought it might be an initial or something."

"That's the symbol of the Cardinals, hun. They're a gang. You are now involved in gang affairs." Patrice could be incredibly blunt when they wanted to be.

"*What? How?* I just slept with a pretty woman!"

"Yeah, and now she probably thinks you're a spy. She and the Cardinals work for the church. They handle everything the holy people don't wanna dirty their hands with."

"Are we talking about my ex-wife?" Anton inserted himself into the conversation. He was constantly inserting himself into things, and Darcy had yet to decide if this was something she liked about him or not.

"I don't know, what's your ex-wife's name?"

"Winter."

"So, I slept with your ex-wife."

"What is she doing sleeping with girls half her age?"

"She thought I was a messenger—"

"You are a messenger."

"She thought I was a messenger for her specifically, and I was not. And now she thinks I'm a spy, and my life might be in danger, according to your gentleman wife."

"My gentleman wife is usually correct. But you're not going to die. When we took you in, so tiny and fragile and stupid—"

"That was three months ago, Anton."

"—*so incredibly stupid*…I made a promise to myself, and also to René, and to God, that we weren't going to let you get hurt because of that stupidity. You keep throwing yourself into situations you don't know how to handle because you're used to dealing with small-town problems."

"Fun fact—" René popped her head into the room because she was an insufferable gossip.

"Oh, now René's got opinions," Darcy muttered.

"You can't solve all your problems by running away from them, Darcy-baby." René continued as if Darcy had not spoken.

"I can try! And what do you know?"

"Everything. I'm brilliant and a chronic eavesdropper, and I also had a phase very similar to what you're going through now. Ah, the joys of being twenty and having bad taste in women." She draped herself dramatically against a wall, sighing theatrically until Darcy cracked a smile.

"She's right. You can't solve your problems by running away every time," Patrice said. Darcy only glared at them.

Anton placed a friendly hand on Darcy's shoulder. "That's why we're kicking you out."

"*What?*"

"Anton, be nice!" Patrice smacked Anton upside the head. "Don't listen to him, hun. We're not getting rid of you."

"We just think it might be a good idea if we sent you to some friends on the other side of town," René added quickly.

"When did you come up with this plan?"

"About ten minutes ago, when you came home after another fight you learned nothing from," said Anton.

"But—"

"It'll be good for you. You'll get to see more of the city. Besides, we've got work to do." Patrice cut Darcy off by hugging her to their chest. "We're not ditching you for shits and giggles, Darcy-babe. Autumn is rest time for most of the trading barges and caravans. But now that hurricane season is over, the boats are out again, and they need security. They're not gonna let us bring our adoptive whatever-you-are with us on a three-month haul to the Yucatán."

"I could learn from you!"

"You'll learn more by staying in town, practicing those fighting forms I showed you and lying low."

René joined the hug. "Look, you're trying to run down the clock until you can join the Academy, right? This will keep you alive long enough to do that."

"But—"

"Darcy, it's for the best."

She hated it when Anton was right.

"So I agreed with them, because they're a lot smarter than me, and I went and stayed with a friend of theirs for three months, and I even managed to keep my job, which was great. But then, on the day I go back to visit the auncles—"

"That's not a word."

"Is now. Anyway, the day I went back to visit them, I got yelled at! Again! It was my own fault, but still!"

March

"What did you do this time?" Anton looked tired.

Darcy paddled in the water next to the newly returned houseboat. She opened her mouth, but Anton held up a hand.

"Get out of the water before you start talking. Your mouth could run on forever and a day."

"Well, do you want me to explain myself or not?"

Patrice, who had a sense for these things, appeared with dry clothes.

"I wanna know why we leave for a couple months, and the first thing I see when we get back isn't my good liquor, but fucking Royalists at our house sniffing around for you at an ungodly hour of the morning."

"To be fair, I was going to come over and say hello anyway. Things just happened—"

"And why did you swim here if no one was chasing you?" Patrice, as always, asked the sensible questions.

"It's a good way not to be seen. Wait, what do you mean, *Royalists*?"

"I mean Royalists, a gang that you should absolutely not be messing with, both because you're an idiot and because I hope you have principles."

"There's more than one gang?"

"Honey, do you pay attention to anything?" Anton began one of his now-familiar *Darcy-girl-how-are-you-this-dumb?* lectures. "How have you been working six months as a messenger—someone who is practically paid to gossip—and not know about the founding institutions of this town?"

"I thought the founding institutions were the Academy and the book barges?"

"Hell no! It's the church and the people with money! How have you managed to get both of them on your ass?"

"She was using me as a front for stolen goods!" Darcy decided then was a good time to have a little cry; it had been a long day, and she'd been broken up with again, and she'd really missed her auncles.

"What?"

"Who'd you sleep with this time?" As always, René appeared when gossip became inevitable.

"Her name is Anne, and I thought she was so nice! She was interested in me! She liked to hear about my job and all the gossip I was collecting, and how I'm going to be at the Academy next year, and she wasn't associated with Winter at all—like she knows *of* her, but she hates her, and that's good because I love making fun of my exes with my current girlfriend—"

"Hun, I love ya, but get to the point," Patrice said with a soothing hand on Darcy's head.

Darcy sniffled pathetically. "She asked if I'd go pick some stuff up for her 'cause she was busy one time, and then it happened again, and then it happened again, and she said I was better at bargaining than her, and I am not immune to flattery, so I kept going and picking up her shit from this guy she knew, and that went on for like two months, but I got cornered by half the market this morning because it turns out everything she was buying was stolen! And she was blaming me! She only wanted me because I'm gonna be at the Academy, and she wanted an insider there!" Darcy collapsed into Patrice's chest.

They petted her hair. "Hun, this is a situation that absolutely couldn't have been avoided, you're fine."

"P, stop lying to her," Anton snapped.

"Oh, be nice! It's not her fault she's an idiot." René was *also* blunt when she wanted to be.

"René!" Darcy whined, already embarrassed and sad enough without being called an idiot.

"She's joking, hun," Patrice said.

"No, I'm not." René took Patrice's slap to her shoulder with no remorse.

"Can't I come with you on your next haul? Maybe you can leave me in Panama somewhere. I'm obviously not meant for this life."

"We can't bring you."

"And stop being dramatic. You're not gonna die."

"*But you said there's gangs after me!*"

"And if you lay low for a while and don't cause any trouble, they'll lose interest."

"That's what you said last time!"

"Well, this time, you can stay with someone else. There's a lot of rent houses on the east end. You could stay there for a few months. Different part of town, a change of pace, and as long as you don't stick your nose into anything, you should be fine."

Darcy nodded and reluctantly agreed.

"And then you stuck your nose into more things."

"I stuck my nose into *you*."

"You've stuck in more than that." Connie makes some *very* rude hand gestures.

"You're asking for it!" Darcy begins tickling her, and it's a good half hour of laughing, throwing pillows, and making out before they settle down again.

"Okay, okay, I know this part of the story." Connie adopts her own storytelling voice: "The silly young thing stays at a rent house, gets on friendly terms with the landlord, and keeps practicing her fighting. She's getting pretty good with her fists and a knife, which is why, when the extremely pretty wife of said landlord goes missing and it's assumed to be a kidnapping, he offers the silly young thing three months' free rent to bring her back. And the silly young thing goes and gets herself tangled up in a political conspiracy. Again."

June

"Explain it to me again." Darcy gestured at the very pretty lady who might just have been able to solve all her problems. Said pretty lady was very tall, with loose, dark curls pulled back into a ponytail and a large number of tax documents in her hands.

"I arranged the kidnapping myself. I'm trying to nail my idiot husband for some of the stuff he does on the side and get his money. Problem is, everyone he works with keeps to themselves. I don't even have names for some of these people. Like the broad who runs the Royalists—"

"Her name's Anne. She makes most of her cash by reselling stolen goods. Decent lay."

The pretty lady's face glowed with surprise. Darcy blushed. "*Oh, we're friends now,*" the pretty lady said. Darcy blushed harder. "Any chance you know anything about their finances?"

"I can tell you what bars they frequent and their shopping patterns and who's dating who." Darcy's job had made her supremely nosy.

"I stand corrected. We're *best* friends. I'm Constance."

"I'mma call you Connie."

"No one had ever called me Connie before."

"And that's why I'm gonna call you Connie for the rest of our lives." Darcy kisses Connie briefly. "The hardest part was explaining it to the family."

"She seduced you!" Anton accused.

"A bit. But we have a plan!" Darcy tried to bring her uncle's attention back to her brilliance, but Anton was already on a roll.

"You've pissed off the Academy and the two biggest gangs in town, and now you've got a hit out on you because an older woman seduced you. If you were smart, you'd leave town."

"I'm not leaving without Connie."

"Oh, you're *serious* about this girl." Patrice realized, surprised.

"Yeah, *and we have a plan*!" Darcy repeated.

"This will go well." Anton tried to leave the room.

"Shut up. I want to hear it." René didn't physically restrain her spouse, but it was a near thing.

"We want to turn them against each other. Everyone thinks I'm working for someone else, which is funny 'cause I lost my job this morning, so I'm not working for anyone."

"You lost your job?"

"I'm a liability, apparently. Anyway, all we need to do is convince both the gangs and Connie's shit of an about-to-be-ex-husband that the others have sensitive information on them and get them at each other's throats enough that they forget about me! Maybe I can make Winter and Anne fight each other." That was a lovely prospect.

"And what about the man who put a hit on you for seducing his wife?"

"We're gonna blame him. The story—" Darcy paints the picture: "A man with a reliable source of income from the rent houses wants to secure his place in the city. Take out some of the bigger players, you know? He's got a lot of contacts, but the contacts are a double-edged sword. When everyone knows you, *everyone* knows you. So what does he do when he wants to start shit? He hires a newly arrived out-of-towner to cause problems with the gangs and steal information. But he doesn't tell his hire that, no, he just tells poor little me to go places and say certain things to certain people." At this point, Darcy started smiling, because if there was anything she could do, it was tell a story.

"Darcy-babe, that just might work. Who'd you blab to, and what help do you need?" Patrice places a hand on her shoulder.

"Just the mayor, a couple pastors, and the members of the Academy staff that would speak to me. Connie fake-cried to a some people about how her husband's business interests got her kidnapped. If you could pretend to be some bodyguards we hired to keep her safe because we were just *so* worried, that would be great."

"Darcy, you're a good girl." René patted Darcy's shoulder.

"Also, me and Connie are engaged."

"*WHAT?*"

September (Again)

"And it worked."

"And it worked! Showed up with half a dozen recommendation letters from town officials, you know, as a show of gratitude, with only a few bruises from a fistfight, and they let me in. Now I'll even know how to fight on top of my other obvious skills."

"You better keep practicing telling that story, because you're gonna need to tell absolutely everyone. You took down a town's political system just because a pretty lady asked you to."

"And I'd do it again." Darcy smiles at her wife, the manic energy of storytelling leaving her, replaced with something softer as she contemplates what might come next. "Look at everything it got me."

Spongeunction   *"untitled"*
_____
Next page
Spongeunction opted not to share the inspiration behind this artwork.

Heartbeat

– E. V. Dean

An agonized scream fills the air. Athos whips his head around to find the source, giving up the small advantage he's gained on his two attackers, but how could he not? He knows the voice so well—it's Aramis. And he's hurt. Was it his stomach, the blade piercing his vital organs? Or was it his heart? No, Aramis is still standing, though as if held up only by the tip of the sword dug into his thigh.

He won't be standing for long. He needs help—the one thing Athos can't offer right now. He tears his eyes away from the red soaking Aramis's trousers and back to the two blades that crave to turn his own shirt the same shade. He dodges the swordsmen and dives between their thick frames.

Athos twirls on his heel, and with a wide swing, he jams his sword into one man's arm. The other stabs at him, and Athos narrowly blocks his blade.

What follows is a flurry of blocks and parries; facing two swords with just his one, Athos's only saving grace is the inexperience that his adversaries share in team fighting. With his arm raised against one strike, his heart's out in the open, waiting for the taste of steel that never comes.

Or maybe they don't want to kill him. It had been self-defense when Aramis had thrust his sword into their friend's heart, but now it's life or death. Maybe they're only out for Aramis's blood—merely keeping Athos occupied while their remaining friend exacts revenge.

Athos has to reach Aramis.

He kicks out, his boot connecting with an ankle, and his opponent goes down.

Aramis collapses into the dust.

Aramis's attacker towers above him like a lighthouse, eager to shatter Aramis against his rocks. He kicks Aramis's side with a heavy boot, cursing in his fallen friend's name. Avenging with bruises before stealing Aramis's last breath.

Aramis is unmoving; he doesn't reach for his dropped sword, still loyally near his palm. The attacker raises his blade, the final rays of orange sun gleaming on its edge.

Athos has to save him—he must reach the killer before he strikes Aramis's heart. The tip of Athos's sword seems almost to touch the man's side when he is yanked backward. An arm snakes around his neck, holding him in place, and the tip of a blade bites into his back.

He kicks and elbows, trying to wriggle out of the hold, but even if he could, he wouldn't get to Aramis in time.

The sword begins to plunge—

A *bang* rips through the air as the bullet tears into the would-be killer. Another bang, and he stumbles a few steps backward. His sword clinks against the ground, surprise on his face, his eyes fixed on the shooters. On Porthos and d'Artagnan, muskets in their hands. He collapses to the ground with a loud *thud*.

Now, the remaining two appear to not like their odds. They could easily knife Athos, but they let him go instead. They won't leave this place alive otherwise.

Freed, Athos shoots to Aramis's side, trusting Porthos and d'Artagnan to deal with the scoundrels.

"Aramis!" Athos drops to his knees next to him.

Aramis's voice slurs when he speaks. "Athos…"

He's breathing rapidly, mouth agape, and half his face is bloodied by a streaming gash on his forehead. One eye is sealed shut, but the other is wide open and locked on Athos.

"I'm here. You're safe."

Athos squeezes his hand, then slips out of his grasp, shifting to take a closer look at his torn thigh. The ground has turned a gruesome shade of maroon, and he fears that soon there will be more blood outside of Aramis's body than inside it.

The laceration itself looks manageable: it's the length of a finger, the edges clean-cut. It won't be any different from tending a soldier's wounds after the dust of the battle settles. Never mind that Aramis isn't just any soldier.

But all Athos has are his own hands, his own clothes. He slips his coat off and yanks at the sleeve of his shirt until the stitches give in and the fabric tears off. He presses it to the wound, and Aramis jolts, a scream torn from his lips. Athos's fingers slip on the slick blood, and he has to hold Aramis's leg with his other hand to keep the makeshift bandage in place.

"I'm so sorry," Athos huffs.

D'Artagnan arrives, then, out of breath as he kneels on Aramis's other side. "You hold," he commands Athos. "I'll tie it."

As Athos applies pressure, d'Artagnan pulls off his belt, then wraps it around Aramis's thigh and fastens it on top of the impromptu dressing, freeing Athos's hand.

"Porthos went to personally escort the king's surgeon," d'Artagnan adds.

"Only the best for our friend," Athos says and gives Aramis a soft smile.

But Aramis doesn't seem to see him anymore; his open eye glides around, unable to focus.

"How bad—?" he asks, his words slow, as if forcing his tongue to move takes more effort than he can spare.

"It's not that bad," Athos says, trying to comfort both Aramis and himself. "You'll be fine. It's just—"

"—trifles?" Aramis supplies.

Athos could swear there's a ghost of a smile on Aramis's lips.

"Yes, it's trifles," Athos says.

It's Athos now who finds Aramis's hand, to let him know he's right there with him. He doesn't let go even as Aramis's head droops to the side, both eyes closed.

"Room?" Athos shouts to the innkeeper. Aramis is cradled in his arms, his head resting on his chest; d'Artagnan follows right behind them.

Athos should have sent d'Artagnan ahead to make sure there'd be a place for them. If he has to, he'll lay his friend on the nearest table and get rid of all the staring patrons, politeness be damned.

The room they're led to is small, the bed taking up half the space, but it's warm and clean and it's the best they can get for Aramis right now. Athos sets him down gently, and they undress him to assess him for other wounds. They pull off his boots, remove his coat, and peel off his bloody shirt. But aside from his thigh, his face, and a cut on his shoulder, there's only bruising.

The innkeeper's daughter brings warm water, and they clean the blood off their hands. Even as they scrub, it remains under their fingernails, in the creases of their skin—it's everywhere but in Aramis's veins where it should be.

How much did he lose? Is there a limit, a line beyond which there is no turning back? There must be.

Did he cross it?

D'Artagnan has to be thinking the same. He casts a careful glance at Aramis, then back to Athos. "You meant it, right?" he asks. "When you said he'd be fine?"

There's something almost childlike in his voice—as if he's holding onto hope but his grip is slipping, and he needs someone who knows better to give him a hand.

But Athos doesn't know better. Not anymore. Athos had fainted from blood loss in the past, but it couldn't have been more than a few minutes before he woke up with the king's surgeon stooped over him. With Aramis, much longer than that has passed already, and there's no sign of consciousness.

What if they got to him a few drops of blood too late because Athos wasn't fast enough or strong enough?

Everything in him wants so desperately to tell d'Artagnan, yes, he'll be fine. But instead, he says, "Take care of the shoulder."

D'Artagnan must realize that's the most he's going to get from him, because he gets to work and remains quiet.

In the silence, Athos is swept up in his own thoughts. He'd escalated the squabble into a fight, like a hotheaded fool. What the hell got into him, he doesn't know. It had been such a nice afternoon: just the two of them, dining and chatting as they waited for Porthos and d'Artagnan to join them. A nice afternoon could have become a wonderful evening, the innkeeper's finest red wine flowing into the late hours.

And now, because Athos had been so easily provoked, Aramis lies there, his breathing so shallow that, even as Athos leans close to his lips, he can barely feel any air coming from between them. His skin—what isn't covered in bruises and drying blood—is almost as pale as the white sheets beneath him.

Athos cups Aramis's jaw as he wipes the blood away with a wet cloth. He moves gently across his cheekbone, his hairline. His touch is as gentle as he can manage, as if it could cause agony, even though Aramis is deep in his slumber and he can't grunt or flinch or feel a thing. It's good, Athos tells himself. He's not in pain for a while.

Selfishly, though, he'd rather have his groans and screams than this uncertain silence.

He carefully wipes the blood from Aramis's eyelid so that when he wakes up, he can open both his eyes and focus them properly: on Athos, on his surroundings. On the world that is too close to slipping away from him. Athos makes sure there are no cuts around his eye, but luckily all the blood came from the gash on his forehead. Aramis will be inconsolable about the scar, as if that small mark could make him any less beautiful.

Athos buries his fingertips in the soft curls at Aramis's temple to keep his head steady. He can't risk reopening the wound and costing Aramis more blood. Should he leave it to the surgeon? Where is he, anyway? It feels like too much time has passed, and Aramis is fading away with every second.

Athos glances at d'Artagnan to check on his progress and finds his eyes fixated not on the shoulder he's tending, but on Athos's hands: on his thumb stroking Aramis's cheekbone every time his other hand dabs at the wound. A small, tender comfort Athos has given unconsciously, and now that he's been caught, he freezes.

Is it wrong? The heat flooding his stomach tells him it is. He holds his breath, unsure whether to pull back or keep from making sudden movements, and the moment lasts forever, until d'Artagnan realizes he's been caught, too. His eyes flick to Athos's, then quickly away.

Before either of them can say anything, the door opens, and Porthos announces, "The surgeon's here."

It takes a lot of convincing for Athos to let Porthos take care of his back wound. He'd forgotten about his encounter with the tip of a blade entirely. With his whole being focused on Aramis, he didn't even feel the pain. It's barely more than a prickle—it doesn't need all the fuss, and the fuss doesn't take his mind off Aramis even for a second.

But it does help pass some of the long time that the surgeon spends in Aramis's room.

When the surgeon finally comes out wearing an unreadable expression, Athos is crowding him before he can even close the door.

"How is he? Did he wake up? Is he going to be all right?"

To Athos's frustration, the surgeon doesn't seem in a hurry to answer. He takes his time closing the door before turning to face the three of them.

"I stopped the bleeding and closed the wound," he says, then pauses. Athos somehow restrains himself from grabbing him and shaking him like an apple tree for the answers he wants.

Porthos puts his hand on Athos's shoulder to calm him. "So he's going to be all right?"

"I don't know."

They're not words Athos expected to hear from a surgeon. What was all his medical study for if he doesn't know the answer to such a simple question? "He lost a lot of blood. He might recover, or his organs might stop working. It's out of my hands now."

His organs? Athos swallows in disbelief. "So whose hands is it in?" Even as he asks the question, he already knows the answer. Were Aramis awake, he'd be chastising him for his doubts. But he's not awake, and his organs might shut down.

The surgeon offers his prayers.

But Aramis's life is worth too much to wage on a prayer.

"Make sure he stays warm," the surgeon instructs. "If he makes it to the morning, he'll have a much better chance."

With that, he leaves the three of them and goes to the room Porthos had rented for him so he could be nearby. But with a diagnosis like that, with Aramis's recovery or death being out of his hands and in God's, would there be anything left for him to do if Aramis started slipping away? Or will his only use, the next time he enters Aramis's room, be to check for the lack of his breath and heartbeat, and announce Athos's worst fear coming true?

Athos can't think that way. He must have faith, must pray and hope that God makes an exception for Aramis. Why shouldn't He? Aramis is the man of faith, the temporary musketeer, always on the verge of quitting the sword to join the monastery.

Athos should have let him go the last time Aramis was so set on giving himself over to the service of God. If Athos hadn't been so selfish, Aramis would be far away. Athos would miss him every second, but at least he'd be safe: walking, talking, praying—instead of needing others' prayers.

Athos rushes into the room, Porthos and d'Artagnan close behind him. They take the seats around Aramis's bed, as if there is anything for them to do besides stare at him. His leg is freshly bandaged, but his eyes are still closed, skin so white it's almost translucent, and the only sign of life is his shallow breathing.

"We should watch him in turns," Porthos suggests.

Athos shakes his head. "No. I'll stay," he says. "I won't be able to sleep anyway."

"You think we will?" d'Artagnan says wryly.

Of course they won't. How could they, if at any moment death might reach out its clawed fingers and drag Aramis away? How could they risk falling asleep only to wake up in a world without Aramis in it?

Athos can't begrudge his friends wanting to stay, but he isn't sure he can bear their presence. He whispers the words he wants to scream out: "You're not the ones responsible for this. It's my fault."

He'd told them the story while Porthos patched him up, but he hadn't told them the *entire* story. He hadn't told them the insults the men had hurled at them, and how they affected him more strongly than they should have. How he hadn't thought clearly before drawing his sword. Nor had he told Porthos about Aramis's palm on his shoulder, trying to stop him, before the only option left was joining him.

Athos can still feel the weight of that hand.

"What's your fault?" asks Porthos dismissively. "That you didn't stop Aramis from defending his honor, too? A *musketeer's* honor?"

Honor? He's had honorable fights aplenty, but this one was different. Athos should have scolded the men for their jeering laughter and the words they'd thrown at him and Aramis—could even have threatened them for offending the king's musketeers. He should only have fought had they remained disrespectful.

But upon hearing their words, his skin had flushed with heat. His head had filled with the buzzing of a thousand bees, his hand itching for his sword.

And then the men had grabbed the bottle they'd been sharing and hurled it to the floor, spattering Aramis's boots with red wine...

"It doesn't matter," Athos says firmly, ending the discussion. "I'm staying here. You two take the other room and get some rest."

Perhaps it's selfish of him, but he doesn't care—as long as he can tell himself it's about responsibility, instead of it being because he needs to be by Aramis's side in what might be the last hours of his life.

The time ticks by slowly, as if each break between Aramis's breaths takes forever. Eventually, the rowdy sounds of revelry downstairs die away as guests shuffle to their rooms for the night.

Silence falls over the inn.

Aramis's heartbeat is as loud as a hammer, as hasty as a galloping steed and just as steady. It has to be a good sign. Athos can't help glancing to the window, into the endless darkness beyond, hoping for a miraculously early sunrise. As if the first rays of sun, harbingers of the morning, could cure Aramis solely because they'd mean he'd made it through the night.

But it's a long way to go until then.

"You know *all for one* doesn't go for petty brawls, right?" Athos whispers, hardly breaking the unbearable silence.

And yet, Aramis's blade was out almost as soon as Athos's. And if it hadn't been for him, it'd be Athos lying here now—or in the deadhouse. Still, if it meant Aramis's recovery, Athos would switch places with him in an instant.

"There are no 'Inseparables' without you, Aramis," Athos says, his voice wavery. "We need you here, so you'd better fight like hell to come back to us."

Athos takes Aramis's hand—it's so cold. Was it this cold before? The surgeon instructed them to keep him warm, and Athos is failing at that vital yet simple task.

He gathers every blanket and cover he finds in the room and lays them over Aramis. But those will do little to give him back the heat he's lost.

Athos can't give Aramis his blood or his life, but he can offer his own warmth.

Carefully, Athos slips into the bed and settles under the blankets, his shoulder pressed along Aramis's. At first, he can feel the cold emanating from his friend, but soon his own body warmth cocoons them both.

When he's lying this close, Aramis's heartbeat is a comforting rhythm. Athos can listen to it with his eyes closed and be assured that Aramis is still alive.

"Aren't you going to say goodbye?"

Athos's eyes snap open. Did someone say something, or had he imagined the sound?

He's not at home. A foreign ceiling hangs above him, painted silver in the fuzzy moonlight.

It takes him a moment to remember.

He turns his head, but the space beside him is empty. "Aramis?" Athos tries to sit up, but the weight of the blankets on top of him won't let him move.

"I'm here," Aramis says.

Athos blinks, and the room comes into focus. Aramis stands a few steps away from the bed, fully dressed in pristine clothes, both his legs steady.

"How are you—?" Athos trails off. He doesn't know whether he's asking how Aramis is feeling, or how he's on his feet.

"I'm well," Aramis says solemnly. "Very well. I'm not in any pain."

Something sinks in the pit of Athos's stomach. If only he could crawl out from under all these blankets holding him down, he could reach out to Aramis and touch him, make sure he's really all right.

"I was so worried," Athos finally says. "I hate seeing you in pain."

"And I hate worrying you," Aramis says with a small smile. "I won't do that anymore."

"Come, lie down," Athos says uneasily. "You need to rest." He tries again, in vain, to get up, so Aramis can have the bed.

Aramis just shakes his head. "I have to go." He shouldn't even be standing upright.

"Go where?"

"Where I'm supposed to be. With God," Aramis says as if it's the most obvious thing in the world.

"To the monastery?" Athos furrows his brow. "Surely it can wait a week or two…"

Aramis lets out an amused huff and crouches close to the bed, his eyes level with Athos's, a condescending smile on his lips.

"You still don't understand? Listen."

Athos strains his ears, but there's nothing to hear. No other voices, no morning ruckus or birds in the trees.

There's no thumping of the heartbeat that lulled him to sleep.

There's only silence.

"No," Athos whispers. He understands now: Aramis isn't going to serve God.

He's going to meet Him.

"Aren't you going to say goodbye?" Aramis asks again.

He straightens and turns away. Athos strains to move his arm, to stop him, but his fingers only graze Aramis's.

"No!" he yells. "Aramis, come back!"

His own screaming awakens him. He'd rolled over in his sleep, and now his head is resting on Aramis's chest, ear pressed tight over his heart.

But the heart is quiet and still.

"Please, no! You can't leave me," he begs, clutching at Aramis's shirt.

This must be another cruel dream, and he'll wake up any moment now to Aramis, safe and sound. He holds his breath and listens harder, waiting for the tiniest *thump* beyond his ribs.

Please beat, please beat.

The words drone in his head, and his fist hammers against Aramis's rib cage to the missing rhythm, only half registering that he must be hurting Aramis.

But he can't hurt him. Not anymore. His hands can't draw bruises nor give him comfort.

Tears well up in his eyes, and his voice shakes. "I'm begging you, God, give him back."

Does this count as a prayer? Or should he kneel and put his palms together, like a child about to go to sleep?

Does it matter? Isn't prayer in the words, in the thoughts, in the intentions?

"What do you want him for?" he cries. "You don't need him as much as I do!"

He can't bear the thought of waking up tomorrow, and every day after, knowing Aramis won't be there. He needs his smiles and words, his warm touches, the comfort of him near. With him gone, it won't just be the Inseparables that get broken apart, it'll be Athos's heart, too. Aramis isn't merely a friend—hasn't been for a long time, has he?

The way Athos feels has been something he couldn't name, but now it comes to him, burning bright and fiery, the easiest words he's ever known.

"I love him," he breathes. It becomes a desperate litany: "I love him, God. I love him. I love him. Please, don't make me lose him."

He can't stop the tears that soak through Aramis's shirt. It doesn't matter. Soon they'll have to change him into his best clothes and put him in the ground. He'll turn cold as the night air. His beautiful face will bloat and rot and fall away.

And Athos will have never spoken those words to him.

"Aramis, please, I—"

A loud sob escapes his throat as two pairs of arms wrap around him and pull him off Aramis.

"Calm yourself," d'Artagnan says, struggling to drag him away. "Let the surgeon through."

Athos averts his eyes as the surgeon goes to Aramis's side. He doesn't want to see him press his ear to Aramis's chest only to pronounce him dead. He doesn't want to hear those words.

Instead the surgeon says, "His heartbeat is weak but even."

Athos slumps in his friends' arms, as stunned as if someone has slapped him across the face. Athos could swear Aramis's heartbeat wasn't there when he'd listened for it.

Did his fist bring him back, or his fervent prayer?

He needs to get to Aramis, but the surgeon isn't done with his examination. He's looking over Aramis's skin and fingernails, into his mouth, his eyes. He decides that Aramis hasn't gotten worse. That time might be a friend after all, and not an enemy.

Once the surgeon shuffles out, followed by Porthos and d'Artagnan, Athos can at last kneel by Aramis's bed and put his head to his chest.

There it is: the quiet but distinct thumping of his heart.

Despite Athos's desire to be there when Aramis woke up, the stress of the night had taken its toll on him. The next thing he knows, Porthos is gently shaking his shoulder, and Aramis is beaming tiredly at him from the bed.

Athos, Porthos, and d'Artagnan spend most of the afternoon taking turns doting on Aramis and letting him rest. Although eager to return home, they decide it's better to let Aramis get his strength back before moving him.

The whole time, Athos is wary of each glance and word thrown his way by his companions. Did Aramis hear him in his dreams? Did Porthos and d'Artagnan hear his confession as they entered the room last night? They must have—they must have been right at the door as Athos cried those words. Would they remain so restrained if they disapproved of him for it, or would they have confronted him by now?

But they don't mention it as they recount to Aramis everything that he'd missed, nor do they say anything when Aramis discovers the bruises on his chest that weren't the result of the fight. The closest indication is the gentle way Porthos squeezes Athos's shoulder as he and d'Artagnan leave for supper. It feels almost encouraging.

This is the moment Athos has been dreading and waiting for: him and Aramis alone, both of them conscious this time. In the daylight, with Aramis safe and on the mend, all of Athos's desperate courage has dissipated and nerves have filled the space where it had been.

"I hope the bruises don't hurt too badly," Athos says, gesturing at Aramis's chest.

Aramis lets out a huff. "No more than everything else."

Athos drops his eyes to his hands folded in his lap. Of course, short of breaking his ribs, Athos couldn't hurt him more than the fight had. The fight he'd started. The reason for his sudden anger and loss of control had been a mystery to Athos until last night's revelation. But his feelings are hardly an excuse.

"I'm sorry," he says. "I was an idiot for pulling out my sword—you almost died because of me."

To Athos's surprise, Aramis scoffs. "You think I didn't want to put them in their place, too?"

Athos's eyes snap back to Aramis. Athos hadn't considered that Aramis might have wanted to fight them as well. Why would he? Was it the musketeer's honor…or could it be something else, something akin to Athos's own feelings?

What a preposterous thought.

It had to be the offense, not the mockery, that had gotten to him.

Yet as Aramis holds Athos's gaze, unblinking, a flicker of sadness appears in his eyes before Aramis at last turns away.

"They don't get to judge us for who they think we are," Aramis says firmly.

It takes a moment for the words to fully sink in, the "us" resounding like a confirmation. Or close to one, close enough to turn Athos's doubt into a resolution. Hadn't he grieved over the idea that he would never have the chance to tell him? If there were even a chance Aramis might feel the same, wouldn't it be better to take a risk than to keep his lips sealed forever?

"There's something I want to tell you."

Aramis quirks an eyebrow at him. The pinks and oranges of the setting sun paint his face with the warmth and color that's yet to return to his skin. Even now, with the bandages and bruises, he looks beautiful.

"Last night, when your heartbeat went missing…" Athos wishes he'd prepared better. "I was so sure you were dead, and I—"

"—and you decided to bring me back by punching me." There's amusement in Aramis's voice, but the inquiry hasn't gone from his brow.

Athos huffs out a laugh, and he doesn't mind the interruption—the reminder of how easily

Aramis can make him smile. "I tried praying, too," Athos admits. "And almost losing you made me realize…" He takes a steadying breath and looks Aramis in the eye. "I love you," he says. "Not just as a friend."

In the tense silence that follows, he tries to read Aramis's face, but for the first time, he can't. "I think I have for a long time. I know it's not right," he adds quickly, "and I don't demand that you feel the same way. Just say one word, and we'll never speak of it again. Your friendship is more than enough, and I cherish it too much to risk losing it, but I needed you to know—"

"Athos."

Athos stops talking. He avoids Aramis's eyes for fear of what he'll find in them, his gaze wandering over the pattern of the knitted blanket instead.

Aramis continues, "I think you've just said more words than I've heard you say in a year." He sounds…amused.

Athos lifts his eyes to meet the new, unexpected softness in Aramis's stare. Too surprised to speak, Athos says nothing.

"I'm glad you told me," Aramis says.

Athos blinks. "What are you saying?"

Aramis reaches his hand out to Athos, and he takes it without hesitation. "What I'm saying is…" Aramis pulls Athos's palm close and presses it to his chest. Beneath his fingers, there's the unsteady *thump* of Aramis's flustered heart. "My heart is beating thanks to you."

And there's something more, something that doesn't need to be said out loud—it's in the tenderness with which his eyes gaze into Athos's.

It beats for you.

Amalia Zeichnerin   *"Three of Hearts"*

I am part of a polyam[orous] polycule and thought, why not depict three queer musketeers in a polyam relationship? I didn't have any specific musketeers from literature or pop culture in mind and wanted to include a Black person because so far, I haven't seen any Black musketeers in stories.

When we lit up the night sky

—J. D. Rivers

Tags

warnings: violence (non-graphic descriptions)

relationships: established relationship, friends to lovers, m/m, m/m/m, polyamory, twosome to threesome

character features: criminal, veteran

other tags: action and adventure, angst, grieving, miscommunication, mistakenly believed to be dead, non-fanfiction story inspired by source material, past tense, science fiction, third person limited point of view

Inspiration

J. D. Rivers opted not to share the inspiration behind this story.

Closing the door felt final, and Elenar didn't know if he should exhale or inhale.

The glider hummed at the end of the path. Arden had already started it up and was shoving their bags into it.

At their backs hung an Imperial Planet Buster, like a ragged third moon between the white, fluffy clouds.

It wasn't there as a response to the recent talk of pirate activity.

Elenar drew a shaky breath. The air tasted of rain, heralding the coming spring flood. The small green fruits on the orange trees were in dire need of it; they should—

Ah, no, that was over now. Five years; they had only had five years.

Elenar exhaled, and despite everything, excitement curled low in his belly.

Down the hill, flashing purple military lights crawled nearer. They were cutting it close. He hurried to the glider, strapped himself in, and floored it.

As Arden pointed them through the maze-like roads of the surrounding farms, a triplet of Veter Hunter ships passed them overhead—sleek and arrow-like, hulls gleaming in the sun.

Veter and Empire on the same planet, and the signature on the official peace treaty wasn't even a week old.

Elenar swallowed. "Well, I guess that confirms our status as war criminals. Do you think the Veter have nicer cells than the Empire?"

Arden didn't chuckle—he hadn't spoken a word since the Planet Buster had appeared. He shrugged and fiddled with the radar, zooming in and out, turning the landscape this way and that. It made Elenar dizzy, which Arden knew. Elenar tamped the flash of annoyance down, focusing on the route.

They thundered down the last farm roads, out into the open land beyond. Grasslands stretched away on either side, and mountains rose in the distance. Elenar wondered if they could drive fast enough to escape to the stars.

The silence was getting to him. Arden had never been the most talkative, but he always voiced his opinion. But Arden hadn't said much in the last weeks—months, even.

Elenar tried again. "I'm betting the Veter want to know the secrets we pilfered from them. I'm sure they want to know exactly what we've seen in their space."

"They're no innocents," Arden mumbled.

Elenar glanced at him, noting Arden's pursed mouth and narrowed eyes. "No one was."

Once, they had been soldiers—the highest decorated agents of the Imperial Celestial Fleet. They had been "The Indestructibles," taking on the most dangerous and suicidal missions because Elenar had a bone to pick with the Veter. "The Invincibles," surviving even the greatest odds against them because Arden had contingency plans for contingency plans. "The Inseparables," because Darmos had led them on every mission.

They had danced through the stars and lit up the night sky.

And then three became two—one never returning from his last mission.

Afterward, to find peace, Elenar and Arden had left the military and their nicknames behind. They had settled on a backwater planet tending orange trees.

Beneath those same trees, Arden had made Elenar laugh for the first time since Darmos's death. Beneath the swaying white blossoms, they had kissed for the first time. And beneath the tender green leaves, a delicate new hope had unfurled in Elenar's chest.

Elenar flicked his eyes to Arden again, who still studied the radar as if it was a particularly difficult code to decrypt. His gaze took in his dull eyes, his frown, his turned-away body. A shadow had replaced him.

The grasslands shifted to sand and gravel, leading them down a dried-up riverbed through the towering stone walls of a canyon.

"We're here," Arden murmured, lacking any emotion, his shoulders sloped inward.

Elenar stopped the glider and opened his mouth to ask what the plan was, but Arden was already grabbing his pack and climbing out, not sparing Elenar a glance. For a split second, Elenar thought about flooring it, driving and driving, never stopping again, leaving it all behind. Just like Darmos had left them. But could he really be that callous?

Elenar followed Arden to two scrubby bushes that hid the entry to a small cave. They slipped in, their steps echoing along a dark path until they emerged into a domed room. Lights flickered on, and Elenar stopped at the sight of a fighter ship.

"How did you get your hands on a 147-x Shadow fighter?" Elenar asked as Arden pulled his pad from his bag. "They decommissioned them all after the armistice." He walked closer, reverence in every step.

Arden colored and typed something into his pad before answering. "An old contact tipped me off…" He shrugged.

Elenar ran his fingers over the synth-metal, brushing the serial number on a side panel. He read the numbers three times to be absolutely sure.

"This is *Milady*. This is Darmos's ship…" He trailed off, his fingers on the numbers that were engraved in his soul. He looked at Arden, but his eyes were on the cockpit, his gaze far away.

"Yes, it was," Arden said wistfully.

Elenar caressed the hull. Every scratch, every bump, every chafe was a testament to his own memories. They told of battles, of adrenaline pumping through his veins, of laughter over the comms and tears that no one witnessed, of kisses in the dark of a never-ending night.

"*Proximity alert*," the AI in Arden's pad said.

Arden cursed, checking his pad. "You remember how to fly this thing?" He rapped his knuckles against the hull.

Elenar threw him a wolfish smile. The excitement from earlier unfurled through his body as he knocked against the synth-metal. It almost felt like coming home.

Being a humble orange farmer had dulled Elenar's skills, but after a few adjustments, the *Milady* was almost docile in his hands. It was like riding a bicycle—if the bicycle could fly and shoot down other bicycles.

Calm settled inside Elenar, soothing an itch that had gotten increasingly difficult to ignore.

With both of them strapped in, Elenar in front and Arden squished in the back seat, Elenar squinted at the narrow cave opening. His fingers hovered over the flight controls. "How did you get this thing in here?"

"I collapsed the entrance. We'll have to leave the hard way." Was there a hint of excitement in Arden's voice?

"You're kidding." But even as he was saying it, Elenar was already running the necessary calculations.

A sound, almost a chuckle, escaped Arden, his breath moving the hairs on Elenar's neck. It was more intimate than anything they had done in weeks.

"Time to bust out the wrecking ball," Elenar said, unable to hold in a grin.

He engaged the thrusters, retracted the landing gear, and balanced them over the ground. The heat of the engines would gather in the small cave and overheat the fighter in minutes; he needed to work quickly. He aimed and fired, breaking down the stone around the passage opening to widen it.

The cave walls shuddered.

Elenar switched to the second laser to give the first one a rest. "How tight is the canyon?"

"You need to make a hard turn or we'll take damage to the nose or the stern."

"Aye."

Small stones and rubble rained down on them, drumming against the hull. Warnings indicating that the second laser was overheating appeared on the cockpit screen.

"Come on, baby, you saved our asses before—you can do it again."

Another few seconds, and there was light at the end of the tunnel. Elenar revved the engines. Laser fire from outside beat down the passage.

Grinning, Elenar let the fighter fly, and the waiting soldiers scrambled out of their way. He flew a tight turn, and then they were gaining altitude fast. Elenar drew the stick back, pointing the nose up, until the blue sky filled his entire vision. He laughed madly, the prickling sensation of joy running along his nerves. He might have joined the Imperial fleet to get revenge against the Veter, but this—the freedom to touch the sky—was why he had followed Darmos and Arden to every hellhole and back.

"I programmed a course in." Arden's voice had an odd quality, almost detached. "It will take us to the next system. You can go wherever you want from there."

"What? What do you mean, wherever I want?" Elenar tore his eyes from the sky, trying to get a glimpse of Arden's face, but the seat was in the way and Arden seemed to be shrinking back.

"*Incoming,*" the AI proclaimed.

"Eyes front," Arden said.

Elenar cursed, turning back to the radar. Dot after dot appeared behind them, gaining on them. Elenar pressed his lips into a thin line and made for the outer layers of the atmosphere.

Laser fire answered their escape attempt, but soon their pursuers fell away.

"Warning: reaching critical heat levels in five minutes."

The fighter groaned around them. The 147-x hadn't exactly been made for a planetary launch; it needed a special devil-may-care attitude to get them through the last stretch. Elenar tried to remember the calculations. "Will the *Milady* hold up?" He flicked over the readings, adjusting speed and angle, keeping the nose up.

"I checked her regularly for fractures and recalculated the heat levels with this planet's atmospheric composition," Arden answered.

"So, fingers crossed, and a prayer to the lords."

The fighter shuddered, rattling his bones, and the metal body bowed against the resistance. The stick jerked in Elenar's hands, and he threw all he had behind it, as if he was snapping off the roots that had bound him to the planet. He tightened his jaw, his teeth grinding together.

"Warning: reaching critical heat levels in one minute."

Elenar wondered what going out as a plasma ball would feel like—being a pulsing ball of energy and heat, slipping between the stardust as atoms, returning to where they all had come from. Was that what Darmos had felt when the Veter took out his scout ship?

"Cleared. Heat levels normalizing. Ship integrity at 83 percent."

It was almost disappointing to see the stars.

The ship trembled one last time and fell into a steady hum.

Elenar slumped in his seat. He had forgotten how physically taxing flying could be, and yet he had never felt better. "Are you still alive?"

Arden snorted.

"Incoming."

The radar filled with dots.

"Looks like they're desperate." Elenar rolled his shoulders back and cracked his neck. "Any last words?"

Arden whispered, "All for one."

Elenar revved the engines. "And one for all."

The comms crackled to life. "This is the Imperial Planet Buster *Cassiopeia* of the First Celestial Fleet, hailing the Shadow fighter. Identify yourself."

Elenar's finger hovered over the comms switch.

"Whatever you want to do, I trust you," Arden said. Elenar desperately wanted to see Arden's expression: was he excited, resigned, detached?

The *Cassiopeia* repeated their hail.

Elenar sighed, took the engines down a notch, and flicked the channel open. "This is First Lieutenant Elenar Windrunner, previously of the Second Celestial Fleet. Let us pass."

There was a long pause, and then a voice neither of them had ever wanted to hear again filled the cockpit. Sounding amused, a man said, "Windrunner. And let me guess: Greenwood."

General Arvent Solmier, once Private Solmier, had been a greenie with a tooth gap and too-long hair. He had run with them for three years, and though he had moved on through the ranks, they had remained friends.

And then he had commanded Darmos's ill-fated scout mission, and nothing had been the same again.

"I have a proposal," the general said into the silence. "The Empire needs soldiers like you. We may be at peace with the Veter, but we still have enemies, and you have proven your loyalty. I would like to reinstate you both into the fleet, each with your own command. Defend the home worlds against invasion. Against the injustice of them being taken in a power play. We would also overlook some, shall we say…indiscretions…from war times."

Elenar snorted, while Arden muttered, "What the hell…?"

Loyalty. Justice. The greater good. Elenar had once believed in those words, had fought by them. But now all he wanted… What *did* he want, exactly?

A new row of dots appeared: Veter Hunters and the larger motherships. They kept their distance; one wrong move and the armistice would be dust.

"Arden, do you really think I'd want to go somewhere without you?"

"Time and place, Elenar." Arden's voice was tired.

"Gentlemen," the general said impatiently, "my offer is time-limited. What is your answer?"

"Incoming."

The space in front of the cockpit rippled and warped, and a massive ship moved through the tear, broadcasting: "This is the *Ghosthunter*, and we claim this Shadow fighter as property."

Solmier sputtered down the comms before the *Cassiopeia* closed their line.

A minute later, the *Ghosthunter* was towing the *Milady* in; whatever proof their captain had presented must have been enough.

The main hangar was bustling with crew working on an eclectic collection of different fighters and shuttles.

A heavyset woman waved them out of the cockpit. In lieu of a greeting, she said, "The boss wants to talk to you." She pointed to a lanky youth who tapped something into his pad. "Follow him. No sense in running; the crew is advised to use force."

"Aye," Elenar and Arden said as one, falling into soldier mode. The youth turned and fast-walked them through a dizzying number of dark-gray corridors. Elenar tried to memorize the way, but it was impossible. Arden probably had it down, but Elenar couldn't catch his eye; his gaze never left their guide's back.

Elenar wondered what kind of power play they had been snared in. *Ghosthunter* wasn't aligned with the Imperial naming scheme for ships; the ship was most likely a mercenary or pirate. Why would they pick them up? Or was this just about adding another fighter to the collection in the hangar?

The youth, who hadn't said a word, stopped in front of a door and pressed a button. It took a full heartbeat before the door slid open. The youth pointed inside.

They stepped through and froze.

The impossible had happened.

Behind the desk, grinning broadly, sat the deceased Captain of the Second Celestial Fleet: Darmos Mountainmover.

"Long time no see, my friends."

Elenar blinked. This couldn't be right. Darmos was dead—the fleet had confirmed the kill. Heck, the Veter ship had confirmed the kill.

Before Elenar could think of what to say, Arden said, "Looks like the rumors were true."

Eleanor rounded on Arden. "You knew?"

Arden's shoulders did something between a hunch and a shrug. "My contacts couldn't confirm it for sure."

"Your contacts..." Elenar closed his eyes and exhaled, remembering how Arden had sprung into action the moment the Planet Buster appeared and that he'd had a Shadow fighter ready. The dark rings under Arden's eyes had had nothing to do with their relationship, and everything to do with secrets and half-truths. It all pointed to one possible explanation: Arden was back with the rebels.

Had everything been a lie? Had Elenar kidded himself that they had actually built something together? Had they *ever* had "something"?

Forget the relationship. "How long have you been working for the rebels?" Elenar ground out.

Arden looked at the floor.

Elenar balled his hands into fists. "What the hell? Solmier could blast us out of the sky for treason! And why, by everything holy, didn't you tell me about *him*?" Elenar pointed at Darmos, who watched them with an amused smile.

"By the lords, Elenar, let it rest." Arden's gaze was imploring.

"Answer me!"

"Because you would have left me!" Arden shouted, and then he deflated, sinking into himself. "But you've already left me, so it doesn't matter."

"Gentlemen."

Elenar whirled on Darmos. "And you!" He blinked, and his hands trembled. "You..." Darmos moved fast, enveloping Elenar in his arms, pulling him close. "You left me. How could you? You left *me*."

"I'm sorry." His voice was gentle.

Elenar caught Arden's gaze over Darmos's shoulder. He closed his eyes against the devastation he found there.

Elenar had calmed down, taking one of the chairs, while Darmos perched on his desk. Darmos had been slow in letting him go, and now Elenar missed those arms around him. He suppressed a flicker of guilt at the thought.

"Why didn't you come for us?" Arden asked suddenly from where he was leaning against the wall.

Darmos's eyes went to him, and regret flashed through them before everything smoothed out to a neutral expression.

"You had each other, and I'm not the same as I was before," Darmos said.

"Didn't we have a right to know you were alive?" Elenar asked.

"No," Darmos snapped, and Elenar shrank back at the harshness. Darmos exhaled and looked away. "I was more dead than alive. The pirates picked me up, put me back together." He tapped his fingers on the desk. "Their cause resonated with me."

"If you haven't come for…us—why are you here, Darmos?" Arden asked.

"Would you believe me if I said I'm trying to prevent a war?" Darmos said, his gaze steady.

Arden snorted, and it made Elenar want to smack him over the head.

But Darmos only sighed. "The Empire and the Veter established a demilitarized zone between them, washing their hands of the people there and leaving them to fend for themselves. We help those that want to stay, and resettle the others."

"It sounds noble," Elenar said, and Darmos chuckled. It was a beautiful sound. Giddiness bubbled inside Elenar. Three hours ago, he had stood in an orchard inspecting orange trees, and now? He still felt the Shadow fighter around him, the power at his back, and the freedom of the sky. He could almost touch the stars again. "Let us help."

"No," Arden said sharply. "Whatever you are doing, Darmos, leave me out of it."

Darmos crossed his arms, raising an inquiring eyebrow.

"Preventing a war?" Arden shook his head. "You have an entire fighter battalion in your hangar. And this"—Arden made a sweeping hand gesture, indicating the three of them—"wasn't a coincidence."

Elenar turned to him. "What do you mean?"

"There was a tracker in the Shadow fighter." Arden's narrowed eyes were on Darmos.

"I hid it in the software. The whole ship was a beacon every time it was powered up. You were a good teacher with that kind of thing." Darmos's smile was smug.

"But why?" Elenar asked, seeking out Darmos's gaze.

Darmos linked his fingers together, and his face was solemn as he looked between them. "I need you."

"You mean Elenar." Arden scrubbed a hand over his face. "You know what? I'm done with this. I'm done with him, and, by the lords, I'm done with you."

The comms crackled to life. "Captain to the bridge!"

Darmos furrowed his brow. "And there goes Solmier's patience." Smiling thinly at them, he said, "You two are welcome to join me."

The bridge was as black and gray as the corridors, designed for utility, not beauty. A metal walkway ringed the entire bridge with manned stations, and two metal stairways extended down at an angle. Between them was a small platform with a seat; Elenar guessed it to be the captain's chair.

While Arden remained by the elevator doors, Elenar followed Darmos down the stairs. Darmos didn't sit down, but he put a hand on the back of his chair. Standing this close to him, Elenar could feel his body heat seeping into him, making him tingle all over.

"Lieutenant Banra," Darmos said, "report."

The woman at the flight console stopped studying calculations and turned. "We have ten minutes to hand the fighter and the two pilots over. They weapon-locked the drive. As soon as we fire up the jump, we're toast."

"What about the new modifications? Do we have a chance?"

Banra shook her head. "The new tech is still too unstable. We need a marker for the instant jump."

Jump engines calculated the entry point into normal space when they started up; the downside was that the start-up sequence took longer. With the help of a marker and another jump-capable drive, the sequence could be nullified. The marker was placed outside the ship, and it poked the machine to do the calculations. The moment the engine started up, the jump was executed. The method had risks; there was a high chance of the marker being shot down.

"Can we use an automatic marker?" Elenar asked.

"Negative. The Planet Buster engines cause too much interference," Banra said.

"I'll do it."

They all turned to the bridge door where Arden was standing, his lips pressed into a thin line, his gaze hard.

"You?" Elenar asked.

Arden rolled his eyes. "Yes, me. We can use the *Milady*—she's Imperial tech. So we can glitch it out of the radar for one minute. That should be enough time to get the data and do the jump."

Elenar frowned. "What about you?"

"What *about* me?"

Elenar pinched the bridge of his nose. "How will you get back?"

"Do you even care?" But before Elenar could shout at him, Arden held up a hand. "Forgive me. I'll piggyback ride."

"Will that work?" Darmos asked Banra.

She considered it. "It could, actually."

"Time to move, then." Darmos walked up the stairway and took Arden's face into his hands, scrutinizing him.

Arden shook himself free. For a second, Arden's hand seemed to reach for Darmos, but then he turned and was gone.

"Elenar," Darmos said, in the same tone of voice he used to use when one of them was about to do something spectacularly dumb.

Elenar walked up to the bridge door, stopping at Darmos's side. "You said you're not the same as you were before, but you're wrong, Darmos. You haven't changed one bit."

Darmos chuckled and said, "All for one."

"And one for all."

As Arden was about to climb into the cockpit, Elenar grabbed his arm to stop him. "I'll fly."

Arden paused. He didn't let go of the ship, but he turned to Elenar.

"We can shout at each other later," Elenar said. "I'm the better pilot—let me go with you." Arden didn't move. "Look, we're the ones Solmier wants. We got them into this mess, so it's our duty to get them out again."

"Darmos invited the mess," Arden pointed out.

It was a fair point, but nevertheless—this was Elenar's wheelhouse. "Let me make sure that you will be safe. Please."

Arden finally moved aside, creating space for Elenar to climb in.

Elenar was speeding through the pre-flight check when an "I love you" was whispered into his ear; it shivered down his spine.

"*Milady*, this is the *Ghosthunter*. Are you ready to move out?"

It took Elenar a second to open the comms. "*Ghosthunter*, this is *Milady*, ready to move out."

"We will open Landing Dock Five halfway so you can slip out. Initiate the glitch sequence one second before leaving; we will start the counter. From there it's radio silence," Banra advised them.

There was a pause, and then Darmos's voice came through the comms. "Elenar, Arden. Come back in one piece."

"Aye," they said in unison.

"All for one."

"And one for all."

A moment later, they were out in the stars again, dropping beneath the *Ghosthunter's* belly. The cockpit filled with its engine hum and Arden's typing as he ran the calculations. When only the hum remained, Elenar licked his lips and seized the moment. "Do you really think I'd leave you behind?" Elenar hadn't taken Arden into his bed because he had been lonely. Arden had made him laugh, had made him feel alive. But when had they last laughed together?

The silence stretched for so long that Elenar thought Arden would never answer.

"You're not happy," Arden said. "Not anymore." A sigh. "And I—I can't go through losing either of you again."

Memories trickled through Elenar's mind: the discovery that Arden had acquired the *Milady*, the devastation in Arden's eyes, his insistence that Darmos had only come for Elenar, his aborted hand gesture on the bridge. Following the news of Darmos's death, Arden had let Elenar grieve in peace—but perhaps he had been hiding himself away, his own grief as overwhelming as Elenar's had been.

Elenar wondered why he had never seen it.

"You love him."

"Sometimes I wish…that we—" A series of pings stopped whatever he wanted to say. Arden grunted, "Data sent."

Radar activity caught Elenar's eye; dots around the Imperial Fleet began moving closer.

"*Weapon lock*," the AI calmly declared.

"The *Ghosthunter's* jump drive is firing up," Arden said. "Get ready for the jump in three…two…one…"

The space around the Shadow fighter bent, and everything shifted as they slipped away. Elenar clenched his teeth and held the fighter in position to ride the fold-wave of the *Ghosthunter*.

"*Hit detected. Engine One failure.*"

To compensate, Elenar wrenched the stick to the other side. They needed to stay on the fold long enough to come out close to the *Ghosthunter*.

Then the second engine collapsed under the strain, and they were catapulted out.

Elenar used the thrusters to stabilize them. Darkness stretched around them, and fear gripped Elenar; with no engine power they would drift aimlessly through space until a celestial body caught them in its gravity or, more likely, they froze to death—but then the *Ghosthunter* unfolded not far from them.

"*Ghosthunter* to *Milady*, are you still alive?" Darmos sounded anxious.

"Aye," Elenar groaned.

Darmos chuckled. "We'll tow you in."

Elenar closed the comms. "That was worse than the time we were almost eaten by giant clams," he grumbled.

"It was you. *You* almost got eaten," Arden pointed out, with something that sounded like a snort.

Elenar laughed. It felt good.

Elenar was seated on the couch in Darmos's quarters, his skin still buzzing from the action. He was meant to be here in the thick of things, but Arden…? He looked up at Darmos as he handed him a glass of amber liquid. Elenar took the glass, and the door buzzer sounded. Darmos turned and went to let the late-night visitor in.

Arden shuffled around awkwardly on the threshold before slipping into the room, the door closing behind him. Darmos stepped aside, and when Arden caught sight of Elenar, his shoulders slumped as if he were a puppet whose strings had been cut.

Arden licked his lips. "I won't disturb you for long. Darmos, if you could let me out at the next station, I would be grateful. I have contacts who will pick me up."

Even before Arden had finished, Elenar was on his feet, anger vibrating through him. "You just told me you loved me, and now you want to leave me? Do I mean so little to you after all?"

Arden looked down at his hands. "I tried so hard to be enough. And yet you looked out the window into the sky and you wondered—don't you deny it! You wondered if the stars still tasted the same. If they still spelled your name." Pain flashed across Arden's face, the small flicker of ease from earlier gone. "I'm tired. I can't take it anymore. Leave me behind—let me go, both of you."

Elenar's anger dissipated to nothing. "Arden…"

"What do you want from me, Elenar?"

Elenar hesitated. How could he put everything he had felt in the last hours into words?

Darmos reached over, touching his arm. "Elenar, answer him: what do you want?" Darmos was watching them, his expression the one he had always worn in the fleet when he wanted to get to the bottom of things.

Elenar swallowed. "The stars had always promised me freedom. Out there nothing held me back—it was only me and the sky. Blazing through the universe with an unshackled heart, bound by nothing." He looked at Darmos, and then at Arden, his heart constricting at the pain he saw. And yet, he walked to him. "Everything comes second to that feeling." He caught the tremble in Arden's body he couldn't suppress, saw a new hardness in Darmos's eyes when he glanced at him. He ached for them. "I want that freedom, Arden." They were now inches apart.

"I'm sorry," Arden breathed. "I can't do it. I can't watch you and Darmos… You were mine, and you still love him, so it's only natural that you be together…he can give the stars back to you. But I can't stay and ask myself every second, every minute, if you're going back to him. I don't even know who I'd be more envious of." He shook his head. "I'm sorry," he said again.

"Arden," Darmos said, his voice gentle but firm. He stepped into their space, and it felt like a comfort. "No one has to choose."

Arden froze; his eyes went wide, but hope flared inside them.

Elenar touched Arden's cheek, and Arden leaned into it. He kissed Arden's temple, then whispered against it, "I'm freest with the ones I love, and I love you both. You allow me to fly with a free heart."

"Darmos," Arden said, stunned, his hand searching for the other, "do you really mean it?"

Darmos caught Arden's hand, smiling at him. "I loved you for so long, but you were impossible to read—always focused on your contingency plans. So I didn't allow myself to think there could be more." His tone was wistful. "And then I fell in love with Elenar, too, and he made the first move."

Arden blinked, astonishment in his eyes. "So…us three? Just like that?"

"It won't be so different from before," Elenar said with a chuckle.

"One for all," Darmos whispered, squeezing Arden's hand, his eyes bright.

"And all for one," Arden said, leaning his head against Elenar's.

Elenar, grinning broadly, snaked a finger into Darmos's belt loop.

They were the Indestructibles, the Invincibles.

The Inseparables.

And together, they'd light up the night sky.

Tags

warnings: death of a parent (off-screen), harm to animals (mentions of), micro-aggressions (misogynistic), misgendering (unintentional), period-typical misogyny, violence (non-graphic descriptions)
relationships: f/m
character features: masquerading as a person of a different gender, original characters introduced to the canon setting, orphan, servant, soldier, trans male
other tags: canon compliant, flirting, france, getting together, historical, paris, past tense, pining (mutual), third person limited point of view

Inspiration

A. L. Heard opted not to share the inspiration behind this story.

The Musketeer's Daughter: The Tale of Jacques Toussaint

— A. L. Heard

The letter arrived by courier, postage paid. Jacqueline could read, but slowly and with great effort. After her chores, she stole away to work it out.

> *April 12, 1665*
> *Mlle Toussaint,*
>
> *It is with deep regret that we inform you that your father, M. Toussaint, was killed in the line of duty. An honorable death. He was much admired among the Musketeers for his bravery and skill. We offer our deepest condolences and the remainder of his unpaid salary (fifteen livres), which you may retrieve at your convenience at our headquarters in Paris.*
>
> > *All the best,*
> > *M. de Tréville*

Jacqueline read it three times before resigning herself to the truth: she had no blood relations left in the world. As a child, Jacqueline's father had found a family in the Parisian countryside to take her in. Famille Lavigne clothed her, fed her, treated her as their own, but as much as they cared for her, Jacqueline never truly felt part of the family. And now here she was, orphaned.

Alone.

❧

Francois Toussaint had been a doting father, visiting in the frigid winter months when he could escape his duties for weeks on end. They would spend whole evenings together. It was then he taught Jacqueline her letters.

And the sword.

Giulia Malagoli   *"A Toast to Scars"*

Previous page

I remember my first meeting with The Three Musketeers was an anime that portrayed Aramis as a woman dressing as a man to be part of the musketeers. I think that was the first time I realized someone could be a different gender than what they appeared to be, and years down the line it stuck with me. Thus, I thought to paint Aramis as a trans man, with his scars proudly on display as they are celebrated by his companions.

"Ladies don't fight," she'd whispered in awe as he handed her his saber.

"Ladies of the court have that privilege," her father agreed. "The rest of us need to be able to protect what's ours. No child of mine won't be able to defend herself."

He even taught her to load and shoot his musket. She'd proven her skill by killing a stag, and ever after joined the Lavigne men on hunts.

Yet her father had neglected to teach her one thing: who her mother was.

She'd asked, as any curious child would, but he'd always waved off her pleas. "Later" or "when you're older."

There would be no more "laters." The loss of this knowledge, paired with the loss of her beloved father, drove her to Paris. She wanted answers, to feel closer to him…and she couldn't deny the necessity of recovering his final funds. Money had never greatly concerned her; now it consumed her thoughts almost as much as questions about her parents did.

What's my mother's name? Did my father die quickly or linger in pain? Can I afford a proper meal? Was my mother green-eyed like me? Did my father think of me as he died? What will I do after I've spent the last of my livres?

Around and around the questions went.

When she arrived at the Musketeers' headquarters, there was a bustle of activity as men came and went. One man hustled by and nearly knocked her over. Another looked at her and spat on the ground, whether in disgust or warning, she couldn't say.

A clerk assisted her with the payment but couldn't answer her questions. There was a book with notes on every musketeer who'd ever enlisted: when they'd joined, their promotions and honors, and their ultimate deaths, discharges, or retirements. Her father's information was recorded there, his forty-two years condensed into two lines of text.

Francois P. Toussaint, August 20, 1645. Order of Saint Jerome-LeMieux, commendation of his peers for bravery, personal thanks of the Duke of Longueville. Killed in action, April 2, 1665

Nothing about his life before enlistment. Nothing about his life outside of his duty. Nothing about his death other than that it had occurred.

"Is that all?" Jacqueline pleaded. "Did he have any…personal effects?"

The clerk seemed put out, but he went to the barracks and returned with a bundle, then claimed there was a fee of ten deniers for her to collect it. She contemplated snatching the bundle and making a run for it. She might be faster than the pock-marked clerk, but there was a courtyard full of musketeers. Odds against her, she paid the fee and left.

Jacqueline wasn't sure what she'd expected—a diary detailing her mother's identity and location, perhaps?—but reality fell pitifully short. The contents of the bundle included: her father's musket, saber, and uniform; a well-worn book of poetry; a deck of cards missing a jack and two; and a bundle of letters from Jacqueline.

Jacqueline shuffled the cards absent-mindedly as she thought.

She had seventeen livres. She could go back to the Lavignes…or she could stay in Paris. If she could find men who knew her father, she could question them about his romantic liaisons and hopefully learn about her mother. But staying required money. While she could sell her father's weapons for a pretty penny, she could no more part with her arm than with these last reminders of her dear papa.

She needed a job.

A plan in mind, she blew out the bedside candle and cradled the letters to her chest. Her papa had loved her. She would discover the truth, and all would be well.

Coming by a job was surprisingly simple. She inquired with the innkeeper, who directed her to a wealthy family seeking a maid. They readily took her in—a harried housekeeper barely interviewed her and didn't even consult the master of the home—and the matter was settled.

She hadn't expected how different household work in the city would be from the work she'd done back home. Specific clothing must be worn (two ill-fitting dresses were provided—one too short, one too wide). One's head must be bowed when members of the family were present (they rarely were). She'd never known there was one right way to clean anything (clean was clean, after all). A sense of inadequacy grew as she re-learned what she'd thought she already knew.

Each night, as a dull ache settled in her knees and hands, she'd look out a narrow window at the moon and regret her choices. In those moments, alone in the attic, she would dig out her father's deck of cards and shuffle them until she fell asleep, the cards slipping from her hands and cascading around her in the dark.

"I didn't know him," the clerk said dismissively. It wasn't the same young man she'd spoken to originally, but he was equally unhelpful. As were the musketeers in the courtyard. Most hadn't even bothered to return her greeting. Once they deemed she wasn't a damsel in distress, she might as well have been invisible.

"Yes," Jacqueline acknowledged, "but perhaps you could find someone who *did*—"

"Mademoiselle," he said stiffly. "I have important business to conduct." The counter was bare. "The others here have important work to do." Guffaws sounded down the hall. "You've been given your father's effects and pay. I don't know what more you want, but you won't find it here." And with that, he turned on his heel and marched off with his nose in the air like he was Captain of the Guard.

"Bricon," she cursed under her breath.

Outside, a group of men gathered around a fresh-faced youth barely older than herself, and yet they hailed him with respect. She stood at the outskirts and reflected on how well they treated him and how ill they'd treated her. She cursed again and stormed away.

If I were a man, she thought, *they'd welcome me, too. They'd be fawning over me, begging for the chance to tell every story they'd ever heard about my papa! If only—*

She stopped short. A dog that had been sniffing at her heels startled, barked, and ran off, but Jacqueline paid it no mind.

An idea was forming. A dangerous, impossible idea. It grew in her mind's eye without her intentional direction until it was a living, breathing thing that demanded attention.

She had her father's uniform. His musket. His saber.

He'd trained her.

She could read. She could fight. She could shoot.

Why couldn't she...?

"I've gone mad!" she exclaimed.

Those nearby looked her way. She waved sheepishly and scurried off before anyone had a chance to agree with her.

The more she envisioned herself posing as a man, the more she liked the idea. It scared her how tempting it was. Worse, she was certain she could pull it off. Her voice wasn't high pitched, her bosom wasn't ample, and with loose enough clothing, her few curves would be indistinct. Many men wore their hair long. Besides, the ruse wouldn't be for long. Once she learned what she needed, she could return to the familiar safety of her sex.

"What a lovely job you've done!"

Jacqueline nearly dropped the rag she was using to polish the silver. Her eyes widened as she saw Camille Moreau, daughter of her master and the only member of the family to have noticed they'd hired a new maid. Quickly, she curtsied and kept her head so low that her chin touched her chest.

"Merci," she mumbled.

Her cheeks burned, though she didn't know why. Mademoiselle Moreau's full attention unsettled her. The freckles, the black hair left free to fall over her shoulders, the crystal blue of her wide eyes framed by long lashes...Jacqueline credited the butterflies in her stomach to how alluring Mlle Moreau was. They'd rarely crossed paths at first, but recently they saw more of each other. It was as if Mlle Moreau sought out Jacqueline. Though likely a coincidence, the possibility made Jacqueline's hands clammy.

Politely unaware of Jacqueline's awkwardness, Mlle Moreau gracefully sauntered closer.

"I trust you are acclimating to city life," she said, her accent pristine and perfect. Her expression was one of sympathy as she took in the dark lines under Jacqueline's eyes. "It must be so different from the country, so lonely by comparison. Why, I live with my maman and papa and have my circle of friends, and half the time *I'm* in want of companionship."

Jacqueline was indeed lonely. She smiled shyly and kept her eyes fixed anywhere but on Mlle Moreau. "I do miss it sometimes. Not that I wish to go back!" she added in a rush. "I'm very grateful for this position and your family's generosity—"

Mlle Moreau silenced her with a wave of her hand. "We're the grateful ones. You're so hardworking! And, might I say, much kinder than the last maid. She barely spoke a word. You needn't stop missing your family on our account."

Wringing her hands, she muttered, "They weren't my family."

Not missing a beat, Mlle Moreau said, "Perhaps not, but you can still miss them. It was your home your whole life, wasn't it? I can imagine how I would feel to leave this place." She gestured at the spectacular dining room.

Jacqueline too wondered how it would feel when she left the Moreau household—an eventuality that was likely nearer than she cared to admit.

She offered more thanks for Mlle Moreau's attention and excused herself back to her work; as the other woman left the room in a swish of skirts, Jacqueline watched her with a sense of longing.

"I'd like to enlist," Jacqueline stammered to the old officer at the barracks. After a week of indecision (and after secretly trying on her father's uniform, inspecting her shape by candlelight to see if she passed as masculine), she'd finally found the courage to return.

The officer looked up, the laugh lines on his face twisting into a surprised frown as he scrutinized her. From head to toe, he examined the too-large hat and the awkward way the musket hung across her back. The sword at least was comfortably situated at her hip, though she'd had to make new holes in the belt to make it fit. Her hair was a mess, resting in a ponytail with the last few inches cut off haphazardly. The clothes were as clean as she could manage, but ill-fitting. The boots she'd purchased secondhand from a cobbler made her walk with a slight limp because one was too tight.

She stood there, ramrod straight and praying. Perhaps she could claim hysteria if she were caught. What was the worst they could do? Beat her? Put her in the stocks? Send her to the mad house? Kill her?

With growing fear, she realized that those were all very real consequences of discovery.

"Name?" he asked with disinterest.

"Jacques Toussaint. Son of—"

The man quirked his head, a smile pulling at the corner of his lips. "Francois? I didn't know he had a son!" Then he clapped Jacqueline hard on the back. "And you have his things! How have you been here already and no one's told me?"

"My—my sister—she collected—"

"But of course! Your father, he spoke of a daughter, but I could've sworn… No matter! Come, let's get you a fresh uniform!"

Simple as that, she was one of them. She hid behind a door as she changed into the new, only slightly smaller uniform and listened as the officer went on about her father's extraordinary talent for cards. One year he'd nearly doubled his earnings through gambling and had been able to buy his daughter new clothes. ("He must have gotten you something as well, lad. You'll remember better than I!")

In the yard, she proved she knew the basics of swordplay and earned praise ("You look just like your father…though perhaps a little shorter."). She was regaled with tales of thwarted bandits and plots unraveled, all with Francois Toussaint at center stage.

When it came to the paperwork, she was sorely disappointed. There was a section that asked for her lineage, and she pointedly looked at the friendly officer.

"My mother…" she prompted.

He scoffed. "No need to worry about such trifles. Half the men here are bastards. Leave it blank. No one's interested in mothers anyway. Put your father's name and that he was a musketeer. That's a good lad. You write well!"

While the acceptance and success had bolstered her spirits, *that* dampened her mood considerably. She wondered if it was worth coming back. The officer went on about a prank he'd pulled on her father and his retaliation, and she resigned herself to returning in a few days. She did enjoy hearing about her father; others might know about her mother.

She went back to the Moreau home that evening and sneaked into the stables. The horses ignored her, and the stableboy was asleep on a stool. She had no idea how he'd react if he awoke and saw a musketeer; she suppressed a giggle as she dug her dress out of the straw.

As she slipped out of her disguise and back into her own clothes, it didn't feel like she was becoming herself. It felt like a different disguise. One she was accustomed to, yes, but now that she knew how it felt to wear someone else's life, she noticed the veneer of this one. The pieces of Jacqueline Toussaint that were too loose, too tight, or simply misshapen on her.

The dissonance nearly overwhelmed her, and she lingered in the empty stall. With shaking hands, she packed her overstuffed bag with her musketeer paraphernalia. When she later hid them under her bed, she acutely felt that she was hiding herself away as well.

Three days later, the same officer greeted her at the headquarters, telling her new stories of her father (still nothing about her mother) before he threw her in with the other recruits. She learned an advancing guard and how to hold the musket so she could fire while moving.

The other recruits were impressed. She basked in their praise and reveled in their camaraderie. It was so different from the muted friendships she'd had with country girls. This was…more real. Like every interaction was in full color instead of dull grays. She left that day almost drunk with happiness, and she knew she would return.

And she did, again and again. She worked quickly so that she could sneak away to headquarters. On the days she simply couldn't go, she practiced swordplay in the barn. The stableboy would watch her with wonder as she parried invisible opponents and practiced her footwork the way other women practiced dancing.

Her fellow musketeers always rejoiced at her return. They begged her to move into the barracks, and her heart yearned to accept. It would be dangerous, yet it felt inevitable all the same.

Being a man was…exhilarating. The thrill of being *noticed* by men was heady. No, she corrected herself. It wasn't their notice. Plenty of men had tilted their hats to her in the street, or at the other extreme, given her winks as they made rude gestures. It was the respect in how they treated her now. As an equal, a person of note. Not just a fixture or object. She was no longer some nameless woman.

She was Jacques Toussaint, son of Francois, a musketeer.

More and more, she found herself slipping into Jacques…and she wasn't sure she'd mourn if, one day, she had to say good-bye to Jacqueline.

"Jacqueline!"

The strangeness of her given name clashed with the excitement of hearing it from Mlle Moreau. Suddenly, she was overcome with the image of Mlle Moreau approaching her when she was Jacques. The longing she'd felt made sense through that lens, her unwitting pining for the beautiful young woman before her… As Jacqueline, it was a confusing mess that would never find any satisfaction. As Jacques, she might stand a chance.

"Mademoiselle," she said with a curtsy.

"I haven't seen you in days!" An adorable pout made Jacqueline's heart leap.

"I've been given leave for personal business," she stuttered. "I'm sorry for the inconvenience, m'lady."

Mlle Moreau laughed, a melodic trill. "You're always apologizing! I missed you, that's all!"

"Missed me?" She flushed as heat coiled through her. "I'm sor—" She caught herself and laughed with Mlle Moreau. "Well, I am sorry, for I fear it'll become permanent. I'd been looking for information about my mother, and…" And what? She could hardly admit the truth. If she said too much, Mlle Moreau might put the pieces together. It wasn't fair to ask her to hide Jacqueline's secret.

To her surprise, Mlle Moreau took Jacqueline's hands in hers and squeezed. "You must be making progress! That's why you came to Paris, isn't it? Once you've finished, will you return to the country?"

It was the perfect alibi. She could leave, and the Moreaus would never suspect a thing.

"Yes." Her voice was too thick, too much like Jacques's, so she swallowed a lump in her throat. "Within a few weeks, I believe."

Mlle Moreau's look of genuine sorrow almost made her change her mind. "I'll be sad to see you go, but I wish you all the best!"

"Merci, Mademoiselle."

There were few things about Jacqueline's life that she would miss; Mlle Moreau was chief among them.

After two weeks in the barracks, being a woman was a distant memory. Surrounded by men and the constant refrain of "Jacques" and "il," it was easy to adopt them even in his own head. Jacques dressed as a man, acted like a man, *was* a man. Jacqueline had, for the few in Paris who'd even known her, disappeared.

He'd never felt more like himself nor felt so close to his father. He pretended his cot was the very one his father had used, that his place in the dining hall was one his father had favored, that every day he walked the same paths Francois had.

His mother continued to elude him. The musketeers offered what they could, but details were scant and contradictory. One man insisted that Francois was enamored with a blonde woman and kept a lock of her hair. Another claimed he'd seen Francois with a woman of small stature who wore her hair in tight, dark curls. Yet another was certain he'd never heard Francois speak of a woman and was shocked when one day he'd proudly announced that he was a father.

"He might as well have plucked you from the Seine," the man mumbled into a mug of beer, scowling at his cards. "Merde, I fold. You play as well as him. I'm not losing more money to a Toussaint."

The recruits saw little action, but occasionally they would pair up to patrol the streets. Here too Jacques garnered more respect and recognition than he'd known as a woman, and he relished each time someone nodded his way, delighted in tipping his feathered hat back at them.

The day was warm but cloudy, the threat of rain keeping the streets empty. He and another recruit, Monsieur LePont, were helping a young boy who'd dropped his basket of apples when they heard the *boom* of a gunshot.

Jacques didn't hesitate. He ran, hand on his hilt, and shouted for his comrade to ready his musket.

They soon reached the ruckus outside a small church. A woman hid in a carriage while two armed men attempted to wrench the door open; the horses whinnied in terror, cornered between overturned carts. A footman lay dead in a puddle of blood.

"En garde!" Jacques shouted as he charged.

The men froze in shock, giving Jacques the opportunity to get the jump on one. In short order, he'd slashed the man's arm and thigh, but then the other man drew a dagger and sword. Jacques retreated a few pieds to defend himself and to draw him away from the carriage. He fell into the rhythm of a fight. His footwork was perfect, his jabs and blocks exemplary. The adrenaline thrumming through his veins gave him preternatural instincts on when to duck and jab. The other man was a hulk of muscle, but Jacques was quicker and more skilled. Before fatigue could set in, he knocked the man to the ground, disabling him with a sharp jab of his hilt to his gut.

The man wheezed as he collapsed, making no move to flee.

Too pleased with his victory, Jacques had forgotten the first man. Nearly too late, he raised his sword to block—

BANG!

The roar of a musket ripped through Jacque's ears as surely as the bullet ripped through the man's chest, traces of red staining outward before he tipped forward and collapsed at Jacques's feet.

"Mon dieu…" Jacques cast a thankful look to LePont. "I thought he'd run away."

"A smarter man would've." LePont shrugged. "But a smarter man wouldn't be such a poor thief."

Jacques sheathed his sword. The footman attracted his attention; there was something familiar about the lifeless body sprawled across the dusty cobblestones.

The carriage door rattled as the woman inside shook it desperately; Jacques and LePont rushed over.

"All is well, Mademoiselle!" they called as both musketeers worked the door off its hinges.

"Mademoiselle," Jacques said and offered his gloved hand inside. "You're safe."

Dainty fingers with polished nails and chestnut skin clutched at him. She trembled, but she regained her courage after Jacques squeezed gently, and a beautiful woman emerged: yellow muslin gown with silver trim, slender figure supported by a corset, stunning blue eyes.

Stunning…and familiar.

"Merci," said Mademoiselle Moreau. She looked between them; her eyes lingered on Jacques. "To whom do I owe my life?"

Panic spiked through him. But he might yet be safe—he'd given his family name to the house, of course, but with Mlle Moreau he'd simply been Jacqueline. So long as he was careful not to give his full name, perhaps she wouldn't make the connection.

"I am Monsieur Toussaint," he said with a sweeping bow, praying his disguise was good enough. He pitched his voice even lower and pulled his hat farther over his brow. "This is Monsieur LePont. At your service, m'lady."

Thankfully, the street soon filled with musketeers. Jacques was able to defer to his superiors and escape to headquarters. Their comrades congratulated them for their triumph, yet Jacques felt like a fraud.

May 27, 1665
M. Toussaint,

I hope this letter finds you well. First, let me express my unending gratitude for your rescue last Tuesday. It was your duty, I know, but I'm no less thankful you were there (and so skilled with a sword!).

I confess, I write to you for more than gratitude. I've thought of you constantly. I dream of your bravery and long to see you again, so that I might properly thank you for all you've done for me. If such a meeting can be arranged, please send word! If not, I'll quietly nourish my tender thoughts for you in secret.

Warmest Regards,
Camille Moreau

Jacques couldn't believe the words. It wasn't uncommon for a lady to fall for her rescuer. Many of the men in the barracks had lovers who'd been impressed with their courage (or their uniform). Yet he couldn't believe his luck! The lovely, kind Camille Moreau, enamored with him!

He didn't reply. Tempted though he was, a relationship would be too risky. Mlle Moreau would certainly recognize him if their paths crossed again. If she learned of his deceit, any tender feelings she held would be instantly gone. In her justifiable embarrassment, she might even threaten to expose Jacques.

It was better to remain quiet and re-read the letter each evening.

Because of their successful rescue of Mlle Moreau, Jacques and M. LePont were given commendations and assigned additional patrols. While none were so eventful as their first, Jacques stopped a pickpocket and helped return a lost toddler to his mother. There was nothing more from Mlle Moreau, and Jacques grieved the life they could never share.

Yet her presence was constant, as if he were haunted by her. He dreamed of her, longed for her. Why, even now he was imagining her before his very eyes! He could see her clearly—hair plaited neatly, dress a deep purple, a look of determination lighting her features—as she marched into headquarters. Ah, what a wonder that would be!

The vision didn't disappear when he blinked. She continued to march toward him across the courtyard. In fact, his fellow musketeers moved out of her way. Was his longing so strong he'd manifested an apparition of her?

No, the reality was worse.

She was there in the flesh.

It was too late to flee; Jacques stood dumbly as she approached. Only after she stopped before him did he remember his manners and bow.

"Monsieur Toussaint. I don't mean to intrude," Mlle Moreau said with a faint blush that obscured her freckles. Jacques had the urge to lean in and kiss the trail of freckles running along her arms to see if those, too, would disappear. "I said I wouldn't bother you if you didn't write back, and you haven't..." Never before had Jacques heard her fumble for words. "But I found information for you. About your mother."

Jacques jolted in surprise. "My mother?" he choked out.

Every musketeer knew of his search for his mother, but how did Mlle Moreau know?

Mlle Moreau retrieved some papers from her pocket and offered them. Jacques was shocked to the core when he unfolded the first parchment and discovered a letter addressed to Mlle Moreau from the Lavignes.

"I—I don't—" he stammered. A wild part of him wanted to tear the paper apart, to destroy the evidence of any connection between himself and the family that raised him.

Curiosity stilled his hand as she continued.

"When you left, I was worried. I spoke with the housekeeper and then contacted the Lavignes to inquire if you'd returned home safely. They wrote that you hadn't returned, and they suspected you wouldn't. They also kindly provided what details they could about your parents."

"But…you and I…we didn't meet until the robbery—"

"Monsieur Toussaint," she said seriously. She looked around the courtyard before leaning in and whispering, "Jacqueline, I knew it was you at once. I was surprised, but relieved you were doing well." She stood straighter and batted her eyes coyly. "Why, I think it was fate that brought us together again so that you could rescue me and I could give you that."

Jacques stared at the words in front of him, then flipped to the next parchment. It was a certified note from town hall detailing the circumstances of a birth some sixteen years ago.

"Your mother was the daughter of a wealthy, respectable merchant. It might be my romantic heart, but I suspect your father planned to leave the musketeers to be with her. She died in childbirth, though, and he was forced to find other arrangements."

He read the note in disbelief, then looked at Mlle Moreau in awe. She had used her connections to help him, and it appeared she'd done so even when she'd still believed him to be simply a maid in her household.

"It's Jacques," he finally said. He clutched the papers to his chest and felt a renewed surge of affection for Mlle Moreau.

"You're rather fortunate, you know," she said coyly. "Your birth was merely recorded as 'a healthy babe,' with no mention of whether it was a boy or girl. I read the registry myself."

Jacques's heart skipped a beat. "Oh?"

Mlle Moreau stepped forward and took Jacques's free hand in hers, a brazen move that doomed him: he would follow Camille Moreau to the ends of the Earth.

"I do believe you could claim your inheritance from your mother's family," she said. The words were said innocently enough, but there was a wickedness in her eyes. "I would very much like to help."

Jacques gulped. They were on the precipice of something, but he had to ask.

"In your letter to me. You knew…who I was. Before. Yet you spoke of your feelings—"

"Feelings I held when you were a different person, living in my family's home. Feelings I harbor still. Feelings…I hope are returned?"

How could there be any doubt?

"They are," Jacques said in a rush. "I must say how much I admire and respect—"

She lifted his hand to her lips and kissed it—a strange inversion to any observer.

"Good," she said. "Now let's get you that inheritance so I can convince my father to let us marry."

Mon dieu, I'm in trouble, Jacques thought. *The best possible trouble.*

Jupiter V   **"*The Blade of Resolve*"**

Next twelve pages

There is no greater inspiration for this story than The Three Musketeers by Alexandre Dumas. I'm not sure who said it on the Discord server (99% sure it was Unforth), but someone mentioned that at this point there have been so many adaptations of the story that the original tale is more-or-less forgotten…typically usurped by the most recent movie adaptation.

With that in mind, I returned to the original text with the intention of twisting it in an anachronistic new direction, with a more colourful and diverse cast of characters. I was particularly amused by our hero's yellow horse, and their particular style of…problem solving.

Sadly, we don't have the time to tell the whole story, but I hope you enjoy this brief glimpse into d'Arta's world, and her first epic meeting with the iconic Three Musketeers!

* *Editor's Note: "Unforth" is the online pseudonym of the anthology's lead editor Nina Waters.*

The Blade of Resolve
BY JUPITER V

PARIS ~ 16xx

Aaah, I see. You had a letter of introduction, and lo—

I believe it was *stolen*.

Poor fortune, for one hoping to join rank with **The Musketeers!**

Ah . . .

No matter! Sir Achilles was an outstanding Musketeer. We would be remiss to turn away his daughter.

Though, without the letter, you will need to squire for some time . . .

Say, how is that sassy old man ?

hm?

Monsieur de Tréville

1

There! In the Market Square!

...your dad?

And probably stole my letter!

It's that annoyingly hot scoundrel who insulted my horse!

Oh! Leave off, Young d'Arta!!

Pardonnez-moi, monsieur

That one is

WAY out of your league

!!!

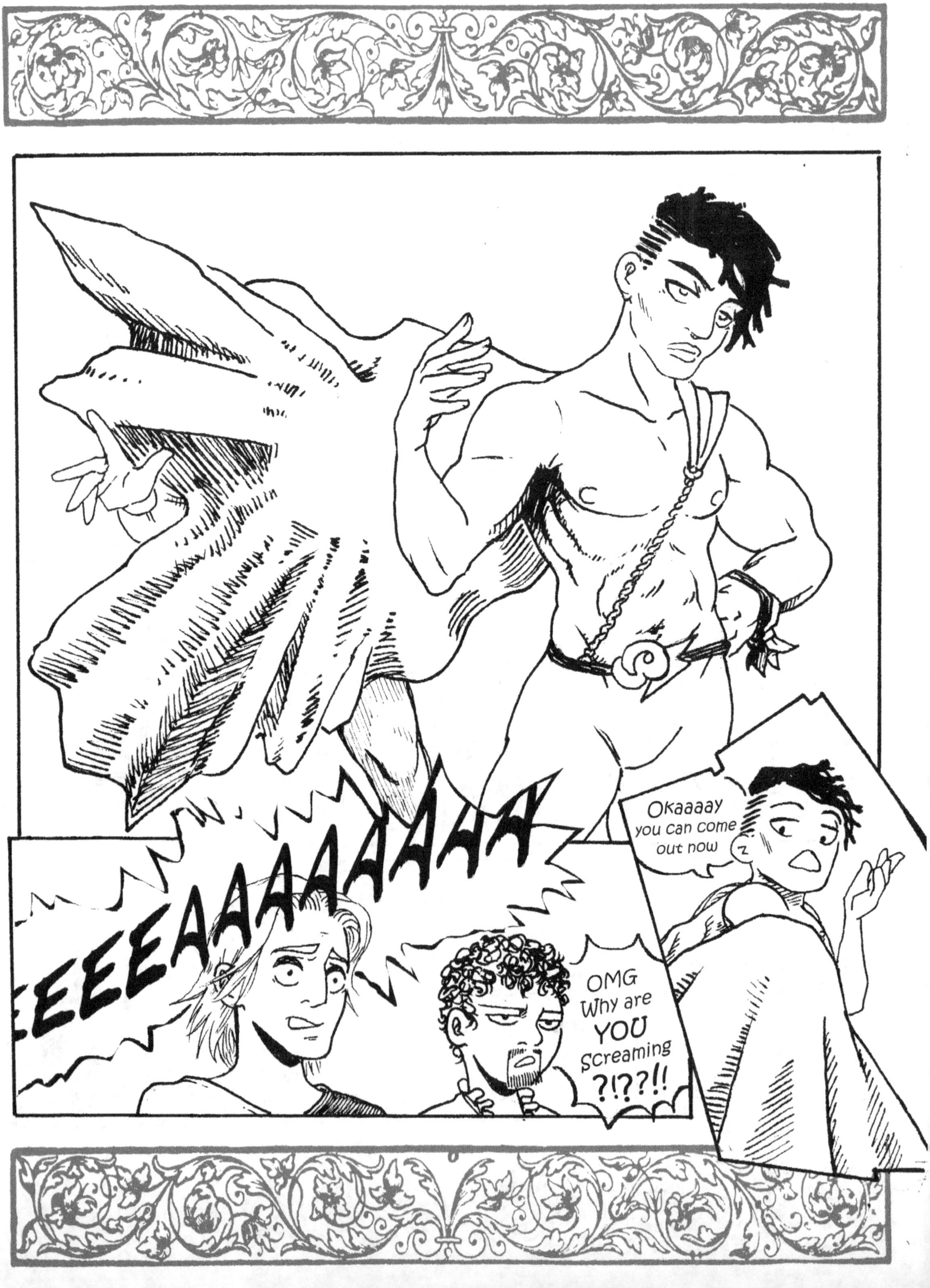

This isn't where I came in . . .

Oh!

Pardonnez-moi, Mo-

Um . . .

Oui? Puis-je vous aider?

Fated Encounter Challenge

– Xianyu Zhou

(0) 20th Street

The city is so strange, Dottie thought as she was pushed along by the crowd. She tried to take in everything at once: the window displays in the shops lining the street, the flashing lights from all sorts of advertisements, the scent of coffee coming from an indiscernible direction, and the people. Gosh, there were so many of them!

Someone bumped into her with a disgruntled noise, and it made her stomach squeeze with excitement and worry.

Growing up in a small town, she'd always wondered what it felt like when-ever she saw pictures of large crowds on the news. Now that she was in the midst of a near-suffocating press of human bodies, she was giddy and awe-struck, marveling at the mind-boggling number of people. She couldn't even tell the color of the pavement between all the shoes!

But that was also the reason for her worry. She had never been in a crowd like this. She kept feeling like she was about to do something wrong and garner judgmental *tsks* from everyone around her.

Between being hypervigilant about not stepping on anyone's foot and be-ing distracted by the liveliness of it all, Dottie nearly walked past her first destination.

Right. I have a plan, she reminded herself as she tried to wriggle her way out of the flow of bodies.

Dottie's plan: attempt *and complete* the 20th Street Fated Encounter Challenge.

The challenge was deceptively simple: visit three shops in succession and buy some-thing from each of them, then sit in front of the fountain at the end of the street. Sup-posedly, she would then meet her "fated one."

Dottie wasn't actually interested in meeting her "fated one." She'd never been inter-ested in romance much; she just liked the idea of it, fascinated by its affect on people. What she really wanted was to debunk the urban legend around this challenge.

Allegedly, the challenge was exceptionally hard to accomplish. During her research, Dottie had come across personal accounts of mishaps that had happened to people while they were attempting the challenge. Some said their belong-ings went missing without a trace, while others claimed to have been pushed by myste-rious forces that caused them to fall over and hurt themselves, cutting their trip short.

Dottie thought it sounded as if that had been cooked up by the shop owners to at-

Tags
relationships: customer/employee, f/f/m/nb, polyamory, pre-relationship
character features: aromantic, character has a different gender than in the source material, customer service representa-tive, non-binary
other tags: alternate universe, anti-soulmates, attraction at first sight, coffee shop, florist shop, getting together, meet awkward, modern, past tense, puzzles and games, third person limited point of view

Inspiration
I wanted to make the silly meet cute that the original characters had Even Sillier :3.

tract visitors and boost their business.

Nonetheless, Dottie was adamant about seeing it for herself.

Even if it was a load of hot air like she thought, she would have a nice day out enjoying the city. So really, she had nothing to lose.

(1) Or Me Café

Changing her direction proved a much more difficult task than expected. Despite her best unobtrusive wriggling and side-stepping, she still had people running into her and scowling irritatedly at her "excuse me"s.

After a few long minutes of awkward shuffling, the mass of bodies eventually spat her out near the queue for the café.

A wave of confusion swept away Dottie's sigh of relief as she looked around. The end of the queue was nowhere to be seen. She had to find the start of the line—spotting the vague shape of a counter through the café windows—and follow the semi-organized arrangement of people around the corner of the building.

She cautiously made her way behind the building only to find that it was even less obvious who was queuing and who wasn't. After standing around awkwardly for a long moment, Dottie sucked it up and tapped the shoulder of a lady in a red coat. "Excuse me, is this the line for the café?"

The lady gave Dottie a slow up and down stare, her mouth curling into a cold smile. "Duh," she said, rolling her eyes before turning away.

Dottie blinked, the thanks on the tip of her tongue melting away in confusion. She shuffled into place behind Red Coat Lady, looking around to make sure she hadn't accidentally taken someone's place.

When no one met her questioning eyes, Dottie turned to her phone to ease the awkwardness. She looked up the café, wanting to make sure she had the right one, but by the time the map of the area loaded, she was already standing directly under the big sign that confirmed she was at the right shop.

The glass doors of Or Me Café were propped open with two bricks, allowing a cacophony of conversation and machine noises to spill out from its packed interior.

Dottie stared as she stepped past the threshold. The shop was filled to the brim. Every seat was taken, and there were even people who were standing about, sipping their drinks as if it was the most natural thing.

Her first thought was, *That doesn't seem to be the right way to enjoy a meal.*

Before she could properly ponder about café customs in the city, she was interrupted by a man squeezing past her, trying to cut in line. She reached out, intending to haul the man back by his collar and give him a piece of her mind, only for the man to trip on one of the bricks propping open the doors and fall flat on his face.

Dottie watched, too shocked by the sudden turn of events to do anything as the man groaned in pain. The crowd tittered without anyone stepping forward to help him up. She was about to put aside her pettiness and give the man a hand when a harried-looking worker with his arm in a sling came by and tonelessly said, "Sir, could you please move out of the way?"

"Next!" the barista shouted, and Dottie quickly hurried to the counter, glad to escape the situation.

She ordered, fumbling over the fanciful names on the menu and the barista's rapid-fire questions: What type of milk did she want? What size drink? What kind of sugar?

"Anything else?" the barista asked with a bored expression.

"Uh, well, the brick at the door is a tripping hazard?" Dottie tried.

The barista snorted. "Only to idiots who don't watch where they're going," they said, handing Dottie her receipt. "Your order will be called shortly."

She looked at the receipt, then at the barista. "The brick—"

The barista made a shooing motion at her, then looked over her shoulder, addressing the next customer. "Welcome to Or Me. What can I get you today?"

Dottie tried—she really did—to get to the counter with a plaque that read "Pick Up," but the throng of people coming and going pushed her farther and farther away. No amount of cautious protesting made them give way, even when she yelped because her foot had been stepped on.

When her name and coffee order were called out, all she could do was stick her hand in the air and wave. She couldn't tell if anyone at the counter had seen her or, with how turned around she was, if she was even waving in the right direction.

Frantic apologies spilled out as she pressed forward with renewed effort. She held her arms in front of her chest, receipt clutched tightly in her fist, and winced at the feeling of other people's bodies running into hers. *Don't trip. Don't trip*, she chanted without looking where she was going, eyes fixed on where she placed her feet.

"Coffee and pastries for Dottie!" someone called again, and Dottie looked up for one second, tiptoeing to peek past a tall man on his phone.

"Here! I just—I can't—" she shouted back, shoving past the man in a moment of triumph only to run straight into someone else.

The crowd stopped pushing, and she watched as the people quickly parted around her and the other person—the harried-looking worker from earlier with the injured arm in a sling—in slow motion. The tray he held tilted, and the used cups and plates went flying, crumbs and murky liquid spilling out in arcs, one of them headed right for Dottie.

All she could think about was the resigned expression on the worker's face that spelled out, "Yep, this might as well happen, why not," as he tipped backward and Dottie tipped forward, getting a cold stream of liquid right down the front of her shirt. They ended up in a heap on the floor.

"I'm sorry! I'm so sorry!" Dottie scrambled to get up. The man's face scrunched up as he muffled a grunt of pain when Dottie's weight shifted before she finally straightened up.

Dottie could hardly care about her ruined shirt, even though it was one of the nicer ones she owned, when the man—Athos, his name tag read—looked so deathly pale. Still, his pallor didn't dim the displeasure written in the furrow of his brows.

"A-are you okay?" Dottie asked, kneeling beside him, her voice getting quieter as she realized the pointlessness of her question. She wanted to help him up, but her hands fluttered; she was unsure where she could place them. In the end, she started collecting the broken bits of ceramic instead.

Even with her head lowered in shame, she saw how Athos glared at her, muttering something along the lines of "I'm having *such* an amazing day at work" under his breath.

"I'm really sorry. I didn't see you. I just wanted to get to—" Dottie started, mumbling. A realization dawned on her. Her head snapped toward the counter, but her view was obscured by the rippling wall of legs. "My coffee and pastries!"

Athos sat up, picking crumbs from the fabric of his sling, looking as if he was about to say something before Dottie shoved the tray of shards right into his chest (and his injured arm, presumably; Dottie wasn't paying attention). Whatever he had to say quickly dissolved into a choked noise that was drowned out by the way Dottie shouted, "I'll be right back!"

For all intents and purposes, Dottie did want to return to ~~the crime scene~~ where she had left Athos as quickly as she could. But as fate would have it—or rather, as the curse of the challenge would have it—she found that she was missing two of her pastries. The set she ordered had three pastries: an egg tart, a chocolate puff, and a milk bun. Yet, there was only an egg tart in the paper bag.

She scrutinized the people standing around the counter, looking for some damning smudge of chocolate at the corner of their mouths. But everyone looked normal, sipping at their own drinks and chowing down on their own pastries.

She tried to flag down a barista, but none of the three bustling away behind the counter gave her any attention, not even the one who had placed an assortment of paper bags and cups—and notably a tiny cake box—right in front of her and yelled out the orders in a deafening volume.

"Excuse me, my order—" Dottie started, only to be interrupted by a middle-aged man who squeezed himself between her and the counter.

He reached over the counter, grabbed a cup-holder tray, and started putting the cups into the holder after a brief glance at the labels.

"That's not your order, sir," Dottie said with a frown as the man picked up a cup with "Constance" scrawled on the side and started to leave. Her ears were still ringing from the barista's yell, and she had clearly heard them mention that the order for Constance came with a cake.

"Mind your own business," the man groused, slipping into the crowd before Dottie could stop him.

The barista from earlier came by and deposited more cups and paper bags on the counter with another yell, then turned back to their work without even a glance at the people who descended on the orders.

Dottie sighed, knowing that her missing pastries were a lost cause. She grumpily trudged back to where she expected Athos to be, only to find that the mess had been cleaned up and the man was nowhere to be seen.

Missing person or not, Dottie had a challenge to complete. The challenge specified the challenger should have a meal in the café, and that's what she did, standing firmly at the spot where she had tripped, buffeted by the crowd as she gnawed on her egg tart between sips of coffee.

A coffee and an egg tart counted as a meal, right? Even if it didn't, Dottie could hardly muster up the enthusiasm to make another order.

When she was done eating, she scrawled her name, phone number, and a short apology on the grease-stained paper bag, put the half-used pack of paracetamol she carried with her into the paper bag, and handed it to the barista that had taken her order. The barista rolled their eyes at her explanation but accepted the paper bag without a word.

Dottie thanked them cheerfully, fingers crossed behind her back, hoping that her message would get to Athos.

(2) Bloom Florist

Dottie exited the café glumly, absentmindedly dabbing at her stained shirt with a wet wipe.

She wasn't convinced that the challenge was cursed, but there was a thread of doubt weaving around her thoughts. It sounded absurd that visiting some stores could result in mishaps, but after what happened in the café, it seemed less impossible than before.

Of course, Dottie thought there was a logical explanation for her unpleasant encounter. The café was near a bus stop and a subway exit, and it was a little before midday, prime brunch time. Naturally, it would garner a crowd. And accidents were bound to happen when there was a crowd.

Since the next shop she was visiting was farther down the street and brunch time was almost over, there should be a lower chance of a crowd there. Plus, it was hard to think of a florist shop being as busy as a café. Therefore, it was unlikely for any mishaps to happen there.

As expected, the crowd thinned as she went down the street. The frantic feeling that came with having so many bodies in one space dissipated, and people's footsteps slowed. The street seemed wider without the crushing foot traffic, the open space allowing Dottie to see the colorful shadows cast onto the deep-gray faux cobble.

Dottie's footsteps came to a stop when she looked up and finally noticed the rows of tiny flags stretched between the tops of the buildings on both sides of the street. She watched the flags flutter in the breeze, took in a few much-needed deep breaths, and let her shoulders come down from where they were tensed around her ears.

Now that she wasn't as high-strung as before, she understood why it was a popular spot with the locals.

It was beautiful.

"It is indeed beautiful!" A boisterous voice echoed her thoughts.

Dottie snapped out of her daze, glancing around to find the source of the voice. It wasn't difficult, as the person spoke again in the same loud voice. "Look at the color. It's to die for." The woman twirled, showing off her dress, sequins shimmering in the sunlight.

The dress looked like something from a fairy tale, something a princess would wear. Though, perhaps not to a bustling shopping area. The skirt was a huge puff of something gauzy and delicate, the frills at the hem almost touching the ground.

Dottie was about to convince herself that the dress was just something for a photoshoot when the woman put an apron over her dress and bid farewell to her audience before she disappeared into a shop. "Bloom Florists," the plaque above the shop read.

What a coincidence, Dottie thought, tossing her dirty wet wipe into a trashcan.

Bloom Florist was Dottie's next stop.

Dottie looked at herself and grimaced. The wet wipe seemed to have made the stain worse. She was in a sorry state. The woman probably wouldn't comment on it out of politeness, but Dottie couldn't help but want to look more presentable around someone like her.

She sighed, pulling a scarf from her bag to wrap around her shoulders, making sure it covered the stain as much as possible. It was the best she could do.

Dottie was relieved to find the shop relatively empty when she pushed open the door.

Empty of people at least. The little shop was overflowing with flowers. The shelves lining the walls held arrangements in mismatched pots and vases, and flowers and greenery burst forth from their containers on the floor, reaching out to touch Dottie as she walked by. There were even pots of orchids hanging overhead, which Dottie nearly knocked her head into.

"Hi! How can I help you today?" Dress Lady greeted from behind a large bouquet of flowers.

"Uh, I'm looking for something simple? For…" Dottie's face went hot at the thought of the silly challenge. It was one thing to attempt it and perhaps review it on her social media, but it was another thing entirely to tell someone she was doing something as cheesy as that.

"For the Fated Encounter Challenge?" The woman asked, her mouth—painted dark plum—quirked in a smile. "Oh, don't be embarrassed! Plenty of people come around to try it out. The mix-and-match stuff is this way."

Dottie nodded, tucking the scarf more securely around herself as she trailed after the woman.

"Everything on the wall is ten stalks for five bucks," the woman said. "I'll be right over there." She pointed toward the mass of green leaves.

Dottie stared at the wall covered in stalks and stalks of flowers. The choices were overwhelming. "Oh, uh, Miss…"

"Poppy," the woman prompted.

"Miss Poppy, do you mind picking out something for me?" Dottie asked hesitantly. "If it's not too much trouble!"

Miss Poppy laughed, a hearty, joyous noise. "Of course."

Dottie smiled in relief, watching with interest as Miss Poppy set down her basket and laid out some brown paper on a nearby tabletop. She deftly picked out sunflowers, roses, lavender, and another yellow flower Dottie didn't know the name of, trimmed the stalks, and wrapped them up, winding a ribbon around the bundle.

"Sunflowers for happiness, yellow roses for friendship and joy, daffodils for—"

A loud, childish shriek and quick pitter-patter of tiny footsteps interrupted Miss Poppy mid-sentence. There was a forceful bump against Dottie's thigh as she turned to look, and she caught sight of a little boy, no more than ten, running past and careening into the large puff of Miss Poppy's dress.

The old habit of being around the village children made Dottie fix a stern look at the boy, "Hey, you bumped into me quite hard there."

The boy stuck his tongue out at her before darting out of sight.

"I know his mother; don't worry. I'll go get him." Miss Poppy put the bouquet in Dottie's arms and walked away as a series of clanging noises sounded from the back of the shop. "Just leave the money in the pink pot on the counter."

Dottie nodded, watching Miss Poppy disappear behind some large leaves before she carefully stashed the bouquet into her bag and picked her way through the shop, looking for the aforementioned counter.

She was about to count out her money to put it in the pot as told when the kid from earlier ran into her again, yanking her bag off her arm and spilling some of its contents across the floor.

Before Dottie could react, Miss Poppy strode toward her and the stunned boy, who was still clutching Dottie's bag.

"You little rascal! Come here," Miss Poppy bit out.

She stalked forward, stepped on a pen that had fallen out of Dottie's bag, and slipped, comically flailing her arms as she fell.

Dottie didn't even think before reaching out, trying to pull Miss Poppy to her feet. Miss Poppy reached for her, too, managing to grab Dottie's shoulder.

Ultimately, it didn't go like the scenes in dramas do. For the second time in a day, Dottie found herself on the floor. At least this time there weren't any liquids.

The boy laughed in demonic amusement, saluting Dottie before dashing out the door with her bag.

"My bag!" Dottie yelped, watching the boy sprint away.

She got up, paying no attention to her scarf slipping off her neck, one end of it still stuck in Miss Poppy's grasp. "I'll be right back, I promise!" she said over her shoulder, the bell on the door ringing as she chased after the boy.

(3) All Night Hobby

The little bag thief was a bullet in the wind, darting between people on the street with Dottie on his heels. She would've caught him—she had practice chasing after their farm dogs back home—if he hadn't thrown her bag into a random shop and run in the opposite direction.

"You rascal! You better hope I don't see you again!" Dottie yelled between heavy breaths, stomping her feet in frustration at the absolute mess of things, ignoring the judgmental glances from the passersby.

She trudged over to the shop her bag had been unceremoniously tossed into, intending to grab it and head back to the florist, but her bag was not at the doorstep of the shop as she'd expected.

She took a tentative step into the shop, peering around for her bag. Upon coming up empty, she took another step and peered under the tables that held boxes of…games?

Someone cleared their throat as she peeked under table number two, and she straightened up, her cheeks flushing in embarrassment. Partly because she realized how strangely she was acting, partly because the person—Aris, their name tag read—was very good-looking.

"I—I lost my bag?" Dottie said, hands coming up to cover the stain on her shirt. "A…kid threw it in here."

Aris's mouth flattened, and though they said nothing, Dottie wilted under that pointed gaze. "A staff member probably put it in the lost-and-found closet. Follow me."

They turned on their heel, flicking their silky, long hair over a shoulder as they strode away. Dottie couldn't help moping about how much of a mess she was in comparison, especially when she could hear the whispers of the shop's customers.

"What are they doing? Isn't the shop closed for the demo?" Dottie overheard, and she tried to not look in the direction of the crowd.

Out of the corner of her eye, she could see tables and chairs and cardboard standees of some game characters with big swords. There was another worker in the crowd, marked by the apron he wore, talking about the game presumably, his voice getting quieter and quieter as the crowd's unhappy grumbles drowned him out.

Dottie shrunk into herself. She didn't mean to interrupt their event. She just wanted her bag.

The backroom was larger than expected. Aris headed for the rack next to the door and pulled out a cardboard box, thumping it on the nearby desk. Her bag was right on top.

"This is it," she said, reaching for it. "Thank you for your help. I'm so sorry for interrupting your event."

Aris blinked at her slowly, that minute expression freezing Dottie's hand awkwardly in mid-air. "What's in it?"

"Uh," Dottie's mind went blank. She could barely think with Aris staring her down. She glanced around the room, spotting a mirror hanging from a hook. "A yellow mirror with flowers?"

Aris dug around the bag gently. "There's no mirror here."

Right. Right. It must have fallen out of her bag at the flower shop. The flower shop!

"There's a bouquet in there with yellow and pink flowers!" she exclaimed.

Aris handed her the bag, and she hugged it to her chest immediately. "Thank you."

"You should check if there's anything missing. In case it fell out when they put it in here," Aris said.

Dottie peeked into her bag, spotting her wallet. That was all she cared about really. Even if anything had gone missing, she wouldn't know if it was lost here or at the florist. "Everything is here. Thank you, and sorry for the trouble!"

She didn't catch the expression on Aris's face as she walked away as fast as she could without breaking into a run.

Dottie swore she was watching where she was going, but something caught her foot, tripping her, and she bumped into a display shelf, sending dozens of boxes clattering to the floor.

She looked around, finding that she was being watched, snickers and quiet whispers going around. No one stepped forward to help.

She picked up the boxes, putting them back on the shelf. Aris reappeared just as she replaced the last one. They squatted down, wordlessly picking up the broken pieces of the display unit.

Dottie felt a twinge in her nose and at the back of her throat. As if things couldn't get worse!

Aris rose without a word, heedless that something had fallen out of their pocket as they took away the broken display.

Dottie sniffled and picked up the item.

It was…a condom packet.

Her ears warmed, and she quickly hid it in her palm, clutching it tightly as she followed Aris. They made their way behind the counter, setting down the broken display as they dug around trays of office supplies.

"T-this fell out of your pocket," Dottie said, thrusting out the hand that held the condom packet and squeezing her eyes shut.

"Not mine," Aris said flatly. "Please keep it away."

Dottie cracked open an eyelid to peer at their expression. "It fell out of your pocket," she insisted.

"You must be mistaken," Aris said. "If it isn't yours, I suggest you throw it out. There's a garbage can outside the shop. It is inappropriate to wave that thing in my face."

Dottie scrunched her nose. *Fine then*, she thought, stuffing the condom into her pocket. An awkward silence stretched out as she waited for Aris to ring her up for the damage.

"Why are you still standing here?" Aris said instead. "Look, I can't take a condom from a customer even if it's mine. So, just throw it away."

"Aren't I supposed to pay for that? I broke it," Dottie huffed, ignoring the awkward lump in her pocket.

Aris glanced at the broken toy rapier. "It's fine. You don't have to."

"I insist." It had been an accident, but paying was still the right thing to do. She wouldn't feel good about herself otherwise. "How much?"

The crowd tittered again, and Aris glanced at them quickly before sighing, "200 bucks."

Dottie gamely nodded, pulling out her wallet.

"Goods sold are not returnable," Aris said again.

"Just let me buy the thing," Dottie grumbled.

Aris thankfully did not say anything else, dutifully swiping Dottie's card and slapping a "Sold" sticker onto the box.

Dottie barely kept herself from running out of the shop. There was a prickly feeling behind her eyes like she was about to cry, and the last thing she wanted to do was break down in tears in front of a random person she'd just met.

(4) The Fountain

Dottie's feet brought her to a fountain, and she sat heavily on one of the benches surrounding it. She stared unseeingly at spurts of water, trying to breathe and re-center herself after a near meltdown.

Bit by bit, she calmed down, her consciousness coming back to her body slowly.

She was exhausted after the ordeal of the day. Never had she had an outing that wore her out so thoroughly. *What was the point of all this anyway?* she grumbled to herself.

The price tag on the box caught her eye: "All Night Hobby, $200."

Wait, All Night Hobby? Wasn't that the last shop in the challenge?

I've…completed the challenge?

She'd been looking forward to this challenge since she'd moved to the city a few weeks ago. Despite being uninterested in romantic relationships, she loved things about romance, and she loved the hustle and bustle of a city, and this challenge had seemed like the perfect combination of the two.

But after everything she encountered, she could hardly muster any happy feelings about her experience. If anything, she was disappointed about how her adventure had turned out.

To hell with that ridiculous challenge. I'm going home. Dottie stretched her arms to the sky and sighed.

Well, she was going to fix the mess at the florist, then go home. Her sofa was calling to her.

"Excuse me," a disjointed chorus of voices called out.

Dottie turned to look, finding three familiar faces.

There was Athos from the café holding a pastry bag and a coffee cup.

And Poppy from the florist holding Dottie's scarf and a basket containing the assortment of things that Dottie had dropped.

And Aris from the hobby shop holding a…gift card?

Dottie blinked, perplexed. *The challenge said fated one, not fated* three!

She waved awkwardly, forcing a smile onto her face.

Aris spoke first, looking uncomfortable as they held out the card. "Buy something that isn't broken next time."

Dottie took the card hesitantly, warmth settling in her stomach at the sentiment behind those stilted words.

Poppy tsked, slinging an arm around Dottie's shoulder. "Let's go tell the rascal's mom on him and watch him get scolded while we snack on popcorn."

It sounded ridiculous, but it eased the tight feeling around her throat.

Athos let out a sigh. "Don't take the challenge thing too seriously. It's just a dumb gimmick."

Dottie nodded, accepting the coffee and the bag of pastries.

Perhaps Athos was right, but surrounded by the three of them, Dottie thought there might just be something more to it.

VI

L'AMOUREUX

XX

LE JUGEMENT

Allergy Girl and the Hate Arrangement

— R. L. Houck

Christa paused in front of the glass door, confirming the store's hours.

Three Petals Flower Designs
Mon–Fri 8 a.m.–6 p.m. & Sat 9 a.m.–3 p.m.

It was 9:15 a.m. and while she hated to get up this early on one of her Saturdays off, she also hated waiting in lines. Squaring her shoulders, Christa grabbed the door handle and pushed her way inside. She discreetly rolled her eyes as a little bell above the door gently tinkled. So quaint.

The shop was small, located in the downtown sector where all the business fronts were "charming" and "old-fashioned." Charming and old-fashioned were *not* Christa's style. She would have picked another place, but honestly, every flower shop she'd ever walked by looked the same. This one was closest to her apartment, so it was the best option.

"Welcome to Three Petals Flower Designs. How can we help you?" A woman popped up from behind the counter as Christa approached, making her momentarily pause. Christa was tall for a woman, standing at 5 ft. 8 in., but the shop worker was several inches taller. It wasn't common to meet a woman who made Christa feel small. The shop worker also had eyes that were a lovely shade of blue and cheekbones for days, but Christa forced herself back to the task at hand. She wasn't here to ogle the potential owner.

"Uh—yes. I'd like to order an arrangement. Oh!" Christa exclaimed. She pointed at the woman's left arm, exposed by her cap-sleeved shirt. "Nice tattoo."

While looking at the tattoo, Christa noted that the woman's nametag read "Portia." Christa idly wondered if the name was inspired by Shakespeare. Portia turned slightly to better expose the fiery phoenix winding its way up her arm. It was an amazing piece of art, tail feathers trailing down to the top of her hand and beak arching up to her shoulder.

Amy Alexander Weston

"Mousquetaires de Marseille" & "D'Winter de Marseille"

Two previous pages
Amy Alexander Weston opted not to share the inspiration behind these artworks.

Tags

warnings: dead-naming (accidental) **relationships:** customer/employee, f/f, siblings, triplets **character features:** allergies, character has a different gender than in the source material, customer service representative, tattoos, trans female

other tags: alternate universe, attraction at first sight, florist shop, getting together, the language of flowers, meet awkward, modern, past tense, pining, third person limited point of view

Inspiration

I've always been fascinated by the language that exists in the sphere of flower gifting. I thought it would be interesting to see d'Artagnan starting a revolution in a modern, every-day setting. I considered what he could use to spark that revolution and thought of something as simple as giving a bouquet of flowers. Thus the seed of the story began to germinate.

"Thank you. What kind of arrangement?"

Christa opened her mouth and promptly sneezed. "Oh, geeze. I'm sorry," she said, rubbing her nose. "Um. You know how flowers can mean things right? Of course you do. Well, I want an arrangement that secretly means 'fuck you.' "

Portia blinked, and her bright-red lips curved upward on the left in a smirk. "Like—as in an invitation? Or, 'fuck you, I hope you die in a fire'?"

"Oh God, no—the second one!" Christa exclaimed. "Definitely the second one. Scarlett, this bitch at work, stole my promotion. We were both up for the position of executive assistant to Louis, our branch's president. I was the shoe-in, but she miraculously got it. I don't even know how! I have way more experience and an actual degree in the field. Plus, I know Louis appreciates the work I've done on some lower-level copy, and this is all irrelevant and you totally don't care," she said, seeing Portia's eyes start to glaze over. "Anyway—I need the arrangement to still look nice because Scarlett will now sort of be my boss."

She sneezed again and then sniffled, feeling a little congested. "Damn it. Um. Nothing extravagant, so she doesn't think too much of it and start to investigate the different types of flowers. But nothing too small either. Just the right size for a backstabbing executive assistant."

"I got you, girl." Portia bent her head and wrote some things down on a pad. A few strands of her black-tipped blonde hair fell into her eyes, and she distractedly brushed them away. Hm. Normally Christa wasn't into such bold makeup and presentation choices, but they really fit this woman. "Take a look at these pictures. Size wise, you'll probably want the medium. That seems like what you're going for."

Christa shook herself out of her musings and leaned over to look at the laminated sheet. Then she promptly sneezed three times in a row. "What the fuck?" She rummaged in her purse for a tissue and blew her nose. When she glanced up, she saw Portia looking at her askance. "What?"

"Maybe you should have taken some Benadryl before walking into a flower shop if you have allergies."

"I don't have allergies," Christa insisted, waving a hand through the air. She turned her attention back to the sheet. "You're right. The medium looks perfect. What kind of flowers are you thinking?" She cleared her throat, the back of it a little itchy.

"Well, we need some orange lilies to start. They traditionally symbolize hatred and disdain. Yellow carnations also mean disdain. Petunias—okay, yeah, you are totally allergic to something in here, babe. You need to go," Portia suddenly announced. She grabbed a business card and shoved it at Christa. Then Portia came around the counter and took hold of Christa's shoulders, gently propelling her toward the door.

"No, I'm fine!" Wow, her throat felt a little like sandpaper when she raised her voice.

"Your eyes are swelling up," Portia said, opening the door and practically shoving Christa out. "Go home, take some Benadryl, and call us. I'll keep working on an arrangement, and we can handle everything over the phone. I'm not having you die in my shop. Out. Go."

The door slammed shut behind Christa, and she forlornly looked through the glass. Portia stared back and pointed down the street, mouthing "go!" Considering Christa's eyes were starting to water, she thought the shop owner probably knew what she was talking about.

Ugh. There went Christa's day off.

Christa went back to her apartment and nearly cried when she looked in the mirror. Her face had broken out into a blotchy, swollen mess. She kept sneezing, and her sinuses were blocked up. Benadryl wasn't something she routinely took, but she did have some in her medicine cabinet. Within half an hour, she was snoring on her couch.

Several hours later she emerged from her antihistamine-induced coma feeling groggy and gross. But her face was no longer swollen, and she could breathe properly again. So, apparently, Christa was allergic to flowers. Or at least one particular flower. Who knew? No one had ever bought her flowers before, and she wasn't a woodsy girl. Christa liked walks and bike rides, but that was around the city. Now she knew what to stay away from: every single flower shop in existence.

"Oh, you have got to be kidding me," she muttered, checking her phone. It was 3:10 p.m. The flower shop was closed. She didn't have to be at work until 9 a. m. on Monday, so maybe she could call as soon as they opened. Or she could just order from an online service and never speak to the shop owner at Three Petals again. Portia probably thought Christa was an idiot.

Unfortunately, after searching several websites, she discovered that the earliest an online service could deliver was Wednesday. Christa really wanted something for Monday, so she reluctantly placed an order, noting that she could cancel up until noon on Tuesday. She'd see if Three Petals could make and deliver an arrangement any earlier.

Monday morning finally arrived, and Christa stared at her phone, watching the numbers flip from 7:59 a.m. to 8:00 a.m. When they hit 8:01 a.m. she pulled up the shop's phone number and pushed "Send."

Fortunately—or not—the person who answered was a man.

"Thank you for calling Three Petals Flower Designs, Athos speaking. How can I help you?"

For a moment, Christa was taken back. " 'Athos'? As in 'The Three Musketeers'?"

She heard a brief sigh. "Yes, my mother is an English literature professor."

"My apologies," Christa replied. "I'm sure your childhood was—colorful."

"You have no idea. What can I do for you?"

"Yes, uh—I was in on Saturday and talked to Portia about an arrangement, but I had to leave because I'm apparently allergic to—I'm not sure. All flowers, for all I know. Anyway—"

"Oh, Allergy Girl and the 'Fuck You' arrangement. Yeah, Portia was worried you'd ended up in the ER since you never called back," Athos said.

"No, no, I was fine. More like a Benadryl coma." Great. Christa had an official nickname at the local flower shop. *Not* the type of infamy she had been aiming for in her life. "I really did mean to call back, but I fell asleep after downing half a bottle."

"Understandable. Well, Portia—"

In the background, Christa heard a voice call out something. Athos moved the phone away, but Christa could still hear him speak.

"Yeah, it's the Allergy Girl. What? No, she's fine. She's calling about the arrangement. I don't know! You talk to her! Hey, ma'am, I'm giving you over to Portia."

A moment later, there was a scratching noise, and then Portia's voice came through the speaker. "Hey! Glad to hear you're alive!"

"Yeah, thanks," Christa replied, feeling sheepish. "Sorry you had to see me blow up in real time. I've never had an allergic reaction like that before."

"Guess you should stay away from your rival's arrangement. I put together something for you. If you want to give me your phone number, I can text you a picture of it from the shop's mobile."

In the background, Christa heard Athos say something before Portia moved away. "Portia, we don't have—"

Christa barely heard. She was too shocked. "You—you actually already have an arrangement made?"

"Well—yeah. You seemed pretty intent on buying one, so I figured why not? Arrangements last several days in the fridge so it's still fresh," Portia explained. "If you like it, I can catch Aramis before he heads out on his deliveries, and it'll arrive today."

"Yes, I'd love to see it." Christa recited her phone number. Then she blinked down at her kitchen table. "I'm sorry, did you say 'Aramis'?"

"Yup. That's my brother."

"Is Athos your brother too?" Christa cringed. Wow, way to be nosy.

"Mmhm. We're triplets," Portia said, tone proud.

"Your mom must have been so bummed to not have another boy so she could name you Porthos," Christa commented.

"Heh. You know your Dumas. She *did* originally name me Porthos. I'm trans-gender, and that's my dead name. I've disappointed my mother in many ways, but that's got to be the worst."

Christa immediately sobered. "I'm so sorry," she said, voice quiet. "It must be rough not having parent support when you're trans."

"Oh, no! Mom's been very supportive of me being trans. I just meant the name change. For an English lit professor, she has a real hard-on against Shakespeare," Portia said. "It was one of the main reasons I chose the name."

Christa didn't want to bring the conversation down by discussing unsupportive parents of LGBTQA+ kids. Instead, she jumped on the mention of Shakespeare. "Well, Portia is a kick-ass character too," Christa said.

"Right? Thank you!"

"You're quite welcome. Oh! Phoenix! Is that why you chose the tattoo? Never mind, you don't have to answer that. I apologize—I'm being super nosy," Christa said, immediately backtracking.

Portia laughed. "You're fine. That is exactly why I chose the phoenix: rebirth. And those pictures are sent; tell me what you think."

A few seconds later, Christa got a text message from an unknown number. She opened it to see a gorgeous flower arrangement shown in several pictures taken from multiple angles.

"Wow. This is beautiful," Christa said, voice faint from awe. "Are you sure this says, 'I hate your guts and wish abstract misery upon you for the rest of your natural existence' in flower language?"

"…in so many words, yes," Portia said, sounding amused.

"Awesome. Put it on the delivery truck for today. The card will just say, 'Congratulations, Scarlett!' I'm ready to give you the address and my credit card information," Christa declared.

"Besides the whole allergy thing, this has got to be the easiest transaction of my life. Thank you so much."

"We aim to please," Portia responded. Her voice was warm, and it sent a pleasant little buzz down Christa's spine.

But she had just downed two cups of coffee back-to-back, so it was probably just that.

A week later, Christa was dropping off some paperwork to Louis's office. Scarlett wasn't at her desk, so she hesitantly knocked on Louis's door. He looked up, and when he saw her, he waved her in. A wireless bud was in his ear, and he was nodding and making "mmhm" sounds every few seconds. As Christa was about to turn around, Louis held up a hand. She paused.

"Yes, Robert, I'll be sure to let them know. Right, right. I'll see you tonight. Bye." He clicked off the earpiece and glanced up. "These the new figures?"

"Yes, sir."

He paged through the sheets and nodded. "Thanks for bringing these by, Christa. Could I ask you a personal question?"

Before Christa could catch herself, she looked at him askance. Then she schooled her expression into something more professional. "You may. I can't say I'll answer."

"That's fair. If someone were to buy you flowers, would there be a particular kind that you liked?"

Christa burst out laughing. She couldn't help it. So much for being professional. At least she managed to muffle her laughter quickly, however. "I'm sorry. I'm so sorry, sir. It's just that when I went to order Scarlett's congratulatory arrangement, I discovered I'm violently allergic to some sort of flower. I'm a little gun-shy around flowers at the moment."

Louis looked disappointed. "I see. Well, I'm sorry to hear you had that reaction. I was going to ask Scarlett, but she seems to have disappeared."

Christa watched a morose expression form on Louis's face, and she instinctively took a step forward. "Did you know there's a language behind flowers? It's not just how they look, but what each type and color represents. If there's someone important in your life you want to send a bouquet to, I could arrange something for you."

"Could you?" Louis looked up, and his gloomy expression turned hopeful. "There's this woman I met several weeks ago who is coming to the banquet tomorrow. We've had two dates already, and I'd like to give her something—nice—when I pick her up."

Christa raised an eyebrow. "Just 'nice,' sir?"

A delicate pink bloomed high across Louis' cheeks, and Christa had to fight back her smile. "Well, perhaps a bit more than just 'nice.' "

"I have just the thing in mind. Well—I don't. But I know someone who will."

An unfamiliar male voice picked up at the Three Petals flower shop. Christa assumed it was Aramis, the final triplet. Or maybe they had other employees.

"Yeah? Whaddya need?"

Wow. Christa hoped it was Aramis, partial owner of the shop. Otherwise, the employee needed to work on his phone-answering skills.

"Hello, yes. I purchased an arrangement about two weeks ago and worked with Portia. My name is Christa Donnelly, and I'd like to place another order."

There was a pause before the man spoke again. "Oh, so you're Portia's Allergy Girl, huh?" The man's voice was suddenly a lot warmer. "She was hoping you'd call back."

"She—was? Did I not pay enough?" Christa was confused. Surely they'd have contacted her if there had been a problem with the payment, right?

He laughed. "No, you paid enough money. Portia! Allergy Girl is on the line!" he shouted, directing his voice away from the phone. Then he brought it back to his mouth. "I'm Aramis, by the way. Her brother."

"I figured. Nice to meet you, such as it is. No other siblings?" Christa rolled her eyes. She really needed to stop being so nosy!

"Nope, just us three. I think we were more than enough for Mom. Athos said you seemed to know literature."

"Ah—yeah. I graduated with an English lit degree, but it never really got me anywhere. I wanted to go directly into editing, but I ended up as a glorified secretary in an editing company instead. It's decent money at least, and I have my foot in the door," Christa said with a self-deprecating laugh.

"Gotta follow your dreams. You—"

"No one wants to hear about your horticulture dreams, Ari!" Christa heard Portia's voice come closer, and then there were sounds of a scuffle. "Go water some plants or something."

There was a beat of silence before Portia spoke into the phone. "Hey, girl—how can I save the day again?"

Christa couldn't help but smile at the jovial note of the other woman's voice. "Hi, Portia! I wanted to order another arrangement, and you were the first person I thought of," Christa said.

"Aw, I love that you thought of me," Portia said with a delighted laugh. "What did you need?"

"It's more flower language. I wanted a bouquet that speaks of a crush, admiration, affection—you get the idea."

"Yeah? You have a special someone in mind?" The jubilance of Portia's voice dimmed, and Christa found herself shaking her head even though she was the only one in the room.

"Oh, no. No, it's for my head boss. Louis, actually! The branch president. I mentioned him when I first came in—my rival works for him. He's picking up a date he's really serious about for a big work banquet tomorrow night and wanted to give her something extra special. I thought you could create a bouquet that included a tag that listed the symbolism of each flower?"

All she heard was silence. "—Portia? Are you still there?" Christa checked her phone to make sure the line was still connected.

"Yes! Sorry, I was just acknowledging someone that came in." Portia's tone brightened again, sounding almost relieved. Christa decided it must have had something to do with the other customer. "Yeah, yup, we can absolutely do that! Where would you like it delivered? To you or your place of work?"

"Oh, to me. I don't trust the people at work not to lose the bouquet. And if you could send me another picture via text ahead of time, that would be great too. Knowing your skill, I'm confident it will be gorgeous, but Louis hoped to see it. He wants to wear a matching flower on his lapel. He's ridiculously adorable," Christa said. She pulled over her notepad and absently jotted down a few notes about her own outfit. Definitely no flowers for her, but new heels? Absolutely.

"No problem. I'll get right on it!"

Christa received several texts as she was finalizing her makeup before the big event. She couldn't quite tell how wide across the bouquet was and wanted to ask. Meaning to call, she accidentally hit the Facetime button instead. To her surprise, Portia picked up.

"Uh, hi? Oh, wow. I guess you're going to the banquet too, huh?" Portia's eyes were wide as she looked at Christa's dolled-up face.

"That I am. I have to hold my boss's hand. He'd be lost without me. My immediate boss, not Louis. Louis is actually quite competent, which is fortunate since Scarlett is very much not." She wasn't still bitter about her lack of promotion, oh no.

"You look beautiful." Portia's voice was a little awe-struck.

"Thank you! Although, anything is pretty in comparison to the balloon-face I was the last time you saw me. Anyway, I called because I wanted to know how wide the bouquet is."

Portia blinked and then took a few steps closer to the table where the bouquet still rested in a vase. She held her hand over top of the flowers for comparison. "I'd have to get a ruler for an exact measurement, but no wider than about one and half lengths of my hands. 'course I still have big ol' man hands. These don't exactly shrink when you start taking hormones."

"That's all right. The better to hold someone with," Christa said absently as she eyed the bouquet in relation to Portia's hand. "Okay, I think the bouquet should be just right. I wanted to make sure it wasn't too flashy, you know?"

She glanced at Portia and saw the woman was blushing. It was a good look on her, Christa decided.

"Yeah, no, I—I get that. I'll have Aramis deliver it shortly," Portia said, averting her eyes. "You said the banquet is at 8 p.m., right?"

"Yeah. I always get my makeup done first. I like to let it settle a bit, see if I need any touchups before I head out. Aramis has plenty of time," Christa reassured her. "I'm leaving here at a quarter to 7. You really saved me again, Portia. You're a great florist! I'm always going to use you if I need flowers in the future."

"Right. Thanks." Portia's smile slowly dropped. "Well, it's been nice doing business with you again." Glancing down at the floor, she blindly reached out and ended the call. Christa stared at the phone for a moment, confused, then she gave a little shake of her head. Putting the odd interaction out of her mind, she went into her closet for her dress.

At 6:15 p.m., Christa's doorbell rang. She rushed to her door, peered through the peephole, and observed a tall, dark-haired man holding the same bouquet she had seen in the Facetime call. She assumed he was Aramis; he certainly had Portia's cheekbones. Just to be safe, though, she kept the deadbolt chain on and cracked the door.

"Yes?"

"Delivery for Christa? I'm Aramis. We spoke earlier on the phone," he said.

Their voices matched. "Never can be too sure," Christa said, her tone perking up. "Oh, these are beautiful! Portia did an amazing job!"

Christa carefully took the bouquet and placed it in a vase she had waiting on her dining room table. When she turned around, Aramis was giving her a doubtful look. "What?"

"Was it really such a good idea for you to handle that? Did you take some Benadryl?"

"I took some non-drowsy Claritin, thank you very much," Christa announced. "Do I really have the moniker of 'Allergy Girl' for life at your shop now?"

"Pretty much," Aramis said, shoving his hands in his pockets. His eyes narrowed as he scanned Christa from head to toe. She was wearing a slinky black dress which—while tasteful—accented the dip of her waist and the curve of her hips and bust. Yet his gaze didn't feel lascivious. If anything, it felt dismissive. "Hey, so—if you hurt my sister, Athos and I will kill you. Fair warning."

Christa had been reaching for her purse, ready to grab some cash for a tip, but his words caused her to come to an abrupt halt. "I'm—I'm sorry?"

"You heard me. She's fragile. She may look tough, but she doesn't handle rejection well."

"I—what? Dude, you have totally lost me. Portia is lovely, but neither she nor I have made any overtures," Christa protested.

Aramis raised his chin. Then he grunted, turned on one heel, and left the apartment. Christa stared after him, mouth open, until she could no longer hear his steps in the hallway. Then she threw her hands up in the air. "What the fuck?"

Early Monday morning, Louis called Christa up to his office. When she passed by Scarlett's desk, Christa noticed the surface was noticeably absent of all materials. And of Scarlett.

"Good morning, sir! How was your weekend?" Christa chirped, shutting the door behind her as Louis indicated.

"It was good. I wanted to thank you again for arranging that bouquet of flowers. Teresa loved them and thought they were beautiful. The card with the meaning behind each flower was the crowning touch," Louis said with a wide smile.

"I'm glad to have been of assistance. Is there something else you needed?"

"Yes, actually. There is. As you walked in, you may have noticed Scarlett's desk was empty. She was transferred to our sister location today. Robert Eckles was looking for a secretary, and I thought she would be a better fit for him. As such, I have an immediate opening for a personal executive assistant. Would you be interested?"

Christa mouth opened on a small gasp before she managed to close her lips together in a giddy smile. "I would love to, sir. Any reason you thought of me?"

"Well, I know you applied for the position. Between us, I had originally chosen you, but my father liked Scarlett more. Dad still has some say in things around here," Louis said, expression rueful. "Scarlett portrayed herself very well in her initial interviews, but her skills are better suited for office coordination. I like my executive assistant to do more than that—to be able to contribute to my work. Scarlett wasn't giving me what I wanted, and I needed some time to prove that to my father. But I think an English literature major may have some insight into the intricate details of the editing world, don't you?"

Don't squeal. Don't jump for joy, Christa firmly told herself. "Some," she replied calmly. "And the rest, I'm eager to learn."

Louis smiled. "That's what I like to hear."

☙ ♡ ❧

Three Petals called just as Christa was clocking out on Friday.

"Christa speaking."

There was silence on the line for a moment. "—Christa?" Portia's voice was quiet and uncertain.

"Yes, Portia."

"I—uh—this arrangement just got delivered to the shop—in my name. And it's—"

"Is it pretty? The shop wouldn't text me like you guys did. And I didn't have time to run over and see it myself," Christa said, grabbing several files and placing them in her bag.

"It's—fine, I suppose. I could have arranged it better. It's just—the purple lilacs and the white gardenias—did you choose them for the aesthetic or—?"

"Oh, no, I chose them for the language. Did they not put that on the tag? I asked them to. Your shop is far more accommodating than theirs; I'm going to leave them a bad review," Christa remarked. "Anyway, it was my way of saying, 'Hey, I like you.' So, I was wondering, would you like to go on a date with me sometime?"

She shut down her computer and waved goodbye to Louis before walking to the elevator. The whole way, there was silence on the other end of the phone. Christa purposely stood off to the side of the elevator doors, not wanting to get in and potentially lose Portia. "Portia? Are you still there?"

"Yeah—yes! I— What—what made you—?"

Christa smiled down at her shoes. "Well, you did save my life by shoving me out of your shop. And then gave me your personal cell-phone number so you could text me pictures of the 'Hate Arrangement.' "

"—you knew about that?"

"I figured it out eventually."

The next bit of silence lasted even longer. "You remember that I'm trans, right?"

"Yes, and—?"

Christa heard a shaky sigh echo over the line. "Just checking. Aramis thinks you're going to hurt me. Says you're too fancy for someone like us."

"What does Athos think?" She resettled her bag on her shoulder.

"He reminded me that dead bodies make good fertilizer and then wandered off."

Christa threw her head back and laughed. "I mean, honestly—if someone's going to get hurt, it's going to be me. I just have to forget my Claritin one day, and I'll end up as plant food."

Portia made an upset sound. "Don't even joke about things like that."

"Sorry. Listen, Portia—it's just one date. Maybe we have nothing in common to talk about, and we'll go our separate ways."

"That's true. So—what do you want to do? Nature walk?"

Christa snorted at Portia's sly tone. "Bitch. You're going to give me a run for my money, aren't you?"

"Would you have it any other way?"

A slow smile spread across Christa's face. She didn't do "charming" or "old fashioned"—but she sure liked "feisty."

"Never."

Midnight Silver   *"Affaire D'amour"*

Affaire D'amour is inspired by warm, content, sun-kissed moments of quiet reflection that allow a little soul searching to take place and maybe the spark the boldness to seize a moment and follow the heart.

Fast Times at Treville High

— Aeryn Jemariel Knox

Tags
warnings: harm to animals, homophobia
relationships: found family, friends, m/m
character features: gay, lesbian, student (high school)
other tags: alcohol use (casual), bullying, getting drunk, getting together, high school, love declaration, meet awkward, misunderstandings, modern, non-fanfiction story inspired by source material, present tense, third person limited point of view, underage drinking

Inspiration
Aeryn Jemariel Knox opted not to share the inspiration behind this story.

This time, it's going to be different.

It's senior year. He's supposed to own the school. Big man on campus. But it's hard to own anything when he doesn't stay anywhere longer than six months.

His boots squeak on the speckled tile of Treville High School, West Dundee, Illinois, his sixth high school in four years. They all have the same tile, the same shitty metal lockers—blue, brown, gray, and now orange—their slamming doors echoing down the hallways. The people are the same, too: same cliques, same fashion trends. As he's ping-ponged his way from city to suburb to boonies and back, Dorian has watched the ebb and flow of social hierarchies as if through a pane of glass.

They're just coming back from winter break but are already embroiled in the new year's drama: who's kissing who, who's on drugs, who made the cheerleading squad. Why would anybody notice the gangly, long-haired new kid with the third-hand Jansport and army-surplus overcoat?

This is Dorian's last chance to be anything more than a vague smear on somebody's memory.

For now, though, he needs to find his first classroom. He shoulders his way through the press of adolescents, one eye on the room numbers and one on his own shoes. When he bumps into a solid body, it's not really a surprise. He bounces right off and lands with an *oof* on the tile.

"Watch it!" she snaps. "You got milk on my leather, you dick."

Pride and tailbone smarting, he eyes her ripped black skinny jeans, patterned buzzcut she definitely fashioned herself, and the safety pins and studs she's stuck through a leather jacket that still creaks like it's new. Milk drips down the front in translucent smears.

She's just a punk.

He can deal with punks.

"The fuck are you doing drinking milk in the hall?" Dorian claps back as he regains his feet. He's taller than her, but not by much, and she has a lot of muscle on him. "Besides, it looks like you've already fucked it up."

Her eyes flash with a satisfying glint of rage. "You got something to say about my jacket?"

In for a penny. Dorian puffs up his chest, grips his backpack strap tighter, and says, "There's a joke in here somewhere about milk and leather and calling you a cow, but honestly? Not worth the effort."

That does it. Her nostrils flare. She starts to launch at him, her expression tight and bulldoggish. But before she can do more than shove her carton at a wide-eyed bystander, a sharp whistle-blast cuts through the student murmur.

"All right, all right," the teacher says—no one Dorian recognizes, but if he had to guess, he'd say calculus. "Portia. We have talked about this. We will be civil. And you—" She turns, hesitates.

"Dorian." He's well accustomed to that blank space where his name should be.

"Ah, our new transfer. Well. The sooner you learn to keep your nose clean, the better."

Dorian snorts, but he doesn't feel like getting detention just yet. He keeps his mouth shut.

With a stern glare, the teacher wades away through the crowd, the circle of students dispersing in her wake. But the girl in leather—Portia—doesn't let Dorian off so easily. She grabs him by the elbow.

"After classes," she says. "By the bleachers. We'll finish this."

"Fine," Dorian gripes, determined to figure out where the bleachers are before then.

With one final posturing thrust of her shoulders and chin, they part company to the ringing of the bell.

Third period. English.

Either the school lost his transcript again or all English classes blur together, because he could swear he read *The Count of Monte Cristo* in sophomore year. A few chapters, at least. A few chapters is all he gets through of any given book.

But the girl next to him seems invested. She scribbles notes like she's hearing the Sermon on the Mount, not the half-baked ramblings of some fool in a sweater-vest. It's irritating. The scratch of her pen. *Itch, itch, itch, itch.*

"You know," he says, leaning close. "Edmond Dantes is just asshole 19th-century Batman."

The girl gives him a sharp look. "So what?" she says. "I don't see you taking notes."

Dorian shrugs and kicks his chair back on two legs. "Yeah, because I'm not a teacher's pet."

She openly glares now. "Who *are* you?" she asks, but the teacher's voice cuts across any further talk.

"Miss Auteville. Do you have something you'd like to add?"

The girl blanches but recovers quickly with a flick of her straight black hair. "I was just remarking on the similarity between Edmond Dantes and masked vigilante characters in modern literature and cinema."

A few people in the class laugh; somebody mutters "*Batman*" from the back row. Before Dorian can move past flustered shock, the teacher continues.

"Now, that is a fascinating comparison. Thank you, Athena."

The second the teacher's back is turned, Dorian drops his chair with a *clank*. "You did that on purpose."

"Did what?" Her smugness knows no bounds.

"You stole my idea."

"You didn't seem to care much about it."

Dorian scoffs. "I think you're a goodie two-shoes who didn't like getting called out."

"A milquetoast take on one of the most studied books in French literature does not make you smarter than me."

"Then why did you steal it?"

Blithely, she spins her notebook around. Dorian first glares at her, then down at the page full of tidy penmanship. He reads for two seconds—long enough to catch the gist—then swears under his breath.

Tugging her notes back, she gives him a cool, measuring look. "You're new this term, aren't you?"

"What gave it away?"

She nods. "Meet me by the bleachers after school."

With a skeptical eyebrow, Dorian asks, "You want to fight? You?"

"Don't be absurd."

A loud clearing of the teacher's throat finally puts an end to their conversation. Dorian spends the rest of the class drawing spirals on the desk, wondering what he's getting himself into.

Whoever thought gym class right after lunch was a good idea deserves a kick in the face. "Lunch" consisted of half a bag of Doritos and a Cherry Coke, and Dorian feels sick.

At least part of that is because of the boy in front of him. The class is spread out in a rough grid on the waxed wood gym floor, and the teacher has them doing fucking *yoga*. This dude's long legs and bubble butt in nylon shorts are directly in front of Dorian's face, and there's nothing to be done about it. He's just glad his own shorts are loose.

Worse, the guy manages to make eye contact while they're both folded almost in half. Dorian drops his head quickly, but he's been caught, and he knows it.

Not good. He swore he wouldn't get the shit beat out of him this time. Not for this. Let it be for something he's done, not for something he is.

They move on to dodgeball, but that barely helps. Dorian ends up directly opposite the gorgeous boy with the flop of dark hair and the amazing legs, and he's definitely got Dorian's number. He's glaring across the court as if he either wants to blow him or blow him away, and Dorian's not lucky enough for option one. After a few volleys, Dorian starts to itch under the collar. Leg-boy hasn't taken his eyes off him. Not once.

"*What?*" he asks with his shoulders and his eyebrows. But Leg-boy just scowls and fires the ball in Dorian's direction.

Somehow, he makes it through the game with his balls intact, but the after-gym showers are always the worst part. *Eyes on the floor. Don't look.* A lesson learned the hard way.

He manages to avoid Leg-boy until he's navigating back to his locker with a towel around his waist, hair limp and damp around his face. Leg-boy is equally undressed, water droplets beading on his olive skin, and he plants himself directly in Dorian's path. Dorian keeps his eyes carefully above the chin, though his heart kicks like a mule and his toes curl into the grout lines.

"Do we have a problem?" the boy asks. His voice is bass-drum deep. Dorian swallows.

"Nope."

Leg-boy squints at him. "You got something to say to me?"

"Not while we're both naked," Dorian says, and immediately wants to curse his stupid lips.

"That so?" Leg-boy moves a step closer, close enough that Dorian can smell the water on his skin and feel the residual heat of the shower. He swallows again; the tension in his belly turns sharp. "Does it make you uncomfortable?"

"Uh." That's all that comes out this time. It's for the best.

Leg-boy laughs, a knowing little huff. "You want to take a swing at me? Fine. Bleachers. After the last bell."

"I'll be there," Dorian manages through a tight throat. His brain immediately conjures visions of a much more pleasant kind of rendezvous, but the withering look that Leg-boy gives him as he wanders back to his own locker puts the kibosh on that little fantasy.

If he survives his first week at this cursed school, it will be a miracle.

As the last bell rings, Dorian stands in an empty bathroom peering into the spotty mirror, fists against the cold ceramic edge of the sink. Three separate people want to decorate his face, all at the same time. He's a scrappy asshole, but he'll be lucky if he can get out of this as more than bloody pulp.

Whatever. He's gotten this far on a devil-may-care attitude. Maybe if he can take the punk chick—Portia—the other two will fold. Athena hadn't looked like the fighting type, and Leg-boy…that's another story.

The others have already gathered by the time he finds the bleachers, the three of them in a loose clump under a banner proclaiming "*Go Muskets!*" strung across the back of the sagging wooden structure. The football team is practicing at the far end of the field, but the bleachers themselves are empty.

Portia catches sight of him first. "Look who didn't chicken out," she shouts, deliberately loud enough for his ears.

As one, the others turn to Dorian, who feels his legs turn to jelly and his stomach to ice. He should have expected this.

"You all…know each other?" he asks in a tremulous voice.

"Yeah. We freaks gotta stick together," Portia sneers. "Didn't think this through, didja?"

Dorian shrugs his shoulders up tight. "You're the ones who wanted to pick fights, not me."

"But you're the one who needs an attitude adjustment," says Leg-boy, somehow even more gorgeous in ripped jeans and a well-worn black hoodie. He's got his thumbs stuck through ragged holes at the wrists. Dorian bites his lip and finds something else to focus on.

"Where the hell did you come from, anyway?" asks Athena.

Dorian shrugs again, shoving his hands in his pockets, eyes on the scuffed grass. "We move around a lot."

"Hell of a first impression—" she says before Portia cuts her off.

"Doesn't matter. I owe you one." Portia shoves her way forward, cracking her knuckles against the palm of her other hand, posturing accentuated by the spikes in her leather.

Dorian wants to run—his legs quiver with the urge—but he roots to the ground. Bends his knees, curls his fists. If he's going down, he's going down like a man.

As it were.

Before she can take her first swing at him—

Thud!

A football flies through the air between them, landing in the mud at Leg-boy's feet and stopping Portia in her tracks.

From across the field, a voice shouts, "Hey, gaywads!"

Dorian turns, fury in his veins. *Now* he wants to fight.

It takes a second to realize the jab wasn't aimed at him.

One of the jocks from football practice jogs up to them with a sneer on his face. Dorian doesn't know him, but instantly hates him thanks to a lifetime of torment at the hands of people like him. From his tidy haircut to his expensive cleats to the name "Bishop" emblazoned on his jersey, Dorian hates him. "Think you can throw that all the way back here? Maybe get your dyke friend to do it."

Portia surges toward him, all her anger redirected. The other two hold her back by the arms, but that leaves nobody to stop Dorian from advancing. "Why don't you shove it in your ear, jackass? Maybe it'll grow into a brain."

The jock's lip curls in a dismissive half-laugh. "Who's this chump?"

"New kid," says Athena, eyeing him with an expression he can't be bothered to interpret.

The jock's sneer turns into a real laugh. "You already hanging out with these weirdos? Get better friends."

"Better to be freaks than Daddy's little rich brat," Dorian snaps.

"You shut your mouth—" The jock starts after Dorian, but a sharp whistle from the coach stops him in his tracks.

Athena throws the ball at his feet. "Just take it and go, Reggie."

The jock gives them one last look, spits in the dirt between them, and turns to jog back across the field.

Dorian doesn't dare look back at the trio until he feels a hand on his shoulder. It presses his coat into his skin, cold from the light drizzle that's started to dampen everything. He hadn't even noticed.

Leg-boy stands close enough that Dorian can see the hazel-green of his eyes; his heart skips a beat. "You didn't have to do that," he says, still guarded.

Dorian swallows, then shrugs. The hand drops away, leaving the warm shape of his palm to be filled in by the rain. "Yeah, I did. Is what he, uh. Are you—?"

Color floods the boy's cheeks. "I thought you knew that."

"How could I?" Dorian asks.

"The way you looked at me in gym." Now it's Dorian's turn to flush while the boy visibly musters his courage. "I figured you knew I was gay and were going to kick the shit out of me for it."

Summoning his own voice, Dorian stands a little taller. "I thought you knew *I* was gay and wanted to kick the shit out of *me* for it."

The grin he gets in response is shy and aimed at his shoes. Dorian's heart flutters up into his throat, and he cracks an answering smile.

"I'm Adrian," the boy says. "You shouldn't hang with us if you want to make any other friends. Something tells me that's not a high priority for you, though."

Dorian laughs, relief pushing it out loud. "What makes you say that?"

"You got yourself into three fights on your first day," Adrian says.

"In fairness," Athena chimes in, "I never really wanted to fight. I was going to ask about your *Monte Cristo* essay."

A few more of Dorian's nerves escape on a giggle.

Portia is still studying him, sullen but curious. When Adrian gives her a significant look over his shoulder, she says, "I'm still mad about my jacket."

"Yeah. I am sorry about that," Dorian says. "It was an accident."

One last side-eye, and she shrugs. "Eh, to hell with it. Leather jackets are supposed to get fucked up, anyway."

The term gets better after that. They are still outcasts in a school where there is little worse one can be, but at least they're outcasts in company. Classes fail to spark his interest, but his verbal sparring matches with Athena help him figure out what to actually say in his essays. There's nothing to do in this town, but Portia always manages to drum up an afternoon's entertainment.

And then there's Adrian.

Dorian's not sure if it's a matter of convenience, given that they may be the only queer boys in the entire school, but he's in no position to ask stupid questions. Their stolen moments remain a bright spot during his days and a tantalizing temptation during his nights.

Unfortunately, none of his friends are in Mr. Winters' Biology class.

Reggie Bishop is.

And today, he's elected to sit directly across from Dorian.

It's lab day; they're supposed to be dissecting sheep hearts. Reggie hasn't even touched his before he starts in on Dorian.

" 'Sup, new kid?"

Dorian's eyes roll. "Is that the best you got?"

Reggie blows his perfectly parted flop of hair away from his eyebrow. "I think you and I got off on the wrong foot." When Dorian doesn't dignify that with an answer, he continues. "You hear about Rockfort's party on Saturday?"

Dorian had heard that it was happening, but the effect it had on his life was a short, succinct *zero*. "I guess." Dorian frowns down at his heart—firm and cold, squashed sideways from being packed in a bucket with a few dozen others—assuming the conversation to be over.

"I can get you in," says Reggie.

He's overly casual as he says it, like a rich man offering a peasant one of his many gold coins. Dorian barely glances up, reaching for the probe. "Why the hell would you do that?"

"It's not my fault the bull-dyke found you first. I'm trying to help salvage what's left of your social life."

"Out of the goodness of your heart?" Dorian's eyebrow cocks higher than he thought possible.

Reggie sits back a little, twirling a T-pin between his fingers and idly examining the heart in front of him. His nose and lip curl in disgust, and he slides the tray a little farther away from himself. "Pretty much, yeah."

" 'Pretty much.' "

"Nothing wrong with a little tit for tat. I help you; you help me. Save the party, get the girl, y'know. Or the guy, I guess. Whatever." The disgust doesn't go anywhere, it just moves.

Dorian waits him out, still probing the heart in his hands.

"We need supplies," Reggie finally says. "Nobody knows you, so you're the only kid in town who can get away with using a fake ID."

Pretending to scan the next steps of the dissection, Dorian contemplates. For just a few seconds, he thinks about it. Crashing a rich kid's house party…they could definitely get up to some mischief. Maybe Portia would think he was cool for once. And maybe there would be a dark closet or a basement with a nook under the stairs. Somewhere he could pull Adrian by the hand, and they could—

But no. One look at Reggie's smug smirk, and he knows.

"Thanks," Dorian says, "but I'll pass."

Reggie's smirk evaporates. "What? Didn't you hear what I said?" He leans forward again, elbow almost knocking his tray to the floor. He's got his scalpel clutched in his other hand, still perfectly clean, and for half a second, Dorian's worried he might actually use it. "You really gonna spend your whole senior year with a handful of freaks? Don't you want to actually do something here?"

Once more, it tugs at him. The fear of a life forgotten.

"I said no," he repeats. "Find another mule."

Reggie may have the perfect nose, perfect jaw, perfect teeth, and perfect hair required by his perfect rich-boy quarterback role, but in that moment, his snarl makes him the ugliest soul Dorian has ever seen. "You'll regret this," he hisses.

Heart pounding on his tongue, Dorian picks up his scalpel. The blade trembles as he makes his incision. "Hey, how's that homecoming game plan working out for you?"

Reggie blinks. "What plan?"

"Y'know. With the laxatives. And the—"

Reggie slaps one hand on the table so hard, the rest of the class goes quiet. Even Mr. Winters looks over at their table. "Mr. Bishop, I don't see any incisions happening over there."

"Sorry, Mr. Winters," Reggie says. It's almost alarming how quickly he can switch from dangerously unhinged to golden boy and back again once the class's attention has moved on. "How do you know about that?"

Heat creeps up Dorian's neck. He's not about to say what he and Adrian had been doing under the bleachers while Reggie and his minions sat overhead hashing it out. "I've got ears."

"If you tell anybody, I will—"

"You'll what? Uninvite me?" Before Reggie can respond, Dorian presses on. "I don't care what you think of us. But I can guess what your father might think if he knew you were planning to cheat by poisoning the other team."

Reggie's gaze goes flat and cold, but then he scoffs. "Like he'd listen to *you.*"

Dorian just shrugs, turning his attention back to the splayed-open heart. "It's your juvie record." His hand doesn't shake much when he makes the next incision, but it is a struggle to stay focused when Reggie finally jabs his scalpel into the meat, bringing forth a gelatinous gloop of dark-brown blood the texture of cottage cheese. Dorian bites down hard on his lip to keep from laughing.

After class—and an extremely thorough hand-washing—Dorian lingers long enough to be sure that Reggie is out the door ahead of him. His path crosses with Adrian's at the end of the hall, and every part of him quivers as he approaches. Adrian's watching for him. Their eyes lock, and his smile is sweet.

As soon as Dorian gets close, Adrian's nose wrinkles. "You stink."

Shrugging his backpack higher on his shoulders, Dorian dips his chin. "Formaldehyde."

"Seriously? Cool," Adrian says. The walk to their next class is short, but they make it last as long as they can. There are other kids on all sides, jocks and cheerleaders, band kids and burnouts, scrawny freshmen looking lost. Inside the maelstrom, nobody notices how close they stand. Nobody sees when Adrian's wrist crosses under Dorian's, the meat of his thumb barely brushing Dorian's palm. He hopes to God that nobody is watching when he turns his hand back to meet Adrian's, or when the very tips of their fingers—clammy, fumbling, scared—press together, interweave.

If it's going to be them against the world, there's nowhere Dorian would rather be.

"Who needs prom, anyway?" Portia crows from the top of the slide. "Bunch of pissant heteronormative jerks doing the leave-room-for-Jesus shuffle under the basketball hoops? Boring."

She's a swirling, upside-down squiggle, just like the rest of the world. Dorian lies flat on his back on the merry-go-round, long hair dragging in the sawdust. It feels dangerous. So does the sparkle-fizz of Miller High Life in his stomach. And the way Adrian's feet are hooked around his own in the middle of the spinning steel.

Athena cackles from the swings off to the side. "You're just mad because Kitty went with Reggie Bishop."

"No," Portia protests. "I wasn't even going to bother asking Kitty."

Dorian's ankles knock against Adrian's. "It's all a bunch of bullshit, anyway," he says. "Manufactured social hierarchies showing off their hollow gains."

"It's the Great Gatsby all over again," Athena says, hopping off the swings. Striking a pose and a dramatic tone of voice, she wails, "Oh Portia, green light across the water, will I ever reach you?" Her hand reaches toward Portia's perch; Portia gives a raucous laugh and slides down, metal booming and rattling.

"Don't start," Dorian moans.

"Y'know what?" Portia says as she pulls another beer out of the cardboard box. Dorian's still not sure where she got it, but it's flowing sweetly in all of their veins. "You know fucking what?"

"What?" Dorian and Adrian ask together. Dorian is starting to feel sick. He has no idea how he's going to get off this carousel. He closes his eyes to block out the spiraling trees and ash-and-orange clouds beyond, but that only makes it worse.

"We can make our own prom," Portia says.

Athena scoffs. "You're drunk."

"And why not? Look—" Portia gestures at the spinning carousel. "Dancing. And hey!" She lunges at the slide, beating it with the palms of both hands. "Music!"

"You're gonna get the cops called on us," Athena scolds.

"And—" Suddenly solemn, Portia picks up the paper bag that had once held beer and Cheetos. "A crown fit for the illustrious Queen of the Prom!"

With a shriek, Athena speeds off into the dark beyond the playground, kicking up a spray of wood chips. Both girls disappear beyond the orange globe of the well-lit playground, cackling and screaming as they play chase like the children they still ought to be.

Dorian hauls himself up at last, using the steel handrails to right himself. The world tilts, dizzy, nauseous, and he laments that he has to disentangle his legs from Adrian's. But Adrian is moving, too, hopping off the carousel without seeming any worse for the wear. Dorian, meanwhile, struggles to drag his feet in the mulch while the ghost of carbonated booze wails inside him.

When his foot finally hit something solid, it's Adrian's ass. He's planted in the bark, looking dazed and woozy. Maybe he wasn't unaffected after all.

He still summons a smile for Dorian. "You all right?" he asks over his shoulder.

Dorian nods, then shakes his head. "Think I'm gonna be sick."

Adrian clasps his ankle in sympathy. "Stay there for a bit. I'll fetch Her Majesty and the Jester."

Dorian manages a weak laugh and does as he's told. The steel railing is cool against his forehead; he lets himself drift.

He thinks of Adrian's face so close to his own. He thinks of Reggie Bishop and Kitty Beaucomp, King and Queen of Normalcy. He thinks of his little band of weirdos, the punks and the poets, the *queers*. He wonders about the vagaries of fate that brought him here to this school just in time to meet them. He wonders about the future. They graduate in a few weeks. This summer will be spent in Athena's basement playing D&D—and then what? Where will they all go?

"Gotcha!"

Dorian startles out of his half doze when Portia pins Athena to the ground nearby. Adrian is handing Portia the paper bag while Athena laughs like a madwoman, only nominally struggling. "By the power vested in me by the Church of Queerdom," Portia intones, her booming voice carrying across the park, "I dub thee Queen Athena of AP English Lit!" This gets her another peal of laughter from Athena. "Long may she reign!"

There's a moment—Athena's giggles have died down, but Portia is still looming over her—when Dorian wonders if they're about to kiss. It wouldn't surprise him.

Then Athena wriggles; the paper bag fails to stay on her head. "All right, okay, let me up." She still doesn't sound as put out as she'd pretended to be, and she accepts Portia's hand to lift her out of the dust. "Who ever heard of a prom queen covered in wood chips, anyway?"

"Better than whatever Kitty's wearing, that's for sure," Adrian drawls.

Dorian is on his feet before he's quite sure they'll hold him. Still swaying, he crosses to where Adrian stands on the foot of the slide, stopping along the way to scoop up the beer box. There's one can left rattling around in the bottom, and he liberates it.

Adrian watches him approach, a question on his full lips.

"And you, Adrian," Dorian says. His voice hardly trembles; he can push through. "To you, I make a toast!" He cracks the can of Miller with one hand, tugging on the tab with a fingernail. "To the sweetest pretty boy that ever haunted the halls of Treville High!" The girls cackle behind him, and warmth melts Adrian's countenance. "To you, my king, I pledge fealty. For as long as you'll have me—" As the words fall out, Dean knows they're too much, too sincere, even for a bit. But there's no way out now except through. In for a penny. "I dub thee King Adrian, long may he reign, or whatever." And he dumps the Miller box over Adrian's head. Peals of laughter sound from Portia, a snickering snort from Athena, and Dorian pounds the beer in his hand to cool his flushed face.

"Thank you," he says as he finishes the foamy brew. "I'll be here all week."

Refusing to meet Adrian's eye, Dorian escapes toward the bushes outside the playground lights.

Footsteps follow him. "Dor— Hey, wait!"

"Mm—gotta—" Dorian holds up one finger. Maybe he will throw up now.

Adrian catches his arm. The Miller box didn't last long, thank goodness. "You okay?"

"Yeah, just—too much beer. And spinning."

"You gonna hurl?" Adrian asks.

The grip of Adrian's hand above his elbow grounds him, steadies his stomach and sends his heart racing. "Maybe not," he says. "Sorry—about—whatever that was."

Adrian's shaking his head and holding on tighter. "No, the—the feeling's mutual," he says.

The carousel spins the other way. "What?"

He lets go, but Dorian is stuck watching his expression, the careful hunch of his shoulders as his hands tuck into his jean pockets. "You know why we're out here, right?"

"Yeah, 'cause they wouldn't let us go to prom."

"No," Adrian shakes his head. He's backlit in orange and planes of shadow, but Dorian can see the shine on his lips. "We could have gone to prom if we'd wanted, but not—not right. And being right is more important than doing what we're supposed to do. You know? The normal scripts don't work for us, so we have to write our own, and that's scary as hell. But it's also kind of amazing, don't you think?"

Dorian's heart pounds harder.

"And I think—if we get to choose our own family—I don't want to lose this one. I don't want to lose you."

It's too much. "Man, I was kidding—"

Then Dorian has to shut up because Adrian's lips are on his, soft and warm and more real than ever before. And no matter what else life throws at them, he's sure of one thing:

They will remember each other.

Jennifer Smith **"Knight and Squire"**

Jennifer Smith opted not to share the inspiration behind this artwork.

Sword Dancer

— J. D. Harlock

Tags

warnings: death of a parent (mentions of), death of a sibling (implied), violence (non-graphic descriptions) **relationships:** f/f **character features:** bipoc **other tags:** break-up, duels, fantasy, first person point of view, non-fanfiction story inspired by source material, past tense, politics, religion, reunions,

Inspiration

This short story was initially pitched as a short comic to the *Sharp Wit & the Company of Women* anthology by Extra Pages Press. On Wikipedia, I had read that an Ottoman Sultan had for a time banned sword dancing in the Middle East as it was believed that dancers collected the swords that were taken from Ottoman soldiers to arm a resistance against the Ottoman army. The lunar theme that's featured prominently in the story was inspired by my dabbling in lunarpunk at the time, and earlier drafts had more elements in line with that style, even though this technically isn't a lunarpunk story. I did consider setting it in a pseudo-futuristic fantasy/sci-fi hybrid like Star Wars or Adventure Time, but eventually decided against it.

Prologue

Under the auspices of the sacred stars, I basked in the luminescence of the sister moons that came together in cosmic harmony, aligning for an instant—one brief moment in an eternal dance—only to part and realign again in a different formation a decade later. On this night, as in the decades prior in the Emirate of Qamarayn, the Izhar was to take place, I leading for the first time. Bless Yarih and Astarte, my passions had prevented me from participating in the prior two, but now, with the recent passing of the Emir, I had found a steadfast resolve to stand on this terrace and oversee the arrangements for a third—as my brother had, and our father before him.

How I wished it was transpiring under different circumstances…

Part I: The First Izhar

After the Emirate of Qamarayn had fallen under the heel of the Sultanate, the Emir had found himself in the throes of invaders from the north and the pressures of the High Porte. Though it pained Father in ways I would only come to understand later, subjecting himself to the will of the Sultan was our only recourse, and he readily acquiesced even though it entailed his utter humiliation. To commemorate the memorandum, the Sultan had agreed to stand as audience to one of our oldest customs, the Izhar, where I was to perform for the first time.

Except, when it began, I was nowhere to be found.

I'd chosen to hide myself in the mashrabiya, where I came across a strange girl lit by the luminescence of the vines that climbed through the lattice. The shadows of their blossoms on the stones shifted in the breeze as she gazed out at the palace gardens, lit by fuchsia orchids and violet roses.

At that moment, I came to understand beauty, and I was frightened by it.

"You're not supposed to be here," I said, backing away.

"Don't worry." The girl turned to me, and I was struck by her radiant crimson ferace, embellished with candescent pleats. It wrapped her body loosely, effortlessly reaching the ground. "The Sultan instructed me to come here. I am Anbara bint Jazzar. Who might you be?"

I stood there in my paler ferace and çarşaf, modest in its embellishments, and knew the true status Yarih and Astarte had bestowed on me and my people. The girl's peçe was draped over by a yaşmak made of fine silk that clung, gold glistening in the moonlight, to her statuesque features. Though she vexed me, she was so beautiful. I couldn't look her in the eye.

"I am Nahla bint Hamad," I said, then turned from her gaze.

"Ah." Anbara bowed her head politely. "You're the Emir's daughter. Why are you not preparing for the Izhar?"

"I'm afraid, Sultana," I stammered. "A lot is expected of me, and I'm afraid I can't meet those expectations."

"I see." Anbara smiled. "Then I allow you to forsake this one. If anyone were to ask, let them know the order came from the Sultan himself."

I fell to my knees. "Thank you, Sultana. Thank you for your generosity."

"Excellent." Anbara straightened her back. "Now, that is all well and good but"—she calmly unsheathed her pusat and pointed it at my outer garment, the blade gleaming in the moonlight—"who allowed you to wear that?"

"Sultana," I muttered, feeling a shame I never had before. "These are the clothes of an Emira of the Qamarayni Emirate."

"Oh, I see." The Sultana's façade faltered. "It would be best to replace it with a skirt and cape."

Fearful of rapprochement, I threw myself at her feet and asked for forgiveness.

"It's all right." The Sultana smiled. The blessings of the sister moons shone onto me through her. "This was not through any fault of your own, but Father expressly forbids the women of his palaces from wearing clothing not in line with what the Sultanate has deemed fashionable."

In private, Brother had instructed me to allot the Sultan and his coterie the respect I would show Father. However, in that moment, the precocious feelings that—unbeknownst to me—had been fermenting for years were released in a flurry of anger as she made light of me and my people.

I finally met her gaze.

"This is not his palace, and we are not his women."

But Anbara, amused, turned from me to admire the moons on the Goddess's night.

"As of the signing, you are."

Bless Yarih and Astarte, the celebration held on that Izhar was, by far, the most elaborate the Emirate had witnessed during my father's reign. Though it was my first, I could tell from the excitement that exhilarated the staff and advisors that it would be unlike any experienced before.

Neath the glare of the purple roses, the royal guard lined up in front of each other in the palace courtyard, close enough that their shoulders touched. Then the court poets pronounced verses to inaugurate the proceedings; the gathering repeated them and tossed pink petals into the air. Behind the Izharis, players picked their ouds and a drummer beat the takhmeer to control and unify the motions of the dancers. Their slender bodies glided across the polished marble, vined blades carefully maneuvering in and out of each other's way with a swift, calculated elegance. The Sultan and his coterie were entranced, staring in awe.

From his cushion, Father's eyes, unmistakable in their pride, followed my brother as he stepped through the dance bearing our ancestral scimitar. But, as Brother and the guards approached the Sultan and his coterie with their hands held out, alarm wrested Father's face.

"What is the meaning of this?" The Sultan's personal guard drew their kilijs, directing them at the royal guard—and my brother froze in fright as the priceless heirloom that our forefathers had built this Emirate with fell to the floor with a pathetic *clank*.

"Forgive me, Your Excellency." My father knelt before the Sultan. "The Izhar requires that the swords of all who attend be taken and incorporated into the performance. It really is a sight to behold, if you will but allow it…"

This was the first time I'd ever seen my father lower himself in such a way, and I held my breath, worried that no sooner had I lost my mother, I would lose my father and brother too.

"Padishah…" Anbara rose. She moved forward carefully to address her father, and the intensity of his expression faltered. "There is no reason to fear the ritual. It'd be foolish for them to try and harm us—mad, even."

The Sultan chuckled, amused. "You have much to learn." He turned and gestured toward my father and me. "Shall we allow them to continue? Or would you prefer an Emirate all to yourself?"

Befuddled, Anbara straightened her back, glancing at us—at me—before she finally responded: "Padishah, it would not be wise—" she stuttered, the effortless fluency that defined her speech gone. "If our allies in the region find out we haven't kept our word and have dissolved our latest, hard-won alliance, it could make them uneasy."

The Sultan studied his daughter as if he was unsure of what to do with her, then broke into a fit of laughter.

"Excellent observation, my daughter. You will make a fine addition to my court." He turned to his coterie, who were startled. "Let us continue the—what do Qamaraynis call it?—Izhar?"

It was not until the ceremony proceeded that I realized no one had dared to retrieve the ancestral scimitar.

Interlude

As I was about to part from the terrace to begin preparations for this Izhar, I noticed one of our watchmen riding from the hills toward the capital's gates. I motioned to call over the wazir, but then spotted the extravagant procession that trailed behind the watchman at a leisurely pace, its strange beasts outpacing his mule without urgency.

Before I could process what was happening, the dragoman at its head sounded the imperial horn, shattering my thoughts. I called urgently for my scope and inspected the center of the proceedings where I'd noticed a behemoth of burden, hoping to glimpse whoever the Sultan had sent on this night of all nights.

It was the monster known throughout our region as the General. She sat on a lavish cushion of silk and velvet, stirring the beast with a steady grip and stern expression that gave no hint of the perverse delight I knew she derived from the entire charade. Spearmen flanked her sides, and regiments marched behind her. These were not the Sultan's guards. These were his soldiers. The royal porters sounded the drums, then turned to me for further instruction as my wazir, Kassem, rushed out to the balcony for my commands. With the prospect of conflict and no defenses to speak of, I signaled them to open the gates, allowing the General and her army inside.

Kassem and I greeted the General with much fanfare beneath the steps to my father's throne, exalting her presence and the auspices of the High Porte. These senseless courtesies were interminable. Once concluded, the palace guard escorted her to my private chambers, where we did away with all pretenses.

"How dare you?!" I held myself back from lunging. "You've embarrassed me in front of my subjects. I am the guarantor of their safety, and you marched into my Emirate prepared for war!"

But the General didn't seem perturbed by my outburst and carried on in as formal a manner as one could in light of the situation.

"I demand an audience with you and the wazir." Her hand hovered over her sword. "The Sultanate is reconsidering its strategies in the region."

"Now?!" I stomped and threw my hands in the air. "With all the time in the world, now?"

The General chortled. "Oh, what could you mean?"

Her sneer of cold command pricked me, letting the blood from my veins. In the midst of all this pomp and circumstance, here in the haven that once housed my family, in the temple that once venerated our Goddesses, in the monument that once celebrated my people, I could strangle her.

"Why would you do this to me?" I cried, but she just scoffed.

"Laudable words coming from the woman who abandoned me and left me to die."

"Do you not recall what happened—the way you had begun to act—that twist that curled in your smile with every victory, every conquest?" My chest collapsed inward. "I never abandoned you. You were gone long before that."

I expected the General to retort with venom, but she glared, then turned her scarred face away as if she couldn't look me in the eye anymore.

"To think that only ten years ago, we'd sworn our lives to each other."

I performed the sign of the crescent.

"That was another life."

Without another word, I retreated to my chambers for my next move.

Part II: The Second Izhar

I missed the second Izhar when I was lost at sea on our return voyage. Father had asked me not to leave his side, and Kassem had gone down on his knees, beseeching me not to abandon the Emirate after the tragedies that had befallen it. But I was young and full of love and life, yearning for an existence outside of the mountains—one that promised endless adventure on the high seas.

I could have drowned on that stormy night when the skipper ran to secure the bow and hard winds knocked him from the deck right before my eyes. He'd have been gone if not for the rope around his waist that he had tied to the mast. I ran over to heave him back in, struggling to hold on, but the more I fought, the more he threatened to pull me under.

The rope snapped.

Realizing we would both be lost if I carried on, the first mate struggled to release himself from my grip. I begged him to have faith in me.

Before I could resign myself to the inevitable, I was pulled away by the captain with the force of a fiend far more feral than that of nature's disasters.

Later, inside the captain's quarters, I sat sulking as she stomped around, the rage palpable in her seething breaths. But, before she could lay into me, a knock sounded from the door. Marching toward it, she unlocked and opened it. The first mate was caught off guard by the fierceness of her expression.

"Captain—" The old man fumbled with his words. "I wished to make sure the Emira was all right."

"Did you now?" The captain glanced over at me. "What say you, Nahla? Are you all right after the stunt that nearly cost you your life?"

I looked away, ashamed of my failings, as I always was, but that didn't stop her from pressing further.

"Did I not order you to stay inside?"

Though she thought she could intimidate me with her performance, the annunciation of the word "order" brought me to my feet.

"And what does an order from you mean to a Qamarayni Emira?"

Intrigued, the captain treaded slowly toward me, breathing down my neck. I stood firm, frightening the first mate more. He always trembled at the first sight of conflict between the two of us. Slowly backing away, the captain turned to him, glaring, until he ran off, tripping over himself. She then raised her head high. I raised mine and unflinchingly met her gaze, expecting a fight, until she burst out laughing and lunged toward me, our lips locking in a passionate embrace.

"That man must be beside himself with fright," Anbara whispered into my ear, laughing. "You could come off a little less feisty."

"Me?" I exclaimed in jest. "You could come off a little less demented when you're mad."

Anbara tilted her head. "I have every right to be mad. Do I not?"

"No," I responded, chuckling, but Anbara snapped back with the ferity of a lioness.

"I am the Sultana," she declared for the first time in years. "You'd be wise to heed my orders."

I flinched, shaken by the intensity of her glare, and remained silent, expecting her to reveal that this was another performance. But it only occurred after my fear registered in her eyes. I sat there, unconvinced, shivering like a frightened kit whose owner had lashed out at her.

"I apologize." Anbara could not bear to look me in the eye. "That shouldn't have happened."

Before I could forgive her, she walked past me, finally noticing the color of the light coming from the window. "Is that—?"

"Yes," I cut her off.

"How does it feel to miss the second one?"

"I don't know." I turned to it, more out of obligation than religious fervor. "I guess I don't have any thoughts other than it feels peculiar."

Anbara walked back over to me with careless ease. "Perhaps your mind is preoccupied with other events." She reached for my hand, intertwining it with hers.

"Perhaps." I smiled coyly. Though I wished to stay mad, I was at ease again, and I hated myself for it.

"Do you think it'll be like this forever?" Anbara finally asked, and I wanted to say yes, but only ten years ago, I'd stared up at the same sky and told myself that I'd lead the next Izhar, and instead I'd run off to the sea.

Cupping my chin, she apologized again, and as I had before, I forgave her in spite of my trepidation. Leading me toward the sole window in the room, she embraced me in the moonlight just in time to see the sister moons come together in a new formation. We stared up at the starry sky, coarse hands interlocked, scorching hearts intertwined, and lucent souls about to part.

Part III: The Third Izhar

To think we were once sisters-in-arms—fire-forged lovers who'd sworn an oath out in the west for our homelands, our people, and each other. But one couldn't have told by the smug gaze that seemed to mock me underneath Anbara's scar. The servants had been instructed to prepare the council chamber for an impromptu meeting, arranging the divans, carrying in the customary trays of dates, and pouring gawas of sherbet without a word. Whatever this was about, the matter needed to be settled now.

Leaning back on the divan set out for her with arms stretched wide, the General seemed to encompass the entire room as the wazir and I sat there caged and cornered—prey in search of an escape.

"You were never one for formalities, Nahla." The General ripped a chunk of the date in her hand, crunching audibly with her mouth open. "I would've never figured that you'd bother following in your father's footsteps."

As always, she knew just the right words to irk me and seemed keen on doing so, but as Emira of the Emirate of Qamarayn, I held my head high and maintained my composure.

"With the passing of the Emir and his successor, I alone could ascend to the throne."

"All the better." The General flicked the seed onto the floor and picked another. "I hope you prove a more capable successor to your father than your brother did."

My grip tightened under the table, but Kassem calmly placed his hands on mine.

"Let us redirect our attention to the border delineations." The old man leaned over the table. "We believe what the Sultan is asking of us is rather…excessive."

"Some would say it's unbecoming of him." I smirked back, and her expression mangled into a sneer.

"Naturally." The General scoffed. "The Sultan has given me free rein over these lands, and I've determined that direct oversight would be best suited to the Qamarayni Emirate."

Before I could stand, Kassem rose and nodded agreeably. "Naturally, but"—the quill in his hand quivered ever so slightly, and I realized he was as rattled as I, perhaps more so—"in all my years as wazir, the Sultan has never asked such concessions from us. The Emirate has offered more of its soldiers to the High Porte than any other wilayat has."

"And?"

Kassem was slighted, but the old man pressed on, incapable of making sense of who, or what, he was dealing with. These formalities were more of an annoyance than an obligation to the General, who'd gone from detesting tradition to accumulating enough influence that she derived a twisted pleasure in affronting those in power who'd once snubbed their noses at her.

"And why must we relinquish our arms?" He shook his head. "To the west, we are exposed to the sea, which is out of the Sultanate's reach. The High Porte cannot hope to protect us, nor can it arrive in time if the unthinkable happens."

The General tilted her head. "And if it didn't?"

"Pardon?" Kassem asked innocuously, though I suspected he'd caught on to the General's machinations.

"What would that matter to the Sultan?" The General rested her chin on a curled fist. "Up here, on the slopes of the mountain, the High Porte has not been able to exercise its due influence, and we feel that our subjects have been given free rein. If we don't proceed with these measures, you might as well not belong to us, even with the risks involved."

Bewildered, Kassem turned to me and nudged his blue turban toward the mashrabiya at the other end of the room.

"If you'll excuse us."

The General promptly redirected her attention to the gawa of sherbet, masking an amused smile. "You're excused."

Taking the lead, Kassem slid one of the windows open, and the moonlight poured onto the balcony. I ushered him toward the railing, and we leaned over, hoping the General wouldn't hear what we had to say nor read our lips as I had taught her in another life.

"Your dealings seemed to have soured since you last crossed paths."

"I had hoped that, when we parted, I would not have to see or hear from her again."

Irritated, the old man gritted his teeth, quipping: "Care to share the story?"

"I would rather not."

For the first time in years, I was conscious of my personal dealings, and I didn't wish to linger on them, as I had preferred not to since Anbara and I had parted. Though I was irritated by his lack of respect for my privacy, Kassem had the right to ask now that our bickerings had poured into the Emirate's affairs. But that stormy night we'd parted…I dared not think of it. I dared not speak of it. I dared not relive it, lest I remember the blood and thunder under the violet moons that left her a scarred, sad creature, and left me forever shrouded in its shadow.

I had resolved to escape her suffocating grip, aware it'd be my life if I were caught. After she'd fallen asleep, I'd left our chamber and readied one of the rafts under the cover of night. Anbara soon confronted me, sword in hand, just as I was about to lower into the raft. Perhaps she had known my intentions all along.

I'd had neither the spirit nor sense to draw my scimitar; instead I'd fumbled with my shibriyeh. That pitiful dagger was all I'd used to fend off the lioness charging in my direction. Our blades had clashed, and, in panic, I'd swiped at her face, drawing her blood and her ire. Shoving me into the raft, she'd moved to strike me down, but I'd kicked her back onto the ship and made quick work of the rope.

The image of her scarred face staring me down as I drifted into the sea still haunted my nightmares.

"Nahla," Kassem's eyes narrowed. "You don't cry or complain of the injustice that she's hoisted on you."

I didn't respond. The change in his tenor caught me off guard. The old man raised an eyebrow, as he was prone to doing. I could tell he'd more or less put together what had transpired years ago on the open seas.

"This is no time to dwell." I sighed, and Kassem finally understood, taking a deep breath and letting it all out in one long, uninterrupted sigh.

"To think that the sultan's daughter would lash out like a petulant child over a lover's spat."

"You could say we were more than lovers."

"I could if I wanted to be dragged to Bab Al Najoom and have my tongue flayed." Kassem flailed his arms before remembering who he was speaking to and collecting himself. "Is there no recompense?"

"I'm afraid not."

From the corner of my eye, I could see her savoring each sip as she pretended not to look at us.

"To think that this would occur on the night of Izhar!" he exclaimed, and I wondered how the event would unfold this time.

"Might I suggest you return to the table?" the General called out. "There are far more important matters the High Porte must attend to in the region."

"A moment, Sultana," Kassem called back, then whispered into my ear. "If there's anything that can be done to stop this, we must act now, before it's too late."

In the courtyard, the royal guard lined up in front of each other once again neath the roses, and for the first time, I positioned myself at their head, proudly unsheathing my ancestral scimitar. Breathlessly, the court poet pronounced the verses, and in unison, the guards and I recited them by heart as petals were flung at us from all corners. Behind us, the players frantically picked their ouds and the drummer thrashed the takhmeer, restraining and disciplining our motion. The General's eyes followed my every step, and I could feel her predatory thirst again taking over that gaze.

I led the guards to her and her coterie, and we held out our hands. With a sick, mocking smirk on her face, she made the customary move to pass me her pusat before latching on to my arm with the other and dragging me toward her, placing the blade at my throat. On alert, the guard turned to the wazir for guidance, who shook his head slowly. I stood still, refusing to struggle, waiting for the right moment. Satisfied with my acquiescence amidst utter public humiliation, the General signaled with her head to her coterie, who promptly passed my men their swords. I was let go, and I stood up, motioning for her pusat, but she chose to snub me again by sheathing it.

Now was not the moment, I had to remind myself.

But how I wished it was. I led them back, my eye fixed on her every tick, wondering how she thought she could touch me again.

As I raised the scimitar to the sister moons at the point they came together once again, high above us in the heavens, the guard dispersed around the General and her coterie, spinning in perfect synchronization until our swords were aimed right at their throats.

Unsure of what to make of our "customs," the coterie glanced at each other nervously as if wondering if this was part of the performance, but the General knew all too well it wasn't, and she broke into a fit of laughter.

"Are you mad, Nahla?"

I gritted my teeth.

"I am the Emira, and you will address me as such, Sultana."

"You are nothing but a puppet whose limbs are flung wherever the High Porte wills." The General rose, fearlessly unsheathing her pusat again. "There are thousands of my men camped outside the city gates. Do you expect them to stand idle if you kill me?"

Though I wanted nothing more than to pierce her heart with the same scimitar my ancestor had established this Emirate with, I reined in the relentless rage that would drive me into inhumanity as it had her.

"I don't intend to kill you, Anbara."

Hearing this, the coterie shared curious stares until Kassem chimed in:

"Sultana, there is no use. You are to be bargained with for the future of our Emirate. I've sent word to your guard outside that any machination will result in your unceremonious beheading."

As he stuttered, the General chose not to pay him any heed. Eyes bulging, her face contorted in a glower that made her men pale with fright.

"You are a coward." She spat onto the ground. "You were *always* a coward."

My grip on the handle tightened.

"Just like your father and brother who went down like curs!" The General heaved, baring her fangs "Duel me, or I'll kill you where you stand."

"Then"—I finally lunged at her, my blade clashing against hers—"have at it!"

The intensity of the engagement sent sparks flying as I slid my scimitar off her pusat and went for her arm. Letting go of the sword, she backed away, pulled out a yatagan, and seized on me with that curved ivory knife. I deftly slid myself out of each stab, whirling and twirling with the swiftness of a swan as the lioness pounced on me relentlessly.

Frustrated with my evasion, she kicked me in the stomach, and I fell to the floor but managed to grab her blade-hand before she could plunge the length into me. Moonlight shone on us in the quadrangle as I struggled with the hand. No one dared intervene, fearing for their lives. This was not unlike our scuffles as children, and as Emira, I was ashamed I'd acted out of petulant spite. I was remiss to have indulged her wrath. I could've called for my guards to restrain her, but the vines of vengeance had their thorns in me. Latching on to her dagger arm, I redirected the yatagan ever so slightly so it was thrust into the Earth, right by my face, grazing it—scarring it. Then, with a handful of sand, I blinded her and threw her off me. Retrieving my scimitar, I stood over her, pitying the sad wretch she'd become, and raised my sword to strike her down. Gasps and whispers from our audience did little to deter me until I gazed up at the sky and remembered that the moons had come together once again on this sorry night.

This was not the way, I conceded. My fealty was to my Emirate and my people—not my worst inhibitions.

Sheathing my sword, I called for my men. "Take her away…"

The royal guard ran over to surround her as Kassem instructed the servants to treat my wounds.

"Kill me," Anbara goaded before breaking down into tears, but I couldn't bear to look at her any longer. "You've done it before. You left me for dead. Don't let your feelings get in the way now. You coward."

"I am no coward." I met her vapid glare one last time. "I am the Emira of Qamarayn, and you'd best mind your tongue, prisoner."

It was a sorry sight. The munificent procession that had entered my gates, ready to subjugate me and my people, left them with the head of each soldier hung in shame, their bodies stripped of their weapons and armor as they were forced to walk back to the High Porte to deliver my message.

My people rejoiced in the street, the sound of their merriment serenading a night the sister Goddesses had, no doubt, blessed. Though they were able to rest easy for the first time in two decades, and I finally felt I had a grasp on my own Emirate, I pondered what would become of us when Bab Al Najoom received word of what had transpired here tonight?

How would it all come together? Would it unravel?

Only Yarih and Astarte knew, and it was up to me to repay their favour in kind.

As I gazed up at the moons, parting again—not for the last time—I held out hope for my people and myself, knowing that the moons would one day realign and wondering what unique formation they would take.

Index

About the Creators

Aceriee

Hi! I'm Aceriee and I draw sometimes. I've been drawing all my life, but after falling into the Supernatural fandom in 2014 I've mostly focused on fanart.

Other Duck Prints Press Publications: *And Seek (Not) to Alter Me*, Croissant and Coffee Enamel Pin, Bubble Tea and Donut Enamel Pin, Eerie Animal Enamel Pins

Cris Alborja

I'm an illustration and comic artist from Spain. I've got a nursing degree, but I decided to pursue my passion. I have studied Illustration at EASD Pablo Picasso in A Coruña and comics at O Garaxe Hermético in Pontevedra. I have done cover art for an anthology called *Infiniteca* by Retranca Editorial and comics for *Altar Mutante*, *Nai dos Desterrados*, and *Abraxas en Cuarentena* fanzines, as well as in *Gaspariño 21* by Retranca Editorial.

Other Duck Prints Press Publications: *And Seek (Not) to Alter Me*

bloomingtea

Téa is a hypothetical writer and artist, a professional procrastinator, and a merch hoarder. When they aren't working on personal projects, they moderate zines and bake the same loaf of bread over and over again. From their pile of WIPs, they've managed to self-publish one book and are currently working on other manuscripts to eventually release into the world. Until then, they remain the worst gamer on Twitch and like to spend their free time ranting about books and thinking about fictional lawyer video games.

Other Duck Prints Press Publications: *This is bloomingtea's first contribution to the Press.*

C

A massive drinker of coffee and a lover of old TV shows and movies, C is a small-time concept artist and illustrator who likes to dabble in all things literature and history. When she's not busy drawing and nodding along to Bruce Springsteen while researching the Kentucky Cave Wars, she's trying to save up for grad school to become to a forensic artist so she can draw some more.

Other Duck Prints Press Publications: *This is C's first contribution to the Press.*

Aria L. Deair

Aria L. Deair is an author who has been writing and (while cursing her excessive comma usage) publishing fanfiction online for more than sixteen years. Freelance writer by day and author every other hour that she isn't sleeping, she spends her days courting carpal tunnel and "forgetting" to wear her wrist brace.

As a proud member of more fandoms than she can count, Aria can be found blogging about some of the writing that she is avoiding doing at arialerendeair.tumblr.com.

Like a dragon with her hoard, she can be found in her New Hampshire apartment, surrounded by notebooks (most of which are empty), half-filled mugs of tea, and some of the comfiest blankets that have ever existed. Disturb her at your own risk, especially during NaNo season.

Other Duck Prints Press Publications: *And Seek (Not) to Alter Me*, Heated Desperation

E. V. Dean

E. V. Dean is a writer with a decade of fanfiction writing under her belt. She's embarking on her original fiction adventure with the angst tag kept within arm's reach. Her favorite excuse not to write is watching Jeopardy.

Other Duck Prints Press Publications: In the Moonlight

Amy Fincher

Amy Fincher (she/her) is a producer and artist with over a dozen years of experience in the video game and animation industries. She has contributed to various AAA and indie titles, including the Civilization, XCOM, and Skylanders series. Amy is currently working on *Open Roads* as Executive Producer. When the mood strikes and time allows, she teaches art classes and takes on art commissions on the side. Her hobbies include learning aerial silks, collecting aesthetically pleasing empty containers, looking at shiny rocks, and taking very long naps.

Other Duck Prints Press Publications: *And Seek (Not) to Alter Me*

Rhosyn Goodfellow

Rhosyn Goodfellow is an author of queer romance and speculative fiction living with her spouse and two dogs in the Pacific Northwest, where she is sad to report that she has not yet mysteriously disappeared or encountered any cryptids. Her hobbies include spoiling the aforementioned dogs, drinking inadvisable amounts of coffee, and running unreasonably long distances very slowly. She's secretly just a collection of loosely related stories dressed up in a meat suit.

Other Duck Prints Press Publications: *She Wears the Midnight Crown*, The Fairy Garden

Catherine E. Green

Catherine E. Green (pronouns: xe/xem/xyr or they/them/their) is an agender person, one who's had an on-again, off-again love affair with writing. Xe began writing when xe was a wee thing, when xyr other major pastimes were playing xyr mother's NES and roughhousing with the boys next door. It's only in the past few years that they have begun writing consistently and publishing their writing, fanfiction and original writing alike.

Outside of writing, xe is a collector of books and sleep debt and an avid admirer of the cosmos. Playing video games, reading a variety of fiction genres (primarily fantasy, queer romance, and manga and graphic novels of all kinds), and working on wrangling their own personal data-archiving projects occupy most of their free time. Xe has also started meeting up with a local fiber arts group and is excited to be crocheting xyr first scarf.

Other Duck Prints Press Publications: Of Loops and Weaves

J. D. Harlock

J. D. Harlock is a Syrian-Lebanese-Palestinian writer and editor based in Beirut. In addition to his posts at Wasifiri, as an editor-at-large, and at Solarpunk Magazine, as a poetry editor, his writing has been featured in Strange Horizons, Star*Line, and the SFWA Blog. You can always find him on Twitter and Instagram posting updates on his latest projects.

Other Duck Prints Press Publications: Little Witch's Apothecary, An Odd Gathering of Peculiar Cats, Solarpunks: Viva la Revolución

A. L. Heard

A. L. Heard is an aspiring writer from Pittsburgh. She's been writing fanworks for over a decade and self-published her first novel, *Hockey Bois*, in 2021. Some of her short stories have been published through the indie press Duck Prints Press, where she also contributes as an editor. Ultimately, though, she spends her free time writing about characters she adores in worlds she'd like to explore: contemporary romance, historical fiction, science fiction, and fantasy. In between writing projects, she works as a language teacher, plays hockey, tours breweries with her boyfriend, and spends her evenings playing dinosaurs with her two sons.

Other Duck Prints Press Publications: *Add Magic to Taste, He Bears the Cape of Stars*, In Which James Willoby Enjoys a Ball Far More Than One Should, The Princess and the Maze, Princess Antonia Del Montari, The Offered Ones, Snowbound and Love Sick

D. A. Hernández

AKA Mitch, an author who works as a teacher, reads fanfiction compulsively, tells anyone who will listen about their weird dreams, takes long naps, and once in a while manages to write a story or two. You can find another of their stories in the Duck Prints Press anthology *She Wears the Midnight Crown*.

Mitch's playlist includes metal, pop, electronic, bluegrass, reggaeton and cumbia.

Other Duck Prints Press Publications: *She Wears the Midnight Crown*

R. L. Houck

R. L. Houck (she/her) still has one of the first stories she ever wrote as a seven-year-old in elementary school. It was about flightless penguins reaching the sun and a good indication of her boundless imagination and her love of animals. The latter became a full-time veterinary career; the former keeps her occupied with fanfiction and original fiction in between appointments.

Identifying as asexual herself, she is fond of exploring characters on the asexual spectrum in her writing. She has a tendency toward erotica, and her modus operandi could best be described as "smut with feelings." However, she also enjoys writing about found families and fluffy meet-cutes. Anything goes, and she is very grateful to Duck Prints Press for allowing her to place well-known and respected characters in flower shops and space…and officially publishing those exploits!

Outside of writing, she enjoys snuggling on the couch with her dog and four cats, watching zombie or other disaster movies and TV shows. A native New Yorker, she currently resides in Virginia but dreams of one day retiring to Portugal.

Other Duck Prints Press Publications: *And Seek (Not) to Alter Me*, Awkward and Oblivious, Fortune Favors Felines, No One Right Way

Lucy K. R.

Lucy K.R. (she/her) is technically in existence. Every time she is free, she writes. Sometimes when she is not free, she also writes. This has occasionally created problems. She is fortunate to be supported (read: enabled) by her enthusiastic fiancée Tomo, a loving OG family, and a lively found family as well.

Eager for a change after a decade of waitressing, Lucy K.R. took the chance in March of 2021 to make her first steps into the world of published work. Prior to the success of the largely fabricated German translation of the short story "die Karaoke-Königinnen," she was best known for her work on Mageling: Rise of the Ancient Ones and in the Duck Prints Press anthologies listed below.

In her stories, Lucy K. enjoys writing evil ideas as gently as possible, portrayed through unexpected lenses. She would like to acknowledge that she has never written a biographical statement that did not turn out weird, beg your indulgence, and express her hope that you enjoy her work in this anthology. The people at Duck Prints Press have been a delight, and she is deeply grateful to be included!

Other Duck Prints Press Publications: *And Seek (Not) to Alter Me, She Wears the Midnight Crown*

Aeryn Jemariel Knox

Aeryn Jemariel Knox first identified as a writer in second grade. With both parents involved in theater and a house full of bookshelves, they grew up surrounded by stories, and as soon as they could hold a crayon, they felt the urge to tell their own. In 2001, they discovered the wide and wonderful world of fanfiction; since then, they have gone by Jemariel in fandom spaces across the internet, engaging with their favorite media and communities in the best way they know. Previous fandoms include Star Trek (The Original Series), Torchwood, and BBC's Sherlock, but their most prolific writing and strongest community ties are in the Supernatural fandom. Now, nearly a decade after their last original fiction attempt, Aeryn is eager to explore the wider writing world.

A native of Portland, Oregon, Aeryn currently lives in the suburbs with their husband and 17-year-old cat. For a day job, they work as a tech writer and general paper-pusher for an energy drink factory. Their favorite stories, both to tell and to read, are stories about love, identity, and magic.

Other Duck Prints Press Publications: Pas de Deux

Kou Lukeman

Kou Lukeman is an artist, composer, writer, and video-game developer. His long-term goal is to someday lead a video-game company that makes video games by queer and neurodivergent people. Kou identifies as queer and neurodivergent, and is proud to be both. He is an avid Final Fantasy 14 player, a huge Kingdom Hearts fan, and video games have inspired Kou to create from a very young age. While his main creative interests tend to be in queer and neurodivergent horror, Kou also dabbles in fantasy as a genre. He is currently working on releasing his first few games and a graphic horror novel about neurodiversity and queer people in society.

Other Duck Prints Press Publications: *This is Kou Lukeman's first contribution to the Press.*

Annabeth Lynch

Annabeth Lynch is a genderfae (she/they), bisexual author who writes mostly queer stories, preferring to write marginalized characters finding love. She lives in North Carolina with her husband, daughter, and two very overweight cats.

Other Duck Prints Press Publications: *She Wears the Midnight Crown*, Away With the Fairies, The Problem with Wishes

Giulia Malagoli

Giulia Malagoli (she/they) got into art because of generally friendly competition with a classmate in middle school, and now she has an entire bachelor's degree in Concept Art to show for it.

For about ten years, she has been hopping through fandom spaces—from video games, to comics, to movies and TV series—and has drawn inspiration from each of them for both fan and original art. The result is a passion for character design and for art that weaves a story into its visuals, with a whole lot of feelings about the role of The Narrative to boot.

To chase this passion Giulia has moved from their home country of Italy to the United Kingdom and back again. They now work as a freelance illustrator with enthusiasm, always scraping some time at the end of the day to keep up with fandom friends.

Other Duck Prints Press Publications: *This is Giulia Malagoli's first contribution to the Press.*

Sebastian Marie

Sebastian Marie (he/him) is an engineering student with a lot of opinions about dragons, pirates, and sword fighting. Track him down on Ao3 or Tumblr and he'll share these opinions gladly, just be prepared for music and some excited shouting. His original works often combine fantasy and dystopia into what he calls "queer fantasy hopepunk," something that will be explored in his future novels. He loves to write conflicting traditional and non-traditional family dynamics, especially where they intersect with queer relationships. And if he can throw werewolves and brujas into the mix? So much the better. When not writing, frantically studying, or reading, he can be found singing loudly, sewing impractical coats, and going on long rambling walks while plotting stories (and occasionally falling into rivers).

Also, he's also the guitarist and one of the lyricists of folk punk band Here Be Dragons, who hope to have their debut EP out near the end of Fall, 2023.

Other Duck Prints Press Publications: *She Wears the Midnight Crown*

Nova Mason

Nova Mason spent a significant portion of her childhood fantasizing about dragons, spaceships, and other worlds. She is now, allegedly, a grown-up, with two kids and more varied interests. Dragons, spaceships, and other worlds are still pretty high in the list, though.

Other Duck Prints Press Publications: *And Seek (Not) to Alter Me*

MidnightSilver

I'm MidnightSilver (they/them). I'm a freelance artist who specialises in fandom art, most often inspired by Supernatural the TV show, and I can usually be found illustrating stories for independent authors—my favourites are those that combine adventure/magic/horror with a boatload of feels! As a bi, non-binary, mixed-race person, I don't believe in restrictive boundaries, and I love tales that highlight diversity and freedom of expression while incorporating the fantastical and magical elements that I fell in love with when reading stories as a child. It's my aim to take all the many wondrous worlds and people with whom we visit when lost in book pages at 2 o'clock in the morning and to share them with you in visual form. It's a project I never tire of pursuing.

Other Duck Prints Press Publications: *This is MidnightSilver's first contribution to the Press.*

Sage Mooreland

Sage Mooreland (they/them) is a city-dwelling gremlin from Chicago. They are embarking on the adventure that is their 40s equipped with three amazing partners, one very ridiculous eighteen-year-old biological offspring, and a fleet of teenagers and twentysomethings that adopted them through work over the last several years. Sage put themselves through the torture of grad school and now holds a bachelor's in English and a master's in English and Creative Writing—Fiction, to which they say, "Now I have expensive pieces of paper that make it seem like I know what I'm talking about."

Sage has been writing since they were wee small, entering their first writing contest in fifth grade/at ten years old. In high school and college, they made small offerings to school literary magazines, and they have done eighteen years of National Novel Writing Month. As their writing career grows, they hope to provide stories that are entertaining, caring, inclusive of all, and full of the stuff of which dreams are made.

Other Duck Prints Press Publications: Bubble, Bubble

D. V. Morse

D. V. Morse (she/her) is a writer of fantasy and science fiction, generally (though not always) with some romance in there somewhere. She's been in various aspects of healthcare for a couple of decades, most recently nursing. A lifelong New Englander who has been writing for as long as she can remember, she loves to find the liminal spaces in the local landscape and find the stories lurking within. She also loves playing with fiber arts, cycling through knitting, crochet, cross-stitch, and blackwork.

Other Duck Prints Press Publications: Got You Covered, Let the Solstice Come

MouMouSanRen

MouMouSanRen (she/her) was born and raised on unceded Matinecock territory in what is now known as Flushing, New York. She has been published in multiple non-fiction magazines including Polygon. Aim for the Heart is her fiction debut. She resides in her native Queens, practicing martial arts and taking care of her dogs.

Other Duck Prints Press Publications: *This is MouMouSanRen's first contribution to the Press.*

J. D. Rivers

J. D. writes speculative fiction where they fall deeply and madly in love and find a dead body, not necessarily in that order. She collects hobbies as others collect books and has an unhealthy addiction to watching competitive cooking shows.

J. D. lives close to the woods with her husband and the cutest dog in the world.

Other Duck Prints Press Publications: *He Bears the Cape of Stars*

Veronica Sloane

Veronica Sloane has authored a novel, several short stories, some poetry, and twenty-two years' worth of fanfic. She lives with one lovely spouse, one rambunctious clever child, and one sleepy cat.

Other Duck Prints Press Publications: *And Seek (Not) to Alter Me, He Bears the Cape of Stars*

Jennifer Smith

Smith has been drawing since a young age. With a focus on traditional drawing techniques, she has recently started using digital mediums to imitate traditional styles. Her focus is portraiture and landscapes, especially with watercolor. You can find more of her art on her Tumblr.

Other Duck Prints Press Publications: *This is Jennifer Smith's first contribution to the Press.*

Spongeunction

Thanks for reading my bio! My name is Sponge, and I use they/them pronouns! I am currently studying for a Game Arts degree through online courses at SNHU. Along with working at a thrift store, I enjoy working on projects with others. Based in Northern Wisconsin, I majorly entertain myself through art and media pertaining to it. On the long list of my hobbies, I enjoy staying active as well as collecting. I am an avid, crazed Sanrio fanatic with a long list of fandoms dating all the way back to when I was ten. I may be more reserved, but I love making new connections through creation! Meeting like-minded individuals working toward a common goal has been the most fulfilling experience I have had to date. As a young artist, I have dabbled in vending at conventions, game art, and selling my own merchandise online. I hope to one day chase after my ambitions of artistry full-time through a studio! Thank you for your support and interest in my work!

Other Duck Prints Press Publications: *This is Spongeunction's first contribution to the Press.*

Shea Sullivan

Shea Sullivan is a life-long writer living in upstate New York. As a late-blooming queer person, she enjoys writing about complex characters coming into themselves and finding comfort in being exactly who they are.

Shea's day jobs in computer programming and middle management have molded her into the patient, sarcastic, big-hearted, frustrated human she is today, but it's what she does outside the 9–5 that really excites her. When she's not writing, she can be found painting, napping, making quilts, watching documentaries, and trying not to adopt more animals, usually with a cup of tea in hand.

Other Duck Prints Press Publications: *Add Magic to Taste*

Toby.exe

Freelance animator and illustrator based in the UK. He/they LGBTQ+ friendly little goblin who plays excessive amounts of DnD and loves to play Live Action Roleplay events all over the country! If I am not at home drawing, I am out and about playing a variety of fantasy characters in the woods and hitting people with silly foam swords.

Other Duck Prints Press Publications: *This is Toby.exe's first contribution to the Press.*

Jupiter V

Hailing from Kjipuktuk/Halifax, Nova Scotia (that's in Canada), Jupiter V is an artist, musician, and creative crackerjack with a career spanning over a decade. Cutting their teeth designing award-winning gig posters, they've gone on to illustrate for film, graphic fiction, children's literature, and more. At times, they have been caught painting murals at the circus (?!) and whooping their child mercilessly in Rivals of Aether.

Jupiter is currently toiling away at their next graphic work of fiction, Wizards 99k, as we speak.

Other Duck Prints Press Publications: *This is Jupiter V's first contribution to the Press.*

Amy Alexander Weston

Alex, AKA foxymoley, (she/her) is best described as a jack of all trades, but practices digital art more than anything else. She just wants to make things and change the world for the better.

Other Duck Prints Press Publications: *And Seek (Not) to Alter Me*

Amalia Zeichnerin

Amalia Zeichnerin (she/her) lives in Hamburg, Germany. She is a disabled queer woman with a chronic illness and lives in a polyam polycule. Amalia mostly writes original fiction (SFF, cosy Victorian mysteries, queer romance) in German and has also one English Star Wars fan fiction on AO3, with one of her favorite shippings, StormPilot. Amalia also likes to draw and paint, especially fantasy world maps, character portraits, and sometimes also fanart. Amalia's hobbies include pen-and-paper RPGs and LARPing; these also have inspired some of her writing and artworks.

Other Duck Prints Press Publications: *This is Amalia Zeichnerin's first contribution to the Press.*

Xianyu Zhou

Xianyu Zhou is a translator and aspiring garment and plushie cloning specialist hailing from a coastal city in the tropics. Despite staying a 20-minute drive away from the nearest beach, they have yet to visit one, preferring to dwell in their darkened room luminated by a table lamp and ever-shifting RGB of a CPU fan. They have the tendency to accidentally wander into new and exciting forays such as joining Duck Prints Press (and enjoying it!), learning to sew (stitching and unstitching the same part of a "coaster" for the nth time) and working on their language skills (watching shows to scrutinize and take notes about how their subtitles are written).

Xianyu's contribution to the anthology was their first publication and they have reportedly made a party hat for their computer to celebrate the occasion.

Other Duck Prints Press Publications: Irreverence, This Treatment for Chronic Pain has an Unbelievable Side Effect, Urchin Juiced

Jagoda Zirebiec

Hiya! I'm Jagoda or MizuShiba. I am a game dev artist currently working on a few unannounced titles. In my spare time I love to join collaborative projects like this or charity zines. This is my first project with DPP and hopefully not last!

I'm located in Poland and currently live here with my family. Aside from art, I'm interested in collecting dice and playing ttrpgs with friends.

Other Duck Prints Press Publications: *This is Jagoda Zirebiec's first contribution to the Press.*

Backers

Our Top-Tier Patreon Backers:
Anonymous Backer

Sam Brown

Tina Houck

jumblejen

Aria L.

A. Reilly

Karen Welborn

Our Premium Kickstarter Supporters:
Alex Gruendl

Tam J Guy

Kimberly M. Lowe

PoToOoOoOoO

Rachael L. Young

About Duck Prints Press LLC

Duck Prints Press LLC is an independent publisher based in New York State. Our founding vision is to help fanwork creators navigate the complex process of bringing their original works from first draft to print, culminating in publishing their work under our imprint. We are particularly dedicated to working with queer creators and publishing stories and artwork featuring characters from across the LGBTQIA+ spectrum.

Find us online at our website https://duckprintspress.com/ or on social media:

Bluesky: https://bsky.app/profile/duckprintspress.bsky.social

cohost!: https://cohost.org/duckprintspress

Dreamwidth: https://duckprintspress.dreamwidth.org/

Facebook: https://www.facebook.com/duckprintspress

Instagram: https://www.instagram.com/duckprintspress/

ko-fi: https://ko-fi.com/duckprintspress

LinkedIn: https://www.linkedin.com/company/71237377/

Mastodon: https://pettingzoo.co/@duckprintspress

Patreon: https://www.patreon.com/duckprintspress

Pillowfort: https://www.pillowfort.social/duckprintspress

Pinterest: https://www.pinterest.com/duckprintspress/

TikTok: https://www.tiktok.com/@duckprintspress

Tumblr: https://duckprintspress.tumblr.com/

Goodreads: https://www.goodreads.com/user/show/129902473-duck-prints-press-llc

Storygraph: https://app.thestorygraph.com/profile/unforth

If you enjoyed this story, don't forget to leave us a review!